THE BOOK
OF
SIN

"I'd rather be a sinner with an aroused soul, than a saint with sexual constraints . . ."
Cairo

ALSO BY CAIRO

Passion Island
Prison Snatch
The Pleasure Zone
Dirty Heat
Between the Sheets
Ruthless: Deep Throat Diva 3
Retribution: Deep Throat Diva 2
Slippery When Wet
The Stud Palace (ebook original)
Big Booty
Man Swappers
Kitty-Kitty, Bang-Bang
Deep Throat Diva
Daddy Long Stroke
The Man Handler
The Kat Trap

WITH ALLISON HOBBS
Sexual Healing

THE BOOK
OF
SIN

A NOVEL BY

CAIRO

Pleasure House Publishing

Library of Congress Control Number: 2021908027
ISBN: 978-1-7370201-0-3
eBook: 978-1-7370201-1-0

PRINTED IN THE UNITED STATES OF AMERICA

10 9 8 7 6 5 4 3 2 1

Cover design: Shevinton Graphic Design

THIS BOOK IS DEDICATED TO

You, the readers . . .

ACKNOWLEDGEMENTS

What's good, my freaky peeps? As always, this literary journey would be nothing without all of you. So, thank you! I continue to deliver you the kinda *heat* you desire because you allow me to be as nasty as I wanna be. So as long as you keep reading, I'ma most definitely keep writing. On God. Now step into the flames . . . and let's get nasty!

Zane, Charmaine & Sara: I appreciate you. Thank you for believing in me and my vision over the years. And for allowing me the creative license to be as wild and as raw as I wanted to be. I am eternally grateful for your support and encouragement throughout my literary career. Though my literary journey has shifted, I do hope to continue to make you all proud.

And, as always, to you, the naysayers, my style of writing still hasn't changed. So why are you still in ya feelings? The hate you give only gets me off more. Now who wanna catch deez *nutzzzzz?!*

One luv—
Cairo

Sin was everywhere.
It consumed the air around you. Melted over
your flesh. Seeped into your pores.
Crept into the hidden spaces of your heart.
Then filled your womb with the promise of
something deliciously decadent.
It was toe-curling sensations.
It was long, *deep* strokes.
It was shameless fucking.
It was cunt-clenching euphoria.
It made you claw at the sheets, and mewl
out in sweet, agonizing bliss.
Oh, yes . . .
Sin.
It was more than an act of transgression against divine law.
It was unrequited lust.
It was guilty pleasure.
It was unrestrained passion.
It was the darkest parts of one's desires.
It was erotic energy.
Unadulterated temptation.
It was six-three.
Long-tongued.
Tatted.
Shouldered-length dreads.
It was chords of muscle wrapped around chocolate skin.
It was nine-thick reasons to make a
woman denounce her religion
and, yet, still cry out to the Lord to save her soul.
Welcome to the world of Sin . . .

PROLOGUE

"SPREAD YOUR PUSSY, baby," he urged, his heated words suddenly becoming a thick blanket of arousal.

His broad, veiny dick surged upward as she used her delicate fingers and stretched for him, her scent rising, swirling around him. She was ridiculously aroused by him, ravenous; her golden-brown cunt splayed open on display, all slick and glistening, full of need and want.

"That's right, baby," he coaxed. "Get my pussy ready." He fisted his dick, stroking it a few times, the sight leaving her breathless.

"My pussy . . ."

Lord Jesus, he was putting claims on her, her sex—her sweet honey-hole. Her pupils swallowed the color of her eyes, her nipples tightened. That knowing caused her skin to heat. Because, goddammit, she wanted him. To own her, mark her, to feel his heartbeat inside her pussy.

She writhed, her heart-shaped ass lifting up off the mattress, wanting him, his magnificent dick, embedded in her deeply—so, so deep.

Balls deep.

She found herself choking on her desire for him. She'd never wanted—no *needed*, to feel someone inside of her as badly as she did this very second. Never had she craved for the stretch of her pussy over a hard dick as much as she had this very moment. Something had come over her, as if she'd been somehow possessed.

Goddamn him.

The wet tip of her tongue peeked out to tease him. "You see how wet I am for you?" she breathed out in a heated whisper.

He was tempted to stare down at her opened pussy lips, but instead he gazed more directly in her eyes. "I don't need to look." His eyes seemed to glow with hunger as they locked with hers. "I can smell how wet you are."

And wet she was.

For the love of God why wasn't he fucking her already? What in fuck's sake was he waiting for? Couldn't he tell, *see*, how badly she needed this. *Now.*

Lord knows, she needed him to ravage her, to do all types of nasty, smutty things to her. Blindfold her. Spank her. Lick her. Suck her. And, most importantly, *fuck* her until her pussy went numb.

Yes, God, Jesus . . .

She swallowed. And then, finally, her lips moved, her words were nearly soundless. "Fuck . . . me. *Please.*"

A corner of Sin's lips curled into a smirk as he ignored her plea, finally glancing down at her glistening petals. Her clit was a little pink berry he would have happily suckled against his tongue had he been in the mood. So instead, he ran his thumbs up the wet channels of her folds. He'd known she was on the prowl from the moment he'd spotted her sauntering into the lounge, the sway of her hips as she made her way to the bar, her luscious tits spilling out of her low-cut dress, which fitted perfectly over her curves. Her second skin now tossed over in the corner of her hotel room, a crumpled mess, along with her cunt-soaked panties.

"You want this dick?" he murmured, wanting to hear her say it, to beg for it.

"Oh, God, yes," she whimpered, nearly pleading. *"Please."*

He curled his thumbs into her pussy, stretching her just enough to see how wet she was and his dick twitched as the sight of creamy heat trickling out of her body greeted him. The sweet stench of her arousal caused him to wet his lips. He wouldn't lick her there but, surely, he'd taste her. He loved the taste of pussy. Loved how it soaked his mouth and tongue. But tonight, wouldn't be a night of pussy eating.

So he pulled his thumbs from her body, and sucked one in his mouth, while using the pad of his other to paint her full-lips, before slipping it into her mouth.

She sucked and licked, hungrily.

"Yeah, that's right. Eat up that sweet cream."

She moaned over his finger.

"I want you to imagine this dick sliding all up in your pussy," he taunted, "stroking your walls, making your toes curl."

She swallowed audibly, and then blinked, before taking him in. His hooded eyes draped in lashes thicker and longer than her own made her pussy quiver. She blinked a few more times, and then she saw the pale flecks of gold circling the black depths of his pupils. Those dreamy bedroom eyes fixed on her, their intensity heating all over. And his chiseled jaw—Lord, it was enough to send her over the edge. He was ridiculously handsome, his body sculpted perfection from genetics and hours of weight training.

She couldn't help but wonder how many other women felt this way about him. How many of them had he bedded in his lifetime? How many satin sheets had he left stained with his sweat and seed and masculine scent?

"Play with your clit," he coaxed softly, reaching for her breasts with his strong hands, gently kneading each swollen globe. Her nipples beaded, and then he stroked them into hard nubs.

She gasped, her hand languorously sliding to her clit. With her nipples between thumb and forefinger of each hand, he pinched, then dipped his head and flicked his tongue over each one, before pinching them again, sending a flood of sensation from her clit straight down to the tips of her painted toes.

He would have sucked them into his mouth, licked over her soles, and nibbled on her heels, had they been prettier. He loved pretty toes and soft, pretty feet. Hers were simply . . . *okay*. Not mouthwatering, and definitely not worthy of *his* mouth.

Juices trickled out of her as she drew sensual circles luxuriantly over her clit, then over the front of her slit. She slid her middle finger in, her hips slowly rotating.

"That's right, baby," he said throatily. "Fuck yourself for me." His upper lipped curled into another sexy smirk as he slapped his heavy dick over her clit, smacking it until it puckered. "You wanna be my whore for the night?"

"Yes," she murmured on nothing more than a puff of air.

His grin deepened. "Yeah, just what I thought, you little filthy whore. You want this big, black dick stuffed inside your sweet, slutty hole?"

Her lips parted; her eyes darkened.

A pulse beat fast at her throat.

She secretly loved being called dirty pet names.

Bitch, slut, whore . . .

How had he known?

Her mind quickly swam back to the start of the evening trying to recall if she'd mentioned how her penchant for name-calling made her hot. She licked over her lips; flashes of his long, thick dick stretching her mouth from earlier, its bulbous head plugging her esophagus, drool pooling from her gaping mouth.

God, yes . . .

Her tongue flicked over her lips again. His taste still lingered, and it made her burn hotter for him. She stretched an arm out, frantically reaching with wet fingers, for his dick—all fat and long and veiny, bouncing with his pulse.

He caught her by the wrist. "Nah, you dirty, little cunt. No touching this dick." And then he leaned down and whispered in her ear. "The next time you feel this dick, it's gonna be sliding inside of your tight little pussy, stretching you until it burns."

She moaned, the erotic sound of his words causing her toes to curl.

"I'm going to fuck your orgasm loose," he warned, using only his hips to run the shaft of his erection over the seam of her pussy, up and down it, "and then make you cream all over this dick."

She swallowed, catching her breath as she eyed him as he reached, finally, for the condom—ribbed, for extra pleasure—and then tore it open with his teeth, and then slowly rolled it down his shaft.

It was sweet torture watching. And the breath she thought she'd caught stuck in her throat as she stared down at his bobbing dick, fully sheathed. It stood upright, deliciously thick. Bottle-thick. She wanted to reach out and cup his balls, but she groaned at the sight instead.

"Mmm . . ." her hips moved involuntarily.

"I'm going to fuck you hard," Sin rasped, lifting her legs and then bending them so that either knee was nearly flush to her ears. Her pussy opened to him, ready and wanting. "And then," he whispered, his tone full of conviction and promise as he pushed inside her, "I'm going to fuck your whole body inside out."

She gasped as her pussy took all of him, her eyes aching with the sweet burning of his dick as he went deeper, harder.

Filling her. Stretching her.

Pushing her through the heat, before sending her up in flames.

ONE

Never, ever, ignore a woman's body . . .

That was Sin's motto.

He lived by it. In fact, it was the driving force behind why he loved bringing mind-numbing pleasure to a woman. It made his dick hard, just the idea of being the creator of such bliss, knowing he was the orchestrator of every sweet sound of her sighs and moans, her soft chants, her whimpers, and her whispery pleas for more—more dick, more hands, more mouth, more lips, more tongue . . .

More orgasms.

More him.

They always wanted more of *him*.

Her body sated, her orgasm still filtering through her core long after he slipped out of her, because he listened. Because he was acutely aware that if a man paid attention—if he really, really, listened—a woman's body would tell him everything he needed to know, long before she ever opened her mouth.

There was a sense of power in being able to anticipate a woman's needs, her desires, the naughty punishments she craved, the dirty words she longed to hear, and then giving her exactly what her body ached for.

For Sin, there was something unexplainably feral about taking control of a woman's body, owning it, stripping her of her inhibitions, then giving her license, the sexual freedom, to give into her darkest desires.

If only for a night . . .

⌀

Sin awoke to an incessant pounding at his temples. It was early Wednesday morning and, instead of taking himself up to his hotel suite once he'd checked in last night, he'd spent the better part of his evening unwinding with a couple rounds of Jose Cuevo. Shit. He took a deep breath and shut his eyes again. He should have drunk more water before he finally climbed into bed a little after two A.M. Or taken an aspirin. Instead, he'd been enticed to a night of pussy. He came. She came.

Again.

And again.

And again.

The pussy had been wet. Yet, it could have been better. Creamier. Maybe with a bit more grip. Still, it'd been good enough that he'd gone through three condoms—Magnums, of course, finally fucking her to sleep before creeping out of her hotel room. But it hadn't been about him. It was about her. She'd needed it. Needed to feel special. Needed to feel that her needs were all that mattered.

They *did* matter.

And he'd delivered.

He always did and said all the right things. Things that made a woman weak at the knees and nearly forget her name. He filled places inside of a woman that had been left hollow and aching. He made love to a woman's body from the inside out, touching her, surrounding her, spreading heat and sensual energy all around her.

Last night had been no different. Admittedly, he'd wanted her naked from the moment she'd invited him up to her room. And he'd wanted to give her everything her body hungered. It was his duty as a hot-blooded, hard-dicked man, to bring an asking, willing, woman the pleasure she sought.

He'd been sure to tell her explicitly how wet she was, how sweet her lips tasted, how good she felt wrapped around his dick. And then he'd stroked her until he made her dizzy with pleasure, until every synapse, every nerve ending, exploded through her body, and she sobbed.

Without blinking an eye, he'd caressed her afterwards, kissed away her tears and then held her until she'd drifted off to sleep before easing out of her bed, slipping back into his clothes and leaving her lost in her dreams, lightly snoring.

But that was last night—well, earlier this morning, and today he hoped he wouldn't run into her. He'd seen the neediness in her eyes, her vulnerability, her silent wanting. Behind her teary-eyed gaze, he'd caught a glimpse of the broken, lonely woman she'd tried to hide behind a pound of mascara and mink lashes.

And then . . .

There'd been the wedding band that she'd brazenly worn.

But he was neither the judge nor jury of anyone's life choices. Nor had he been put on this earth to become anyone's therapist.

He allowed women to be who they were, who they needed to be.

And yet he knew, was very much aware of the fact, that—if he didn't have dick control, pussy would be his kryptonite. It was a pussy that he'd come out of. And it would probably be a pussy that he'd end up dying in.

Sin chuckled, shaking his head. And then he closed his eyes, and finally drifted back to sleep.

∽

One hour and forty-five minutes later, he stretched and yawned, then slowly opened his eyes, again, to slivers of light streaming in through the curtains.

Rising up on his elbow, he reached over and retrieved his iPhone from the nightstand, and then looked at the time. 8:43 A.M.

Fuck.

He'd overslept. Something he rarely did. The headache was now slight. But thanks to his liquid friend, Jose, coupled with his fifteen-and-a-half-hour flight to New York and then his greedy dick wanting to oblige his romp for the night with several rounds of deep stroking, he roused reluctantly.

His internal time clock was still set to the South Pacific. Exactly seventeen hours ahead of New York. And he was feeling it.

He groaned and ran a hand over his dick. His morning hard-on needed release. He gently rubbed his heavy balls, sighing. Busting a morning nut would have to wait if he wanted to be on time for his meeting. He knew he'd be late for his eleven o'clock appointment if he didn't get himself out of bed.

And yet his dick jerked, reminding him of its need to come.

Sin shook his head and sighed as he threw his legs over the edge of the mattress. *Not now,* he thought looking down at his erect appendage, before pushing upward, stretching as he went toward the bathroom, his meaty dick bouncing, his size fourteens sinking into the carpet with every step.

Once inside the bathroom, he relieved himself, holding his hard dick in such a way, careful to not allow urine to spray all over the place. He couldn't help but sigh with relief as he emptied his bladder. His eyes rolled up into his head in bliss. When he finished, he flushed the toilet, and then started the shower.

"Ain't this some shit?" he muttered as his dick jerked. His morning piss had done nothing to deflate his erection. He swiped a thumb across the head and hissed in pleasure.

Shit.

He was going to lose the battle at trying to tamp down on his overactive sex drive. There was no getting around it. He'd have to stroke one out.

Yes, he had a high sex drive. He was insatiable. And he enjoyed self-pleasure just as much as he loved having sex, if not more than.

He found masturbation satisfying when he wanted to be alone with his fantasies swirling around in his head. And this morning would be no different for him.

He would give the beast what it wanted.

Release.

As steam slowly rolled around the bathroom, Sin brushed his teeth, gargled and then stepped into the large tiled space. He rolled his shoulders under the heating spray. Six jets of pulsating water flowed over him in all directions as he grabbed a complimentary bottle of shower gel sitting within a niche in the wall. He poured some into his hand releasing a citrusy sandalwood scent. Sin frowned. He didn't particularly care for the scent, but it'd have to do.

Rubbing his hands in soapy circles over his chest, over his nipples, and then down over the deep ripples of his abdomen, Sin's hands slid back over his pecs. He closed his eyes and imagined his hands being replaced by some faceless woman's tongue. He flicked his neatly trimmed fingernails over his nipples, causing his dick to become thicker, harder. But instead of soaping up his dick and stroking out his release, he tortured himself further by sliding his sudsy hands to his groin area, in between the creases of his muscular thighs and then over his scrotum, where he lingered, teasing himself there.

Blood rushed to the tip of his dick making its bulbous head more swollen, more sensitive. He knew if he hadn't been pressed for time, he could get himself off like this. Bust his nut without ever touching his dick.

He reached for more gel and squirted more of its cool content into his large hand, finally deciding to end the sweet agony of his self-torture. He grabbed his shaft and, at first, leisurely slid his hand up and down its length with long, slick strokes until his need to orgasm intensified, until a strangling surge of heat splintered through his body.

"Aah, shit," he muttered. That first stroke always felt so good. All the way up, then all the way down. He closed his eyes. Licked his lips. Imagined his dick sinking deep into some sweet, tight, wet pussy.

With one hand placed on the tiled wall, Sin's other hand moved faster on his turgid flesh, his rhythm matching his rapid desire for release. Seconds later, his balls clenched and he groaned throwing his head back as his orgasm erupted.

"Ahh, fuck," he growled out, his body jerking. A thick nut spurted into the tub, then washed with the sudsy water down the drain.

Sin stroked his shaft a few more times, shaking out the remainder of his orgasm, before dropping his grip from his half-hard dick, rinsing his hands, and then turning of the shower.

He was still keyed up, his plump, meaty dick far from flaccid, but his balls felt lighter. He felt refreshed, reenergized, and ready to take on the day.

TWO

"SIN, MY DARLING," the woman of nearly every man's fantasy said as she stood to her feet and made her way around her sleek desk to greet him with an embrace.

"Nairobia," he breathed out, before wrapping her in his strong arms and kissing both of her cheeks. "It's good seeing you."

He hadn't seen her in close to three months, since her last visit to Passion Island. Aside from being the founder of Sweet Pleasures—a multi-million dollar California-based production company, the former porn star/world-renowned sex goddess reigned over two of the world's most coveted adult-only private clubs—the one here in New York, and the other in the South Pacific (on *her* private island)—both catering to the dirty desires of the rich and freaky. And membership alone was a small fortune well worth every dollar spent for access to unlimited salaciousness. Debauchery. Sweet release.

An all-out upscale, anonymous fuck-fest for the men and women bold enough to indulge their libidos. And Sin had flown into New York to meet with her to discuss the possibility of managing her soon-to-be third club, The Pleasure Chest, in Vegas once it opened in the fall. An invitation and opportunity extended to him by her.

He was already in her employ as a pleasure consultant on Passion Island—a title she'd crowned him with when she'd hired him nearly three years ago, a position that afforded him an abundance of pussy, catering to the needs of married (happily, or not) women who longed for a night (or many nights) of wild abandon, while they sifted through the woes of matrimony during their six-week, all-expense-paid stay.

And, although he was flattered that Nairobia had chosen him as her first pick to operate her upcoming endeavor, he wasn't so sure he was ready to give up his carefree life on the island. The tropical paradise, nestled in the South Pacific, had become a place he'd surprisingly fallen in love with.

Come to think of it, he wondered why she hadn't asked him to manage her club on the island instead. Even though someone was already managing it, he believed he could manage it better. And he didn't understand—at first—why she had flown him in instead of simply meeting with him the next time she'd visited the island until this very second.

Nairobia Jansen always did things her way, on her own terms. Period.

"Mmm," she purred, bringing him out of his reverie, her body sinking deeper into his arms, her hands sliding over the muscles in his back. She reveled in his masculine heat, breathing in. He smelled of seduction and, one of her favorite scents on him, Creed Aventus.

She felt the muscles in her pussy pulsing as she stood back and allowed her gaze to journey over him from head to toe. Her hands eased over his biceps, and she gently squeezed. He was thick and strong, hard and muscular, just the way she liked it.

"You smell delectable, my darling. Just the sight of you warms my loins." Her voice, low and hot and sweetly seductive, swirled around him, teasing and tempting. "If I weren't already fed, I would clutch you into my moist valley and ravish you. Milk you, right here. Every time I see you, my *kut* creams, my love, at the thought of having you."

The confession sent a jolt of electric heat straight to the tip of his dick.

"You're about to make the temperature rise in here," Sin said huskily.

"Mm, *ja*. I love it hot, my darling," she said, and then inched up on the balls of her feet and sweetly kissed his cheek, before quickly stepping from his embrace as if she knew he was tempted to grab her by her luscious ass and cup her there, tightly pulling her back into him, up against the throbbing pulse in his groin.

Nairobia quickly composed herself and then swept an arm out toward a set of leather chairs. "Come. Sit, my darling."

Sin eased by her, stuffing his hands down into his front pockets. She waited for him to fold his long, muscular body into his seat and then sauntered to the edge of her desk, but not before Sin's gaze locked onto the sway of her hips.

Man, oh, man.

That hypnotic ass, firm and perfectly round tapered down to sleek thighs that he suddenly imagined having spread wide for him, again.

It had taken every ounce of his restraint not to leap from his seat, tear his pants down, lay her back on her desk, and plunge into her, fucking her so deeply that she would feel his dick stroking her soul. But it was the voice in the back of his brain reminding him of the reason for his visit, this meeting.

Sin swallowed as her plush ass pressed against the edge of her desk. She crossed her legs at the ankles and then spread her arms out in back of her over her desk.

The way she was sitting would have given him the perfect view of her pussy if she'd pulled back her daringly high slit and spread her thighs.

But she hadn't.

Nairobia smiled. "I trust your flight was pleasing, no?"

Sin nodded as she looked at him, her enchanting gray eyes,

piercing through him. And then he ran a hand over his dreads and tried extremely hard to keep his gaze from the pointed tips of her breasts, their peaks stiff against the sheer fabric of her dress. The sight made him want to run his tongue over the tips, suckle her.

He swallowed the thought along with the drool slowly pooling in his mouth, and said, "Yes, it was. As always."

She smiled at him. And then she wondered why he hadn't taken himself off the market, yet. Was he as selfish as she? Did he enjoy multiple lovers more than he did the possibility of having one lover with multiple talents?

"Are you not ready to give up this salacious life, my darling?"

The query caught Sin by surprise, random as it was, and his forehead creased in question. "Give up my life for what?"

Nairobia pursed her lips. "For love? For a woman to inch her way into your heart, my darling? Do you have no desires to spill your seeds into a lover's womb and watch your love take root and bloom inside of her?"

Sin gave her a blank stare. He'd never given thought to having a family. Hell, he'd never had a relationship. Didn't even know how to have one. Sexing, *fucking*, was all he knew how to do. It was all he ever wanted. Yet, on occasion he indulged in cuddle time, but not often. However, if he were completely honest, he enjoyed the feel of a woman lying in his arms, her warm body sweetly pressed into his. But never for more than a night, and he saw no forever in his lovemaking. A night or two of unbridled passion, it was all he had to give.

Nothing more.

Pseudo-intimacy with a mixture of some kink was good enough for him.

So, he was more than happy with his current No-Strings-At-tached lifestyle. But he knew if he ever allowed himself to open to a woman, she would need to be someone who understood that what he had to offer her was limited. She would need to want whatever he was willing to give. Want to lose herself in whatever parts of himself he was willing to share, whatever wickedly sinful pleasure he could bring. And *that*—the pleasure, was the only thing he offered without boundaries.

It was limitless.

"Nah, I'm good on that," he said flatly.

"You are good on a lot of things, no?" She cocked her head to one side, eyeing him intently.

"Only on those things that matter," he said confidently.

"Good fucking always matters. And you, my darling, in all of your fine, deliciously endowed masculinity are a hot commodity."

Sin felt his dick stirring as he stared at her wicked, beautiful mouth, remembering how deep she'd taken his dick the last time they'd been together, nearly a year ago. And like her *NY Times* bestseller, *Good Pussy*, Nairobia Jansen was exactly that.

Good pussy.

Nairobia flicked her tongue over her lips again, and Sin bit back a groan. And then swallowed against the lust. Christ's sakes—that tongue. And now he couldn't stop thinking about all the nasty little tongue tricks she'd performed on him, his balls, over the head of his dick. The way her tongue had caressed his skin, wetly bathing every part of him.

So here he sat, his dick coming alive, gritting his teeth for strength. He had to be strong. He knew she was toying with him, like she did with all of her prey. But she was baiting a tiger, one unleashed and untamed and unafraid to strike if he allowed himself to, if he gave into his carnal cravings.

Shit, whom was he fooling? The woman was a seductress, for fuck's sake. She lived to seduce. He knew better than anyone that she had legions of admirers, fans, and—hell, probably—a shitload of stalkers, too. Men who obsessed over her and fantasized about having her in their beds, even if the majority of them could never match her sexual prowess.

Still they daydreamed. And imagined. And got off on the fantasy.

Truth be told, she'd been one of his secret fantasies long before he'd ever been graced with the reality of knowing her. Pleasure— her porn name—was what he'd known her as, before the formal introductions. And her potent bedroom skills had taken the word *pleasure* to new heights once she'd lured him into her seductive web.

"If you cannot bring me pleasure, if you cannot make my kut *cream and cry out to you, my darling, then you cannot work for me . . ."* those had been her words to him during his interview for his current position, before she brazenly stepped out of her gauzy gown, spreading herself open to him and then telling him to feast on her goodness.

And in the red haze of his lust, he'd fed on her luscious cunt for what felt like hours, sucking and licking and drinking in her sweet, tangy flavor, before finally sliding his dick deep into her plush body, her wet clutch taking everything he had to give.

Sin blinked out of his reverie only to find Nairobi smiling, her gaze latched onto his lap, acutely aware of the bulge in his pants. She imagined it pressing violently against the zipper of his pants, desperate to burst out through the fabric—for freedom, for pussy . . . for good loving.

She licked over her lips, teasingly, once again.

Sin smirked. He knew her well enough to know this was a game to her. It always was. She enjoyed the game of seduction. It aroused her knowing she had a man's dick hard without ever touching him. Her pussy was probably already soaked, he mused, matching her with a grin of his own.

She oozed sex, hot, kinky, delectable sex.

And he did as well.

Still, this was also about control. She was testing him, his ability to deny her, temptation in its greatest form. And yet, through the lushness of her dark lashes, Sin felt her gaze undressing him.

"Your hard dick longs for the heated clutch of my *kut*, no?"

Sin opened and closed his legs, the answer swelling in his

lap. Nairobia inched closer, her crotch nearly eye-level. He willed himself not to touch her, but she felt him straining toward her. If he leaned forward, he could kiss her there, over the flimsy fabric, her sweet cunt just a tongue swipe away from his mouth. Sin breathed her in, and then swallowed another groan.

"Don't tempt me," he said low and even, as Nairobia leaned into him, bracing both hands on the armrests of his chair, she pinned him, caging him in his seat with her seductive charm.

"Oh, my darling, temptation is what I live for. Do you know why I choose you?" The question could have held double meaning had Sin not known her better. She was referring to the position.

Sin nodded. "Because I am good at what I do."

"Yes, my love. That is true. But it is not the reason I *choose* you. I choose you because you are *sin*, my darling. And what better place to have *you* than in Sin City, a world of glitz and glitter and all things dirty, my darling."

What was he to say to that?

He regarded her thoughtfully. "Sounds like you've given this a great deal of thought."

"I leave nothing to impulse, my darling. I have not built my empire on whimsical decisions." Nairobia paused a beat, and then she continued in her native tongue, *"je goed bent lul, je bent goed liefdevol. U bent onvergetelijk neuken."*

Simply put, she wanted him because he was good dick.

He was good loving.

He was unforgettable fucking.

Goddamn . . . shit.

He loved it when she spoke in her native tongue. And he knew whatever she'd said in Dutch was something dirty the way her warm, moist tongue seductively slid over her lips again.

For a fleeting moment, he imagined her spreading open her pussy to him, wet cream running from her as his tongue licked luxuriantly over her clit.

"You smell like heaven," he said huskily, fighting hard to shut off the switch to his erotic thought.

Nairobia's fingers twitched, wanting to touch him, to grab a handful of his magnificent cock. Instead, she leaned forward, planted another kiss to his cheek. And then she released the arms of his chair, freeing him from her alluring heat, easing back against her desk.

"I *am* heaven, my love." She sidled around her desk, "but then," she continued wickedly, before slinking into her chair, "you already know that." She shuffled a stack of colored folders on her desk and then placed them into two neat piles. "Now, my darling. Let's get down to business."

Sin's smile was crooked, his appreciative gaze lit with something more than lust. Nairobia was used to being in power. Men did what she wanted, when she wanted, how she wanted.

Sin respected that about her, her need for control.

In that regard, they were more alike than not. The way her sensuality, her sexuality, yielded power over men, he held the same type of control over women. Because like her, the only thing he had to offer women, the only thing he wanted to give them, was his body, his sex, and lots of unforgettable pleasure.

His gaze lingered on Nairobia's face.

Any man whom she allowed in her world would need to know that his purpose was for only pleasing her, at her whim, for as long as she wanted, desired. And when he was no longer needed, he would be replaced.

Including him.

THREE

ENTER IF YOU DARE. LEAVE BEHIND YOUR APPREHENSIONS. SURREN-
DER TO YOUR DESIRES . . . AND STEP INSIDE THE PLEASURE ZONE . . .

Sin pulled out a silky domino from a gold box, which had
been given to him earlier in the day by Nairobia, and tied it on. A
mischievous grin eased over his lips as he glanced up at the elegantly
crafted sign, which hung above the club's enormous door. *Enter if
you dare* . . . he repeated to himself, before stepping into the club's
Italian marble foyer.

Tonight, Sin was at Nairobia's New York-based adults'-only
club to take in the sights and, perhaps, indulge in some of its
pleasures. Though he'd heard lots of underground chatter over the
years about the hedonistic playground, this was his first time inside
the erotic sex club. It was exactly what he'd heard it would be: the
underworld of taboo sex all under one tantalizing roof. And, so far,
from what he was seeing, he was impressed.

From the marbled floors and the swathes of billowy ivory silk
that covered the walls to the draped candlelit booths and gas-lit
torches lining the walls, from the enormous candles flickering about
the expansive space to the oversized white leather sofas and armless
chairs, the first floor was chic, sophisticated, and very sensual.

Huge statues, along with life-size erotic paintings of men and
women in coitus, depicting a variation of lusty positions, were
situated throughout the club. And there were dozens of exotic-look-

ing, red-bottom-heeled model types from all ethnic backgrounds donned in pasties shimmering in Swarovski crystals and matching thongs, wearing elaborate bejeweled masks, working the floor. Their male counterparts, chiseled-chested and tall, were clad in loincloths and wore red silk domino masks.

Mesmerized, Sin took it all in.

Ta-Ku's "We Were In Love" floated out of the world-class sound system and Sin watched as three naked women dusted in gold, wearing six-inch gladiator sandals and diamond-studded collars, seductively swayed their hips, their arms moving sensually up over their heads. In synchronized motion, the three women swayed and dipped at the knees, then swirled their hips.

Bare-footed, naked bodies airbrushed in gold paint were posted up throughout the exquisite space as human statues, holding gold candelabras.

It was clear that Nairobia had gone to great lengths to ensure all those in the club's employ were beautifully built. Sin had thought he'd seen it all at her club on Passion Island, Club Passion, but The Pleasure Zone proved him wrong. She'd pushed the sexual boundaries, and left nothing to the imagination.

The club oozed sensuality.

The vibe was seductive.

Everyone seemed to be floating.

On lust.

On salacious thoughts.

On forbidden desires.

Sin stepped further inside, and then breathed in the aromatic scent perfuming the air from the massive floral arrangements. Under the glow of sultry lighting, he took in the wall of water cascading behind the sleek, curved bar before glancing up at the vaulted ceiling and then latching his gaze on three large, white Persian carpeted cages suspended in the air by thick ropes of metal chain.

He stood captivated by the sight of caged lovers hovering in the air fucking and sucking. Arousal shot straight to his groin, and his dick swelled against his jeans, the head of his dick now hanging out from the leg of his silk boxers. He cursed himself for wearing the wrong underwear.

"Enjoying the view," came a masculine voice in back of him over the music.

Sin glanced over his shoulder, and caught sight of Nairobia's once dutiful assistant and (one of her many) part-time boy-toys, Josiah. He'd recently been promoted to manager of The Pleasure Zone, responsible for overseeing every aspect of the club's nightly function. And, although, he still pleasured Nairobia as she saw fit, being her human sex-toy was no longer his primary role.

Josiah gave him a knowing look. Dominican and Haitian, he had skin the color of milk chocolate, and stood an inch taller than Sin. And, though leaner, Sin noticed the way his black T-shirt—the words THE PLEASURE ZONE scrawled over his chest in gold-foiled lettering—wrapped around a thick wall of muscle.

"Yeah, man," Sin said as he shoved his hands into his pockets in an attempt to mask the heavy bulge between his legs, "it's definitely a sight to behold."

Josiah grinned, the small diamond hooped earring in his left ear sparkling against the club's lights. "This is just the warm-up. You haven't seen anything, yet. Let me give you the full tour."

Sin obliged, following the six-foot-four hunk through a haze of scantily clad partygoers. He caught the back of Josiah's neck and couldn't help but notice a panther's head tattooed on the back of his neck as they headed toward a spiral staircase that wound up to the second, third, fourth, and fifth floors.

Sin shifted his attention back to the dance floor, where a sexy bronze-skinned Latina, tall and regal, caught his eye. She wore five-inch thigh-high stiletto boots, corset, ultra-short shorts and opera gloves—all leather. And black. Her cleavage spilled out over the top of her corset. Her lips were painted red, and shellacked with gloss.

Around her neck she wore a diamond choker, and her long black hair was pulled back into a sleek ponytail, and behind her left ear she wore a bright red rose. And in her hand, she held a riding crop.

She gyrated her hips, taunting her admirers, as she danced with a masked, bare-chested man. She moved into him, pressed her pelvis into his body, and then she brought her lips to his neck and bit the skin over his jugular, before licking over it. The man threw his head back and then growled when she stepped back, raised the crop up high and, with a quick flick, struck him over his right nipple.

The man's dick hardened beneath his loincloth.

If he weren't so dominant, Sin mused, if he had a submissive masochistic side, perhaps he, too, would have happily considered allowing the beautiful woman to whip a nut out of him—or not. He chuckled to himself at the ridiculous notion of him getting beaten and then fucked. Yeah, picture that, he thought as they made their way up and around the spiral staircase.

On the second level, there was a bubbling fountain in the center of the floor, flames dancing across the water's surface, and more oversized sofas. Gas lamps lined the walls, and the hedonistic sounds of primal fucking echoed over the music.

Sin had wanted to stop and take in the sight of three men dicking down a thin brunette. The busty vixen was taking the dick like a pro, mewling out over a mouthful of dick as the two other hunks plugged her ass and cunt with their dicks. All three men had found a rhythm, thrusting and retreating, fucking her orifices mercilessly.

Directly across from the foursome, situated on a silk-covered pallet, a short, stocky man was pushing a thick-hipped woman, with skin the color of brown sugar, to her knees in front of him. Beneath her was a man on his back, his face between her legs, his hands pulling open her ass.

The man standing in front of her slid his hand down into a

pair of leather-zippered boxer briefs and seconds later pulled out his thick, uncut dick.

His veined length bobbed.

Beckoned.

And the woman drank in the sight, running her hands up the chords of muscle in his brawny thighs. His hand tangled in her hair as he cupped the back of her neck, guiding his dick to her mouth.

"Suck it," he commanded.

The woman parted her lips and enticed the head into her mouth. She sucked him slowly as he held still in front of her. He was thick in her mouth, and the woman closed her eyes, seeming to relish in the full stretch of her mouth.

"Cock whore," the man growled. "*Shit.*"

Sin watched on, his own arousal beginning to stir as the woman slid a hand between her legs and played with her clit.

"Dick sucking, Cunt," the man hissed, teeth clenched.

The woman's eyes cut over in Sin's direction, and for a second their gazes locked. And then a smile curved her lips as she worked her mouth up and down her lover's dick.

Sin grinned.

Then the woman winked at him.

"Swallow that dick, bitch," the man barked. The woman opened her mouth wider and sucked him in, swallowing him as he strained forward, curling his fingers into her scalp. "F-*fuuuck*," he gasped.

Despite the music playing, Sin could hear her moans of plea-sure and the juicy, wet-suck sounds her mouth made as she bobbed her head with rapid back-and-forth motion. And he swore he could hear the man beneath her slurping, his tongue and lips working hungrily, sloppily sucking and licking over her folds.

Josiah slid a glance his way. "C'mon, man," he finally said, walking off. "There's more."

Sin simply nodded, and trailed behind him, prying his eyes away from the erotic scene before him. The voyeur in him wanted to stay planted, perhaps get a closer look, but his tour guide was more focused on whisking him through the club rather than allowing him to soak in the *fuck*tivities.

"The third floor," Josiah explained as they climbed the staircase, "is where we host our live shows."

Sin burrowed his brows in confusion. "Live shows? Didn't we just walk past several *live* shows? How much livelier can it get?"

Josiah chuckled, opening the doors to the space that held stadium-style seating. "Man, anything goes behind these doors. But here is where stage performances are hosted." After Sin peeked inside, they continued down the hall to a set of double French doors. "And this is The Playground."

Inside, the space was filled with collars and leashes, sex swings—spinning and bondage type, sex stools, bondage boards, liberator ramps, blowjob machines, and every sex toy imaginable, exclusively from Nairobia's adult-toy line, *Nasty*. There were even mechanical sex machines, something he'd never seen before.

"Damn, man," Sin said, impressed. "I see this club has thought of everything."

"Most definitely. Whatever your sexual tastes," Josiah said as he glanced over at Sin, "there's something naughty for everyone."

Along with the floor-to-ceiling windows and transparent floors looking down the club's five flights, every floor offered a condom and lube station, and had spectacular views of the Hudson River. By the time they reached the fifth floor—which opened up to a five thousand-square-foot rooftop garden with retractable walls and roof, along with an enclosed penthouse lounge, Sin was overly impressed.

He whistled, taking it all in. "Man, this is some view." He glanced down, staring through the floor, before walking over toward the railing and looking over. From what he could see, the members were taking full advantage of their membership privileges in every way imaginable.

"So what happened to the last manager?" he asked, directly. There was no point in beating around the bush. Although this wasn't the club he would be expected to manage, he still wanted to know what had happened, why the previous manager had been replaced by this twenty-something year old. *Kid.* What could he possibly know about the art of pleasure, about forbidden desires?

As far as he was concerned, managing something to this magnitude required the skill of someone who had years of experience in pleasuring, in good fucking.

"He was only meant to be temporary, from the start," Josiah told him. "Lamar owns his own security business. But he'd stayed on for two years longer than he'd wanted as a favor to Nairobia."

"I see. And how'd you end up in the position?"

Josiah regarded him, thoughtfully. "Let's just say, Nairobia knows my talents well. And over the years she's seen my dedication and commitment to not only the club, but to her as well. I started out here as a bartender when the club first opened." He glanced over the railing down onto the club's dance floor. The club was in full swing. Packed with scantily dressed women, heeled and curvaceous, and hard-bodied men thrust in the throes of untold passions.

Yeah, he'd come a mighty long way from being an inexperienced, big-dicked, quick-nutting cabana boy in St. Lucia (where Nairobia had found him) to becoming a virile, insatiable, pussy-pleasing man. He'd surely evolved, matured, into a sexual beast. And he had Nairobia to thank for all that he was.

"I may be younger than most in this business—twenty-eight, to be exact," he added as if he'd read Sin's previous thoughts, "but I *know* the business of pleasure."

Sin gave him a head nod. "That's what's up, man. Congrats, and much success to you."

"Thanks." Josiah gripped the glass railing, and smiled. "So, what do you think so far?"

Sin swept his eyes around the club again, taking in the erotic view from the top floor down. The seduction. The temptation. The deviance. The debauchery.

It all made his dick hard.

"Man, this shit is lit." He glanced over the railing, again, and took in the half-naked dancers, before noticing that the staircase spiraled down to another level beneath the first floor.

Curious, he asked, "So, what's down on the basement level?"

Josiah met his questioning stare. "The Love Tomb," he said, amusement thick in his voice. But his eyes said it all. They grew dark and mysterious. The basement level housed a Roman-style sauna and its heated, Olympic-sized pool. It was also where several passageways led to a variety of chambers, where patrons who craved a bit more kink could indulge their fetishes freely.

"Mind if I go check it out?"

A sly grin curled Josiah's lip. "Go indulge your curiosity. Take in all of its pleasures. But proceed with caution, my brother."

Sin laughed. "I'll keep that in mind, playboy."

And with that, Josiah watched as Sin walked toward the elevator and then pressed the call button. He waited, glancing at his watch.

2 A.M.

The club closed in another four hours. But the drinks poured steadily in abundance, and the club-goers danced and fucked and sucked with reckless abandon, all with the same salacious intentions in mind—to unleash their hidden, freaky desires.

When the elevator doors opened, Sin stepped in. Then pressed the button for the main floor, leaving Josiah soaking in the sights from where he still stood. Sin would have to take the stairs down to the basement once he reached the first level. On the way down in the elevator, all he saw were tongues on pussies, on clits, on asses; mouths on dicks, hot, sweaty fucking in multiple positions—and lots of people climaxing.

He felt his own nut swelling in his balls. He was tempted to make a pit stop on the second floor to get a quick dick suck, but—

The elevator doors finally opened, and Sin stepped out.

He licked his bottom lip in anticipation, and then—without being distracted by the sexually explicit going-ons happening on the dance floor—made his way down to the next level of decadence, where pain and pleasure swirled into one.

FOUR

ELEVEN A.M., THE following morning, donned in a pair of cut-up PRPS jeans, a fitted white linen pullover, which showcased his perfectly defined pecs, and a pair of designer flip-flops, Sin was strolling toward Nairobia's luxury high-rise building in the Tribeca section of New York. "For a brunch meeting," she'd called it. This was his first time visiting her at her home, where the well-heeled roamed. And for the life of him, he didn't quite understand why she hadn't wanted to meet him at her club instead. But who was he to question her? Nairobia wanted what Nairobia wanted.

And she summoned you how she wanted you.

The moment he stepped through the entrance the doorman immediately greeted him. "Mr. Saint-Michael. Welcome. Ms. Jansen is expecting you."

Unsure as to how the middle-aged man knew his name, Sin glanced at his nametag. Stewart.

"Bet you're wondering how I knew it was you, huh?" he asked as he ushered Sin toward the elevator.

Sin chuckled. "Yeah, something like that."

"I'm psychic." He laughed. "And the picture of you sent down by Ms. Jansen didn't hurt." He used his keycard to swipe access to the private elevators.

Sin stepped inside, and then turned to face the doorman.

"Enjoy," he said, giving Sin a slight head nod.

"Thanks," was all Sin could let out before the doors shut.

Sin caught a glimpse of himself in the elevator's mirrored walls. His locs hung loosely down his back for a change. His beard was freshly lined, and his rich chocolate-brown skin looked smooth. He had to admit, he was one sexy motherfucker, if he said so himself.

The elevator dinged, announcing his arrival to Nairobia's penthouse. He stepped out into the marble foyer the second the door slid open. The 21-feet high floor to ceiling windows offered iconic views of the Hudson River, the Statue of Liberty, and the New York Skyline. Sin whistled under his breath at all of its opulence. But, of course, he wasn't surprised. He'd expected nothing less from the sultry, sex goddess.

Mahogany doors slid open automatically, and there she stood, several hundred feet away, beneath an enormous crystal chandelier gleaming with crystal droplets and beads that looked like falling raindrops.

Hand on one curvaceous hip, and draped in more diamonds than clothing, the slit of her sheer dress angled just below her sex. Her mesmerizing gray eyes glinted with sexual interest. Oh, how she always had an interest in fucking him. Her cunt always enjoyed good company.

However, sexing her was the furthest thing from his mind. But that didn't stop his gaze from moving over her body, from the lace bodice of her dress, which dipped dangerously low. Sin tried not to rest his eyes on her cleavage, or voluptuous breasts, or the outline of her dark areolas and thick chocolate-tipped nipples, for too long. But, goddamn, he was a man. Ass and breasts did it for him.

"You like the view, no." She didn't ask it as a question.

Yet he answered. "As always," he said over another smile.

"Then do not stand there. Come to me. Press me into your flesh, my darling."

Sin smiled wide, perfectly straight white teeth flashing as he moved toward her. He found her refreshing. And he loved her hedonistic approach to life and her sexuality. She refused to live her life confined to labels—and fucked whomever she wanted to fuck, when she wanted, however she wanted, with abandon.

That alone was a major turn-on. He inhaled. Suddenly he smelled her, before he reached her. Floral scented. She was a garden of arousal.

He wrapped her up in an embrace. "Good morning," he said. And then he kissed her cheek.

"Yes," she purred, pressing her pelvis into him as she looked up into his gaze. "This is truly a good morning, my darling." Seconds ticked by before she finally stepped from his embrace, reaching for his hand. "Come, my love," she said as she led him further into her palatial home. "I've laid out a feast for you. I do hope you've brought your appetite."

"I'm always hungry," he said in a husky voice, as his gaze settled on the seductive sway of her hips.

"Then I shall feed you well," she said saucily over her shoulder, leading him through the foyer. As they walked, Sin thought he heard what sounded like moans and sultry music drifting from the other side of a set of French doors.

Mere seconds later, the doors opened, revealing an immense dining room filled with some of the most exotic-looking women he'd ever laid eyes on. They all wore elaborate bejeweled eye masks. Some were naked, while others wore sheer ankle-length loincloths and glittery pasties; several of them posing as human statues, just like the ones he'd seen in her club the night before, while others were in the throes of passionate kisses, or engrossed in some form of masturbation.

In the center of her massive dining room table was what she called her human centerpiece—two women in the sixty-nine-position pleasuring one another with their fingers and tongues—situated atop a luxurious white mink throw and hundreds of red rose petals.

A groan nearly escaped Sin's parted lips as he took them all in;

beautiful, shapely women, of all sizes and skin tones. Not only was Nairobia known for surrounding herself around beautiful men and women, but she'd also been known for hosting the most elaborate, invite-only sex parties around the world, before she'd opened her first club.

Abruptly, all their eyes were now on him, every movement and conversation halted. Mouths watered. He suddenly became a succulent slab of chiseled beef being thrown into a den of lust-starved women. Some of the women leered seductively, others licked over their lips. Their dark gazes, hungry and needy—gleaming with lust, showed their desire to touch him, to run fingers and hands over his skin.

They wanted sex with him.

Wanted to be lost in the fullness of him.

To be enveloped by his heat and sensuality.

"My darlings," Nairobia murmured, "I introduce to you this morning's guest of honor, Sin—the epitome of masculinity and sexual prowess."

The women moaned their appreciation. Sin greeted them, and then gave Nairobia a questioning look as hands resumed moving slowly between quivering legs, and tongues swirled over turgid nipples.

"Today," she answered before he could ask, "is about you. First, I will feed you. And then . . ."

She paused, but Sin was still looking at her, his brows creased in question, his eyes now filled with an arousing curiosity.

"And then?"

"And then, my darling . . . *they*"—she swept her arm around the room— "will worship you. And feed your libido."

On cue, a gold glitter-dusted woman in gold strappy heels poured champagne into glittering crystal flutes, while another glitter-dusted woman walked in with a multi-tiered gold platter. Salmon croquettes and mini Asian crab cakes were arranged on the top level. Tuna Crostini and tuna tartare were arrayed on the second; crab salad canapés and stuffed piquillo peppers with goat cheese filled the third. Cheeses and grapes were arranged on the bottom level.

"A toast," Nairobia called, flute in hand. "To passion and never-ending pleasure. And to Sin—the man who knows how to deliver both." Sin couldn't help but grin, glancing around the room, and then at Nairobia, who simply smiled at him.

When the guests raised their drinks, Sin did the same, then brought it to his lips to sip. After the toasts, the remainder of his drink went untouched. He didn't want to be inebriated. He wanted to be present, in the moment, with a clear head and conscience, aware of every detail, of every decision, presented and made.

"You didn't have to do all this," he stage-whispered to Nairobia. But he was glad she had. What man wouldn't want to be standing in his shoes surrounded by beautiful, half-naked women?

"Nonsense," she said, her inconspicuous hand sliding slowly over the back of his shirt, along his spine, until she was cupping his hard, muscled ass. "I long to return you to Passion Island with nothing but thoughts of returning here . . . to me, to *this* . . . eager to take hedonism and eroticism to another level, to push sexual boundaries and give new meaning to the word *sin*. All in my new club."

Sin stood, unblinking, unflinching, a grin on his face. "You're definitely making it easy to consider," he said, his gaze now locked on the two women sprawled out on the table. He felt his arousal stretching to the tip of his dick.

Nairobia looked up at him. "No, my darling. Don't just consider. Accept."

Sin looked at her. "Can I at least give it some more thought?"

Nairobia pursed her lips, and then nodded, before running her hand down the length of his chiseled chest. She removed her hand before she rubbed it over his thick bulge. "Do not make me wait for long."

He kissed her temple. "I won't."

"Very well." She stared at him for a long moment, before her hand touched his face. "Now tell me, my love." She stroked his cheek. "Your night at the Pleasure Zone was all that you imagined it to be, no?"

Sin grinned, and then his tongue ran slowly over his lips, making the women who watched him almost moan. "It was more than what I expected," he admitted, his voice thick with heat from the lingering memory of his night and, now, from the eroticism in the room. "You left nothing to the imagination."

She smiled. "I never do, my darling."

"I see," he said, quickly glancing around the room, before landing his gaze back on her.

"Did it arouse you?"

"What do you think?" he said huskily.

She nodded, knowingly. "And were you able to find release?"

"I found more than enough," he said in a mischievous voice.

"And hopefully you will find—" she ran her hand between his powerful thighs, cupped him there— "more release here."

Sin eyed a woman as she slid her hand over the curve of another woman's ass as she watched him watching them. She smiled wickedly, and then her hand moved to her partner's inner thigh, rimming her slit with a finger.

Pleased to find him aroused, Nairobia removed her hand.

"It looks promising," he answered, as his gaze stayed fixed on the beautiful woman. She slid another finger inside her partner, stretching her, making her moan. Sin imagined the feel of her wetness as pleasure raced through her body. He licked his lips. And, with Nairobia's arm looped around his, he was led around the room, mingling here and there, and sampling the hors d'oeuvres.

An hour later, a door slid open and in walked a woman wearing a mask covered in rhinestones, pulling a beautiful, dark-skinned woman by a leash. Hands tied behind her back, her head was shaved bald, her lips painted in tangerine, the collar around her neck bedazzled in rubies. A submissive.

Shit.

When both women approached them, he watched as Nairobia cupped the sub's breast through the thin layer of her dress and thumbed her nipple until it hardened and jutted outward. When the submissive gasped, Nairobia captured her breath with her mouth, kissing her long and hard until the young woman was struggling to catch her breath. Clearly leaving her in a passion-induced fog.

Nairobia pulled away with a smile, looking over at Sin. "Pleasure is yours for the taking, my darling." She then sauntered around the woman and undid the straps of her dress. And as it fluttered to the floor and gathered at the woman's feet, she added, "All that is here, my love, is for you." And then she turned her attention to the sub. "Now, my love," she said, her lips flush against her ear. "Tell Sin what you desire."

"To taste you," she said softly. She dropped her gaze. She was offering herself to him. Submitting to him. And Sin found himself caught up in the gesture.

"What else do you desire?" Nairobia urged, her lips still next to the woman's ear, slipping her hand beneath the front of her loincloth.

Her eyes lifted to meet Sin's gaze through her lashes. "For you to bathe my tongue with your semen." She shuddered as Nairobia rubbed her clit. "T-t-to have you . . . make love"—she moaned when Nairobia withdrew her hand from her wet pussy— "to my mouth."

Sin stood eyeing her, his dick slowly stretching, achingly aroused. But before he could respond to her, she dropped down to her knees. Parted her lips.

And waited.

FIVE

SIN MOANED IN his sleep.

The once crisp sheets beneath his skin were now twisted around his limbs and damp, his pillows strewn about.

"Take your clothes off?"

Anguished eyes—the eyes of a young boy, pleading, stared back at the young woman. *"I don't want to."*

Whap!

A hand seared the side of the boy's face. *"Do as I say,"* the woman sneered, *"'fore I beat the skin off you."*

With trembling hands, the young boy began removing his clothing. He pulled his Michael Jackson T-shirt over his head, and let it drop to the shag rug. Then he nervously unzipped his pants and shoved them down over his narrow hips. His bottom lip quivered as he stood in his Incredible Hulk underwear.

"And you bet' not cry. You a man now. And men don't cry. Ever. You hear me?"

He nodded.

"Now take off them underwear."

Three sets of eyes stared longingly, waited hungrily; their lusty gazes hazed by weed smoke and brown liquor.

Tears shimmered in the boy's eyes, but he willed them at bay. He didn't cry. He was a man. The air hot and stifling, he tried to focus on the red strobe light swirling around the living room, tried to focus on the green velvet-wallpapered wall, tried to count the album covers hanging from the wall, tried to keep his eyes on anything other than on the leering eyes burning over his trembling flesh.

"*Goddamn, you, boy! You taking too damn long,*" the woman hissed, impatiently yanking down his underwear, freeing his dick from its confinement.

Breaths hitched.

"*See. I tol' y'all,*" the woman said to the three other women, her voice filled with pride. Paper cups filled to the rim with Johnny Walker, the women sat on the edge of the sofa, the plastic beneath them crunching from their shifting bodies. She grabbed his dick. Shook it. Squeezed it. Then stroked it. "*See how fat it is. Watch how big it gets . . .*"

The boy closed his eyes. Bit back a groan. The needle of a record player spun around the grooves of a .45, a man's voice singing about a woman who'd faced the hardest times you could imagine; her eyes fighting back the tears.

". . . *Bernadette, girl, c'mon 'n' get you some of this . . .*"

Plastic crinkled. The woman stood, cup in hand. Braided-wig, big-breasted, wide-hipped, she sauntered toward the boy, the tip of her tongue moving over her bright pinkish lips.

"*Yes, look'a here.*" She fanned her warm hand out over his young chest, fingertips brushing over his flat nipples. "*Ooh, he's a fine, sexy thang.*" Her hand slid over his flat stomach, then lower.

"*Unh-uh, bitch,*" the young woman snapped, quickly snatching her by arm. "*Pay me my money, first.*"

Pink Lips yanked her arm back. "*Bitch, I got your money.*" She slid a hand down in between her breasts, fished out her money, a crumpled twenty-dollar bill. She tossed it. Then she sank to her knees. Licked up and down the boy's young dick until it stretched beyond her wildest surprise. Then she opened her mouth, and swallowed it whole.

Wet.

Warm.

Slurping sounds.

Moans.

A hand cupping his tender sac.

The boy felt himself fading.

Fading.

Fading.

Fading.

Until he'd disappeared . . .

Sin shot up in bed, heart racing; his muscled body slick with sweat. His gaze darted around the hotel suite. His bared chest heaved with breaths; his hands clenched into fists. His body shook with anger, with hurt, with confusion.

He'd dreamt again. Of a dark place. A lingering remnant of a past, of a life he fought to forget, fought to out run. But no matter how hard he tried, no matter how far he ran, no matter how many times he tried to erase it from his memory bank, it and that lost little boy always found him. And no matter how many times he'd wanted to save that little boy, he'd fallen short. Fallen victim to the sensations, to the sounds, of hands and mouths and wet pussies.

He couldn't run from it. Couldn't hide from it.

When he least expected it, the dreams would surely come.

He'd suffer through them, as he'd done with all the others.

Then he'd awaken.

To only find his dick hard, throbbing.

And an array of feelings sweeping through him, like now . . .

Guilt. Shame. Arousal. Hatred.

Yeah, hating himself—for allowing it all to happen, even when he knew there hadn't been a motherfucking-thing he could have done to stop it. Because all he knew was that he had been helpless to it. That he had been forced to surrender to it.

That he hadn't been able to say no.

SIX

SIN SAT IN the backseat of the metallic silver S600 Benz that had picked him up outside his hotel. A pensive look on his face, he stared out of the window, watching as the city passed in a haze of traffic lights, honking horns, panhandlers, street characters, and stop-and-go traffic.

It was a little after eleven in the morning, and midtown was already buzzing all around. Admittedly, he loved New York City. Good, bad, and grimy, there was no other place like the city that never slept. The Big Apple had it all. No matter what time of the day or night, no matter the vice, there was always something going on.

And yet he didn't feel connected to it—to anything, really. But he loved the energy while he was surrounded in it, for the moment. And he was glad to have had a chance to be caught up in all of its hustle and bustle, if only for a few short days. But like the saying went, all good things had to come to an end.

At least for now, he thought inhaling deeply.

His trip had been interesting, to say the least. But, surprisingly, he was ready to get back to the quiet, where he could think.

He had a lot to process, and to consider.

Nairobia had left no stone unturned, turning up her seductive charm at every turn, trying to entice him into staying.

"I choose you because you are Sin, my darling. And what better

place to have you than in Sin City . . . I want you because you are good dick . . . you are unforgettable fucking . . ."

He slowly breathed out through his nose, replaying her words in his head. Yeah, the dick was good, for sure. And the stroke game was superb. But what made it all unforgettable was always the man it was attached to.

He believed *he* made the experience unforgettable. He made it his business to make each experience not easily forgotten. As a man who loved sex, he considered himself a master at giving pleasure. He prided himself on being a skilled lover. After all, he'd had years of experience and a countless number of women to practice on. He'd learned the art of lovemaking and fucking, early in life.

And he knew the difference.

And if nothing else, in spite of whatever he'd gone through in his lifetime, he'd been taught well.

And he—

"Was your time here for business or pleasure?" The driver had a thick Nigerian accent. His eyes met Sin's in the review mirror.

Sin pushed out a breath. "Both."

"And did you enjoy your stay?" the man asked as he sped his way over the George Washington Bridge to New Jersey.

Sin wasn't really in the mood for small talk, but he decided it was better to indulge him than being stuck inside of his own head.

"I did. Thanks."

"What kind of work you do?"

"I'm a consultant," Sin answered, cryptically. He didn't feel the need to go into any further details, explaining what type of *consultant* work he did. Nor did he want to be the topic of discussion, so he took control of the conversation and asked the driver how long he lived in the States, and if he had a family here.

"Seven years. I leave my family to come here to work. Save money. Then send it back home so that my family has a good life. I am here alone. Staying with friends. But I go home once a year."

Sin stared at him. He had to be getting pussy from somewhere. There was no way he was only fucking once a year. He thought to ask, but quickly dismissed the question.

"That must put a lot of strain on your marriage. You know, only seeing your wife and kids only once a year."

"We Skype a lot." He laughed. "And I like lots of Pornhub."

Sin chuckled. "I bet."

"And you? You have wife, kids?"

"Nah."

The driver glimpsed in his rearview mirror again. "Sometimes it's better. It's hard to not miss them when they're not with you."

Sin shrugged. "You're a better man than me. I'm sure they miss you as well." He said that more out of courtesy than care.

The driver laughed. "They will miss the money more."

Sin nodded, then glanced at the sign that read TETERBORO AIRPORT. He couldn't wait to board the plane, and then sleep most of the seventeen-hour flight away.

He was exhausted.

The last three days had been filled with nothing but parties and salacious nights at the Pleasure Zone. And then yesterday's "brunch meeting" with Nairobia had somehow turned into an all-day orgy.

Well, that wasn't quite the word he was going for to describe what had gone down at Nairobia's sex haven since he'd been the only man in the room, doing most of the fucking. But, still, there'd been lots of fucking and plenty of sucking between the women, with multiple female partners being passed around.

It had been close to dusk by the time he'd stumbled out of there. His balls completely drained. After all that, he definitely needed a few days to relax and recharge.

The driver suddenly turned onto a service road, and then showed his credentials after stopping at a security checkpoint, before driving out onto a tarmac.

"Your plane," the driver announced as if Sin didn't already

know that the Gulfstream with the letters NJ—for Nairobia Jansen—entwined on the tail wasn't there for him, waiting.

Before stepping out of the car, Sin thanked the driver and slid him a fifty-dollar bill. And then he gathered his bag and crossed the tarmac to the luxurious jet, which was a much smaller version of the Pleasure Chest, the one used to fly couples to and from Passion Island. The one he'd been known to give its female passengers, who longed to become a part of the secret mile-high club, some of their most memorable orgasms.

Pleasing passengers in-flight to one of the world's most tropical paradises, most times than not, was a part of his job title. And Sin *always* aimed to please.

Sin grinned.

A voluptuous flight attendant stood at the bottom of the steps, wearing a short black dress and red patent leather, pointed-toe Louboutin heels.

Her smooth milk-chocolate skin was flawless. And she wore red lipstick over her full lips. "Mr. Saint-Michaels," she said. And then she smiled. "Welcome."

Sin smiled back. She was also a pleasure consultant on Passion Island, but she mostly worked her sex magic on the flights she was assigned to, providing pleasure to the male *and* female passengers when requested.

"What's good, Mocha?"

"*You*, sexy man," she said saucily. "I'll be your flight attendant. And since you'll be traveling alone, I'll be sure to give you the red-carpet treatment."

"I like the sound of that." It was nice to be in the role of passenger for a change, where his needs would, could, be catered to, if he so chose to indulge himself. Mocha winked and then let him know she was available for anything he might desire during his flight.

"Shall I take your bag?"

He laughed, knowing damn well she had no real interest in carrying his designer duffle bag unless she was taking it home with her. "Nah, I got it."

"Good," she said. And then she gave him a mischievous grin as she headed up the steps and into the plane.

SEVEN

NEARLY SIX HOURS later, the Gulfstream was somewhere high above puffs of clouds, soaring at an altitude of over forty-one thousand feet. There'd been a significant amount of turbulence so he'd been confined to his plush leather seat, where he sipped a bottle of Passion water and flipped through the pages of the latest *Men's Health* magazine. The edition covered thirty red-hot sex secrets and twenty ways to lose belly fat.

Sin shook his head. Just push back from the damn table, mofo, he thought, before coming to an article on erectile dysfunction. He skimmed through the five causes of impotence, thankful that he was still highly blessed and favored with a very, very hard dick.

He couldn't imagine the stress, depression, and low self-esteem that many of the men who experienced impotence were faced with.

It sounded like an affliction. One he hoped he'd never have to suffer through.

Just shoot me.

Life without a rock-solid, harder-than-steel erection was unthinkable. It was a sick, twisted form of cruel punishment.

Sin pressed his thighs together and then blew out a sigh of relief. If he'd been in the comforts of his own place, he would have slipped a hand down in his boxers and fondled himself, his balls and dick, until he brought himself to an erection.

Hard dick mattered.

A big dick mattered.

Good dick mattered.

It was what most women craved. It was what they wanted, what they needed.

The size of a man's dick, his ability to perform sexually, was the center of his existence. It had a stronghold on a man's self-image, of his self-worth. It had the ability to fuck with a man's psyche.

Closing the magazine, Sin stretched his long legs in front of him and rolled his head on his neck. And then he closed his eyes and said a little prayer for all the limp dicks in the world no longer capable of completely satisfying their women in bed.

You can send them to me.

Amen.

He opened his eyes when Mocha came to him. "Hey sexy," she murmured, pulling him out of his thoughts. "Are you ready to eat, yet?"

A smirk on his face, Sin looked up at her. "You, or dinner?"

She puckered her lips. Tilted her head. "Both."

"In that case," he said huskily. "I'll have dinner now. And, perhaps, *you* . . . later."

She smiled, before moving back toward the galley.

Sin sipped the remainder of his water then unlatched his seat belt. He stood and stretched and then toured the cabin. Just behind him, there was a plush leather sofa, a sixty-five-inch flat-screen, a stocked media console and state-of-the-art sound system, and an extended dining table. There was even an area for doing laundry.

In the back of the jet were two suites, each with king-size beds and its own bathroom. Sin slipped inside the main bathroom to relieve himself, impressed by the décor. All white marble, veined with 14kt gold. A white swivel chair faced a white marble vanity that held baskets of expensive toiletries.

He washed his hands and then dried them on one of the fluffy white towels. He stared at his reflection in the mirror. He looked like he felt. Tired. Luckily, there'd be enough time to crawl up in one of those beds later. And he was looking forward to it.

When Sin finally made his way back to the main cabin, Mocha was setting a place for him to sit at the table in view of the TV.

"Dinner is ready, Sir," she said, teasingly. "Is there something special you'd like to watch on television while you dine?" She reached for one of several remotes on the console. "Whatever your pleasure, we have it."

Sin laughed at how serious she was taking her flight attendant role. "Yo, you're really going all out. Relax. You can get off script." He pulled a chair out. "Matter of fact, go grab yourself a plate and let's just have dinner and chill. I don't need you to play flight attendant. And I promise I won't write you a bad review."

She let out a breath. "Good, because I need a damn drink."

He laughed again. "Cool. Then bring back two. And make mine a double."

And for the next two hours the two of them ate, drank, and talked about life on Passion Island.

"Did you know Soul left for California yesterday?"

Soul—not his birth name—was another one of the island's pleasure consultants, and had taken on his moniker after he'd met Sin and his brother, Saint. Over the last three years, most people who'd visited the island had mistaken all three of them for brothers, since he, too, was over six feet, had dark chocolate skin wrapped around thick muscles, and deep searing brown eyes. But his Caribbean lilt, whenever he didn't turn it off, would give it away.

"Oh, word? So he decided to take the job, after all." Sin smiled. One thing about Nairobia she looked out for those who were loyal to her. She'd offered Soul an opportunity to work for her adult entertainment company, Sweet Pleasures. And from what Sin knew about it, he'd be starring in several of her newly scripted adult films. Something Sin was sure he'd rise to the occasion for—no pun intended—with flying colors.

Mocha nodded. "Yeah. He's on his way to becoming the next porn king."

"Right, right. I'm happy for him. But I'm definitely gonna miss his crazy ass."

Mocha smiled, and her brown eyes twinkled at him. And then she licked over her lips. "Me too." She'd never fucked him, but she wished she had now that he'd left the island for new endeavors.

Sin laughed. "I bet you will. Nasty ass."

She feigned insult. "*Nasty?* Not me." And then she laughed. "Besides, I never had the chance to get nasty with him. But you know LaLani did. And she said the sex was good."

Sin shook his head. LaLani was another one of the island's pleasure consultants, who also filled in as a flight attendant when needed. "I figured one of you would have sampled the goods at some point."

She playfully rolled her eyes. "Anywho, he said he was ready to go, to move on to bigger and better things."

"Yeah, I know." Sin sipped his drink. "Good for him. Change is a good look when it comes your way."

"Do you think you could live there on the island indefinitely?" she asked.

Sin shrugged. "I haven't given it much thought. But I don't see my life there for any long period of time. Hell, I didn't expect to be there this long." And, yeah, three years was a long time for someone like him. It was almost a lifetime. "Don't get me wrong, though. I dig the vibe."

Mocha smirked. "I bet you do."

He laughed. "Yeah. What can I say? I enjoy being able to give pleasure." He stared at her. "What about you?"

"Are you asking me if I enjoy giving pleasure? Or if I see myself staying indefinitely?"

"Both."

"Yes, to giving pleasure. And no to staying there indefinitely. I mean. It's cute for now. But I don't see myself being there for much longer, either. I miss my family and friends. I mean, it's beautiful and all, but it's so far away from the rest of the world, you know? And the cell service is so damn shitty. And the fact that there's no cable for television"—she shuddered— "is tragic. I can't even watch *Black Ink*, or any of the *Housewives* shows."

Sin laughed. "Yeah, it's hit or miss. But that's purposeful. The whole point of being on the island is so that you're away from the rest of the world, away from negativity and unnecessary stress while pampering yourself."

Mocha reached for the crystal canister and poured herself another drink. "Yeah, I guess. Still, it gets lonely sometimes. Don't get me wrong. I enjoy what I do. And the pay and perks are great. But, sometimes . . ."

She paused, taking a sip of her drink.

Sin regarded her thoughtfully. He couldn't wrap his mind around the concept of being lonely, probably because he enjoyed his alone time so much. And he knew how to entertain himself, very well. Living as the only child had a way of teaching you how to enjoy being alone, by yourself.

"Sometimes what?" he asked, shifting his body in his seat so that he could face her.

She set her glass down on the table and looked him in the eyes. "Sometimes I wanna be held, you know? It would be nice to have someone to come home to—not that Passion Island is my home, but you know what I mean."

Sin nodded.

"I'd like to have someone I can crawl into bed and make love with."

He didn't quite share that sentiment. The idea of coming home to the same woman, the same pussy, day in and day out seemed monotonous, tiresome, and . . . *boring*.

He wasn't interested. He preferred a revolving door of women—

preferably ones who were nameless and easily forgotten—rather than having one woman trying to smother and trap him.

"So"—Sin looked around the luxurious aircraft—"you're ready to give up all this?"

"If Mr. Right comes my way, then yes. I'd give it all up in a heartbeat."

Sin smiled. "He's out there, baby. Somewhere your Mr. Right is making his way to you."

Mocha gulped down the remainder of her drink. "Well, I hope he hurries the hell up. I need some steady loving in my life, something with substance."

"Maybe you shouldn't wait then," Sin said.

A questioning frown creased her forehead.

"I mean, maybe, you need to hang up this life, and go back home to your family and friends, to civilization, where you can meet a pool of cats to choose from. There's nothing but random-ass dudes, who are typically already attached when they come to the island, anyway. And the rest of us are mostly there for a good time. So your pickings are very slim to none if you're expecting him to show up at your door. If a man of your own is what you really want, then go out and get him, baby. Because he damn sure isn't on the island."

"Maybe I will," she said. She stared at him, wondering. "What if you're my Mr. Right?"

Sin shook his head, slowly. "Nah, baby. I'm Mr. Right Now. And that's all I will ever be."

She shrugged. "Oh well. Can't blame a girl for fantasizing." She downed her third drink, and then raked her gaze over him, head to toe, giving him an *I'm ready to get fucked by you all night* look.

Without missing a beat, Sin asked, "Why you looking at me like that?"

She feigned ignorance. "Like what?"

"Like you want this dick."

She stood to her feet. "Because, Mr. Right. Now," she said, her voice sweetened by lust, "I do." She unbuttoned her dress. "So, since you enjoy giving pleasure so much, how about you share some with me."

EIGHT

MOCHA WAS PISSED.

Sin hadn't fucked her last night, like she'd hoped, wanted. And now she was prancing around the aircraft, pouting that he hadn't given her the dick this morning, either. He chuckled to himself. Women.

Granted, her pussy had been so ready for him. All wet and needy—and, shit, his dick had stretched out ready to put in work. And then it clocked out before he could stretch her open. Hell, it wasn't that he didn't *want* to fuck her down. He'd simply been too exhausted, and didn't have the energy. And the two drinks he'd had hadn't made it any better. It'd made him more tired than he'd already been. Still, he'd given her some form of intimacy, which is what he felt she needed most, anyway, before he'd started to drift off to sleep. And, yeah, his hands and lips and tongue had felt so good all over her, but she'd still wanted more from him. She needed it. She ached for it.

His long, thick dick, she'd wanted it stuffing her holes, mostly her mouth and pussy—but she would have given up her ass to him too—if he'd wanted it, if he'd asked for it. But he hadn't.

Instead, he'd loved on her body with his mouth and then simply held her in his arms, brushed his tongue against hers, kissing her deeply, passionately, while fingering her to an orgasm.

Still . . .

That hadn't been enough.

And, this morning—even after she'd stroked and sucked every single inch of his delicious dick, licking over his hard shaft, trailing her tongue up over that thick, juicy vein until she was swiping it over and around the head—he *still* hadn't fucked her.

"I'll make it up to you," he'd promised, before rising above her. "Spread your legs."

"You better," she'd said. And then she poked her lips out, while spreading her legs.

He'd positioned himself between them and kissed her lips. "You're sexy when you pout."

"Whatever." She sucked her teeth. "I'm so horny."

"I know. I smell you."

She'd swallowed. And then blinked up at him. "So, are you going to fuck me?"

"No." He'd centered his dick over pussy and then pressed his shaft in between her lips, sliding back and forth over her clit and slit. "I'm gonna tease you. Make you nut, just like this." There was no way he was fucking her without a condom, even if he'd planned to. Mocha was the type of woman who Sin fucked on occasion. She was pretty as fuck, and sexy as hell, for sure. But she'd always given him the feeling that she was . . . uh, well—for the sake of not calling her crazy—a bit *touched*. And the last thing he needed was a nutty broad stalking him for his dick. Fine or not, he had to ration out his sex to her. Having good dick was stressful.

Mocha thrust her hips upward, grunting. "Fuck you, Sin."

"I know you want me to, baby. And I will . . ." Again, and again, he slid himself over her pussy and clit. "Next time."

She'd felt herself becoming undone. She'd felt herself melting. Felt herself on the verge of screaming. "You know you ain't shit, Sin. Teasing me like this."

"I know."

"I can't believe you have this wet pussy right in front of you, ready for the taking, and you won't put your dick inside it. What the hell is wrong with you? Why are you doing this to *me*?"

"It's all about you, Mocha. Everything I am doing, is for you." He'd licked his sexy lips, his hips slowly moving back and forth, his dick wetly gliding, gliding, gliding, over and over her pussy; the contact drawing her closer to nirvana. "Am I making you feel good?"

She'd bitten down on her lip. And then grunted out her response.

"*Unh*. Fuck you, Sin!"

"Yeah, I know you want me to, baby. Fuck you helpless."

"I already am. *Helpless*." And then she arched to him, and murmured over and over, "Fuck me, fuck me."

"No," he'd rasped. Then he'd given her a low, sexy laugh. "You should know by now I give you what I want you to have, what I know you need."

"*Unh*. That's . . . *aaah* . . . so . . . *mmm* . . . not fair."

"Who said sex with me would be?"

"You're such a control freak."

"And you're so wet." His hooded eyes flicked over her face, and then lower—to her breasts, her pierced nipples. "And your nipples are making my mouth water." He'd ducked his head and then flicked his tongue over her right nipple, then moved onto her left one, before pulling it into his mouth and sucking on it, hard.

Mocha's breaths came quick as his wet tongue scorched over her nipple, as the heat from his heavy dick seared her labia. Her head thrashed. She couldn't ignore the sensation. Her cunt lips began to swell. Her distended clit became overly sensitive. Still he stroked; still her flesh swelled, her walls clenched.

"This is sexual torture."

He'd abandoned her aching nipples and then nibbled on her neck, and then brushed his lips against her ear. "I know that, too." He moaned low in her ear. "But it feels good. Doesn't it?"

A cry broke out from her lips, her back bowed to get her closer to her orgasm. "I hate you, Sin," she'd hissed, before releasing another cry of pleasure.

"And you should, baby. Hate me. Hate me for making you feel good. For making your pussy so wet when I haven't even fucked you." His voice had grown huskier, thickened by lust.

"Ah-ah . . . *uhhh.*"

He met her heavy-lidded gaze. "That's right, baby. Hate all over this dick."

Her clitoris throbbed.

Her eyes closed.

And then she'd—

"You owe me big time," Mocha hissed, bringing him back to the present.

Sin looked up at her. Hand on one hip, one brow raised, she had a fresh coat of lipstick on her lips. "I promise, I'll make it up to you."

She rolled her eyes. "You better."

"I got you, Mocha."

She leaned in so that her lips were mere inches from his face, and then she spoke low as if someone else, some imaginary person, in the cabin would overhear her. "And when I call you, Sin. I expect you to deliver. Fuck me hard. And deep."

Then she straightened her body, and mushed him on the side of his head.

He laughed, shaking his head as he turned his attention out the window. Stretched out below him was, miles and miles of clear turquoise water. And right in the center of it all was a heart-shaped island, with its leaning palms and powder-soft sands.

Sin sighed. Relieved that the long journey was finally coming to an end. He expected the return to be met with new guests horny and eager to have their sexual appetites fed.

The first thing he'd do when he landed would be to check his messages and any notecards that he might have received to see who wanted him, specifically, to indulge their fantasies and deliver a mind-numbing, toe-curling experience.

Yeah. That's what he'd do. Sift through the freaky requests, and then discard the ones he had no interests in fulfilling.

As the aircraft's wheels lowered and it started its descent, Sin leaned back in his seat, as the pilot's voice came over the intercom to announce that they would be landing on Passion Island in less than twenty minutes.

NINE

"DIRTY, CHEATING BITCH," Sin whispered against her ear.

He'd been back on the island for more than a week, and he'd already had seven fantasy requests. And out of those, two had been requests by men, wanting to explore their bisexual sides. Sin didn't judge, but he'd politely declined, passing those requests on to someone else willing to fulfill those types of desires.

Pleasing only *women* was his sole mission.

"You love being a whore, don't you?" he murmured in her ear. And then he sunk his teeth into her earlobe, his hand between the woman's legs, stroking, caressing.

"Does your husband know what a slut you are?"

Her pussy was so wet and needy.

She hadn't told him her name, but he knew who she was. Alberta Jessups. He knew because she'd been on the flight's manifest to the island several weeks back, and he'd only remembered her because of her strawberry-blonde hair and the fact that she was slightly cross-eyed. But that one lazy eye hadn't taken away from her strikingly good looks and curvy body. She was older, perhaps earlier fifties or so, but her skin glowed and had the unlined quality of a woman who invested lots of money in moisturizers and other beauty products to only enhance her genetic blessings.

He just tried not to look in her eyes for any longer than a few seconds at a time, or he'd start to feel dizzy.

As if she knew, she closed her eyes and shuddered as he filled her with one finger, then two, then—oh, oh, God, no—three fingers. Her pussy drenched him. "N-no," she pushed out breathlessly. "He doesn't know."

Of course, he didn't.

Did they ever?

She'd filled out a fantasy slip and had placed it in one of the islands' many fantasy boxes scattered on the island, where guests could discreetly write out their fantasies, and ask to have them fulfilled by one or a hosts of selected pleasure consultants, spiking up the erotic heat that already spread over the tropical paradise.

She'd wanted to be called dirty names and be hand spanked, and then fucked hard. *I'VE BEEN A REALLY BAD WIFE* she'd written on her note.

"Fucking conniving slut."

She moaned in response. Her body flushed with need. He bracketed her throat with his hand, lightly squeezing, but not enough to bruise; just enough so she couldn't take in enough air to breathe.

Her pussy clenched, juices sliding down the insides of her thighs.

"You like that, huh, whore?" He stroked her, kept his fingers moving over her walls, his eyes on her.

She parted her lips but words didn't follow, just gasps.

Sin knew this was all part of the game, all part of the seduction. It was what she requested. But he couldn't understand why any woman would want to be degraded. At what point in her life did she (or any woman, for that matter) find it endearing to be called all types of filthy bitches, cunts, or whores?

He loved dominating woman, but he didn't enjoy disrespecting them. And yet it aroused him knowing that he was giving her what she needed, what she craved for.

Humiliation.

Domination.

Even if she weren't a true submissive, she wanted to submit. She wanted the pleasure the night would bring, because she thought, she believed, she deserved it as long as she endured the pain.

As long as she was punished, as long as she was debased.

It had to be some deep-rooted psychological shit, he thought. But it wasn't for him to figure out. He wasn't here to save her from herself. He was here to help her play out her fantasy. He'd never hurt her, or any woman, but he'd give them more than what they'd ever imagined they could bear.

Who was he to judge? His dick was hard, and he had a box of condoms on the ready to split her back open.

Pulling him from his reverie, she moaned again and bucked against his touch, pulling his fingers deeper. "Wet, greedy whore," he hissed, finally freeing his hand from her neck.

"Yes, I'm a greedy whore," she murmured, and with his free hand he toyed with her right nipple until it tightened and peaked, and ached for his tongue.

"Is that why you cheat?" He abandoned the right nipple for her left, tweaking it until it throbbed for his mouth. "Because you're a greedy whore?"

He pinched her clit, and she whimpered against the pain, with the pleasure.

"I-I . . . don't . . . know."

He thrust his fingers deeper.

"Don't lie to me, you nasty cum dump."

"Be*caaaaause*," she croaked out; Sin had found her G-spot. "Oh, God, oh . . ."

"God can't help you now, whore." He stroked her there, and her knees nearly buckled. "Tell me why you cheat, you fucking slut."

She grew wetter, hotter. Sin gave her the words she craved. It fueled her need to be reminded of how dirty she was, how trifling she was, how fucking scandalous of a woman she was.

She'd chosen him. Had wanted him the moment she'd laid

eyes on him, because everything about the man was sinful, and—well, because she was a dirty sinner. And she hated herself for it. Fucking her sister's husband, her children's uncle, her own husband's golf partner.

She couldn't stop herself.

She didn't *want* to stop herself. Fucking him, loving him, wanting him. But she didn't want to keep hurting either. Loving him hurt. Fucking him hurt. Deceiving her husband, and her sister hurt. The idea of ending her affair hurt.

Everything about her life hurt. She was surrounded by it. And yet she still wanted him. She hadn't asked for it, hadn't been looking to cheat, and yet when the opportunity presented itself, she welcomed it.

Seven years later and she was still deceiving everyone she loved. He wasn't leaving her sister, though many times over the years she'd fantasized he would. But if he would, she'd throw away sixteen years of her own marriage for him. She'd disrupt her children's lives. Ruin her marriage, and her sister's because she was a selfish bitch.

And now she had to make a decision. Leave or stay.

She'd come to Passion Island in hopes to find a reason to stay with her husband, the father of her two children, the man who'd stood by her side—through the countless doctor visits, the chemo, the hair and weight loss—as she battled ovarian cancer.

Then she thought about her lover, his touch, his voice. And suddenly nothing else mattered. So she somehow felt being here, being fucked by this stranger, being manhandled, and humiliated, would be some sick form of atonement.

Could she atone?

"You want me to fuck you in your cheating ass, you cock-sucking whore?" His gaze held hers, spearing through her soul, burning her from the inside out as his fingers steadily, rhythmically, moved in and out of her body, round and round her pussy, over her clit, then back between her aching lips.

She moaned. And her eyes went wide. She loved big dick, but she'd never been fucked there, in her ass. Maybe she deserved to have her asshole fucked to shreds. It would serve her right for all of her debauchery. For being such a deceitful, lying bitch.

"I, uh—" she started.

Sin put a finger to her lips. Focused his gaze on her good eye. "I'm going to reach down into your filthy soul and fuck you like the whore you are. I'm going to make you cum, and give you everything you wanted to sin for."

His fingers retreated; wet, sticky, and warm.

Her eyes suddenly ached as if she were about to cry.

"Turn around, you fucking whore," Sin snapped, before a single tear spilled. He spun her around toward the sofa, forcing her to bend over. "Spread your legs," he said firmly, domineeringly.

He smoothed a hand over her plump ass, and then cupped her there, squeezed. Then rubbed his shaft along her ass, and a shudder rolled through her body.

Sin stepped back, and then he slapped her ass with a cupped hand, causing her to jump. The sting seared across her skin, finally settling over her clit and making it throb.

"Oh." The word came out a moan.

He smacked her again, harder.

"Look at me, dirty whore."

She turned her head to look at him, her eyes pleading, her hips moving. "Yes?"

Sin smoothed his hand over her ass again, rubbing the reddened skin in rhythmic circles, before trailing his hand along the crack of her ass. His fingertips grazed her hole until his fingers slipped in the heat between her thighs.

"You're wetter than before." His dick jerked. "You like your ass spanked."

She moaned.

Whap!

"Dirty cunt," he hissed, and she clawed the arm of the sofa.

Whap!

"Bitch," he whispered, and she arched into the pain.

She ached in a way she'd never had. The intensifying pleasure, all coiled around a delicious pain, swept through her core, sending sensations rippling through her veins, through every part of her flesh.

Whap!

"Fucking dick sucker," he sneered, and she begged for more. He spanked her again and again, her ass jiggling, her skin gleaming red. She buried her face into the sofa. Bit into the fabric.

"Filthy slut," he muttered, and she writhed beneath the onslaught of his blows to her ass, gasping, tears suddenly springing from her eyes. Sin brought his hand down across her ass in hard, swift, calculated swats, and his dick grew harder from the lascivious sound of hand to flesh, marking her ass.

Her aroused pussy, a fresh wave of heat scented by her sinful desires, frantically clenched as every nerve ending spasmed.

Her ass burned.

Oh, God, yes. This, the pain, was so terribly mind numbing; so good, so exquisite.

Legs shaking.

Eyes squeezed shut.

Mind whirling.

She gasped.

Whimpered.

Begged.

Submitted to the pain.

Gave into the pleasure . . .

And sobbed in the throes of her multiple orgasms.

TEN

"So how was it?"

Sin was on the northern tip of the island, where the sand was pink, and the water a rich turquoise, having drinks at one of the island's beach bars with his brother, Saint. Tall and dark like Sin, he was three years older and a foot shorter. And with the exception of having a neatly trimmed goatee, he was clean-shaven and kept his shaved head bald, mostly because the women loved his perfectly shaped head.

The two imposing, irresistibly sexy brothers hadn't grown up together. In fact, their mother had given Saint to his father, without a fight, once she'd learned she was pregnant with Sin. He was three years old. And, while Saint envied Sin for having lived with their mother, Sin had grown up wishing he hadn't. But that was another story all together. One he wasn't trying to give any thought or energy to.

Sin and Saint where similar in some regards, but entirely different in others. Where Sin preferred causal sexual encounters, Saint had numerous global flings and fleeting relationships, and had managed to sire seven kids, by six different women, in five different parts of the world.

He was the epitome of a rolling stone.

Sin believed in using condoms. Saint didn't. He preferred experiencing the true essence of a woman, capturing her nakedness raw and in its purest, nastiest form. The thought of creaming inside of a woman's body, coating her walls, turned him on. However, the only time he did use condoms was when he was on the island, working, like his brother, as a Pleasure Consultant. But, off the island, in his personal world, that was a whole other story. Condoms didn't exist.

And neither did pulling out.

Sin's brows furrowed. "How was what? Last night?"

Saint had his bottle of beer hoisted to his lips, frozen in midair as he shot Sin an incredulous look. "Nah, fool. How was New York? I know that shit was dope."

"Oh, that." Sin laughed. And then he recapped his time in New York, and all that he experienced inside the Pleasure Zone. "No lie. It makes Club Passion look like a monastery. Real vanilla compared to what I witnessed there." He decided to not mention the brunch Nairobia had hosted in his honor, or the abundance of beautiful women who had been at his disposal.

"Damn, that sounds like my kind of shit. I love it nasty." He narrowed his eyes. "Wait. What happened last night?"

"Nothing earth shattering," Sin said nonchalantly. Loads of feminine laughter echoed from somewhere behind them over the music.

"Nah, bruh," Saint said. "Don't hold back now. I need details." He took a swig from his beer. "Spill it, *muhfucka.*"

As much as Sin enjoyed sharing the sordid particulars of his conquests with his half-brother, he didn't feel like talking about last night.

Sin shrugged. "Damsel in sexual distress meets savior. Savior indulges damsel's need to sin. And then the rest is history."

"And?"

Sin shook his head and grinned, his locs sweeping over his back. "And, let's just say, we have another happy visitor on the island."

"Was it good?"

Sin looked at him, as if he were trying to find the words to explain. "It got better as the night went on," he admitted.

"Did she ask you to bite her clit?"

"Nah. But she did ask me to whip her."

"Whip her, where?"

"Her ass," Sin said nonchalantly.

Saint grinned. "Damn. I hope you tore that ass up. I bet she got wetter with each blow."

"She did."

Unlike Sin, Saint was impulsive and could be unpredictable. He was moody and easily lost interest. But the one thing you could be sure of from Saint was that he did whatever the hell he wanted, however he wanted, whenever he wanted. There were no apologies. No second-guessing. He followed whims. Lived on the edge. And went after what he wanted, before moving on to the next best thing.

And what set them apart the most was the fact that where Sin was sensual and passionate when it came to sex, Saint preferred it rough and nasty.

With a dick two inches bigger and thicker than his brother's, Saint preferred to pound a woman out, with lots of choking and ass slapping. He liked spitting in a woman's pussy, then shoving his horse-sized dick in her. He also enjoyed skull-fucking a woman, holding her by the head and fucking the snot and spit and tears out of her, while his dick stretched her throat and sealed off her airway. When a woman requested his services, she had better be prepared for the fuck of her life. Because when he was done with her, all three holes would be fucked raw, and she'd be wobbling back to wherever she'd come from too worn out, too sore, to spread her legs for anyone else for at least a week.

Truthfully speaking, Saint saw women as a tool to *his* pleasure. And in pleasuring him, they too would be pleasured. He objectified them. Period. And as long as they brought *him* pleasure, he didn't see any reason to not have his way with them.

Wasn't that what women were put here on earth to do, pleasure men?

After Saint drained his bottle of beer, he wiped his mouth and looked at his brother. "These married broads kill me." He shook his head. "They come here under the guise of working on their marriages, and yet many of them end up creeping on their husbands. That shit makes no sense to me."

Sin agreed. But, again, who was he to judge? This was Passion Island. Couples came here for their own reasons, with their own agendas. Many of them wanting vindication, forgiveness, and/or second, third or even forth chances to fix what they saw as broken in their relationships. The road to whatever it was they needed to salvage in their marriages wasn't for him to decide, nor was it for him to judge how they made the journey.

So, if he needed to make another man's woman's back arch and her toes curl, or allow her one night of pleasure to help her live out whatever fantasies she conjured up in her head, then so be it. It was what he was paid to do. To allow women to live out the dark desires floating around in their heads. Period.

"We're not here to try to make sense of it," Sin said, reaching for his drink. "We're in the business of providing a service. Bringing pleasure to those who seek us out." And he believed that wholeheartedly. It was their duty to worship at the altar of the women who sought out their services, where every part of their body was touched and tasted and savored. *That* was how you turned a woman out, giving her a dizzying, toe-curling experience. One she'd never forget.

Slow, sweet, lovemaking.

"Yeah, I guess," Saint said, unmoved by his brother's sentiment. The bartender slid another beer across the bar to him. He gave the curly-haired man a head nod. "These broads out here can't seem to be trusted to stay clear from temptation. Seems like that shit is everywhere." He shook his head, and then gulped down his beer. "Cheating is definitely becoming an epidemic."

"*Becoming*? You think?" Sin said sarcastically. "Man, it already is."

Saint grunted. "These broads out here ain't shit."

He belched and wiped is mouth with the back of his hand.

Sin chuckled. "Says the man with the six baby mothers, and multiple jump-offs in practically every area code." He motioned to the bartender for another drink.

Saint shrugged, glancing over at two beautiful buxom babes perched on stools across the bar, sporting crocheted bikini tops and lots of cleavage. One had the word JUICY tattooed in red ink on the swell of her breast. The other wore a half-sleeve of red roses, which started over her right shoulder and then stopped at her elbow. They both smiled. He smiled back. And then he envisioned himself bouncing them both on someone's mattress, staining up the sheets. There was nothing like getting lost in the feel of two women's hands on him at once, two women working their mouths over his dick and balls, working to pleasure him at the same time.

"It's a dirty job," he said after a beat, "but someone has to do it."

Sin laughed. "Right, right. Thankfully the world is a dirtier place with you in it."

"Exactly."

A few swigs before Saint's beer was drained, another appeared before him. He glanced at the bartender and gave him a head nod.

A highball glass was then plunked down in front of Sin on a napkin. Sin gave the bartender a confused look. "I didn't order this."

He gestured with his head. "From the women at the end of the bar."

Sin tossed a cursory glance in their direction, catching their glassy-eyed gazes. Sorority sisters. Both wearing colorful bikini tops, their breasts on display, barely covering their nipples. One of them was attractive, probably had a husband and two kids tucked away someplace on the other side of the world. She sat perched on her stool, back straight, all prim and proper. The other had heavily painted eyes and wild tousled hair. She looked a bit more uninhibited, but it was clear they were both traveling freaks.

And yet neither of them was right for the night. Still, Sin lifted his drink, and gave them both a head nod.

They both smiled and gave him finger waves.

"They want you," Saint said.

Sin shrugged. "Not interested in doing a lot of work tonight."

Saint huffed. "Man, you tripping. Double the pleasure."

"Double the headache." He shifted his body, his back now to them.

He heard the wild-haired one say, "Oh no the hell he didn't." He'd cost them fifteen bucks, after all. "The motherfucker doesn't even have the decency to come over here and greet us. Bastard."

Saint laughed. "Sounds like she's hot with you."

"She'll be fine. She needs to learn to wait. They both do. I'll make my way over there when I'm ready, if I decide to."

Just then, Saint caught the eye of another woman. She'd been looking over in their direction for a while, so he summoned for the bartender.

"Send the woman in all that red whatever she's drinking."

When the bartender turned to fix whatever she'd been drinking, Saint watched as he set the drink in front of her. She looked like she needed some dick in her life. And he'd gladly give it to her, from the back.

She had her hair dyed chestnut blonde. And he'd never really been attracted to blonde women, anyway, but he had to admit the hair color looked good on her. It had at least four different shades, ranging from butterscotch to caramel and all hues in between, complimenting her copper skin tone.

Saint grinned at her. The woman smiled, and then shook her head, her eyes quickly shifting over to Sin. *Oh.* The message now loud and clear: I'm not interested in *you*, but I'll drink your drink. And then fuck the one you're with.

It had to be the dreads, because it definitely wasn't about the dick. Bitch probably couldn't handle this dick, anyway, he thought as he gave her an acknowledging head nod, letting her know he'd read her eyes and body language.

He chuckled to himself. He'd never suffer a case of blue balls, so it was all good. Pussy was all over the island, and there was always enough to go around.

He wasn't all that interested in her ass, anyway. All he'd done was send her ass a drink, and the first thing the bitch did was jump to conclusions. That he wanted to get in her panties. And he did—but she didn't *know* that for sure. *Bitch, them drawers probably nasty any-damn-way.* And yet he casted her one of his typical bad boy grins, and then turned his attention to Sin, clearing his throat. "Uh, bruh, looks like you have another admirer." He motioned with his head in her direction. "Right side corner; across the bar. And she looks like she might be stacked right."

"Yeah?" Sin said coolly. It wasn't a big deal. He was used to women vying for his attention, one way or another. He waited a few seconds before turning in her direction. One elbow rested on the bar top, and her other hand stirred a drink with the red straw.

Sin caught her eyes, held them.

She was attractive enough. Middle-aged, perhaps early forties give or take. But it was hard to tell given the bar's lighting and what appeared to be good genes. She definitely looked like she took good care of herself.

She smiled and thought she saw curiosity and interest flickering in his gaze as he acknowledged her with a head nod, and then with his signature lopsided grin.

At that, she brazenly swept her tongue over her top lip, catching a droplet of her drink. He lifted his drink in gest, and then slid from the barstool and stood to his feet.

"I'll catch you later, bro," he said.

And then he made his way over to her.

ELEVEN

THE MOMENT HE reached her, she felt herself nearly swoon off the barstool. He was temptation in the flesh, with his sinfully fine self. And those intense dark eyes (Lord, help her!), eyes that a woman could drown in, eyes that had her wanting to lose herself in, made the walls of her sex pulsate. She imagined herself alone with *him*, in a room lit only by candlelight—naked, his body the only thing covering her, blanketing her. His dick, what she imagined would be long and thick—maybe even curved, fucking her so sweetly, so deeply, until she wept from the pleasure of it all.

And now, out of nowhere, he was right in front of her, in all of his pure fineness.

Sin smiled, revealing rows of perfectly straight teeth. He had the whitest teeth she'd ever seen, particularly on a man. And, for some strange reason, his teeth—or the knowing that he took pride in them—made her want to lean over and kiss him, lick over his gums, and then suck his tongue into her mouth.

She raised her glass of wine to her lips.

"Hi, you're Sin, right?"

"The one and only."

"I thought so," the woman said. "I remembered you from the plane ride over"—she looked him over— "without the shirt on, though."

Sin chuckled. "I've been told I look better with my clothes on."

She laughed and reached over and slid a hand over his shoulder and then down over his bicep. She squeezed his arm. "I doubt that very seriously."

"I'm serious," he teased.

She playfully rolled her eyes. "Oh, stop. Whoever fed you that crock of crap had to be dumb *and* blind."

"Duly noted," he said over a chuckle. Then he held his drink up to her. "Thanks for the compliment, though."

She grabbed a bar napkin and dabbed at the corners of her mouth, while lifting her glass to his. Their glasses clinked.

"You're very welcome. I'm Sheila, by the way."

"Nice to meet you." He extended a large hand, and swallowed hers up in a firm handshake, causing a warm, tingly sensation to spread up her arm and then over her breasts. Or was she having another hot flash?

When he finally let go of her hand, it felt as if he'd taken a small piece of her with him, and she wanted it back.

Dusk was starting to set in, and Sheila dragged her gaze away to look out at the ocean. A waning sun cast a glow of brilliance over the calm waters, while small waves lapped at the shore, leaving a cascade of foam over the wet sand.

She shifted her gaze back to the bar and glanced at the bartender who was moving from one end to the other, grabbing glasses, mixers, and bottles. She watched as the man pulled down two highball glasses from the glass shelving and began pouring drinks.

"So, beautiful lady, how long have you been on the island?" Sin asked.

"Almost four weeks," she said, before taking a sip of her drink and then gliding her tongue over her lips.

She caught her reflection in the mirrored wall of the bar, and then Sin's. She flipped her hair over her shoulder, suddenly feeling sexier and desirable, and more alive than she'd felt in years.

Sin took a sip of his drink, looking over at her. "Almost at the end of your stay, huh?"

She sighed. "Yes, and then back to reality."

"Ah, yes. Reality. It sounds so boring. Let's not think about it, yet," Sin said. "Let's stay in the moment."

She pursed her lips. "Mm. Yes. Let's."

Sin smiled. "So, are you enjoying your stay so far?"

She shifted on her stool, and nodded. "Yes, yes. The island is beautiful. So peaceful, and yet so full of . . ." she paused, unable to place a word to it.

"Sexual energy," Sin finished for her.

She laughed. "Yes, that. And lots of passion; I never knew an island could be so erotic."

Sin smiled at her again. "Well, it's what this island is all about. Eroticism, passion—all rolled up into one big bowl of pleasure."

She nodded, knowingly. "It's like nothing I've ever experienced. Every day I'm learning something new, discovering a new part of myself."

Sin cocked his head to the side, studying her. He looked intently into her eyes, and there went that drowning sensation washing over her again. "And so far, beautiful, what have you learned about yourself?"

"Oh, Lord," she groaned, shaking her head. "I don't think you want to turn this into a counseling session."

"It's all good. I'll send you my bill later," he joked.

She chuckled. "Well in that case, only if you tell me some of your deep, dark secrets in turn." Yes, she was flirting with him.

Sin laughed. "Ah, you want my dark secrets, huh?"

Among other things . . . yes! She shuddered inwardly. *Girl, you'd better stop this right now, before—*

"My name speaks for itself," he said over a smile. "My dirty deeds are no secret."

He took a sip of his drink, then set his glass aside, his eyes suddenly flashing a fire that scorched over her body. "Now tell me something naughty about you." Sin smiled again. "The dirtier the better."

Blood suddenly rushed between her legs, and she felt herself swelling with need.

She swallowed, then reached for her drink and took a long swallow of the rich, red wine.

"Um, well, let's see . . ."

I'm so fucking wet.

I swallow.

I love anal.

And—Oh, God—I think I wanna have your baby.

"What," Sin teased, "cat got your tongue? Don't go shy on me now."

Sheila coughed, choking on a laugh. A fresh flush darkened her face, and Sin took pleasure in knowing he'd been the cause of her blushing moment. Still, he decided to not press her more about any of her dirty thoughts or deeds. He'd let her off the hook, for now.

"I'm not that *naughty*," she said once she managed to find her voice again.

"Well, then, perhaps, we'll have to come up with something to change that, before your stay here comes to an end." His voice was husky, his eyes flashing another round of heat over her skin.

"Hmm. Perhaps," she murmured. Without as much of a word, the bartender returned with another glass of wine as if he'd known she would need it.

"Thank you," she said, and then offered him a smile.

He gave her a quick wink, took her empty glass, and then whisked off to the other side of the bar.

She sipped. Swallowed. Tried not to focus on Sin's lips, or the pleasure they might bring. Tried not to linger too long on his big, warm hands, or the idea of them grabbing her ass, kneading her breasts, or cupping her pussy.

She felt another burst of heat climbing up her neck and over her cheeks. Her breaths were starting to come in short, deep pants. Was she having a panic attack?

She cleared her throat. "So, what brings you out to the bar tonight?" she asked, changing the subject. Yet her eyes glinted with a mixture of curiosity and arousal.

"If I told you, would you believe me?"

She blushed again, shaking her head. "Probably not. But, if it sounds good, I might consider it."

"Well," he said, leaning slightly back and sliding his gaze over her body, "then I'll say I came down to get a closer look at the view."

She took another sip of her wine, grinning against the glass.

"Oh, you're good," she said.

"And I get even better," he shot back.

Oh, Lord.

She set down her glass. She wasn't drunk, but she was tipsy enough to know another glass—or two—would have her stumbling back to her villa, or staggering through the sand with her cum-stained panties in her hand. She stared at Sin for a long moment, trying to imagine his thoughts. Were they as salacious as hers? Was he as hot and horny as she was?

The sun drifted lower in the sky.

And the longer Sin sat, the wetter she got. She could feel the wetness between her legs saturating her panties. And Sin could smell the delicious heat of her pussy. He knew without asking, without being told, without exploring the possibility—she wanted some attentive loving.

He licked his lips, and the provocative gesture incited her clit, causing it to tighten. She shifted her ass on the stool, pressed in and shut her legs tightly, trying to rein in her pulsing cunt. It throbbed thick and wet in her panties, begging for attention, for his thick fingers to finger out its juices, for his tongue to lick out her cream, for his dick to pound into her slick heat. Sheila bit back a groan.

She felt her libido floating endlessly around an overwhelming desire to spread her legs to him, right here, right out in the open.

She felt the urge, her hands itching, to reach out, to caress the sharp edge of his cheekbone, to run her fingers through his luscious beard.

"I don't know what it is about you, sexy man," she admitted, her tone low and conspiratorial, "but you're dangerous."

Sin raised a brow. "Oh? You think?" He smirked. "Tell me more."

She raised her glass to her lips and swallowed more wine. "I'm sitting here having all sorts of naughty thoughts."

"The only danger here is you leaving without ever knowing true bliss."

She swirled the drink in her glass, gazed up at Sin through her lashes. "My mind is telling me I should leave."

"Then why don't you?" he challenged. "I won't keep you. But if you stay, I won't tell, either." And then he brushed a finger over her knee. "It'll be our little secret, baby."

Baby.

The word rolled off his tongue like melted wax, hot and raw. And she felt the effects pouring out onto her flesh, searing over skin that longed to be touched, caressed.

Sin grinned. "What if I told you I wanted to make sweet love to you; would you let me?"

Caught off guard, Sheila laughed nervously, and then threw her head back to look up at the sky. She definitely hadn't been expecting that. And more disturbing was the fact that she hadn't expected to feel the heat rise in her cheeks again. A man hadn't made her blush, like this, in—*God, how long had it been?* —years.

"I, uh," she stammered. "I can't."

He smirked. "Are you sure about that?"

With now trembling hands, she reached for her glass of wine again, and took two long sips. "Honestly, I don't know."

"Don't lie, baby. We both know you want me to give your body the attention it's been craving. One long night of untamed pleasure. Admit it."

She swallowed. And then her mouth went incredibly dry. He was too damn fine, too damn sure of himself, too sure of her. She looked down into her half-finished glass of wine and fought the urge to take it down in one swallow. She knew she should gather her purse and excuse herself, quickly, and flee back to her villa without another glance at this fucking sex god, this goddamn Mandingo warrior. This, this, panty-wetting motherfucker . . .

TWELVE

Nails sinking into dark flesh, her pussy was wet and spread wide open. Its pink center glazed with her arousal. Sin pulled back, only slightly. Stirred the lower part of her pussy with controlled strokes. Slow. Determined. His dick churned a delicious heat inside of her, and she groaned.

"Shit. *Uh . . .*" Desperation crawled between her legs, and she arched her body, tried to get more of him, his dick, her pussy trying to swallow every part of him, whole.

Sin pulled back to the tip, and she clutched him wetly. "Greedy woman. You only get as much as I give"—he thrust in deep, causing her to gasp, then quickly pulled back— "when I give it." Two inches in, he teased her pussy in slow shallow thrusts. "You want it deep?"

He slammed in again, and the air around her suddenly exploded, making her dizzy.

Tingles shot up her spine. "Yes."

He drew back, almost completely withdrawing, then eased back in, sinking—this time, three inches in. He pumped her there, in swift shallow thrusts.

"You want it fast?"

"Yes," she answered in a shaky breath.

"You want it hard?"

He slammed back in, his dick stretching down into her heat. He pounded her until she creamed around him.

Disoriented, she arched her body and cried out. "Yes, God, yes."

Sheila lifted her hips, inviting him, silently offering him more, her aroused scent rising and tantalizing his senses.

Sin locked his gaze onto hers; her brown eyes liquid pools of need, pleading for more. He grinned, and then bit into his bottom lip, moving his hips ever so slowly. One inch, two inches, three inches, sliding in and out of her body.

"Please," she begged, her breath catching at the back of her throat as he held her hips with his hands, thwarting her attempt to coax more of him inside of her, his unyielding fingers lightly pressing into her flesh.

"Please, what?" Sin continued stirring is own hips in a slow, sensual motion, his dick pulling out and then dipping only two inches into her steamy, wet cunt.

"Put it all in."

Sheila cupped his ass and tried again to pull him to her, but Sin held her hips in place with his big hands and kept himself still.

"Nah, baby. I control the dick. Do I need to tie your hands up over your head?"

She blinked. She'd never been tied up, and the thought, surprisingly, swept a fresh wave of arousal through her. Still, she shook her head, and moaned. "N-no—don't." She couldn't help but stammer. He was pulling her apart and yet she felt her body shivering with an overwhelming desire she'd never known existed.

Diving back into her pussy, the head of his dick hit the bottom of her well, and she cried out, before he pulled back out and then played with her clit. She moaned again.

"Oh, *Sin*," she whispered over a breath. He pushed in two more inches, then snatched them back. She lifted her mouth to his and placed a hungry kiss over his lips. "Please."

He didn't respond.

Instead, he sank down into her, the base of his dick pressed tightly against her, which put pressure right on her engorged clit. He pumped her hard. He pumped her so fast and so deep until her arousal washed over so fast, like a tidal wave, that she felt herself drowning in it.

"Oh, God, Oh, God! Oh, Sin. Sin, Sin, Sin . . ."

The more she cried out, the more she chanted his name, the deeper he plunged into her with rapid-fire thrusts that caused her ache of desire to spread through her entire being until it bubbled up in the pit of her pussy and swept her under another wave of pleasure.

Sin hammered into her body, the force of his thrust shaking the entire bed, and she drowned in the sounds of his skin slapping against hers, in the wet sloshing of her cunt. Her senses heightened as the room spun.

Her breasts jiggled, her nipples hardened and beaded so tight that they ached. Sin licked over his bottom lip and then lowered his mouth to her right nipple. He sucked it into his mouth and worked her nipple with gentle scraps of his teeth, before plucking it with his lips and then moving onto her other nipple.

She screamed incoherently.

"Come on my dick," he growled. And just as she was about to spiral over the edge of another orgasm, Sin quickly pulled out, causing her to gasp. She blinked several times through a cloudy haze, trying to gather her senses.

What had he done? And why?

He grinned, holding his sticky, sheathed dick at the base and then sliding it back and forth over her opening and then over her clit.

"Goddamn you," she hissed, tears sliding out of the corners of her eyes.

He nipped at her nipple again with his teeth and stretched into her cunt in one deep thrust.

Her eyes rolled back in her head.

For the love of God!

He was snatching her life, snatching her soul, snatching her brain matter.

"Oh, God, oh, God, oh, God . . ."

There'd be nothing left of her when he was done with her.

"Play with yourself," he whispered. "I wanna feel this pussy come on my dick."

She slid a shaky hand between their bodies and swirled her fingers over her swollen clitoris.

Faster, deeper, hotter, higher, Sin sliced into her orgasm, his incessant strokes sawing over her sweet spot, unrelenting, unapologetically.

"Is this what you want?"

"Yes," she whispered, trying to catch a breath. "God, yes."

He pulled back, the head of his dick dragging along her walls and then over her spot. She nearly sobbed. "Oh, God, no, no, no. Don't pull out. Keep fucking me."

"Why should I?"

She let out a breath that she'd been holding in for almost forever. The breath turned into a groan. Pain and pleasure choked her with teasing hands. She wanted to scream out. Curse him. Claw at his handsome face. Yank a handful of his silky dreads from out of his scalp. She was burning with desperation to get him back inside her slick, throbbing cunt, to fuck her with his entire dick—not an inch of it, not half of it. No—hell no! —she wanted every thick inch of him.

He leaned in, nibbled along the column of her neck. "You're not ready," he breathed in her ear, then reached for her clit and pinched it. She groaned again and her walls constricted around him.

"I dreamt about this dick for the last three weeks." Sheila's eyes trapped his. Eyes pleading. Hungered.

"Does your husband know?" He slid his dick back in deeply. She gasped again. "N-no."

He pumped her hard for several long moments, before retreating again, staying at the mouth of her pussy, stroking her there. Her skin flushed hot, and she felt her desire boiling over, searing every part of her body.

A smile curled up the sides of his mouth. "Did you fantasize about me fucking you with this dick, while your husband was fucking you?"

"Yes," she admitted, shamefully, over a moan.

"Do you love him?"

Sin rocked into her body, and she nearly forgot her answer. Almost. But, of course, she loved Seth. He was the father of her four beautiful adult children (three sons and a daughter), he'd never disrespected her or mistreated her, and he had given her a wonderful life, one she wouldn't have had had she married her high school sweetheart. Jimmy the Mechanic. Jimmy had always been all dick and no ambition. He hadn't wanted to go to college. Hadn't wanted to travel the world. Hadn't wanted to dream big. Hadn't wanted to do anything else except fix cars.

Sheila had wanted more. She'd wanted a life of privilege. A life that afforded her the types of opportunities she hadn't been exposed to growing up in a household where robbing Peter to pay Paul was commonplace. No, no, she wanted financial security and the freedom to shop and spend however she wanted.

And, sadly, motor oil and cans of Fix-a-Flat didn't quite fit into her life plan—no matter how much she had loved Jimmy, no matter how much she knew her heart would ache for him. And so she'd ended the relationship in her second semester of college with her sights dead set on a lean, muscular running back with a promising future with the NFL.

With her cunning ways, after months of plotting and scheming, she'd finally snagged him. Married him. And then quickly popped out babies to secure her station, never looking back.

Twenty-eight years later, she was still with him. And, though his dick didn't quite satisfy her completely, he was a good man, a good father, and a loving husband. And she loved him for that. But she wasn't *in* love with him.

Still, she cared deeply for him, nonetheless.

Sin nudged her cervix, bringing her back to the moment. She gasped, sliding her hands over his shoulders and then down his back.

"Y-yes," she finally pushed out over another shaky breath. "I love him."

Sin lifted up on his arms, and stared down at her, his hips slowing down as he moved deep inside her body. "Should I stop?"

The three-lettered word formed in her head, but she couldn't bring herself to speak it into existence. Everything bloomed between her legs. The slow stroke of his dick inside her coaxed another climax from her body, his fingers now on her clit.

She panted and moaned, then sobbed and shouted. Every response being that of pure, unadulterated pleasure caused her body to buck. She was coming hard, endlessly, melting over each thunderous stroke, loving it.

She bit back a scream. Was he purposefully trying to drive her utterly insane?

If so, it was working—thank you, goddamn it! She felt herself going mad, the blood between her legs beating wildly. How could this man fuck her without really fucking her? How could this man— this, this stranger—seduce and torture her so sweetly at once?

This had been the best fuck of her life. One she knew she'd never recover from. She wanted to lie here, lost in his scent and in the sensations spreading between her legs yet she forced herself to breath, in and out, trying to get back to reality.

And back to the reason she was here on the island.

Her husband.

Her failing marriage.

And yet she still begged him to keep fucking her.

THIRTEEN

SIN'S EYES SHOT open.

He blinked at the ceiling, heart racing. Another bad dream about the same helpless little boy he dreamt about most of his life. This time the boy was ten, standing with his arms out, his eyes pleading for Sin, begging him, to grab him by the hands and save him. Sin tried to save him. But, once again, he'd failed.

He always woke before he could get to him.

He rubbed his eyes, then shook his head. He knew that little boy in his dreams was safe now, that no one could or would ever hurt him again. And yet, in his dreams, that same little boy—hurt and broken—would always need saving.

The same nightmare. The same main character. The same struggle. Nothing ever changed, except the varying stages of the little boy's life. It was always the same script reeling around in his head over and over. Voices and sounds and smells fusing, faces blurring, hands reaching and pulling, mouths moving—lips and tongues melding, teeth gritting . . .

The grunting, the crying out, the flood of sensations always woke Sin up before he could rescue that helpless boy.

Still, the visions often swept through him like a winter's storm, leaving him chilled from the inside out, from the memories.

From the images of that frightened little boy.

Frustrated, he threw back the covers and leaped out of bed.

He stood naked in the middle of his bedroom, raking his locs back from his eyes.

Sunlight filtered through a crack in the drawn, blackout curtains. He heaved a dramatic sigh. He knew he needed to do something to get his thoughts in check. He needed a reprieve from his dreams. He'd considered a few times, in fleeting moments, to talk to someone about them. But the idea of giving someone a glimpse into his head, of allowing them to draw out his secrets, was more than enough reason to dismiss the notion.

Besides, he wasn't crazy.

Was he?

Hell, nah.

He had it all under control, his thoughts. His feelings.

Didn't he?

Most definitely.

He knew he wasn't the blame for someone else's dysfunction. He'd learned a long time ago that hurt people hurt people. That damaged people damaged people. And he knew only he could control how he allowed it to affect him. He chose not to let it.

He was—

The loud knock at the door pulled him out of his thoughts. He almost made it to the door before realizing he was butt-naked. He hurried back to his bedroom and quickly retrieved a pair of cutoff sweat pants and a white T-shirt, the words HARD BODY stretched across his chest, from the dresser drawer, before heading toward the door again.

He flung it open.

"Mr. Saint-Michaels?" a twenty-something year old male said, his copper skin shining. He held an envelope in his large hand.

Sin gave him a questioning look. "Yeah?"

He shoved the envelope at him. "Here you go, Sir."

"What's this?" Brows drawn together, he took the envelope,

eyeing the young man as he walked off. Sin shut his door, before flipping the envelope over and pulling the tab to tear it open.

Inside was a crème colored envelope. A gold embossed seal the only thing keeping it closed. He lifted the seal and then pulled out a matching card.

He read the elegant script.

My darling Sin,

Passion lies in the seat of the soul. Without it, we are not alive. We become shells of ourselves, void of desires. Step into the sensual light. Say yes to my offer. And come join me as I take sexuality & eroticism beyond the world's wildest imagination.

With baited breath, I await you.

Een liefde,
Nairobia

Sin shook his head, the corners of his mouth turning upward slightly. She was definitely not going to make it easy to say no. Not that he was planning to. Fact was, he was still on the fence about the whole moving out to Vegas and managing a sex club, but Nairobia had piqued his curiosity. And yet he wasn't sure if he was ready to shake the island's dust from his feet for the Vegas heat. But the opportunity, the change . . . it was too good to pass up.

For most of his life, he'd been a drifter. Never settling in one place for more than a year or two. Being here on the island was the longest he'd stayed anywhere in his entire adult life.

Sin took a deep breath. Part of him wondered why he was still here, but then . . . the other part of him just wanted to stay in the moment and not put too much thought into the whys he hadn't taken off yet.

Obviously, something kept him put, even if he didn't necessarily feel rooted here.

He glanced at the time, and then decided he'd get his day started. First, by doing a few chores around the villa, and then he'd take a long hot shower.

Followed by a visit to one of the most beautiful head doctors he knew.

He needed a distraction.

And he knew exactly where he needed to go to get it.

Passion Hall.

⮢

Dr. Gretchen Dangerfield was at her desk, where most of her counseling sessions occurred on the island. She was finishing up the last line of her treatment note when she heard a tapping at her office door. The door was slightly ajar, and she muttered a curse for not making sure it had been shut all the way.

She was a licensed psychologist and specialized in Human Sexuality. On the crisp white wall in back of her were diplomas from Spelman and Harvard, certificates from various psychology associations, licensures, all showcased in expensive-looking frames.

The long-lashed therapist with her doe-shaped eyes and skin the color of rich creamy fudge was also the woman in charge of Passion Island's couples' retreat. A six-week, all-expense paid relationship boot camp, sort to speak, where couples seeking love, light, and reignited passion were tested, challenged, and dared to step outside of themselves to become better partners, more loving, more understanding, and—hopefully, more sexually giving of themselves.

Her work here on the island—and with the couples who sought to be a part of the experience—was about teaching them how to be more open, more passionate, growing in forgiveness, in love, and in lust for one another.

It was about renewing sexual energy.

It was about inspiring and arousing partners. Pushing their sexual boundaries, while testing their commitments to one another.

For many, it was the fuel needed to reignite their fires, to reclaim lost desires. For others, it was the last stop to finally tossing in the proverbial towel and calling it quits.

Even in divorce, however, in the ending of a relationship, there was liberation.

And she strived to free couples, either together or apart. The choice was always theirs to make.

Dr. Dangerfield sighed. This cycle was finally nearing the end for the three sets of couples currently on the island, and—truthfully, she couldn't wait to see them—well, two of the wives—climb their passive-aggressive asses back on that private plane and return to their pathetic lives.

Crazy bitches.

She shook her head, quickly rereading the assessment part of her note. WIFE REFUSES TO LET GO OF HER INHIBITIONS. FINDS ORAL SEX VULGAR. REFUSES TO ENGAGE IN ANY OF THE COUPLES EXERCISES. CLIENT SEEMS TO HOLD ONTO UNREALISTIC EXPECTATIONS . . .

But what Dr. Dangerfield had wanted to type, instead, was, IN MY HONEST ASSESSMENT, THIS BITCH NEEDS TO LEARN HOW TO SUCK A DAMN DICK AND SWALLOW!

She slid her tongue over her teeth, then pursed her painted lips.

Four weeks on the island, she mused, and this uptight woman had still failed to see the value in a good dick suck.

She *tsked*. She was so over these simple-minded bitches. They lacked desire to learn new things. Lacked openness to exploring new sexual horizons. And they clearly lacked the commitment needed to rekindle the passion lost in their marriages.

And yet women like her were too stuck in denial to either let go of their inhibitions, or let go of their marriages. You simply couldn't hold onto both—the inhibitions *and* the marriage—and expect it to end with a happy-ever-after.

No. At some point, that fairytale ended with someone else creeping into their partner's arms and inside their underwear.

Mmph.

Over the course of her career, Dr. Dangerfield had come across her share of men and women who were selfish lovers. Men, who wanted oral pleasure, but weren't willing to give it. Women, who refused to give oral pleasure, but expected their men to not seek it elsewhere.

And then there were those who simply detested giving or receiving.

It was sickening.

She despised an inconsiderate fuck.

Nevertheless, she loved her work on the island. It allowed her a voyeuristic-view inside every couple's private sex lives. She licked over her lips. Oh, how she loved working with the sexual deviants, the ones who had kinky, secret fetishes that they'd kept hidden from their partners.

Being on the exotic island was like being on a hedonism resort but with therapy.

And lots of hot, nasty fucking—or not.

She kept reading. CLIENT STATES HUSBAND IS TOO ENDOWED.

Then why the fuck did your frigid-ass marry him? She mused. She had to know he had a big dick, long before she said, "I do."

Dr. Dangerfield rolled her eyes, and yet she felt her nipples tighten at the recollection of his eleven-inch dick. She'd had the pleasure of catching several glimpses of the bat-like appendage during her—

There went the tapping again. She blinked away her lusty thoughts, and kept typing. When she didn't respond, the door opened, and the epitome of male eroticism stuck its head around. "Hey, beautiful. Mind if I come in?"

"If I say no, would that stop you?" she teased, looking up from her laptop.

"Probably not," he said, giving her a seductive grin as he pushed farther into the room, in arrogant strides that made it clear he was a man used to doing whatever he wanted. "You do know I've been known to take what's not given to me, freely."

Her head lolled back, and laughter bubbled in her throat. "Well, depending on what it is, taking it without permission, could be construed as theft."

His grin widened as he slid his muscular body in a chair in front of her desk. "Maybe it's *you* I'm trying to take . . ."

Legs spread wide, dreads brushing over his shoulders, Dr. Dangerfield let her gaze drift appreciatively over his muscular frame. Desire nipped at her clitoris.

Sin.

Sin.

Sin.

The man was hypnotic.

There was something about the way he looked at her, his eyes always flickering with undisguised interest, like he wanted to explore every inch of her, like he wanted to slide into her cunt, and then melt into her silken heat.

It made her want to blush.

But she managed to maintain her composure—barely.

"Then it's called kidnapping," she finally said saucily.

Sin's eyes captured hers, and he licked over his lips, almost in slow motion, before he said, "What if I told you I came here to touch you? That I wanted to dive into your body and swim into your soul, would it still be kidnap?"

Dr. Dangerfield felt herself going slick inside her panties, her cunt walls clutched at the ache of arousal.

Oh, he was good, damn good. Smooth-talking bastard!

She wet her lips, the pink tip of her tongue darting out.

Suddenly she had visions of being bent over her desk, her skirt hiked up over her hips, and Sin fucking her—her ass clapping happily around the heavy length of his dick, clutching him, her silky walls bringing him to climax.

And now there was a deep throb spreading through her pussy.

God, she hated when that happened, especially when she didn't have time for a quickie, to soothe the building ache.

Sin stood to his feet, and then he bent forward and planted the palms of his hands on her desk.

Dr. Dangerfield eased her chair back, and then crossed her legs.

The moment her five-inch pump slipped off the heel of her foot and her right leg slowly bounced over her left, he grinned. "You're turned on, aren't you?" he said smugly.

She kept her eyes trained on him. "I wouldn't actually call what I'm feeling at the moment *turned on*," she said calmly.

"Oh, yeah? Then what is it?"

"Amused."

He reared his head back and laughed, exposing his throat. She wanted to lick him there, bite the chocolate flesh and leave her mark.

"Lies," he said. And then he sniffed. "I smell the sweet heady scent of arousal. It's wafting all around me."

Her lip twitched, and she bit back a smile. "What you smell is deodorizer." She tilted her head and then her brows rose. "You know, you should really get that overactive imagination of yours checked. I can give you a referral if you'd like."

"Nah, I'm good on that. How about dinner instead—tonight?"

She looked up at him through her lashes. "Are you asking me out on a date, Sin?"

He didn't date. He fucked. He freaked. He gave a woman something to remember. Most women didn't get a meal—just the dick, but Dr. Dangerfield was special, real classy. And he honestly wanted to spend some time with her. Odd, however, since he'd never really considered spending any time with her one-on-one outside of the bedroom before now.

Still, she was good people, a real chill-type. And, tonight, he was in the mood for more than just pussy. He wanted conversation over a meal with a beautiful woman.

"Nah," he said, his mind already wondering if she were wearing another red lace bra and panty set. She'd had one on the last time he'd gotten her undressed, and the color against her skin had had him drooling. "Just dinner and conversation between good friends, and then . . . perhaps dessert. If you're up for it."

The idea of having him as her dessert sent a flutter of butterflies twirling in her stomach.

She bit back a moan.

"I'm always up for a little dessert," she said in a dreamy voice that suggested there might be room for something sweeter than a chef's pastry. "Tell me what time. And I'm there."

Sin grinned. "I like the sound of that."

Her brow rose. "The sound of what?"

"Compliance, baby," he said, before moving toward the door, his stride full of swag and self-assuredness. "See you at seven."

And all Dr. Dangerfield could do at that was laugh and shake her head as he eased his way out of her office, shutting the door behind him.

FOURTEEN

"SO DO YOU think you'll take the position?" Dr. Dangerfield asked in between bites of her salmon. They were having dinner at a quaint restaurant on the southern tip of the island. The maître d' had seated them out on the veranda, giving them a picturesque view of one of the island's many lagoons. Sin had spent the last ten minutes recapping his time in New York with Nairobia.

"I'm not sure. A part of me wants to. But then . . ." he paused, shaking his head.

Dr. Dangerfield lifted her linen napkin from her lap and lightly dabbed at the corners of her mouth, before dropping it back over her lap.

She met Sin's eyes across the table.

"But then, what . . .?"

Sin signaled a passing waiter. "A bottle of Brunello di Montalcino Costello, please." Once the waiter left, his gaze pinned her. "I hope you're fine with another bottle of red wine."

He'd chosen red over white because it reminded him of her—bold and flavorful.

Vibrant and full of warmth.

"Are you trying to get me drunk?" she teased. "Because if so, I'll have you know, this saintly woman isn't easily taken advantage of."

Sin leaned in and a wide grin spread across his lips. "Baby, you might be a saint in that pretty little head of yours, but you kiss—among other things—like a sinner."

Dr. Dangerfield coughed, nearly choking, over a laugh. "Well, a lady can have her naughty moments. After all, they say a little sinning is good for the soul."

Sin shared a laugh of his own. "I like the sound of that. But, sinning with me, baby, will stain your soul."

Dr. Dangerfield shuddered. "Then stain me," she teased as their waitress, a twenty-something platinum blonde, wandered—gracefully, with her shoulders squared and straight—toward them with their wine bottle. She refilled their glasses, and then set the three-hundred-and-twenty-dollar bottle in front of Sin.

"Can I get you anything else?" She nearly offered Sin her breasts.

She was tall, at least six feet, and slender with smooth caramel skin. And should have been trying to be on someone's runway, Dr. Dangerfield decided as she eyed her, instead of trying to be on her back, spreading her legs.

"Nah, not at the moment," Sin said, and the shameless little hot pocket sauntered off, deliberately throwing her hips as she walked. But Sin kept his attention on Dr. Dangerfield, who fought to keep from rolling her eyes at the thirsty little bitch.

She flashed Sin a bright smile. "Now . . . back to you. Tell me why you aren't sure about taking the position?" she asked, finally redirecting the conversation back to her original question.

Sin took a breath, sat forward in his seat and clasped his hands on the table. "I don't know. As exciting as it sounds, there's a part of me that thinks I'll start to feel trapped."

She nodded, understanding all too well that feeling of entrapment. Sin was a free-spirited kind of man, the type of man who preferred living by his own rules instead of the ones created by someone else.

"But, on the flip side of that, I imagine you'll still have license to indulge your desires."

He chuckled. "Yeah, imagine the endless possibilities."

Dr. Dangerfield shook her head, biting back a laugh of her own. "Mm-hmm. Spoken like a true manwhore."

"Uh, correction, good doctor," Sin said lightheartedly, "I've spoken like a true pleasure consultant. Women have needs. I have needs. And I have an endless need to meet their needs." He reached over and stroked her hand. "Like I do yours."

Dr. Dangerfield's cunt tightened. *And you've done it so damn well.* She shifted in her seat. She didn't have to tell him what he already knew, so she simply let her gaze softly caress his face, her eyes flashing with a heat that kept his eyes drawn to hers. He couldn't look away. He didn't want to look away. He was tempted to lean over and kiss her. But he cleared his voice, instead, and said, "I've gotten so used to doing my own thing. Not being tied to a desk; you know?"

Dr. Dangerfield nodded. "Yes, I do. In between membership screenings and the daily operations, I'm sure it'll be an adjustment. However, I know Nairobia. And I know she wouldn't have offered you the position if she didn't believe for one second you weren't cut out for the challenge."

Sin reached for his glass, and then took a slow sip of his wine, nodding. "Yeah, I guess you have a point." He set his drink down and smiled.

"What? Why are you smiling?"

"Nah, it's nothing." He shook his head, his lips still curled into a lopsided grin.

"Don't do that," she said, feigning insult. "Tell me."

"While you were talking," he stated, "I could hear her in my head saying, 'Pleasure, my love, awaits you. Give into your desires.'"

His lousy attempt of imitating Nairobia's Dutch accent made Dr. Dangerfield laugh. "You have a thing for her, don't you?"

Sin furrowed his brows. "A thing for *who?* Nairobia?"

She raised a brow. "Yes. *Nairobia.* Admit it."

Sin eyed her and then, over a smile, said, "Let me find out you're jealous."

She shook her finger at him. "Oh, no, Mister. You don't get to twist this into some green-eyed monster tale. My soror is an exquisitely beautiful woman. And I love her like a sister," she said, hoping her tone didn't sound defensive. "So, jealous? No. I have nothing but deep admiration in the way Nairobia commands the attention of men *and* women alike. But, if it were meant to be a secret, Mr. Pleasure Consultant, that *you* didn't have a thing for her, you'd be exposed already."

"As in butt-naked?"

Dr. Dangerfield playfully rolled her eyes. "No. As in the naked truth."

Sin cleared his throat. "Okay. Here's the naked truth, Doc—I have a thing for beautiful women. And, yes. Nairobia is exactly that. And yet so are you."

Dr. Dangerfield felt her cheeks flush.

"Nairobia, however, isn't the kind of woman I could ever, realistically, have a *thing* for—as you call it. She's the fantasy every man has. She's like a walking fairy tale, sort to speak."

Dr. Dangerfield couldn't help but smile at the analogy. "That's a new one for the books. Tell me more," she said lightheartedly.

"All I'm saying," Sin continued, "is that Nairobia is the thing—that work of art—that many men covet, and women aspire to be. True, she's a remarkable woman but, then again, so are you. I, like so many other men, admire *all* of her *ass*ets, along with her strength and beauty. Just as I admire yours."

Dr. Dangerfield swallowed. Oh, he was good. So good that she was ready to slide off her chair and slink her way under the clothed table and then slip his dick between her lips.

"Now, how's that for getting naked?" Sin said with an amorous tone in his voice. And then he licked over his lips.

Heat flashed through her. She pressed her thighs together and reached for her wineglass, but then stopped herself and grabbed her water instead. She took a sip. Then another. Suddenly she felt more parched, and yet her panties were nearly soaked.

She sipped more water.

When she saw his gaze following her tongue as she flicked it over her lips. She stared at him, wondering if the gesture had him imagining it was his dick her tongue had been slowly licking over.

As they stared at each other, seconds ticked by, before Dr. Dangerfield cleared her throat and then finally said, "I think you should take it."

Sin gave her a questioning look. "You think I should take what?"

"The job."

"Yeah?"

She nodded. "Of course. If it's in your heart's desires, I say go for it. I think you'd be great at it. Who knows, having your very own sexual playground at your fingertips, may be your calling."

"Is this your way of getting rid of me and all of this good loving," he teased. "You know you'd miss me."

"Behave, Sin."

Sin raised his glass to his lips, only to lower it without taking a drink. *"Behave?"* He chuckled. "Baby, my mother named me Sin for a reason."

Dr. Dangerfield smiled. "Your mother must be a visionary to have had such foresight," she said. And then it dawned on her. In the three years that she'd known him, this was the first time she'd heard him make reference to his mother. He'd always been very private, tight-lipped, about his family life.

She, also, was very guarded about her personal life, so she respected his boundaries. And she'd never thought to pry, never had any reason to want to, until now. Then again, all they'd ever done was have sex. All he'd ever done was touch, uncover, nearly every inch of her body. And not once had she given any real thought to who this enigmatic man really was until this very moment.

But as her curiosity to know more about the woman who'd birthed two sons, naming them Sin and Saint, sat on the tip of her tongue, she decided she didn't need to know any more than what he was willing to share—in his own time, so she bit her lip. She was sure Sin was a man with a story of his own, one she'd hear . . . one day.

Maybe.

"Yeah, she knew the moment she brought me into this world that I wasn't born to behave," Sin finished, bringing her mind back to their conversation. "I was put here on this earth to wreak havoc and break hearts. Her words, not mine."

Dr. Dangerfield chuckled. And then she feigned a shiver. "Ooh, sounds so demonic. Should I schedule you for an exorcism?"

Sin lifted one wicked brow. "Only if it's followed by a night of fellatio."

"Oh, I'm sure something can be arranged," she murmured, shifting in her seat.

Sin reached across the table and slid his hand over hers. "You're a fascinating woman, Doc."

A smile touched the corners of her lips, but she didn't say anything.

"I admire what you do here on the island."

She tilted her head in that sexy way of hers with questioning eyes.

"Helping troubled couples find their way."

"Thank you," she finally said. "It's my gift to them."

"You give them hope, baby."

She nodded. "Sometimes, that's all they need."

Sin finally took another sip of his drink, and her eyes followed the movement of his throat. She wanted to lean over the table and lick him there, over his Adam's apple, over his muscular neck.

He leaned back in his seat, surveying her with appraising eyes, wondering why such a beautiful, sexually liberated woman was still single.

"And what about you, Doc. What do you need?"

Dr. Dangerfield pursed her lips. Though she knew her work with couples was her calling, she so wished she'd been blessed with the gift of discernment where her two ex-husbands, Devon and then Taylor, had been concerned. She'd known from the moment she'd accepted their marriage proposals that they were both wrong for her, she'd known it all along—from the moment they'd started dating, but she'd wanted to prove herself wrong, wanted to give them both the benefit of the doubt, so she'd kept trying to make them both fit, like a too tight dresses shoved in the back of her closet.

Sure, on the surface they'd both given the appearances of having their shit together. Education. Careers. Goals. Financial wealth. A life. And, most importantly, they'd both wanted to be married and raise a family. And yet it had been all smoke and mirrors.

Deceptive bastards.

Had she'd listened to her intuition it would have saved her a shitload of disappointment, heartache, drama, and sexual frustration. Oh and—lest she not forget—the gonorrhea that itty-bitty dicked Taylor had given her.

And though she'd opted to take the high road and not become the bitter, scorned woman, forgiveness hadn't been easy. But a hefty divorce settlement had made the process a whole lot easier.

"Complete transparency," she finally said. "That's what I would need *if* I wanted a man. I would need to be able to have complete trust in the man I've chosen to give myself to, emotionally speaking. Fortunately, I'm not on the market, or on the hunt, for one."

"So you'd want a man who allowed you into every part of who he was?"

Yes. She'd expect him to give freely of himself in every way. "In a magical world, what I would want is a man who is capable of surrendering his heart and loving me without question. But since I don't live my life in delusions, I want continuous access to multiple orgasms."

Sin threw his head back and laughed.

"Jaded, are we?" He raised a brow, waiting for her answer.

Dr. Dangerfield batted her lashes, and feigned indignation. "I beg your pardon, Sir." Though she shamefully had a slightly dim view of relationships—thanks to the shadows of her past, she hadn't completely given up on love. Black love. It existed, somewhere beneath all the bullshit one had to sift through in order to get to it.

"I'm not jaded," she continued. And then she laughed. "I'm optimistically guarded."

"Yeah, okay. Good answer," he replied, gently rubbing his thumb over the tops of her knuckles. "Another reason why I admire you. The way you view life, and love, and the world around you I find it refreshing." He continued stroking her hand. He loved the feel of her satiny skin. And she loved him touching her.

She swiped her bang from out of her eye, glancing down at her half-eaten meal, before gazing up to find Sin staring at her mouth. He knew he should think about anything but her lush mouth right now, but his overheating libido and his growing erection weren't making it easy to focus on anything else.

"And right now, beautiful," he continued in almost a whisper, "I'm admiring the way that pretty pink lipstick is shellacked all over those too-luscious lips. I'm almost jealous."

Dr. Dangerfield's breath hitched as she fused her stare to his; the heat from his gaze made her pussy pulse.

"Is there any particular place you'd like to see it smeared?" she teased in a seductive whisper. And then she slowly, teasingly, flicked her tongue over her top lip.

Sin grinned. Leaned over the table. And then he whispered in her ear, "All over my dick."

She started to say something else, but then the little Amazon waitress-bitch returned to their table. "Is there anything else I can get for you, *Sin?*" she said over a smile, clearly ignoring the fact that Dr. Dangerfield was also still seated at the table.

Girl, go sit your fast-ass down somewhere, silly little twat.

Dr. Dangerfield gave the little trollop a look, then shifted her attention to Sin, who was still looking at her. "We'll take the check," he said, his gaze never leaving hers. "Please."

"Very well then," the waitress said, disappointment laced in her tone. She shot Dr. Dangerfield a dirty look, and then walked off, swinging her hips as she moved toward another table.

Sin shook his head. And Dr. Dangerfield regarded him—this six-foot-three, thirty-eight-year-old chocolate god, thoughtfully. She bit back a smile. Amused, almost, at how women couldn't resist his magnetism. How their lusty gazes crawled up the length of him. How they all seemed so eager to step out of their panties the moment they spotted him.

"Now I'm ready for something sweet," he said huskily, his tone spreading warmth through her entire body.

"Mm," she murmured, wetting her lips. She felt an uncontrollable quiver roll over her body as he gazed at her with those dark dreamy-lashed eyes, wanting and piercing. "What did you have in mind?"

Sin leaned in, brushing his lips against the lobe of her ear, and then he whispered in his rich baritone voice, "You."

FIFTEEN

SIN DESCENDED DOWN and around the spiral stairs, leading the way as he and Dr. Dangerfield made their way onto the sand. He'd decided they should stroll along the beach before heading back to her place for a nightcap of lovemaking.

And she was more than happy to oblige him.

Like dinner, walking along the shoreline would be a first for them, together, that was. And she had to keep reminding herself that this—whatever *this* was—was not a date. No, it was simply two adults having dinner, drinks, a late-night stroll, followed by a night of consensual fucking. So then why did it feel like something more?

She decided to not put too much thought into it. Not to overanalyze it. Just stay in the damn moment.

The second his feet hit the powdery sand he turned and reached for Dr. Dangerfield's hand and helped her down the remainder of the steps.

He glanced down at her feet—those beautiful, perfectly arched mouthwatering feet with ten sweet, succulent toes painted in pink—and nearly groaned at the thought of having them rubbing over his dick, and then stuffed in his mouth. He could already smell them in his face and couldn't wait to suck on the back of her heels, lick over her soles, and then suckle on each of her pretty toes.

"Damn, baby," Sin murmured, pulling her into him the

moment her feet hit the powdery sand. "I can't wait to get those sexy feet in my mouth."

Dr. Dangerfield shivered. She loved her toes, her feet, pampered and loved on—licked and kissed and sucked on.

Sin's hands found her waist, and he pulled her closer to him.

"My dick wants you," he said hoarsely, his eyes hot and hungry. Moonlight illuminated his ruggedly handsome face, and Dr. Dangerfield made a low noise at his words. Sin grinned at the reaction. She liked dirty talk. And he liked talking dirty.

"And I want your dick," she said back.

But he hadn't expected her to grab the crotch of his pants and then reach for his fly, before lowering herself in front of him, her knees sinking into the pristine sand. But right there at the bottom of the steps—beneath a shimmering moon and twinkling stars, she looked up at him through a veil of dark lashes, slid down his zipper, and then reached in and fished out his dick, the scent and heat of his crotch greeting her.

Sin went rigid in her hand. She stroked him up and down, palming the head of his dick, her caress, her hand strokes, gentle and feathery, even as she brushed her fingertips across the heavy sac of his balls, before finally curling her hand around the base of his dick.

A bead of moisture clung to the head, glistening in the moonlight, and she was starved for it. She eased forward and swiped her tongue along the small opening at the tip, lapping his arousal.

He groaned. "Yeah, baby, lick that shit."

She responded by circling the head with her tongue, swirling it around the satiny crown and then lapping at the tip again, before sucking the head of his dick into her mouth; just the tip, sucking lightly, sweetly, at first.

Sin touched her hair. His fingers tangled. Not pulling, just a soft tug that caused her to moan. She was seducing him so fast that he barely had a chance to take control of the situation, and she wanted it that way. She'd always wanted to suck a dick on a beach, but had never done so for various reasons.

No one had been worthy.

No one had been able to ramp up her ho-meter to that level.

No one had inspired her to want to toss that much caution out to the wind.

Until now.

Until Sin.

She'd wanted to suck his dick all night. All through dinner, all she could think of was his thick, hard dick. Long before he'd mentioned dessert, she'd already known what sweet treat she had a taste for. And she was determined to suck it out of him.

Right down to the last creamy drop.

She slid her hands up his calves, then up his hamstrings, stamping to memory every ripple of muscle, every stretch of skin. And then she opened her mouth wider and sucked him inside, inch by delicious inch. Tasting him. Savoring the scent of him. Hands free, she took him to the back of her throat and then swallowed him, her lips pressed tightly to the base, her nose pressed into the thick thatch of curly pubic hairs.

Sin gripped his shoes he held in his one hand, before letting them drop to the sand as Dr. Dangerfield's head bobbed back and forth, her glossed lips gliding over his shaft, leaving his dick slick with her spit.

"Fuck, baby," he hissed. "Goddamn." His dick sank so easily into her throat. He couldn't remember her ever sucking him with such fierceness. He wondered how she could suck him so slutty and still look so elegant, graceful.

"You like that shit?" he asked over a grunt.

She moaned over his dick. Answered him in deed, not with words as her wet tongue lashed along the tip of his dick, sampling more of his arousal, before sucking him back into the waiting heat of her mouth.

Sin cast his gaze downward, his eyes dark and smoldering. He wondered where she'd been hiding this version of herself. He liked her, *this* her, a lot better.

"Slide your fingers into that wet pussy."

Dr. Dangerfield disregarded his demand—or perhaps it was a plea. Either way, she ignored him. At this moment, he wasn't going to be in control.

Not over her.

Not over this.

She covered the head of his dick with one hand, and then gently pulled upward, lifting up his testicles, she licked over each sac, her tongue swathing the ridges, before moaning against his balls.

"Uhn, shit!" He groaned long and low. "Lick them shits, baby."

In her frenzy, she licked and licked and licked. And then sucked one testicle between her lips, and then the other, her mouth quickly filling with drool. And then she was licking over them again.

"You like that," she rasped.

"Fuck yeah, baby," he moaned as she wetly licked over them again and again. And then one ball and then the other skillfully disappeared back into her warm, juicy mouth—

Only to be abruptly set free with a wet *pop*.

And then she was taking his dick back into her juicy-ass mouth, plunging him deeply into the back of her velvety throat, relaxing around him, as she slid her hands around to cup his firm, muscled ass. She closed her eyes as he swelled larger in her mouth, her head bobbing furiously back and forth over the length of him.

"Damn, baby, that neck feels so good . . . ah, yeah, just like that."

She pulled back to run her lips along the side of his shaft—right side, first, then the left side—before swiping her tongue over the head of his dick, lapping at his pre-cum. Then sucking him back into her mouth, causing him to rock his hips in a sensuous rhythm, slipping his dick deeper between her lips, leisurely fucking her mouth. And then she moaned again, her jaws unlatching, her throat opening, her pussy growing wetter, as she sucked him with abandon.

There out in the open for anyone to see as they passed, she sucked him like a woman possessed. Her sucking became more urgent, deeper and faster, wetter, tighter, greedier. She felt the mouth of her pussy pouting with need and creaming in excitement as the head of his dick rubbed against her tongue over and over.

This sweet slice of heaven, this, this . . . mind-blowing dick suck, made her feel naughty, slutty. In this moment, she wasn't Dr. Gretchen Dangerfield, the chic, sophisticated, articulate therapist. She was Gretchen the groaning, moaning, dick-sucking cum whore. And yet all Sin saw when he looked down at her loving on his dick, was a beautiful woman, a woman who knew what she'd wanted.

And then took it.

He grabbed her head as his orgasm neared, his hips working back and forth, his fingers tangling in her hair as he fucked her mouth in long strokes.

Dr. Dangerfield's no-gag skills were pulling him dangerously closer to climax, his legs and ass strained underneath her hands, fire spreading up his thighs as she sucked him feverishly, full-throated and hungrily.

He felt the tightening in his chest.

He gritted his teeth with pleasure.

Felt his toes curl into the sand.

He nearly bit his tongue at how good her mouth and throat felt. And then his body was shuddering, the climax boiling up in his swollen sac.

Fuck she was good—no, great; her tongue and mouth working harmoniously together to bring him over the edge.

"Fuck." He gasped, unable to hold out any longer, though he was fighting like hell not to explode—not yet. He wanted to enjoy her head game a while longer, but her greedy, wet mouth was going to win this battle.

The circle of her lips tightened around his shaft, nearly matching the tightening of her cunt, causing more pressure, more pleasure that then twisted into exquisite heat, pleasure rising up like an erupting volcano.

A guttural sound broke from Sin's chest. Dr. Dangerfield glanced up—her head still bobbing back and forth over his veined length, her tongue swiping over his shaft as she took him to the back of her throat—and saw his head thrown back, the tendons in his neck straining, the muscles in his thighs rippling with strain.

And so she sucked and sucked until his vision blurred—her mouth locked around the head of his dick, her hands gliding up and down the length of his shaft from the base to her lips—and her pussy clenched, her juices soaking into her silky pink thong.

Sin growled, low and feral, his arousal mounting.

And then came the hot creamy treat she'd hungered for, for most of the night, finally hitting the back of her throat; the first spurt, thick and warm. She swallowed quickly to keep from choking, readying herself for more, more musky heat.

Sin's body jerked forward and then came another jet of heat and another grunt. She drank hot spurts of his cum, swallowing, swallowing. Loving the taste of him.

When he was finally spent, she released him, reluctantly, from her drenched mouth in one wet *pop* and then drew back on her knees, gazing at his spit-and-cum slick dick gleaming beneath the stars.

Sin was dizzy when it ended, but he'd never admit it outwardly. And the way his knees nearly buckled; he was surprised to find himself still on his feet. But there he was, heart racing, breath ragged, his dick sucked to completion.

He took a deep, steadying breath, and then it took a few seconds for his eyelids to lift. Staring up at him, eyes glazed, Dr. Dangerfield licked over her creamy lips, and then smiled as she watched him tuck his semi-erect dick back into his pants and fasten them up.

"Dessert was delicious," she rasped as Sin reached down, curled his hands underneath her arms and pulled her to her feet. He wanted to spin her around, bend her over, yank her panties to the side, and then shove his tongue so far up into her pussy that she'd feel him licking around her ovaries.

Instead he bent his head and captured her lips with his, taking her with his tongue, cupping her ass in both his hands, drawing her so close to his body, against his now-growing erection, until she moaned into his mouth. He squeezed her ass as he deepened the kiss. She tasted of dick and nut and lingering wine.

The erotic combination heightened his arousal, causing him to kiss her until she couldn't breathe. Finally, Sin pulled away, taking his tongue and heat with him.

"Now that you've had your taste buds satisfied," he murmured, his tone coated in lust. "It's my turn." He pinned her with a heated stare, one laced with promise and lots of purpose. "I'm going to spread you open, lick you until you cream all over my tongue, then fuck you senseless."

Before she could part her lips in response, Sin bent at the knees, quickly sweeping her up in his arms. Fuck a walk along the beach. He had better things in mind, things that had nothing to do with moonlight, sand, or the ocean. And everything to do with . . .

His dick.

His tongue.

And Dr. Dangerfield's beautiful, wet pussy.

SIXTEEN

DR. DANGERFIELD CLOSED her eyes and relived Sin's lovemaking from the other night. Her body was still sated. Good fucking, good loving. It had been everything she needed. Slow. Reverent almost. He'd stretched her until she felt herself drowning in fire, until she nearly confessed her sins—not that she had many to divulge—in between her incoherent murmurs of pleasure.

"Come for me, baby," he'd whispered as he flexed his hips, driving deeper, the melodic sound of flesh slapping against flesh filling the room. *"I'm not too far behind you. This pussy's so good, so wet for me . . ."*

He'd thrust harder as if he'd felt her orgasm lurking, as if he'd known she was on the fringes of a slow-building tidal wave.

"Let go, baby. Give me all you got."

And then he'd trailed tender kisses from her ear, up her jaw to her lips, before sliding his mouth down her neck, sucking and kissing and licking at her pulse points.

Dr. Dangerfield had nearly croaked out a sob, one of the sweetest agonies as he stroked her to the edge and then quickly backed away, plunging in, then slowly retreating, circling her there—at the mouth of her pussy, taunting her, before slamming back in.

Swish, swish, swish . . .

Her pussy sang out, wetly, as her body welcomed his thrusts.

She'd curled her hands around his neck and held on for dear

life, the waves crashing around her, the heat scorching her, her body exploding in a million different directions.

His mouth had brushed against her ear. *"I've been wanting to tongue you in that sweet ass of yours,"* he'd whispered. *"Would you like that? Me licking your asshole?"*

"Yes," she'd panted.

"Yes, what? Tell me."

"Tongue my ass . . . hole. *Take me however you want me,"* she'd said in a low voice, willing to surrender every part of herself to him in the heat of the moment.

Caught up in the eroticism, of the idea of giving him that part of her, his fingers parting the globes of her ass and tonguing here there, before stretching open the ring of muscle with his invasion, had given new depths to her orgasm.

She'd cried out, her pussy sucking him deeper inside her body, clutching him, milking him, as she climaxed, heat flooding every pore of her body.

Dr. Dangerfield swallowed and then bit down on her lip, feeling a fresh trickle of arousal seeping into her rumpled sheets at the delicious memory. She bit back a moan and then glanced up at the ceiling, before shifting her gaze toward the wall clock, and then sliding it over to the lamp on her nightstand. A sly grin eased over her lips as she finally slipped out of bed and sauntered out of her bedroom, the soft thud of her feet against the teak hardwood floor as she made her way through her villa.

She hummed a sensual melody in her head, then slowly twirled her naked body in the middle of the floor, a hand sliding between her thighs. She brushed her fingertips over her clit, where they lingered as she dipped her knees and slowly thrust her hips.

She teased herself there. And then she sucked in a gasp when she slid a finger inside her body.

She purred low in the back of her throat.

She was floating.

Her pussy was moist.

Her nerve endings tingled.

She knew she was addicted.

To good dick.

To unforgettable fucking.

But thankfully she was able to compartmentalize, to keep that part of herself neatly tucked in a perfectly wrapped box. She knew the difference between a man sexing her and a man loving her. And Sin had sexed her, *down.*

And she'd allowed him to take the *love* she held between her thighs.

Slowly, she pulled two fingers from her cunt and sucked them into her mouth, moaning over the digits, before licking over her fingertips.

Heart racing, pussy pulsing, she finally made her way into the living room, where she opened the drawer to her credenza. She pulled out a remote and pointed it toward a wall and then pressed a button on the base of the remote.

Slowly, the wall slid open, and . . .

There behind the wall was her private suite. Surrounded by plush white leather and erotic sculptures made of alabaster and marble, it was where all the magic happened.

Where dirty deeds were caught and secrets were kept.

Where hidden truths and untold desires unfolded.

She stepped inside. And waited for the wall to slide shut behind her, before glancing over at the bank of monitors that covered a long wall on one side of the room. Each monitor displayed a different angle, a different view of the entire island, along with the inside of many of the villas.

It was here, in her private sanctuary, where she spied on the private lives of the couples that came to the island seeking to reignite the passion in their marriages. It was also where each camera afforded her an overhead and eye-level, front row view of all things dirty and scandalous.

From every angle imaginable, nothing on the island went unnoticed. There were even night-vision cameras to ensure every little wicked deed on the island was captured, including her very own private moments, all available for her viewing pleasure.

She sauntered further into the room, grabbing another remote from off a white marble coffee table. She pressed the ON button and then waited for three large monitors to come alive, before pressing play.

Oh, yes, there they were. Her and Sin, in her bed, candles flickering, the sheets tangled around limbs, plush pillows strewn about, the images of their fuck-fest crisply vivid thanks to spy cameras concealed in the light fixtures, in vents, surveillance cameras neatly tucked in her wall clock and lamps.

She cupped her breasts as she watched her very own porn tape, the view ramping her arousal up, causing her nipples to grow tight. She took her right nipple into her mouth, and then her left, her tongue gliding languorously over each tip as she kept her eyes fixed on the monitor.

Sin had stayed true to his promise and had licked out multiple orgasms and then fucked her breathless. His exquisite dick strokes were always delivered with such precision, such purpose, with such determination, that she feared her pussy would miss him—the dick, if he decided to return to the States to take Nairobia up on her job offer.

And yet she hoped that he would.

Pack up and leave.

She knew it would be for the best—for her, for him—if he left the island. Sooner than later. She wasn't cut out for becoming attached, hooked, or strung out, on a man, or his lovemaking skills.

She'd never allow herself to become one of those women she counseled, women who'd come to the island broken and drained and yet still wanting to fix the men in their lives, still wanting to hold onto relationships and marriages that should have been long given up on. No, no, she wasn't that kind of woman, one who would give more of herself than a man was willing to give of himself. She could not, ever, see herself loving a man who wasn't capable of loving her in the same way. She dared not imagine becoming that type of woman, one needy and desperate and all fucked over, giving a man every piece of her heart until it ended up broken and she was caught somewhere crouched down low in the still of the night, hiding in bushes, waiting to bust out his front windows.

No, no, absolutely not.

She didn't live in delusions. She knew enough to know that Sin wasn't capable of loving anyone except for himself. And she knew allowing herself to want more of him would be more trouble than he was worth. She'd managed to keep her wits about herself for this long, and she wasn't about to allow herself to become unhinged or sidetracked now, no matter how sexy and masculine and powerfully irresistible said distraction was.

She pursed her lips, contemplating.

He was trouble. She knew this. Knew he was guarded. Knew he was incapable of being committed—or monogamous. But she wasn't looking for either of those qualities. So what was the problem?

Nothing. Really.

What she wanted, what she needed, from him hung thickly between his legs.

They were just . . . fuck buddies. Friends with a mutual respect and desire to have hot, passionate sex. No judgments, no questions asked.

Just a fuck-and-go type of thing.

She knew he was only good for deep-dick fucking and yet, somehow, she was aware she was crossing into dangerous territory. And, still, she felt herself more drawn to the man like never before.

Simply put, Sin was a nightmare waiting to happen. But damn him and his thick, delicious dick! But, still hidden deep down in the crevices of her soul, tucked under years of self-help studying and counseling, was a woman who didn't just like trouble.

She loved it.

It made her pussy wet.

Damn him for all of his sensuality and the carnal energy that swirled around him. And goddamn her for wanting to peel back his layers and uncover all there was to know about the elusive pussy slayer.

SEVENTEEN

DON'T EVER GET attached . . .

Not to anyone or anything.

That was something that had been ingrained in him early on. Don't feel. Don't care. Don't trust.

And he didn't.

Feelings made you vulnerable.

Caring made you weak.

Trusting made you careless.

A lesson he learned as a young boy.

"I ain't shit, Sin. And neither are the rest of the bitches in this world. Fuck 'em. Leave 'em. But don't ever love 'em. Don't ever give a fuck about what a bitch wants unless it's your dick. We're all whores . . ."

Words of wisdom his mother had offered one late night, as she stood in the doorway of his tiny bedroom, her eyes, glassy and barely open. She'd stood there in her see-through nightgown with her nipples protruding from its flimsy fabric; a hand on her hip, a joint dangling from her painted lips, marijuana smoke swirling out of her mouth as she spoke.

"Bitches want good dick. We want to be fucked. Long and hard . . . we want to be fucked deep and nasty to forget . . . And you can't be scared of no pussy. You need to know how to use your dick. You need to know how to fuck us. You need to know how to help us forget. You hear me, boy . . .?"

He remembered nodding. And then he remembered staring at her as she stepped into his room. Then everything else went blank.

"I'm teaching you how to be a man. Giving you some of life's hard lessons. You can thank me later . . ."

His mother might have been a whore, but Sin refused to believe—in spite of all that he'd been through—that all women were. He believed they were sexual creatures, some more sexually aware of what they desired, what they needed and wanted; some more hungry, more insatiable, than others. But that didn't make them all whores.

And yet he loved bringing them pleasure more than he could understand, but in the end, he would never feel for any of them. He would never trust any of them.

They weren't worthy.

And they'd never be.

Sin opened his eyes from behind his dark shades and then lifted them from his face so that he could look out into ocean. He inhaled. Held the ocean's breeze into his lungs. And then exhaled.

And then as if his conscience had willed it, Dr. Dangerfield emerged from the water. Gold bangles on her wrists glittered. He blinked. Squinted. Shoulders back, neck long, head high, water cascading down over her curvaceous body, she strutted across the sand as if she owned the world, heading towards—

He blinked again. Then stared at the lovely creature as she came into clearer view. He shook his head.

It wasn't her.

He was almost disappointed that it hadn't been. But then he dismissed the feeling, mentally scolding himself. *What the fuck, man? You're really bugging out here.*

He eyed her as she leaped up into the arms of her male lover, as he scooped her up and swung her around, kissing her.

Newlyweds.

Sin wondered how long their marital bliss would last, before all the bells and whistles of holy matrimony faded, and one or the other did something to fuck it all up, before all the lies unfolded. Someone was bound to get hurt. Betrayal was inevitable. That wasn't pessimism. It was fact. Or at least it was in the world according to him.

Lies and deceit were all he'd ever been exposed to. People played games and toyed with the emotions of others. It was a dangerous game; one he had no interest in ever becoming a part of.

The sound of boisterous laughter stole his attention, pulling him out of his thoughts. Sin shielded his eyes to peer over at a very tanned woman on the right side of him as she peeled off her bikini top and shook her large double-Ds at her three very sunburned male companions as she entertained them with her lousy attempt at seduction.

Instead of finding humor in the act, her shoulders shimmying, her breasts swaying, Sin turned his head as a statuesque Trinidadian woman brought over a passion colada, one of the island favorites—a blend of fresh pineapples, coconut milk, aged island rum, and a dash of grenadine—along with a tray of sliced tropical fruits.

She set the tray of fruit on the small round table. Sin thanked her, and then took the drink she handed him. His third, but who was counting?

He took a sip, and then ran his hand through his locs, before tilting his head up to the sun. *"I fucking hate you . . . but I love how good this dick is . . . ooh, you're a good lil fucker . . ."*

He shook the voice from his head.

He wasn't about to let what was left of his day be ruined by slipping into one of his moods.

Shitty. Brooding. Despondent.

No. *He* controlled how he'd feel for the day. Not his thoughts, not his memories. Period. He downed his drink. Then set the glass down into the sand.

He inhaled deeply. And then breathed out the memories. He shook loose the rest of his thoughts.

They were painful. Haunting.

And the lessons had been hard. Brutal.

And yet here he was.

Breathing.

But was he really living?

Or was he merely a shell of his life experiences?

He didn't know. He didn't want to know. He wasn't interested in picking apart his life. All he knew was that he existed. And, sometimes, he wondered if that was a blessing or a curse.

EIGHTEEN

FUCKING WAS ONLY good when it was fast—and hard.

Sprinkled with lots of dirty talk.

And Mocha had known exactly who to call for just that.

Sin.

He was tender, yet carnal.

And he could deliver the type of pounding she craved, she needed.

Besides, he'd owed her that—a good *hard* fuck. And now she had him here to collect, expecting him to make good on his promise from weeks ago.

Bottom line, when she needed a good fucking, she liked it hot and raunchy. Yet, things had not turned out the way she'd planned, hoped for.

Sin was torturing her.

Dragging out the act. Delaying his sole purpose for being here in the first place.

To fuck her.

He'd been in her lair for nearly an hour, taunting her with his twisted form of seduction. Touching her, caressing her, his fingers dancing over her skin, gliding up her body without ever touching the most intimate parts of her body that needed his touch most.

Her breasts.

Her nipples.

Her clitoris.

Her pussy.

Yes, there. Right inside her wet, quivering cunt—all neglected and empty.

She'd had another scenario in mind when she'd invited him over, one where he walked in, found her naked, and then—without much talking—slammed his dick inside her already wet slit, fucking her mindless.

But this, this shit right here—

Oh, God, help her.

He was killing her.

She curled her fingers into her palms. Frustration and lust flooding through her, she found herself wondering how the hell she ended up on her back, agreeing to be bound to her bedposts.

This was *not* how her night was supposed to unfold.

And yet here she was.

Naked and needy and on the verge of another climax without having one inch of Sin's dick inside her, he slid two fingers down the seam of her pussy.

Mocha moaned, her hips lifting up off the mattress.

He bent and slid his tongue over her nipple, while lazily rolling a finger around her clit. He licked over the other, lapping at it until he tugged the turgid peak into his mouth, suckling it as one would a Hershey kiss, waiting for its sweet taste to melt over his tongue. He nipped, grazing the chocolate nub with his teeth, and the slight bite of pain burst into pleasure causing the muscles in her groin to tremble and spasm.

She groaned; her orgasm dangerously close.

And then he pulled away, leaving her shuddering and arching her body.

Sin reached for one of the scarlet-red scarves he'd brought with him.

"I'm going to give you what you called for," he finally said, taking her right hand and then pulling her arm up over her head. He looped the silk scarf around her wrist and tied it to the headboard.

Mocha licked her lips in unexpected anticipation. Her pussy grew wetter.

She wasn't a true submissive. And she wasn't into bondage much, but every now and again she allowed herself to indulge, to surrender. All in fun, and role-play.

Tonight, however, she hadn't wanted to—give up her control, that was. But Sin wanted her vulnerable. Helpless. Spread open and powerless in her pursuit of nirvana.

"You want this dick pounding deep inside that sweet little pussy?"

Chill bumps shot up her body. "Yes. *Mmm . . .*"

"You want it hard?"

"Yes," she rasped as he walked around her bed to take her other arm.

"You want it deep?" he questioned as he secured her other hand.

"Yes, *Sin*," she murmured over a moan. She knew now she was going to play slave to his master to get what she wanted. "Real deep."

He pulled, testing the tautness. He wanted her secured tightly, but not so tight that her circulation would cut off.

"And I want you to cream all over my dick," he whispered. And then he sank onto the bed beside her, leaning down to cover his mouth over hers. She moaned into the kiss as his tongue swept over hers, and then she swallowed the taste of him into her chest, drinking him in.

His masculine heat filled her lungs, making it nearly impossible to breathe. His hand slid to the wetness between her thighs. She was so, so, wet and ready.

Seconds ticked by—with him delving into her folds, teasing

the edges of her slickened lips, and the kiss deepening, before he finally tore his mouth away from hers, and she was gasping for air.

Sin plunged a finger inside her, and she moaned as her inner walls wetly squeezed his finger.

A smile curved his lips as she shivered with need.

"You want more?" he taunted. "You want this sweet, greedy cunt stuffed with more fingers, don't you, baby?"

He stroked her clit.

"Yes," she said breathlessly.

One finger. Two fingers. Three fingers.

Oh God, oh God . . .

He stretched her, his fingers sliding in and out of her body, then twisting. Heat swept through her core as he brushed over her G-spot. He stroked and stroked and stroked until she was writhing beneath his touch, until her mind whirled and she was begging for him.

"Fuck me, fuck me, *fuuuuuck* me. Oh, God, please. Give me the dick."

Her walls tightened.

She arched her body.

Her legs clamped around his hand. She was teetering on the edge, gasping, drenching his hand with her wet heat.

"Oh, oh, oh, oh, *oh*—"

No, no, no. Again, he'd abandoned her cunt. Left her swinging from the rope of another climax. He exited the bedroom.

Where was he going? He couldn't leave her like this. Trembling and panting and weak with want, every part of her flesh burning with desire. The ache between her thighs sharpened.

She bit back a frustrated scream.

Damn him!

Her eyes widened when he returned, seconds later, holding another red sash.

She stared at his engorged shaft; the sight making her mouth water and her hips undulate.

She swallowed.

"I'm going to blind fold you." He tossed a gold-foiled wrapper on the bed beside her.

She blinked. Shook her head. She'd never been blindfolded, let alone tied up like this, in her own space. This was taking her wild side to a whole other level and—well, quite frankly—she wasn't sure she was ready for this "W-wait, a min—"

"Should I leave and take this dick with me?" he interrupted, grabbing his dick at the base and then shaking it at her.

Her breaths came quickly. There was no way she was letting him walk up out of here, taking all that thick manly goodness with him, without it being shoved deeply, stuffed inside her, ravishing her horny cunt.

She was already precariously hanging off the edge, her orgasm so close that she was aching with need and felt it swelling up in every part of her body. It hurt just thinking about it.

"N-no," she stammered, surrendering. Giving him what he wanted. Allowing him to take her however he wanted. "I want the dick."

"I know you do," he said, his voice low and husky. "Now lift your head up, baby."

Mocha sucked in a breath, her gaze shifting from his swinging dick to the scarf in his hand, then back to that deliciously thick slab of chocolate between his legs. She rolled her eyes. "You're crazy for making me do this. You know that, right? And I'm crazier for letting you."

"Yeah, perhaps," he said thoughtfully as he lifted the sash to put over her eyes. "But know this, baby. I'm here to give you pleasure. But I'll never give you more than you can handle." He tied it tightly in back. Then stood to make sure it completely covered her eyes. Satisfied that she was blanketed in darkness, he told her to lay her head back against the pillow and then he slanted his mouth over hers again.

He kissed her until she relaxed, until she moaned into his mouth.

Slowly, he broke the kiss. And smiled at the vision before him. She looked sexy tethered to her bed. "I wish you could see yourself," he said, admiringly.

Arousal splintered through his body until his dick swelled, thicker, and his balls tightened.

"Well, maybe, if you take off this blindfold I can," she half-teased. She didn't like not seeing what was happening around her, and yet she could feel his eyes burning over.

He traced a finger down her cheek. "When I'm done fucking you," was his response.

And then his fingers made a cage over her throat, and he squeezed, her legs spreading wider as his other hand dipped down to stroke her clit.

Mocha gasped.

And then Sin's fingers made slow, slippery circles, eliciting another gasp from her. "You like that?"

"Yes."

"You want this dick?"

"Yes, Sin," she panted.

"If you want it, then beg for it."

"Fuck me."

Her arousal scented the air around them.

And then the mattress dipped and she felt the heat of his body hovering over her.

"Don't worry, baby. I'ma fuck you. I'ma give you this dick like you've never had it before." She heard him tear open the condom wrapper with his teeth. The image of him rolling the condom over his dick swirled around in her head made her pussy flutter and clench.

Sin tossed the wrapper, then stroked his sheathed dick, holding it close to her opening as he stared down at her. "You ready?"

She was swollen and wet, more than ready for every inch of him.

"Yes," she whispered. "I've been waiting for it all night."

"The wait's over," he said smoothly. "Now get ready for the ride."

He pushed her knees upward, bending her legs, opening her to him. And then he slammed into her, stealing her breath. He pulled out, thrust hard, pulled out again, then fucked her opening with just the head of his dick, before plunging back in, her juices now splashing out around him.

Behind her lids, Mocha's eyes rolled up in the back of her head at the exquisite feel of his dick. He nudged the mouth of her cervix and her cry splintered the room.

Deeper, faster.

Sin fucked her reckless and hard, pounding deeper with each thrust, stretching her wider, forcing her orgasm to bubble up inside of her. He fucked her so good that tears seeped out from beneath her closed eyelids, and she cried out, the sweet burn of his piston-like thrust sawing into her body.

Electric heat sizzled through every nerve ending in her cunt, coiling itself around her clit. She tightened around him.

"Oh, God, yes."

Blindfolded and bound, Mocha mewled out her pleasure.

And then she screamed out his name.

NINETEEN

AFTER AN INTENSE early morning run, Sin had made it back to his
villa, where he'd cleaned his bathroom. And then after a long,
steamy shower, he'd toweled himself dry, then laid across his bed.
His body ached.

He'd needed a massage.

But what he'd needed most was sleep. And so he'd closed his
eyes, and hoped like hell the dreams would stay at bay.

And they had.

Yet he experienced a sense of disorientation when a thrilling
sound woke him.

His alarm.

Shit.

Reaching over, he silenced it with the press of a button. He
hadn't planned on sleeping almost six hours. But he was grateful
he had.

Straining an eye open, he groaned. Sunlight filtered through a
crack in the drawn curtains. He'd nearly slept the whole day away.
A first.

As he lay in bed, he made a mental note to finally reach out
to Nairobia. Although he still didn't have a definitive answer for
her, yet, he felt he needed to at least tell her that. He didn't want
to give her the impression he was brushing her off. But, the fact
of the matter was, he was kind of hoping to put off making any

decisions until after construction on her Vegas club was completed, and ready to open.

He'd been spending the several nights going to Club Passion, not as a participant of its debauchery, but as an objective observer. Taking in every aspect of its inner workings.

Granted, he'd wanted to throw out his willpower to slip his dick between the succulent lips of a few of the female patrons, but he'd thought better of it, quickly removing himself from temptation.

Sighing, Sin threw back the covers and leaped out of bed. He stretched, standing naked in the middle of a dim room. A hand slid over his abdomen and then down over his dick, and then to his heavy sac. And then it dawned on him that he hadn't had any pussy in almost a week. Not since his night with Mocha.

Ah, Mocha.

He shook his head at the thought of their night together. The pussy had definitely been good. But he'd known from the moment he'd left her place that he wouldn't be returning with anymore of his dick.

He'd seen the look in her eyes; the look of desire that went beyond lust. It was a look that told him that if he fucked her again, she'd come unhinged. He'd heard it in her voice. The needy pleas, the desperate cries for more of him.

Maybe she'd only wanted the dick in that moment, but something in her eyes told him she wanted something much more, something he was incapable of giving her.

"What if you're my Mr. Right . . .?"

Women like her didn't ever stick to the script. They veered off from what was expected. Tried to manipulate their way into a pseudo-relationship. He wasn't taking any chances. The best way to avoid chaos and confusion was to simply distance himself from it. And Mocha had the potential to be full of both.

Maybe it was his imagination, maybe it wasn't. All he knew

in that moment was, they could remain cool. But he wouldn't be fucking her again.

He rubbed his eyes, yawning, as he strode into the bathroom to relieve himself. Seconds later, he was washing his hands and then heading back into his bedroom, where he fell onto the bed and stared up at the ceiling.

And then he was up again, pacing toward the window, parting the curtain with one hand. He gazed out at the ocean. It glistened in the sun, like blue diamonds. But Sin was too restless to appreciate it.

He stretched his neck from side to side and stared out at the ocean a moment longer before letting the curtain fall back into place and strolling into the kitchen. A stainless-steel wonder he rarely used, since the villa came with around-the-clock butler service, which was not only convenient but kept him spoiled and far removed from the task of ever having to cook for himself.

Sin reached the refrigerator and opened it up. Sighing, he stared inside at its contents. The refrigerator was full, stocked with mostly fresh fruits and vegetables, along with several pre-cooked fish dishes.

But what he wanted was a cheese steak with lots of green peppers and onions, mayonnaise and ketchup stuffed inside of a soft Italian roll.

He sighed again, knowing there wasn't a place on the island he could go to get one made just right. He pulled out a tray of sliced root vegetables and some homemade hummus, along with a bowl of fish salad, and set it all on the large island.

He returned with a bottle of homemade pineapple and carrot juice, along with a fork. He licked his lips in anticipation as he pulled the lid from off the bowl of fish salad, which was a combination of a white fish marinated in lime juice, with onion, tomato, chili, and coconut cream, and stuck it in the microwave for several seconds. When it was heated, he removed it from the microwave and then pulled out a barstool, and sat down.

His mouth watered as he stuck his fork into the fish dish. Granted, many of the island's dishes had become an acquired taste over time, but he enjoyed the healthy eating over all the fatty processed foods.

As Sin ate, he mulled over in his head what the night's plans would be. Maybe he'd head back to Club Passion again. Perhaps get an anonymous nut off.

Or maybe he'd—

The villa's landline rang, pulling him from his pondering. Sin went to retrieve the phone from off its base. It was an unknown number on the caller ID.

"Hello?"

"I am still waiting, my darling," Nairoiba cooed, her voice flowed through the receiver like warm honey. "Do you intend on keeping me dangling for much longer?"

She wasn't someone who liked waiting around for something she wanted. She was too used to getting what she wanted, when she wanted. And so was he.

"Your ears must have been ringing," he said. "I was planning on calling you before it got too late." He knew there was an eighteen-hour time difference.

"It is early morning here, my darling. Now tell me, Sin. Have you forgotten me?"

"Nah, of course not. Just been caught up. Besides, you are not one easily forgotten," he said, earnestly, chewing on taro leaves covered in ground chickpeas. "I'm still thinking over my decision."

"What more is there to consider, my love?"

Well nothing. And yet he didn't see the need in saying so.

"I guess I'm kinda spoiled here. I've gotten comfortable," he admitted. "And I'm not sure if I'm ready to leave this tropical paradise. The island brings me calm."

"You can always return," she murmured. "And you'll have full use of my private jet, if and when you decide you need a taste of her calming beauty."

"True." He paced his kitchen, and then walked out into his living room. "Listen, I've been meaning to let you know that I've been shadowing the manager at Club Passion."

"So I've heard. I love the initiative, but . . ."

"I was thinking I could work a few nights there until the club in Vegas is ready, instead of going out there to train at The Pleasure Zone. It makes more sense."

"Do not bother with such thought, my darling," she said, dismissively. "I want you here, beside me, every step of the way while my vision for The Pleasure Chest unfolds." She let out what sounded like a soft moan. "No, my darling . . . lick me *there*. More tongue, darling . . . *ja, ja* . . ."

Sin blinked. Was she?

"*Ja, Ja,* like so . . . love all over my *kut* . . ." she moaned low again. And then she was addressing Sin again. "I will not take no for an answer," she said firmly.

"I didn't think you would."

She moaned again. And Sin swallowed, wondering whom the giver of her pleasure on the other end of the line might have been. Then he quickly shook the thought from his head.

"Then what, other than the *calm,* keeps you there?" she asked, over another moan.

Sin rubbed the back of his neck. He didn't have an answer to that. So he simply said, "I'm not going to pretend that I am not interested, because I am. There's really nothing holding me here, except for me."

"Then get out of your own way, my darling. Do not leave room for fear of change to keep you from evolving."

Fear?

He almost laughed. Change was the last thing he feared. He'd spent his entire life evolving, becoming his own man. Moving from place to place. And nothing he ever did was done without thought.

"I'll call you soon," was all he said. And yet, in his mind's eye, he could see her rolling her eyes up in her head, more from whatever pleasure she was receiving than from his response.

She hummed low in the back of her throat. "I'll be waiting." The words came out in what sounded like a purr.

And then the call ended.

TWENTY

AN ELLA MAI mix CD played low in the background.

Skin shimmering in body glitter, six-inch Balmain gladiator heels, Dr. Dangerfield sauntered into her living room area, wearing nothing but a skimpy negligee. She slid a hand over her bare hip as she thrust her pelvis, singing along to the "10,000 Hours" track.

The day had been long, tiresome, and Dr. Dangerfield was glad to be tucked inside the comforts of her own home. After a long, hot bubble bath, she should have been swept away into a deep slumber by now. Instead, she was filled with lots of sexual energy. She felt it traveling through her veins, felt it heating over her skin.

And tonight . . . it was all about her.

She loved sexy heels, sleek and expensive ones, like the ones she had on her feet. Leather straps wrapping up and around her calves and over her thighs like thin, winding snakes.

She ran her hands over her body and moaned as she ran her fingers over her flesh. She loved the feel of her silky skin. She loved being naked and naughty. She loved being sensual.

Dr. Dangerfield loved herself, and she *loved* loving on her body.

"*You know every second adds up to a minute, need ten thousand hours . . .*"

She thrust her pelvis again, then slid her hands down over and around her thighs, before finally lifting her body upright and walking over to her credenza, where she slid open the top drawer, and then pulled out a thin remote. She pointed it at the wall across from her, and waited for it to slowly slide open.

"*Yasss,* girl, sing," she cried out as Ella Mai sang about laying up. She swung her bang from out of her eye and shimmied her shoulders. She didn't get out much, but Lord knew she loved dancing. Dirty dancing. Sultry dancing. She loved anything with a sexy, sensual beat.

More turned on than before, she cupped her breasts, pushed them together, and then slowly tweaked her nipples into rigid peaks. She eyed herself in her mirrored-wall, turned on by the sight of her reflection. "*Yass,* bitch. Sexy ass." She giggled at the thought of someone eavesdropping—or better yet, spying—on her. She'd give them a show for sure. Give them a ballet performance they'd never forget.

Let 'em see all of this heavenly goodness.

She held her hands up over her head and slowly rolled belly. She threw her head back. And stretched out her arms and rolled her hips in a circle. She danced and felt herself up until her whole body heated.

She twirled and twirled, then stopped. Extended her arms over her head, her wrists arched over her head and began a series of ballet moves—going into full *pointe* to *battement* to half *pointe*, then *plié, plié, pirouette.* then double *pirouette.*

Breasts swaying, she moved in light fluttery motion, twisting and bending until the track ended.

Girl, you still got it, she thought as she promenaded into her secret hideaway, and then waited for the wall to slide shut behind her.

It had been a week or so since she'd spent quality time in her secret vault. She stepped further into the plush room. Lit her candles. Then picked up another remote. A panel slid open, revealing her wall-mounted monitors.

"Okay," she muttered, turning each one on. "Let's see what type of sneaky mischief the guests have been up to."

She eyed the live-feeds first, took in the island's goings-on, before venturing her gaze on the surveillance footage of the current couples participating in the island's six-week couple's retreat. She glanced over at a Zone two monitor.

It was for the villa of one of the retreat couples. The wife was bent over the sofa, head pressed into the sofa's cushion, her plump ass up high, while her husband fucked her doggy-style.

Dr. Dangerfield swallowed. And then her pink tongue darted between her white teeth, and she licked her lips, as if tasting his flesh, as if she were licking the back of his balls. Oh, they looked so big, so full. She zoomed in for a closer look. Her mouth watered at the sight of his balls slapping the back of his wife's pussy, causing her own cunt to clench. He pumped his wife hard and deep.

"I need audio," she hissed. "I need to hear you moaning." She rubbed over her clit. "Tell me, girl . . . is he fucking you good? Is the dick touching your soul?"

Her finger slipped inside her body, she was warm and moist, her pussy heating to the idea of seeing him spill his seeds into his wife's pink hole.

"Yes, fuck her. Tight, muscled ass . . ." Dr. Dangerfield imagined for a fleeting moment her nails digging into all that plump, manly ass. She swallowed at the sight of his muscles straining with every thrust.

His body jerked repeatedly, and then he slowly stirred inside of his wife, before pulling out. Dr. Dangerfield nearly climaxed when he knelt in back of her, and then spread open her ass cheeks and pressed his face there, licking out his cream.

She groaned inwardly at the sweet ache that bloomed in her cunt as she looked on with lusty-eyed delight. As if she could smell the scented air around them, she inhaled deeply. She could appreciate the sweet aroma of wet pussy and cum mingling.

She felt herself overheating.

"Ooh, yes, freaky man. Love it."

She licked over her lips again.

"That's right. Clean her cunt out, you nasty nut licker. I'll come back to you two later," she said as she pulled out a skeleton key from out of a drawer in her paneled wall and then walked over to a large cedar chest. She slid the serrated edge in, unlocking her secret treasures, pulling out a black harness and then one of her many dildos. She chose Mandingo—an eleven-inch, lifelike silicone dildo replete with veins and large balls, from Nairobia's *Nasty* toy collection. She attached the dildo to her harness and then strapped it to a leather stool, before climbing up and slowly inching its bulbous head into her wet slit.

"Ooh, yes," she moaned, pointing the remote and then clicking over to Zone four.

To the villa of another struggling-to-salvage-their-marriage couple in search of love and light and long-lost passion. But Dr. Dangerfield was hopeful they'd find their way back to each other before the end of their stay here. That they'd reconnect emotionally and spiritually. She saw it in their eyes; the hope, the want, the desire, the greedy need to find their way back to what they'd once shared.

The husband was out on the balcony smoking a cigar.

Dr. Dangerfield inched further down, moaning as she rocked her hips, until her pussy slid halfway down her silicone dick. "Oh, God, yes. So big. Mmm . . ."

Wait. She stopped moving, her eyes narrowing, her pussy still clenching.

Was that a *blunt* he was smoking?

She zoomed in on him, giving her a close-up of his face as she used her free hand to caress her breasts, alternating between each one to pull at her nipples.

Dr. Dangerfield grunted. She didn't like to stereotype, but when she was right, she was right. "I knew your ass was a pothead," she muttered in disgust. Then when his wife came out on the balcony to join him, she scoffed at the sight of him handing her the blunt. She took two long puffs, and then bent at the hips and kissed him, blowing weed smoke into his mouth. He grabbed her ass, and then slapped it.

Mmph. Weed heads. Now let's see how freaky your asses can get.

Dr. Dangerfield kept her glare locked on them, waiting to see if she would brazenly sink to her knees and suck her husband's dick. Or perhaps he'd slide a hand up her short skirt and finger-fuck her.

When the couple did neither, she rolled her eyes and quickly switched to A-Zone security footage, which recorded the entire island's activities from the last six weeks. Footage she had yet to review before deleting, erasing any traces of her prying, of her sordid breach of trust.

She'd always been a voyeur. Always loved watching others pleasure themselves, and each other. She'd been ten, going on eleven, when her curiosity bloomed, when she'd caught her brother masturbating to porn down in the family's game room, late night when he'd thought everyone was asleep.

In the still of the night, there was her brother on the sofa, surrounded by the glow of only the television in the throes of his self-induced pleasure. Dr. Dangerfield had stood transfixed to the way his hand glided up and down his shaft, the way he'd moaned, his eyes glued to the television screen, while two men had their way with a woman—one man filling her mouth, the other her cunt.

Her young, virgin eyes had darted from the television to her brother's hand back to the television, again and again and again her gaze shifting back and forth until her brother groaned and his body arched and something thick and white shot from his erection.

She'd gasped, clasping her hands over her mouth, before creeping back up the carpeted stairs, back to the frilly pink confines of her bedroom. More curious, more fascinated, more eager to learn and see more.

Little had she known then that that night would be the

beginning of a blooming fetish, hiding in closets, prying into the bedrooms of others. And by the time she'd graduated college and moved out on her own, she'd taken to having hidden surveillance cameras in her own home, replaying her sexual romps for her later enjoyment. And when she'd married, she'd even kept a watchful eye on both of her now-ex-husbands. Though neither had ever gotten caught dragging any of their stray whores into her marital bed, staining her sheets with their sluts' juices, both men had been—*and still were*—lying sneaky bastards.

Dr. Dangerfield threw her head back and moaned, her cunt pulsing around the massive phallus lodged deeply inside her body. She contracted her muscles, becoming increasingly wetter at the slurping sounds her pussy made.

She stumbled on some late-night footage of Sin and Saint engaged in a threesome on the other side of the island with a random hotel guest, with a small waist, big swaying breasts, and a big bouncy ass. She glanced at the date and time stamp—they'd fucked her almost three weeks ago. She watched as they bent the woman like a New York pretzel and had their way with her.

She moaned as if she were there herself, remembering when she'd been fucked by them both, along with Soul. It'd had been a very long night, one that had left her deliciously sore and well satiated.

Soul and Saint might have had the bigger dicks, but Sin, in her opinion, had been the better lover. Unless he was rapidly pounding himself into a woman, Saint knew nothing about being sensual, which is what she preferred. But Sin and Soul had delivered, giving her exactly what she needed, and then some.

She groaned at the memory and then while gyrating her hips, she fast-forwarded through more footage. Oh—mm, yes. She felt herself on the cusp of an—

She blinked.

Finally, there he was. Again.

Sin.

Naked in all of his chiseled glory, and she licked over her lips at the sight. She hadn't seen him, surprisingly, in the last three days. But she knew she'd find him up to no good somewhere on the island. He was such a nasty, freaky motherfucker. And she loved it. Sadly, she believed many people fucked simply to fuck; they fucked to escape, not to please.

Escape from boredom.

Escape from pain.

Escape from sadness.

Escape from loneliness.

Escape from the mundane.

Escape from the expected.

But Sin . . . *mmph*. Now he fucked to *please*.

"Who are you about to give that good loving to now?" she said in almost a breathy whisper. *All that thick beautiful dick.* The sight of it on the monitor made her cunt clench.

When his body shifted slightly to the right, she gasped at the sight of the woman with him.

Alberta Jessups.

"Ooh, you scandalous, cross-eyed bitch," she hissed. And then she glanced at the date stamp in the upper right corner of the footage. She calculated in her head. It'd been taken almost four weeks ago.

"I knew your messy-ass was up to no damn good." She grunted. She had been in her last session over a week ago with her husband professing her love to him, all teary-eyed and snot-nosed. Begging him to give their marriage a second chance. To not throw everything they'd built over the years away on his philandering ways. After all, they had a long history together. Beautiful children. And all the trappings that came along with being successful.

And, most importantly, she'd said she'd forgiven him.

And here this bitch is, with her legs up in the air. Dr. Dangerfield slid a hand between her legs, touched her clit. And then moaned, her eyes locked onto the monitor.

This skank-ass ho . . .

All in sessions playing the devoted wife.

Dr. Dangerfield grunted. She fast-forwarded several minutes of the video, then stopped. Alberta was bent over the sofa, Sin was in back of her, sliding his dick over the seam of her ass.

"Ooh, yes . . ." Dr. Dangerfield tweaked a nipple. "Hope he fucks your ass wide open, you trifling bitch. Mm, yes, Sin. Fuck her asshole to shreds, nasty man."

In the footage, Sin stepped back, and then he slapped her ass with a cupped hand, causing her to jump. Then he slapped her ass, harder, again and again.

That's right, Sin, spank her shit loose.

Nearing another orgasm, Dr. Dangerfield heard the doorbell, and yet tried to focus on bringing herself to climax.

Who the hell had come to her door, disrupting what she liked to call her *release time?* "Mm," she moaned, her fingers moving desperately over her clit. She was almost there. "Ooh, yes, you filthy, sneaky bitch," she murmured as she stared into the monitor. She reached for the remote, zooming in on Sin's ass, the way his muscles flexed as he pumped in and out of that cheating whore's body.

"Fuck her good, Sin . . . mmm, yes . . ."

The sight of his balls slapping over the back of her stretched open cunt, the sight of—

The doorbell again.

No, goddamn you!

And then came the disrespectful chiming again, in rapid succession.

Skin heated, pussy pulsing, she quickly paused the monitors. And then grabbed the remote. She waited for the wall to open so she could slip out of the room, and then slide shut, before calling out, "Just a sec," as she raced to her bedroom to drag on a robe.

Breathlessly, she swung open the door, forgetting all about the juices glazing over her fingers, sliding down her inner thighs.

"Sin," she said, surprised. She caught her breath. "Is everything okay?"

The breathiness of her words, the dreamy look in her eyes, made the ache in his scrotum grow. "Yeah. Everything's good." He peered over her shoulder into her living room, noticed that the interior was aglow with candles, and heard the slow, sensual music. "Did I catch you at a bad time?"

His gaze landed on her lips, first. Wet. Plump. Inviting. And so damn kissable. He had to fight to drag them upward to meet her eyes, instead of taking in the swell of her breasts.

Dr. Dangerfield suddenly felt naked, exposed. And she wondered if he could smell her arousal, could he sense her dirty deeds?

"What brings you by"—she glanced at her watch— "this time of the night?" Unexpected. But very much welcomed.

"My dick," he said over a devilish grin. "Mind if we come in?"

TWENTY-ONE

THE MOMENT THE door shut, Sin followed her through the villa, his eyes drinking in the carnal sway of her hips as she led him to her bedroom.

"What were you doing before I got here?" he asked, wondering if she were wearing panties. "With all these candles lit?" he added.

"Thinking about you," she said, glancing over her shoulder at him.

Sin grinned. "Oh word?" He felt his dick pulse in his boxers. "What were you thinking about?"

"*Fuck*ing you," she said bluntly. Even in its most vulgar form, she made the word sound sexy, made the idea of being wedged deeply between her succulent pussy lips irresistibly hot.

Without warning, Dr. Dangerfield turned to face him, untying her robe. A hiss escaped his lips as he watched it flutter to the floor.

"Is this what you *and* your dick came for?" She slid the straps of her negligee down off her shoulders and Sin watched as the gown slithered down her body, red silk pooling sensually around her feet.

Suddenly, she stood naked.

"Shit." His dick stiffened. "Definitely."

He stared at her breasts, and then licked his lips as her nipples peaked.

"Come here," he said, the dark tone in his voice made her belly quiver, made her skin tingle.

She went to him with deeper intent. Stood before him. Ready. Wanting.

Her lids low, her eyes dark with desire, Dr. Dangerfield lifted her head and eased up on her balls of her feet and kissed him. His mouth opened immediately as she winded her arms around his neck. He twined his tongue with hers, his tongue circling, tasting, craving. Every part of her heated kiss was on his tongue, humming through his body.

She felt so good in his arms, and she tasted sweet, so delicious. He caressed her mouth with his tongue, his kiss stoking her, lighting her up. She matched his kiss with abandon, holding nothing back. Their casual fucking was now not feeling so *casual*. It felt . . . too intense to be anything than.

She groaned into the kiss. God, she didn't know what to call it, this fire that burned so deeply every time he touched her, caressed her, loved on her pussy in long, deep, sensual strokes with his tongue, with his magnificent dick.

The man had a dick made for sucking, for fucking, for coming all over on. She reached between them and felt his hard length with her fingers, wrapping them over his thickness. She slowly stroked him.

"I'm so wet for you," she rasped against his lips. *And from seeing you on the surveillance monitor fucking that undercover skank-bitch, cheating-ass trick.*

Sin breathed in her rich, heady scent, and then his hand eased between her legs, her stance widening for him, inviting him into her sacred space.

Holding him tightly, she slowly eased him back toward the bed. She wanted to be in control tonight. She wanted to call the shots without giving him much thought to consider otherwise. She tugged at the waistband of his cutoff sweats. Yanked them down. Then freed his dick from his underwear.

"I want to make you come."

He teased her with his fingers. "Yeah?"

"Yes," she gasped, grabbing his dick, stroking him. She was so wet, so ready for him. And—damn! The sensual feel of her hands felt so good on his shaft. Gentle and yet firm. How many times had he been stroked like this? Far more times than he could count, and yet this woman's touch felt like it had been his very first time.

"How you wanna make me nut, baby?" He pulled his fingers from her slick folds, pressing them to her lips. She flicked her tongue over the pads of his fingers. The lick aroused him more, made him think about the way her naughty tongue would lick over his crown. "You wanna lick my balls?"

God, yes, she did. His fingers found her pussy again. "*Ooh . . .*"

"You wanna suck this dick into your mouth?"

Her hips rolled to his touch. "*Uh . . .*"

He slid his fingers in deeper. "You want this dick inside you?" He pulled his fingers out, played with her clit.

"*Yesss,*" she hissed out over another moan, louder.

He delved back between the lips of her pussy, his fingers splashing inside her juices.

"Beg me to fuck you." He found her G-spot.

"Oh, no . . . *yesss!*" She gasped out the words. It wasn't a climax. It was a desperate plea, a need so great it nearly made her knees shake. She closed her eyes.

"Look at me," he murmured, his fingers caressing her inner flesh, the pads of his fingertips stroking over silken ridges. She clutched her walls around him.

And then her eyes fluttered opened.

His voice was husky as he stared into her gaze and whispered, "Tell me what you want, baby?"

When the back of Sin's legs finally hit the end of the bed, his world tilted and he was on his back, and she was above him, straddling his hips.

She finally had him right where she wanted.

Beneath her touch.

A touch, a caress, her fingers danced over his skin, causing his balls to fill with a burning need for release. She pulled back and bent down to caress his shaft with her lips, sliding them wetly down to the base of his dick, then tonguing his balls.

Sin groaned. "Fuck, baby . . ."

Her tongue rasped back up his shaft and then over his dick's bulbous head, licking away the salty-sweet droplet of pre-come, before swirling her tongue around the crown. She loved tasting him, savoring him. Another groan fell from his lips as she sucked him deep. Sin bit into his bottom lip, his toes stretching open. She would have loved to make him come with her mouth, and then swallow his climax, relishing in his cries of pleasure as he emptied his sac, but she had other plans.

Keeping her eyes on him, she begrudgingly released his dick, leaving glistening streaks of saliva, as she rose up over him again.

"I want to make you come," she repeated, eyeing him greedily. She rocked her hips over his lap. She felt his body tense. "I want to slide my pussy over your dick until your creamy heat splashes all over me," she continued.

She felt his wet dick throb against her thigh.

He felt her aching heat.

Her bang fell over her eye as she ducked her head and licked over his nipple.

Tensing, he cupped her ass.

"Ooh, yes. Ride that dick, girl . . . I tol' you his dick was good . . ."

He shut his eyes tight, and tried to block out the voice in his head.

"You love it when I take this dick, don't you?"

He stilled, his eyes flashing open. "Stop."

Dr. Dangerfield looked down at him. "Stop, what?"

"You can't be on top." He grabbed her wrists, and then quickly slid from under her. He never allowed a woman to ride him. Ever.

Startled by his abruptness, she gave him a worried look. "What's wrong?"

"Nothing."

"Don't give me that," she said calmly.

She propped herself up on her elbows, gazing helplessly at him, confused, aroused, and questioning. This had been the third time she recalled him abruptly rolling her off of him. The first time had been over a year ago, when they'd been in her villa, her giving him one of her sensual massages. The second time, had been nearly eight months ago, after a night of long-winded kissing, licking, and sucking.

She hadn't given either times much thought, because it really hadn't mattered, until now. It wasn't coincidence that those times she'd tried to mount him, to have him beneath her, he'd shifted the position, flipping her on to her back, then spreading himself over her, pinning her beneath his heat and strength.

"Nothing's wrong," he said, stretching his neck from one side to the other. He felt tension coiling around him. He rolled his neck. "I just like being the one on top."

She frowned. "Did I do something to upset you?" She shook her head, eyeing him as he stood to his feet, pulling his underwear and shorts back up over his muscled ass.

He ran his hands over his locks, pulling them back at his nape. He turned to glance at her. "No."

No?

Was that all he was willing to offer her?

She blinked. "I'm lying here, naked, extremely aroused, telling you how badly I want to love all over you. And then, out of nowhere, you shove me off of you. But *I* did nothing wrong?"

Now he felt like shit. And his deflating dick wasn't too happy with him, either.

It wanted to nut, too.

Fuck.

He sighed. He hadn't come here for this. "What is it you want from me, Doc?"

Where the fuck had he been for the last fifteen-goddamn-minutes? Hadn't he heard a word she'd said?

She sat up slowly. Took a deep, steadying breath. Always being a lady.

Sophisticated. Refined.

"I want you to talk to me, Sin. Tell me what is going on with you? Tell me why you froze under my touch? And why you leave me lying here, soaking wet."

He let out a frustrated sigh. "Let's not exaggerate, Doc. I didn't freeze."

"You did," she insisted. "And I want to know why." And he could tell her before, or after, she orgasmed. She didn't care when he told her, as long as he was telling her.

"Why are you so afraid of not being in control?"

"Ooh, yes, Sin . . . it's so good. I love it when I ride you, like this. Your dick feels so good in my pussy . . ."

He shook the voice from his head. He wasn't going to allow those thoughts to control his mood, or ruin the chance for some pussy. "I'm not afraid. I just like being in control. There is no crime in that."

"No, there isn't. But there is no real reward in stubbornly holding on to it, either. Letting go of some of your control can be liberating."

He cringed, hoping she wasn't about to turn this into one of her counseling sessions. "Why is it so important to you for me *not* to be in control?"

"It's not," she admitted. Although she believed a man should be able to surrender to a woman from time to time. She found it sexy. "But it appears to be very important to *you*. And I want to know why."

"Not now, Doc," he said in a deceptively mild tone.

But she wasn't easily deterred. "All I'm asking is for you to trust me, Sin." She narrowed her gaze at him. "Do you think you can do that, or at least try to?"

Trust.

That wasn't a word heavily used in his world. Trust had been stolen from him a lifetime ago, and it was now nearly a foreign concept to him. He'd lost faith in others long before he'd fully understood the impact it would one day have on his life. And here she was asking him to *trust* her.

Exactly how did she expect him to do that?

Not that he mistrusted her. She'd given him no reason to.

Trust no one.

Especially women. And yet, every time he was with one, he expected her to put her trust in him, to give him the key to open the gates to her deepest desires. Hypocritical he knew. However, no woman ever challenged that.

He had what they wanted, and so they yielded to his expectations, his requirements, without so much as a question.

Women didn't tell him no, and mean it. They denied him nothing. Ever.

Now here she was standing before him, trying to disrupt the controlled order in his life.

His rules, his way . . .

Dr. Dangerfield knew she was pushing the envelope asking for him to trust her. Trust was one of the greatest, most precious, gifts someone could give to another human being. And she wanted to be gifted by him. If only he gave her a chance.

"I'm not asking you to trust me with your deep, dark secrets," she said softly. Although she did want to know the darkest, the ugliest, parts of what made him so painfully beautiful. She wanted to know what really made him tick. Yes, she wanted to get all up inside his head. But for now, she'd happily accept the one hanging between his legs.

"All I'm asking is for you to just give up *some—not* all—of your control in the bedroom. Let me have you in the way I want. Tonight."

His gaze dropped to her breasts and then journeyed along the curve of her hips, before landing in the center of her smooth thighs. That wet pussy of hers, all horny and empty swept around his senses. Her heat and musky scent were getting to him. Sin felt himself calming, relaxing, and growing hungry—for *her*—all over again.

Yet, he was still fighting the will to refuse her.

He sighed. "Listen, Doc. My job is to give your body whatever it craves. Your job is to submit, to give freely of yourself beneath me; not on top of me."

She blinked, and then a hand went on her hip. "Just so we're clear, Sin. I have no problem surrendering when *I* feel inclined to do so. But I *expect* a man to be willing, or at least open-minded enough, to allow *me* the opportunity to take the lead at times. Allow me to be in tuned to his needs and desires as well."

"Nah, baby. We good the way things are. Me on top."

She sucked her teeth. "What are you afraid of?"

Looking down on her, his gaze full of heat, he saw challenge in her eyes.

"Let her ride your big dick, Sin. Let her make you feel good . . ."

He shook the voice from his head again. That was then, this was now. The past was in the past. He could do this. Give her what she wanted. Give her a moment. A brief taste of possession, of having him in the way she wanted, if only an illusion.

He needed to prove to himself that it wasn't a big deal. That he was *still* in control. He stalked over to her, his hardening bulge stretching the front of his sweats. He stroked her bang away from her face, before pulling her into him, staring down at her with smoldering eyes and lids that fell halfway over them. He stared at her mouth, and then into her eyes again.

"I'm far from afraid, baby."

And he'd prove her wrong.

He cupped her nape, and then lowered his mouth to hers, kissing her deeply, possessively, and yet tenderly, while wondering how many other men had kissed her lips before him, and hungered for her taste.

He swallowed her minty, feminine heat, feeling a surge of lust scorching through his veins. And he inwardly admitted to himself that the notion of her grinding on him and making him nut intrigued him.

However, she was the one to break the kiss, nearly breathless, her chest rising and falling quickly. He met her gaze, which blazed with raw desire and passion, a wanting that made him swell thicker.

She stroked him over the fabric of his sweats. "I want you, Sin," she rasped, looking up at him, her eyes piercing him greedily. "Let me slide my pussy over you, and make you come." She untied the drawstring, and then shoved them, along with his underwear, away until they were down around his ankles. "Give me you." She cupped his balls, and he groaned. She sent him a seductive smile, a flash of sexual promise. "Give me tonight, Sin."

TWENTY-TWO

TWELVE MINUTES, AND thirty-four seconds.

That's how long—well, *fast*—it'd taken him to climax. And she'd made him come, *hard*.

But she'd come hard, too, from riding him without penetration, from simply sliding her pussy back and forth over his dick, while licking over his hot skin.

He tried to recall if he'd ever shot his load from a woman grinding on top of him—as an adult, or even as a horny adolescent *without* being inside of her—and concluded he never had. *He* made women come that way; not the other way around.

Until now.

Until *her*.

Damn.

And he was able to allow himself to enjoy it. By staying in the moment.

Without the—

Sin's body tensed. Dr. Dangerfield immediately picked up on the subtle tension that had quickly taken up space in the air around them. She risked a glance up at him and saw that he was staring at the wall across the room, as if his mind had slipped off into another time.

She flicked his nipple with her tongue. "What are you thinking about?" she asked, her voice a mere whisper.

Sin dragged his gaze from the wall, and turned to glance at her, slowly shaking his head. She'd caught him before his mind was able to drift to a dark place.

"You," he said, hoping he sounded convincing. He didn't. But she wasn't going to press the issue, so she simply gave him a "yeah-right" look. And then he smiled at her. "I was thinking, you're a real problem."

He let his hand gently slide her bang from over her eye. The way it hung over that one eye was sexy, but he wanted, needed, to see her eyes, both of them. And then he leaned in and kissed her on the top of her head. He breathed in the hint of hibiscus, papaya, and steamy sex.

She smiled, the gesture injecting calming warmth that flowed through her veins.

"You think?"

He nodded. "Yeah."

She flicked her tongue over his nipple again, her dreamy bedroom eyes locked on his. "I hope that's a good thing."

He wasn't sure if it was or not. But what he did know was, he wasn't going to let himself get reeled into any more of her seductive wiles. She'd had him squirming and moaning like some—

"You can thank me later," she said saucily, cutting into his thoughts.

"For?" he asked huskily, his brow rising.

"The experience."

He laughed. "Oh, really? Is that what you're calling it, an *experience*?"

She smiled. "Oh, not just an experience—an *unforgettable* one. And, like I said, you can *thank* me later." She kissed him lightly on the lips, settled her head back on his chest, and then closed her eyes. There was nothing more to be said.

Sin smiled to himself, his hand skimming over her shoulder. He loved the warm, silky feel of her skin beneath his fingertips.

For a brief moment, the room quieted, save for their breathing, and Sin relished in the silence. Cuddle time, he needed this, not that he'd ever admit it to her. But he was enjoying *it* with her, more than he imagined.

There was definitely a connection between them. Sexually, they were explosive together. Mentally, he admired her strength and determination. She was a go-getter. A woman who danced to her own beat, and he found that in itself sexy as hell.

But, emotionally—well, now, that was an extremely touchy area, one he had no interest in ever exploring. He'd never made genuine connections with women, not on an emotional level.

So, what the fuck was he doing?

He knew he was attracted to her, probably more than he should be. But, hell, all of her sweet, delicate, femininity disguised a woman with a voracious sexual appetite. Beneath all of her charm and grace and mild-nature was a sensual woman who was unafraid, uninhibited, willing to unleash her own desires without limit. And that in itself made it harder for him to resist her.

And yet this, this thing between them was definitely nothing more than physical. She felt good in his arms. *This* felt good—too good. He knew he should stop it, *this*. And yet he still held her closely, melded to his side.

As Sonder's "Care" eased out from the speakers, Dr. Danger-field opened her eyes and stole a glance up at him through her lashes, wanting to engage him in conversation, but not wanting to disrupt the calmness in the room. She was enjoying the intimacy between them, and—God, help her—if she disrupted the energy with her desire to *talk*, to be her probing, curious (and, yes, some-times nosey) self.

She didn't want to ruin the mood, so she decided she'd tread very, very carefully. Allow him to be in control of the dialogue, to give her only those parts of the conversation he wanted her to have.

"I like this," she said warmly, lifting her head from his chest.

Sin smiled. "Me too." He leaned forward and kissed the tip of her nose.

"But what exactly is this?" She shifted her body, so that she was now on her side, facing him. She propped herself up on her elbow, the side of her face cradled in the palm of her hand, her eyes locked on his. "I mean, what exactly is it that we're doing?"

"Fucking," he muttered, regretting the word the second it slipped from his mouth. But the truth didn't seem to bother her. Not much did. Maybe that was why he kept coming back for more of her. She always seemed unbothered.

"Besides the obvious," she said, playfully swatting him with her hand.

He shrugged. "I don't know," he answered honestly. "I really haven't given it much thought." Or had he? "I mean. I dig you, Doc. And I enjoy being in your company. But, other than that—"

She put her free hand up to stop him. "I know, I know. It's strictly sex. A *thing*. And I'm fine with that."

His brows furrowed. *Then stay in the moment and enjoy it.* "So then what's the problem?"

She shook her head. "There isn't one." *Was there?* "It's just that we've been spending a great deal of time together lately, and I feel like I don't know you."

Sin swallowed. It was true. She didn't *know* him. No one did. Not really.

"There's not much to know," he said, feeling his gut tighten. "I live my life in the present." A cue he should probably climb out of her bed and head back to his place, before she started going into therapist mode, trying to unearth his—

"Oh, stop." She playfully rolled her eyes. "There's a *lot* to know about the mysterious, panty-slayer. The magnificent man named Sin."

Sin chuckled, thankful for her lighthearted approach. Somehow, it disarmed him; made him willing to relax. Some.

"Well, I don't know how magnificent I am. But panty-slayer"—he laughed— "now that's one for the history books."

"You're a pussy killer, Sin," she teased. "And I want to know all I can about the man with the—as Nairobia would say, good loving *and* unforgettable fucking."

He smirked. "Oh, you're really pouring it on."

She smiled, sitting up in the bed. "Is it working?"

Sin shook his head, still grinning. He shifted his body, propping two pillows in back of him. He leaned his head back against the headboard. "Okay. What would you like to know?" He stopped her before she could open her mouth. "Tell me now. Is this going to be one of your therapy sessions, or—"

She cut him off, shaking her head. "No therapy session. Just me, the woman you *sex* down nearly every day—or night, wanting to know more about you. The man who has piqued my curiosity for as long as I can remember."

He turned his body, and then cupped her face in both hands. "No therapy. No pressure to answer what I don't wish to."

Still needing control. Fine. She'd take what she could.

"Promise," she said softly.

He then kissed her lips. One gentle kiss, and then he pulled away. "Okay then. Proceed."

She swallowed. The gatekeeper to all things *Sin* was finally allowing her in. She saw this as a small act of trust building. And she'd be damned if she was going to ruin any chance of further moments like this. So she was going to ease into his space slowly.

"When's your birthday?"

"November tenth," he said.

Oh, Scorpio. Now that explained a lot. The intensity beneath his cool, calm demeanor; his unusual emotional depth; his primal sexuality and fire in his lovemaking; the black and white way in which he lived his life, it all made sense.

She smirked. "I should have known."

He laughed, reaching for her hand, and then kissing the inside of her wrist. "Why you say that?"

"You're a tender, attentive lover, but with very dark desires. I think that might have frightened many of the women you have bedded, women who were more restrictive, more inhibited, than you."

"I've only given them what they've wanted, nothing more." Truth was, he fucked women for no other reason than because they wanted him to. They always did.

"Mm, yes, fuck me, Sin . . ."

"See, girl, I told you that young-ass dick was good . . . I taught him well . . ."

She stared at him thoughtfully. "Mm. That may be true. But tell me. What have you wanted from women?"

"Nothing but clean, wet kitty," he said over a laugh. "And lots of orgasms."

She bit back a laugh of her own. "No, seriously. What is it *you* want?"

He considered her, pensively. No woman had ever really asked him what it was that *he* wanted, what it was that *he* needed. The question swirled around in his mind for several ticking seconds, before he admitted to himself, he didn't know the answer. He'd never really given it any deeper thought. As a man, everything given, everything taken, was all that he'd wanted.

It was all that he ever expected.

He stroked the back of his hand over her cheek. "I wanna know something about you. Like what language were you speaking earlier? And where in the hell did you learn to speak it so fluently?" During their earlier sexual encounter, she'd told him in a breathy whisper how good his big dick felt against her pussy as she grinded herself on him.

She rolled her eyes, keenly aware of what he was doing. Trying to dodge the question. "It was Italian. Four years at an Italian boarding school will do it." Her parents had lived and worked as surgeons in Milan during those years, wanting to heal and save lives abroad, while broadening their daughter's cultural horizons.

Sin smirked. "Ah, privileged as I thought."

She frowned. "And what made you think that?"

He shrugged. "The way you carry yourself. Don't take offense. It's everything about you. I bet you were a cutie growing up."

"*Were?*" She feigned indignation. "I beg your pardon. I'm still a *cutie*, as you say."

"Nah. Now, you're a beautiful woman." Then he simply wrapped his arm around her. "You're gorgeous. Head to toe, baby."

She felt herself melting. "That's sweet of you."

"I know," he teased.

She rested her head on his shoulder, and placed a hand on his chest, over his heart. "But don't think just because you butter me up with a few compliments that you're off the hook."

He propped his chin on top of her head. "I already know." For a moment they settled in this position, her in his arms, the palm of her hand gently gliding back and forth over his warm flesh, and the music still playing low in the background.

"I see your face when I close my eyes . . .

Ro James.

"'Cause this love is one of a kind . . ."

Sin liked the song, even though he didn't know its title. He closed his eyes, allowed his mind to absorb the words.

Then she shifted so she could look up at him.

"Where did you grow up?" she asked cautiously.

He knew the questions would come again. He'd expected it.

"Brooklyn." Well that wasn't exactly true. He'd only lived in Brooklyn for about eight years, before hopping on a train headed for Seattle, fleeing memories he'd hoped to forget between the legs of a busty woman, fifteen years older than him.

He was nineteen.

"Oh, nice. So, you have some hood"—she ran her hand over his chest— "beneath all of this chiseled chocolate."

Sin chuckled, his eyes opening. "Some."

"Is that where you were born?"

He shook his head. "Nah. Georgia." He'd been born in Savannah, where he lived until he was nine. Then his mother dragged him to Alabama for a year, before whisking him off to New York.

"Oh, and he's a man with southern charm flowing through his veins. I like you more already."

He laughed again. "Stop."

"You and Saint," she said, furrowing her brows. "I know you're both brothers. But the two of you, although you're both tall, handsome, and very, uh, sexual, don't look much alike."

"I know."

"Who's older?"

"Saint."

"Oh, okay. Do you have any other siblings?"

He nodded. "Yeah. An older sister. Serenity."

Dr. Dangerfield gave him a look.

He responded before she could ask. "Yeah, we all have different fathers."

"I was about to ask if the two of you were close?"

Oh.

"Nah, not really." He hadn't seen her in almost ten years. The last time had been at a gathering where'd she become so inebriated that she accused him of leering at her then twelve-year old daughter, causing a very uncomfortable scene, screaming obscenities and calling him perverted. That was enough for him to never want to be around her again. The distance was for the best. All hadn't been completely forgiven, nor forgotten, but he still managed to call her at least once every few months, hoping for an apology that he knew would never come.

Resentment kept a wedge between them.

She resented him for growing up with their mother. And he resented her for not knowing the type of hell he'd lived through.

"What was her name?"

"Who, my mother's? She nodded and Sin swallowed. "Hope." But there'd been nothing hopeful about her."

"With names like, Sin, Saint and Serenity, she must have been brought up in church."

"Preach, Pastor, Preach! Yes, you better say that . . . !" He cringed inwardly. "I guess you can say that." Until she'd lost her way, until the streets claimed her.

She smiled. "So, you're a man who knows the *Word*, too." She moaned. "You're about to give me an orgasm."

In spite of the slow-building knot in his stomach, she made him grin—and quickly forget. "Oh, really? I'm sure I can give you one in a more creative way."

She licked over her lips. "Well, maybe you can. After we're done . . . *talking*."

He groaned. "Right, right. You wanting to know me." He shook his head. He was already tired of the inquisition. "Anything else?"

"Welll . . ."

"Um. Listen, baby. I don't mean to rush this 'get-to-know-me-talk' along"—he glanced down at his dick— "but you might wanna hurry up before he comes alive again."

She rolled her eyes. "Your greedy friend will be fine. Now tell me. Did you and your siblings grow up together, in the same house?"

Sin sighed, and then he visibly swallowed. "Nah."

"Oh."

His mother had been wild and incorrigible. And fast. Fucking in the church basement was where she'd committed most of her sin. She'd had Serenity by the time she was fourteen, and then two years later, she'd given birth to his brother Saint.

They'd both been taken from her, or maybe she'd given them up. Either way, all Sin knew was, no one had come for him.

Dr. Dangerfield felt him stiffen, and she fought the urge to push.

He bit his lips and looked away, his chest tightening. She'd never understand. So far, he'd left out the nightmarish parts of his life living with his mother, revealing only that she was the woman who'd birthed him.

He felt his eyes beginning to burn. The inquisition was over. He turned to her. Blew out his breath in a long exhale, and then narrowing his eyes, he said in a low, harsh voice, "Some women should never have children. Ever."

His eyes suddenly fierce, Dr. Dangerfield reached for his hand, squeezing, and then she nodded. She understood.

There was nothing more he would offer.

TWENTY-THREE

THE SUN HAD poured like warm molasses over Sin's body as he lay out in a hammock under its burning rays, lounging. Save for the occasional bathroom run and nourishing his body, it was where he'd been all day, chilling, relaxing, dozing off here and there.

He'd awaken earlier than usual this morning. Restlessness had kept him from sleeping in later than he'd hoped for, so he'd peeled himself from tangled sheets around four in the morning, and went for a run along the beach.

He'd run long and hard, his chest nearly on fire, his thighs screaming, before he'd finally made it back to his villa. After he used the bathroom, he'd splashed some cold water on his face, cupped a little more in his hand to swish around in his mouth, then looked at himself in the mirror.

He'd looked tired. And that made him look older. He hadn't been quite sure what had had him thinking about his age, or the fact that he'd be a year older in another eight months, but maybe it had something to do with the fact that, aside from a bank account stuffed with money, he really had nothing to show for his life. Not even a family, aside from Saint and a sister he wasn't really that close with, to call his own. Not that he wanted to be married, or anything like that—hell, the thought unsettled him.

Made him feel suffocated.

And he definitely had no interest in kids for fear of fucking up their lives, or not being able to protect them, to keep them safe.

But still, there was more to life than just that. Wasn't it?

Yeah, yeah, there was.

It had to be.

Because if *that*—having a family, marriage and kids—was what everyone in this world aspired, then something was disturbingly wrong with the world's view of life, of living. And yet something was shifting inside of him. He felt it happening. And, although he couldn't put his finger on it, he didn't like it. It made him uncomfortable.

Talking about himself. Sharing. Exposing. Thinking.

Fucking made him not think. Fucking kept him from sharing.

And yet Dr. Dangerfield had somehow managed to get him to do just that. Oh, she was good—too good. But he was better. Better at detaching himself, better at putting up walls, better at keeping people out of his past, out of those private, personal parts of his life.

It had been almost a week since their *pillow* session. Since he'd told her more than he'd ever told any other woman. But—*shit*. She made it easy to do, to share. She made it easy for him to lose himself in the moment . . . and almost forget about the walls he'd put up. Almost. And *that* bothered him about her. Or was it himself he was really most bothered by?

Hell, if he knew.

He closed his eyes and recalled the smell of her pussy, her breath, the feel of her skin, her pussy. And, yeah, he could go days without seeing her, fucking her, without any thought of her. But then, at the most unexpected times, his body would remember the feel of her skin against his. His dick would remember the feel of her sweet, moist pussy, enveloping him, wrapping it in her heat.

He still hadn't returned her call from three nights ago. She'd left him a message.

"Hello, Sin. It's Gretchen. I haven't seen you in a few days. Are

you avoiding me? And then she'd let out a girlish giggle that tickled his ears as he listened on. *"Silly, I know. But not far-fetched, is it? Well, hopefully, I'll run into you soon. If not, call me. When you're ready to, of course."*

Was he, avoiding her?

He shook his head. Of course, he wasn't. And then, in spite of the unexplainable conflict he was experiencing, he heard her sultry voice, *"Come for me, Sin,"* and a slight smile touched his lips.

He knew what *she* was doing—the Doc.

Trying to dig her way into his head. She was trying to chip away at his skillfully erected wall, to find her way in—into his life, his mind.

And, maybe, try to scheme her way into his heart.

He scoffed. Not a chance in hell of that ever happening. But she could try, he mused. She'd be sadly disappointed. There was nothing there. He was empty. Everything he'd had in him had been siphoned out a long time ago.

And, now, all that was left was—maybe, remnants of—

He sighed. *Fuck this shit.* He wasn't about to stress himself about shit he hadn't had any control over. What he was in control of was now.

And he wasn't about to lose it to a woman, no matter how sensual, intense . . . Damn, she was so fucking smart and engaging, not to mention ridiculously sexy. She was everything any man could ever want, desire, hope for, and yet he wasn't the man for her. The point to this was, he enjoyed fucking her. But he didn't want to hurt her. Because he knew, better than anyone else, that he might fuck up her life.

Sin sighed. This whole shit was making him feel some type of way.

He looked out toward the ocean. Nightfall was slowly encroaching on the day, slicing between cracks of the sun. The sky almost glowed in slivers of color, fighting back the inevitable.

Darkness.

Still, it was a picturesque sight along with a perfect mix of heat and the ocean's cooling breeze. Sin didn't know what he enjoyed most, sunrise or sunset. Truth was, they were both equally remarkable phenomenon. And yet they held different meanings. One, the fresh beginning of a new day; the other—

He climbed out of his hammock, stretched his back, and rubbed a hand over his dick, before heading back inside, determined to empty his mind of any further thoughts of Dr. Dangerfield, her meddling ways, or her good pussy.

He flipped on a switch to the villa's sound system, and then made his way to the bathroom as an Eric Bellinger track oozed out from the speakers. He took a deep breath and stared at his reflection, rubbing a hand over his beard, wondering if he should cut it. But then he thought better of it. Sexy as it might be to have a smooth, shaven face, his beard—along with his locs—was sexier.

Maybe in another life, he'd shed his locs and beard.

Sin shifted his gaze from the mirror. And then after flossing and brushing his teeth, he stripped and hopped in the shower. He groaned as the hot water beat against his skin, slowly melting tension from his body. He needed to call Nairobia, he thought as he reached for a bottle of liquid soap. He still hadn't given her his answer. And he still didn't know why he hadn't. But what he did know was, he didn't want there to be any confusion if he took her up on her offer. There'd need to be ground rules in place. The first being: absolutely no sex between them. The rest of the rules he'd make up as time went on. But there'd definitely be no fucking.

Their relationship would be strictly professional. Period.

He soaped his body up, scrubbed over his skin with a loofah sponge, and then rinsed off, repeating the process two more times, before reaching for his loofah brush and scrubbing his back, then his legs, and finally his feet.

After drying off, he slipped into a pair of black and white basketballs shorts and a white muscle shirt, before—

Damn.

Someone was at his door. Sin thrust his fingers through his damp locs as he ambled toward the door.

He opened the door, and blinked.

"You haven't called me." And just that quick, the decision he'd made to no longer give any further thought to her had now magically unmade itself.

"Shit," he hissed, just as she opened her red silk coat, and let it drop to the ground.

The universe was testing him.

TWENTY-FOUR

THE WETTER THE pussy, the better the taste . . .

That's what Sin believed to be true. And the proof was all over his mouth and soaked in his beard, and stained on his tongue, as he licked over Dr. Dangerfield's clit and then slid his tongue back into her dripping heat, swirling it around inside of her, wanting to taste every inch of her.

His nostrils flared as he inhaled her succulent scent.

He felt like an animal, rabid and starving, and wanted to devour her, to consume the flavor of her swollen sex. He could feel the wet tug of her pussy as he darted his tongue in and out of her, her muscles trying to capture it in its grip, making his hard dick drip with need.

She'd showed up at his door, naked beneath her coat, already with the intent of giving him the pussy. What was he supposed to do?

Turn her away? Hell no. There was no denying, he wanted to be inside of her, fucking her in deep, slow strokes. Marking her core with every thrust, with every stretch, with every length of him. Sin knew her body didn't belong to him; however, he wanted to possess it. In this very second, he wanted to take her pussy and own it.

To impale her, pound her.

To fuck her all through the night, and then again in the morning.

But his own primal need to sink himself into her flesh would have to wait. This was about her. And right now, all he wanted was to give her pleasure with his mouth, his lips, his tongue, and then his hands.

Though his dick throbbed, nearly ached, for release, Sin wasn't in any hurry to end his tongue dance over Dr. Dangerfield's flesh. He wanted to savor her sweet, rich taste, so much so that he laved his tongue up the length of her inner folds, then swirled it around her swollen clit, before sliding it back inside her.

He rasped, "You taste so sweet, baby." He licked over her lips. Up, down. Up, down. And his tongue flicked over her clit, before he tugged it between his lips, nursing on it, loving on it, until the bud swelled and throbbed against his tongue.

Dr. Dangerfield's toes curled; her fists clenched.

She writhed in delight.

"Beg me to stop," Sin dared. The deep timbre of his low voice caused her nipples to tighten. Was this fine-ass man out of his sexy mind? Did he really think she'd part her lips to beg him . . . to stop?

"No," she pushed out, nearly panting. "Don't."

"Don't what?" he teased. He licked her labia. And then licked over the seam of her pussy, catching her nectar.

"Don't stop . . . *that. Mmm*, yes. Licking me . . . *oooh* . . . there. *Uhhh* . . . my pussy . . ."

Her hips bucked off the mattress. Oh, God, he had the most dangerously incredible mouth. She wanted more of it. She arched her back and furrowed her head deeper into the pillow as he continued to dart his tongue in and out of her, taking his time.

She drew gasping breaths and exhaled soft groans that eventually turned sharp with desire as her pussy clenched and unclenched.

"You want this tongue?" he asked, gazing up at her. All he saw was her beautiful face twisted in her budding climax.

"Yes, Sin, yes . . . lick all over my wet pussy."

Her hips bucked wantonly to his mouth as he sucked her there.

Sin's eyes drifted upward again. Her face was etched in ecstasy, her pouty lips forming an *O* as he glided his tongue in and out of her.

Ohgod, yes! Fuck me . . . with . . . that . . . *ohhh* . . . long . . . *uh* . . . delicious . . . *mmm* . . . tongue."

With a cry, she dug her nails into Sin's shoulders and came. Helpless and needy, her body churned, her hips slowly winding as she brought her hands up to her breasts and toyed with her distended nipples.

She attempted to close her thighs as pleasure rippled through her pussy, but Sin's hands forced her legs still.

"Don't," he warned, spreading her wider. "I'm not done having you."

His mouth was back on her sex again, causing another liquid surge of desire blazed through her veins, heating her core.

"Oh, God . . . oh, God, yes. Please," she panted. "*Mmmm . . . ohhh . . . yes . . .*"

Sin growled low in the back of his throat. Her moans were drawing him in, like a moth to a flame. As his lips and tongue leisurely claimed her, her body thrashed against wave after wave of searing heat. Pleasure built, coiling around her body like a spring.

She couldn't remember the last time, if ever, she'd come so severely intense from cunnilingus alone.

He sucked her like a ripe, juicy peach. Wet and sloppily, he wrung out one orgasm after another, feeling her body erupting beneath him with each climax.

"Oh, oh, oh, *ohhhhh*," she mewled out.

She was vibrating.

"You taste so sweet," he whispered over her clit. "So wet"—his tongue lapped her swollen nub— "so juicy, baby . . ."

Dr. Dangerfield's eyes rolled up and then around in her head as he dipped his middle finger between her soft, feminine folds and licked over her labia.

His tongue swipes over her silken flesh were decadent. His long tongue moved in and out of her pussy in a slow, sweet rhythm akin to lovemaking.

His husky groans, the wet-suck sounds of his mouth on her pussy, were music to her ears as she bathed his tongue in her dewy heat. She was so, so, very close . . . nearly at the edge. He was pushing her closer, closer, flicking his tongue over and around her clit, over her pussy lips, time after time, fusing his mouth over her sex, kissing her there, loving her there, until the aching in the pit of her core multiplied, soared.

Then without warning, she cried out and shuddered as she came into Sin's greedy mouth.

Her legs remained splayed.

And there she was. Vulnerable. Exposed. Breathing heavy. Turning her sexuality over to him.

Sin licked the crease of her cunt, then lapped over her drenched labia. "Mmm," he groaned over her flesh. His eyes drifted upward to meet her heated gaze. "You taste so fucking good, baby."

She writhed in response.

Slowly his lips curved seductively. "You want this dick, don't you?"

Yes, yes, yes—hell yes! She wanted his dick. Deep and fast, slow and hard—God at this very moment she'd take it however he was willing to give it as long as he was giving it. Getting fucked was the thing on her mind.

A gentle slid of his finger slid over her slit, and she felt herself clench and then unclench in hungry need.

"Yeah, baby," Sin muttered. "Look at that pretty pussy opening for me."

Dr. Dangerfield gasped. "Stop taunting me."

Sin grinned teasingly, and it held promise.

"Tonight, I'm going to enjoy arousing you, pushing you toward climax, then leaving you clinging there."

A small voice in her head was warning her to stop this madness now, before the knot of desire coiling tightly around inside of her strangled her senseless.

"Fuck me," she pushed out over a fluttery whisper.

What was he trying to do to her? See her lose her mind with want? Well, goddammit, she was almost there. And now he was toying with her emotions—and her damn cunt.

"Fuck me, Sin," she demanded.

"All in time,"—he pushed the tip of his finger inside her pussy "This sweet hole is mine, baby . . ." he curved his finger inside her so his pad pressed against her channel. More sex juices flowed from her quivering cunt, causing her to bite back a sudden wave of anger followed by sharp arousal. She didn't know how much more of this she could stand. Her head whipped from side to side as he blew on her clit, licked it, then blew on it again, toying with it, tormenting it between his teeth as he slowly moved his finger in and out of her body.

Surrender . . .

This was what he wanted.

This was what she offered her clients, what she challenged them to do. Relinquish control, to allow themselves to melt into the pleasure.

"This sweet, luscious clit," Sin rasped. "I'm going to keep sucking on it until I wring out another orgasm, until you flood my mouth with all of those sweet pussy juices."

She gasped.

Suddenly his languid tongue strokes became more fiercely driven, more purposeful. Dr. Dangerfield's body shook and her climax came gushing out of her body, like a tsunami, flooding him.

And she felt herself drowning in it. Then, not giving her a chance to recover, Sin kissed over her flaring pussy as she squirmed with after-shudders. She gasped and froze a moment, then all but melted into his mouth as he licked out the last bit of her orgasm. And then she felt it. The need suddenly rushing through her frightened her. That wasn't supposed to happen. *That* feeling. She knew what this was, what it always was. Noncommittal sex.

And yet she could get used to him licking her, like this, forever.

She didn't want to read too much into it, but something felt different. *This* felt different—for her. But then he kissed her. His mouth covered hers in a heated rush, a gasp, a melding of lips, a groan. The tang of pussy and heated desire swirled around their tongues, flooding her senses.

In her head, Dr. Dangerfield knew this blistering kiss did not mean anything to Sin, nor should it to her. But the swelling in her chest, the pounding in her ears, was evidence that the world around her was slowly shifting in a new direction.

When Sin finally released her mouth and held her face in his hands, staring into her eyes, she drew in a shaky breath, and then she shuddered.

She suddenly felt herself beginning to lose her ability to breath. Heart beating hard, she blinked several times, before shutting her eyes, trying to ascertain whether or not she was on the verge of a panic attack.

Oh, God, no. This can't be happening.

Her worst fear was slowly beginning to manifest itself in the form of a man.

Somehow, she'd gone from enjoying Sin to *wanting* more of him.

TWENTY-FIVE

WHEN SIN WOKE up in the wee hours of the morning, sprawled out in his bed, naked, with the scent of her hovering around him—on his sheets, on his skin, all over his lips—and a hard dick just begging for a third round . . . Dr. Dangerfield was gone.

The sheets chilled.

The indentation of where her body had been was still present.

Sin sighed, wondering what the hell he'd been thinking hoping she'd stayed the night. Not that that'd have been a bad thing. They'd kept each other up most of the night, anyway, feeding each other's hungry need. She'd been ravenous for him. And he'd been starved for more of her.

He chuckled, shaking his head. He couldn't recall who had tapped out, first.

Her. Or him.

Still . . .

The fact that he'd reached out for her—before opening his eyes, his hand automatically seeking her out, wanting the feel of her soft skin beneath his fingers, made him frown.

That wasn't him.

Seeking out a woman in his bed.

And yet he glanced over at the empty spot where she'd been. How the hell had she gotten out of his bed without him knowing it?

He shook his head again.

He was bugging.

Sure, he was in lust. And, yeah, he even liked her. She was mad cool, really easy to get along with, sexy as hell, and the sex was always good. Real good.

That deep, wet pussy and fat, toned ass was enough to drive any man crazy. And last night—after he'd made her orgasm multiple times with his mouth and tongue, he'd finally given her what she'd come for.

The dick.

And the way her body opened to him had made his toes curl, taking in the sight of her pussy swallowing him whole, wetting him with all that hungry want, bathing every inch of him in that silky heat.

Sin licked over his lips at the memory.

She'd been so tight for him. She'd allowed him in as always, allowing him to bury himself inside her body, but last night had somehow been, *felt,* different. Deeper. Being inside of her, he'd felt oddly connected.

Beneath him, she'd writhed, lifted up, absorbing all of him, flooding him, melting over him—all dripping pleasure.

A pleasure that burned him as he groaned and panted and sank deeper, and then still deeper, her legs wrapped around his waist, welcoming his powerful surges by moving with him.

He'd wanted to feel her silky heat raw. Wanted to tear off the condom and plunge into her wet depths, to be bathed in her warm juices.

That pussy's so good. Damn . . .

Sin rubbed over his now-throbbing dick. He tried to recall a time in which he'd replayed one of his sexual liaisons—and there were many, countless and nameless—in his head and his dick hardened. Aside from his encounters with Nairobia and Dr. Dangerfield, there were none.

And, sure, he'd had lots of good pussy, some more spectacular than others. But none had left him wanting more, long after the sex was over.

But sex with Dr. Dangerfield was effortless. They moved so fluidly together. Their bodies melded so perfectly together. He'd be a fool to deny that fact. The chemistry between the two was combustible.

Her pussy, her mouth, always welcomed him in—wet, warm, and readily.

And last night, when he sank his dick into her lush pussy, she had gripped him, milked him, soaking him with her need. Sin had wanted to fuck her so exquisitely deep until he'd lost himself in her body's slick heat, until he'd fucked her memory free of any other man's dick before his.

Something he'd never wanted before. Something he'd never felt before.

Possessive.

Or was he becoming obsessed?

There was something about the way she touched him, gently, sensually. And it did something to him. It warmed him somewhere deep in the pit of his soul.

That troubled him.

It made him weirdly uncomfortable. And yet he couldn't help closing his eyes and conjuring up images of her in the throes of her orgasms. Her eyes had gone all soft and dreamy, as if she'd been transported into another world. Goddamn. She was so fucking beautiful; just all around sexier than he'd recalled from any of their previous encounters.

She was always so tight, so wet, so sweet and warm, her perfect pussy clenching around him, her swollen clit throbbing beneath his touch. She drove him insanely wild.

He'd wanted her to stay the night with him, in *his* bed. This shit was so unlike him. She was fucking him up, confusing him, taking him places he hadn't expected to go. Opening up to her, allowing her slight glimpses into his world. It was all so frustrating, and yet she made him feel comfortable—too comfortable for his liking. She made it easy for him to let his guard down, if only for a short while, and that too bothered him.

Deeply.

He was conflicted in his desires, in his needs. They weren't in a relationship. And, hell, he didn't believe he was wired to be in one. He liked shit simple.

Fuck. Chill. And go.

But still he was sexing her down every chance he got. And now, this new shit of wanting her to stay the night. That had to have been some shit he'd been feeling in the heat of the moment. Yeah, that had to have been it. Nonetheless, he hadn't spent as much time with any other woman the way he was spending it with her.

Seven weeks, though short for many, was like an eternity for Sin. He tired easily; lost interest fast. Truth was, he'd never been with the same woman more than twice—maybe a third time, if memory served him correct. And yet something kept bringing him back to Dr. Dangerfield, pulling him closer to *her*.

Why?

He knew he needed to slow things down between the two of them. But how could he when everything about her was nothing but a flood of sensation? Pleasure searing through his veins every time she touched him, looked at him, and called out his name. Her throaty moans, the flicks of her tongue, the sensual roll of her hips. Her passion unnerved and aroused him like nothing else he could remember.

It was all too fucking good.

But he didn't want to think about it.

Not now.

Not while his dick throbbed for release.

He reached for his phone, and then dialed her number.

"Hello?" she murmured, wondering who the hell was calling

her at . . . she blinked, her eyes slowly focusing on the red numbers flashing on her digital clock.

Six A.M.

"Good morning."

She sat up in bed. He never called her. They'd always either ran into each other or he dropped by her office or just showed up at her door.

She rubbed her eyes. "Sin? Is everything alright?"

"I'm good. Why didn't you wake me, before you left?"

"You looked so peaceful," she said softly. And he'd slept peacefully as well. Something he couldn't recall ever doing. "I didn't want to bother you."

"You should have stayed," the words had come out before he could stop them. Shit.

"I didn't want to. I'm not your woman," she said pointedly. She was sure her voice cracked.

"I would have made an exception."

She shifted in her bed. "And then regretted it. No thanks."

He laughed. "I wouldn't have."

She sighed. "Maybe, maybe not. Now neither of us will know."

"Has anyone ever told you how sexy you sound in the morning?"

She felt her skin heat. "Yes," she murmured. "You, just now."

"Lucky me."

"Yes, lucky you. Now stroke yourself for me. Pretend I'm there in bed with you."

Sin grinned. Although he had both an imagination *and* memories to refer to, phone sex wasn't particularly his thing. He preferred the real thing.

"Nah. Why don't you come back over instead? And then you can stroke me and touch me, however you want."

She moaned. "Sounds tempting. But I want to hear you come for me, over the phone. In my ear."

He groaned. "I can moan in your ear, here."

"No, Sin. I know you're over there with an erection." Her voice had the dreamy quality of seduction and exhaustion.

"Yeah," he murmured. "I'm hard as fuck."

"Mm. I like the sound of that."

"It'll feel better. Back inside you."

"That's not what I'm asking for, Sin," she said softly. "Stroke your dick for me. Let me help you get your morning nut."

Her erotic words made his dick bounce.

"Shit," he muttered.

"Come for me, Sin," she whispered into the phone. "Let me hear how you get that thick, creamy nut."

"Come get it, Doc."

"Give me what I want, Sin."

"I'm trying to. It's here, waiting for you."

"No. I don't *want* to see it. I don't want to feel it. I want to *hear* you come."

He couldn't recall ever having phone sex, especially when pussy was always within his dick's reach whenever he'd wanted it. But there was something soothing and sexy and needy in the way she asked for it that it made him want to give it to her.

She moaned softly in his ear. "I'm playing with my clit, Sin. And I'm getting so very wet for you, imagining my wet, hungry mouth all over your dick. I can taste your arousal, Sin." She smacked her lips together. "*Mmm*, you taste you so good."

His dick twitched.

She was fucking with him. He cupped his balls, massaged them, rubbed them. They were full, heavily reloaded, and ready to be emptied out.

He chuckled. "You're nasty, Doc."

"You have no idea." She spread her legs wider. Slipped two fingers inside her body. And then moaned. She loved phone sex. Loved talking dirty. Loved the way it stretched the imagination.

And, most of all, she loved touching herself.

With a low growl, he envisioned her naked, her fingers sliding into those plump, wet folds—all sticky and wet. He could almost smell the heady scent of her pussy. Almost feel the wet suck and release of it around his dick. That alone was enough to send him toppling over the edge.

"I'm so wet, Sin. Are you naked the way I left you?"

"Yeah," he croaked out, as he slowly stroked his dick. Precum oozed out from its tip, then dribbled down his crown and finally over his hand as he imagined it was his dick inside her, instead of her fingers. Those fucking fingers, fucking what he should be fucking.

"Shit," he punctuated. Then he lowered his voice to almost a whisper and said, "I bet that juicy pussy feels so good right now."

"Mm-hm. It does. I'm so creamy. And hot."

She moaned.

He squeezed his thighs together, pressing them into his swollen balls. He was on the verge of erupting. He stopped in mid-stroke, squeezing the base of his dick. His thighs shook. *Oh, fuck.* It was too late. He bit back another curse.

And then grunted as his nut spurt out of his dick.

Yet, he was still hard, still horny, and still ready to fuck.

She moaned again.

And the sound caressed his ear, vibrated through him, right down into his chest. He hissed, then muttered a curse. "This is bullshit, Doc. No since of you being over there in bed with all that good pussy, while I'm still over here in bed with all this still hard-ass dick. I'm coming over to slide up in you."

Dr. Dangerfield moaned deeply. "It'll be a wasted trip," she warned over a puff of air. "I won't let you in." And then she gasped so close to his ear, he could almost feel her heat.

"I'm leaving now."

"Then you'll be standing outside with a hard, horny dick."

"Don't play."

"I'm already playing"—she moaned— "with this wet pussy."

And then there was a click, followed by silence.

"Hello? You still there?" Sin frowned. "What the . . .?" He shook his head. "Ain't this some shit," he muttered.

She hung up on him.

She hung up?

Sin stared at the phone in disbelief. And then before he could decide what to do next, it rang again. "Yeah?"

"If you want some more of this pussy, Sin, it'll be here for you tonight. Six-thirty. Be on time."

He didn't have time to say a word, because she'd hung up.

Again.

≈

By the time she ended the call, Dr. Dangerfield found herself trapped in thought.

Sin.

Hearing his voice did something to her. It shook her desires loose. Made her feel all frilly and pink, soft and pretty. Well, shit, wait.

She was already pretty. No, scratch that. Fine. She was damn *fine*, a head turner, for sure. No man *made* her feel pretty. But Sin made her feel more desirable than she already felt. He made her hotter, and wetter than any other man had ever done.

Not that she'd had a gaggle of men in her lifetime. She'd been a virgin up until she'd turned nineteen, but (before her deflowering in her sophomore year of college), she'd known how to pleasure a man in other ways without ever letting him inside her panties. She'd fogged up plenty of car windows and had given a few boys in her high school an ear full of dirty talk while she slid her soft body up and down their athletic bodies, grinding her panty-covered pussy over the stretch of their bulges, until they'd cream in their pants.

Oh, sure she'd let them play with her mouthwatering breasts, squeeze her voluptuous ass, and even let them have a quick tit-ty-fuck, if she really liked them. And, sure, she'd been called a dick-tease. Uh. Hello?

She'd had been.

Purposefully.

And she'd proudly toyed with her prey, luring them in for more, more sweet kisses, more grinding, more hand jobs, more creamy explosions.

But her virginity had still been intact.

She'd considered those boys, those chiseled athletes, in high school target practice. She'd used them, always giving them the illusion that they were the ones who'd orchestrated their dirty romps. All the while, she'd been sharpening her seduction skills, mastering the craft of climax.

She'd learned early on that boys, like men, said whatever you wanted to hear as long as they'd thought there'd be something in it for them. Until they grew tired of you. Until you were all used up, and no longer special anymore. Until you were nothing more than an easy lay. Until the next best thing came sauntering in, with bigger breasts, a bigger ass, a wetter mouth, and an even more willing snatch.

Of course, she'd always been above believing anything that spilled out from any of their lips, save for their greedy moans, their shuddering pleas, their needy groans, she knew better. She'd been taught better.

Always make them beg.

Even back then, she knew how to manipulate the male species, driving them beyond wild with hot, burning desire.

Shaking off the memory, Dr. Dangerfield sighed.

Now the task, the challenge, at hand . . .

Sin.

She still hadn't quite figured out how to reach him, how to get him to open up to her, to become vulnerable. He was by far more difficult a nut to crack than she'd thought. She didn't want him to think she saw him as one of her patients, as some case study. No, she hoped, in time, he'd want to see her as a lover, a partner. As someone he would want to build a life with.

But, first, he would need to let her in. Trust her.

He didn't know it yet, but she believed they could be good a fit. If only he opened his eyes and saw her—*really* saw her—for everything she was.

She was more than a sexpot.

She was more than good pussy.

She was a good goddamn catch.

But she would need to exercise patience. And she would do well to keep reminding herself of that. Slow and steady. Ask little of him. Listen to the unspoken. Let him give her whatever little bones of information he'd wish for her to chew on. She would savor every morsel, whetting her appetite, her desire to know more about him.

She didn't know why it mattered, why she cared so much. But she did.

He was so breathtakingly flawed. So beautifully damaged. That she wanted to uncover, unearth, the skeletons of his past.

God, she wanted him to bear his soul, to lay his burdens down at her feet, so that she could help him through whatever pained him, through the hurt, through the darkness until he found his way to the light at the other end, to the love she'd have waiting for him.

However, she suspected if she pushed too hard, if she probed too much, if she didn't balance her concern—her curiosity—with caution, he'd retreat, like most men did.

Too scared to become vulnerable. God forbid he showed any real emotions toward a woman. Yes, if she prodded too deep, he'd definitely slip through her anxious fingers.

She felt her heart thump in her chest. She wouldn't allow it.

No. She'd meet him where he was most comfortable.

Seduction.

She'd lure him in with more than her pussy.

Moving forward, she'd seduce him from the inside out.

That's what she'd do.

Mind-fuck him.

She'd give him just enough to drive him over the edge, and then she'd reel him back in until she had him wanting every part of her, until he finally wanted, needed—nearly begged for—all that she had to give. And if that didn't work, then, dammit, she'd simply have fun trying.

She slid her tongue over the front of her teeth. And then her lips curled into a salacious grin.

She was already wet contemplating it.

Strolling into what should have been a dining room, she sat at her Baby Grand piano, something she hadn't done in—she couldn't remember—and her fingers suddenly glided across the ivory keys as she closed her eyes and hummed Adele's "Make You Feel My Love".

TWENTY-SIX

SIN SAT OUT on the deck of one of his favorite restaurants. Harlots. As with most of the eateries on the island, it overlooked the ocean. But it was the only restaurant that offered authentic Caribbean cuisine and music.

From mofongo, arroz con gandules and pastelón to mango chicken, callaloo, okra, and ackee to pineapple chow; from roti, macaroni pie and cassava to oxtails and butterbeans, Harlots infused Jamaican, Cuban, Trinidadian, Costa Rican, and Puerto Rican culture into each of its dishes.

What Sin liked most was the fact that it only employed Caribbean born workers. And it was one of the Island's most raved about must-try spots. Still, it seemed odd. This one Caribbean restaurant on the farthest tip of the island, with all of its Caribbean flair, minus larger-than-life posters of Bob Marley, surrounded by the rest of the island's Polynesian and Fijian inspired ambiance.

Sin sipped his ginger beer.

A slow-winding calypso groove played from the speakers mounted in the upper corner of the walls. It was still early. Not even noon, yet. And still the energy was already high as several sarong-wearing women seductively danced, their bikini tops barely stretching over cantaloupe-size breasts. Giving anyone who dared to look a front row view of just how nasty they could be.

No matter what time of the day, the place was guaranteed to be lively.

As Saint approached, Sin saw a man running across the sand and then bolting up the steps from the beach three at a time, slinging his arms around a very thick, very scantily dressed woman. She screamed and laughed, trying to break free from his grasp as he planted steamy kisses on the back of her neck.

Sin glanced at his watch just as Saint finally approached the table.

"Hey, man," he said as he pulled out a chair. "Sorry I'm late."

Sin laughed. "Sorry my ass. It wouldn't be you if you weren't."

Saint chuckled. "True, true. But I'm working on it."

Sin gave him a disbelieving look. "Yeah, yeah. I know. You're a work in progress," he said half joking.

"Always. Aren't we all?"

"Well, we all should be."

"Exactly, man. I might have the name of a saint, but I'm too flawed to ever be perfect."

"Ah, finally, you have clarity," Sin said lightheartedly.

"Why you hatin'?"

"You're delusional," Sin countered.

"And I'm starving."

"Our food should be coming out soon," Sin offered, glancing at his watch again. "I ordered it about ten minutes ago."

"My man, always thinking ahead." And then he was craning his head over in the direction of the outside bar.

Sin stared at his brother as he caught the attention of the barmaid.

"So how are the kids?"

Saint grunted. "Big. Bad. Always wanting money."

Sin laughed. "Lucky you."

"Yeah, man. Gotta love 'em." He looked away for a brief second, glancing out at the ocean, before returning his stare on

Sin. "Even though I'm not in their lives like I know I should be, I do what I can to provide for them. You know?"

Sin nodded. At least Saint cared enough about his kids to make sure they didn't want for anything. But he was certain what they'd want more of was quality time with him. Wasn't that what kids hungered most? Having their fathers present in their lives?

Growing up without a father, let alone any real male role model figure could be damaging. Whatever Sin learned about manhood, he'd learned in the streets and on lust-stained bed sheets.

True, Saint's father had become the closest thing to a father, once he moved in with them after their mother had died. And—although there hadn't been much structure and he and Saint were given license to do whatever they'd wanted as long as it wasn't illegal, he'd taken Sin in and raised him as if he were his own.

For that, he was eternally grateful.

"I gotta get back to the States to spend some time with 'em all," Saint said, pulling Sin from his thoughts. "And I hope like hell none of their crazy-ass mothers be on no bullshit." He shook his head. "Let me get a Guinness punch," he said when the barmaid approached the table.

He eyed her up and down. "Damn, baby, you thick. Can I take you home?"

She *tsked* him. "Nuh romp wid mi, bwoy. Ef yah chobble mi, me a guh bax yuh."

Saint laughed. "Girl, you know I like it when you talk dirty."

She rolled her eyes, playfully swatting at him. As she walked off, Saint stared at her heart-shaped ass, the way it sat up on her back, and moved sensually beneath her short skirt.

"Damn. I bet that ass is tasty." He reached over and grabbed Sin's drink, and took a long gulp, before sliding it back to him. "What kinda panties you think she's wearing?"

Sin shrugged. "Hell, if I know." And he didn't care enough to want to know.

"Twenty bucks says she's wearing a thong."

Sin shook his head. "You have issues, man."

He laughed. "Yeah, but at least I don't try to hide 'em."

"Maybe you should."

Saint opened his mouth to say something more, then seemed to think better of it.

Sin reached for his drink and took another sip. Beyond the deck where they sat, water lapped at the sand. Sin stared out at the ocean for several moments, and then glanced briefly at the barmaid when she returned with Saint's drink.

Sin held his breath, waiting for him to embarrass himself by asking her about her underwear choice. He let out a breath when he didn't.

Saint waited for her to be out of earshot, before asking, "Would you rim that? I know I would. I'd tongue the hell out of that."

"Man, you a fool." Sin shook his head, chuckling. "No wonder your breath always smells like hot shit." And then he looked at his half-finished drink, and frowned at the thought of Saint having put his lips to his glass.

Saint caught the look and laughed loudly, attracting the glances of nearby diners. "Man, don't act like you've never licked the brown star."

Sin shrugged. "Nah, man. Can't say I have." Of course, he didn't feel the need to share how he'd licked all up in the Doc's sweet chocolate hole for the first time. He swallowed down the memory, and then he narrowed his eyes. "And I can't believe you out here licking a bunch of random asses."

Saint scoffed. "Fuck no. Only the ones I plan on giving my babies too."

Sin just stared at him. There was nothing else to say to that. "You heard from Soul?" he asked, changing the subject.

"Nope. You?"

Sin shook his head. "Nah," he said, and then he chuckled. "I guess Nairobia has him out in L.A., working his nut sac overtime."

"Yeah, fucking—*literally*, his way into stardom."

When the food finally came, all conversation paused while they savored bites of their meal. Sin had ordered the mango chicken for himself, and oxtails and butterbeans for Saint. They'd taken to having a meal together at least once a week since living on the island together. Something Sin would miss once he left for New York, whenever he decided to go.

Saint looked at him. "So, what's up man? You good?"

Sin drained his glass. "Yeah, man. I'm good."

"You sure nothing's on your mind? You look like you have something you wanna get off your chest."

Sin's brow rose. Was it that obvious? "Nah, not at all. It's all love over here."

A Soca beat hummed from the restaurant's speakers, and Sin watched as a few women rose from their seats and moved their hips to the music. Several others also stood and began jumping up and down, waving their linen napkins in the air.

Saint looked over at them, and then asked, "So what's good for later? You feel like hanging tonight?" He glanced around, and then gestured with his head toward four women at a table to the right of them. They were laughing and talking loudly, clearly enjoying the food, drinks, and music. "We can find some horny, lonely souls to gut out. Send them wobbling back to their hotel with a smile."

"If you want some more of this pussy, Sin, it'll be here for you tonight . . ."

Sin shook the sultry voice from his head, glancing at his watch. "Nah, not tonight. I have plans."

And they were plans he had no intentions of canceling.

Twenty-Seven

HER NIPPLES HARD, her pussy exposed, Sin's dick swelled at the sight, more from memory than what was before him. When he'd arrived at her villa at six-thirty, he found the door unlocked and so he let himself in.

There were candles lit throughout the place, and a note saying, *"I'm in the kitchen. Don't touch. Just enjoy the view."*

When he walked into the kitchen and found her, he damn near tripped over his feet. To his surprise, she was propped up on the granite-top island in a red-laced flyaway, her legs bent at the knee and spread wide.

He'd nearly drooled at the sight of her.

Gesturing toward the chair positioned in front of the island, she'd told him to sit.

But how could he?

Just sit, and not touch?

"Let me have my moment," she'd said as she slid a finger into her wetness.

Begrudgingly, Sin had taken the seat. But he hadn't expected to still be sitting, still be waiting. He shifted in his seat and tried to think down his dick, which wouldn't be eased by anything but a slow deep fuck. He knew there wasn't anything he could say that would stop the inevitable from occurring.

He was going to fuck her, that simple. His dick wouldn't have it any other way, nor would he. The question was, when? When would he dismiss her request for patience, and take over?

Granted, he wanted to give her this moment, her moment—of seduction—because she'd asked for it, before he pounced on her, before he tore off her negligee and mauled her breasts, before he pinned her down and—

"Sin," she whispered.

He swallowed. Pressed his legs shut. "Yeah, baby?"

"My pussy's so wet for you."

"I see," he said coolly.

She stroked over her clit.

"It aches to feel you."

He groaned. *Relax.* He inhaled deeply. *Focus.* He could do this. Give her the sense of being the one in power. The illusion. He'd done it all of his life. Gave women the fantasy of being in control. So this was no different. She was like any other woman he'd been with.

Fuck. Why was he lying to himself?

Dr. Dangerfield was nothing like any woman he'd ever experienced. She was different in every way imaginable. He was drawn to her. She called to him on more than a sexual level. Brought him to a sharp apex of desire in a way no other woman ever had, ever could.

And *that* was the problem.

She slid two fingers into her body, and Sin nearly choked, wishing it was his tongue sliding over the wet, pretty pussy, swiping around the inside of walls.

"Pull out your dick. Let me see it."

Sin grinned. Freed his dick.

It bobbed, heavy.

"Is this what you want?"

Dr. Dangerfield looked over at him, and moaned. "Ooh, yes. It's so big. So beautiful." She dragged her tongue slowly over her upper lip. "Play with it for me."

Sin stroked it gently. From base to crown, then slowly back down. She was really fucking with him, and he felt it deep down in the lower part of his abdomen. The tightening. Fluid seeped out from the tip of his dick.

She watched him as if she wanted to see into him, and Sin felt the intensity in her stare, the heat, the need. So why the fuck was she prolonging shit?

"Close your eyes," she whispered.

He stopped stroking himself and made a face, one filled with disbelief and surprise. Was she serious? Close his eyes on all of *that*?

"You're bugging, baby. You expect me to have my dick in my hand and *not* look at you?"

"Yes," she murmured. "I want you to use your other senses."

Sin frowned. "Nah. Fuck that. I can't touch you. My dick is hard as steel, and now you're trying to run some sensory experiment." He shook his head. "I'm keeping my eyes wide open, baby. You're depriving me of way too much already."

"Please," she added, in almost a plea as she rolled her hips, her fingers going in deeper, finally finding her sweet spot. She arched her back, and let out another moan.

Sin edged forward in his seat, but then stopped himself from rising to his feet.

Dr. Dangerfield's eyes narrowed. "Don't disappoint me, Sin."

He sighed, impatience sweeping through his chest. He bit back a groan. "I'm still seated, right?"

She smiled. "Yes, you are."

"And my dick is still in my hand, right?"

She licked her lips. "Yes, it is. Now close your eyes, and keep stroking all that magnificent chocolate." She flashed him another smile. "For me."

Sin snorted, shaking his head, but he closed his eyes and stroked his dick.

He could feel her smile as her eyes took in his hand, his dick, moving up and down his shaft. "Now listen," she prompted, her fingers clicking wetly in and out of her body.

Sin swallowed. His hand strokes deepened. "Damn."

"You hear that?" *Click, click, click.* The wet click of her fingers filled the room.

He heard the sound of lagoons, of waterfalls, of rain, of ocean waves.

All washing over him.

"Yeah, baby. I hear it." He bit into his bottom lip, and grunted.

"That's the sound of my wet pussy calling to you."

"Fuck." He squeezed his eyes tighter, and groaned. "Ah, shit . . ."

"I want to drown you in my juices. Smother your dick in my heat."

"Yeah, baby . . ."

"Ooh, Sin, yes. Stroke that beautiful dick. Imagine it inside of me, pumping into my pussy, sliding this way and that way, balls deep, baby . . . your hard, muscled ass clenches as your hips thrust, circling in and out of my juicy cunt . . . ooh, fucking me, stretching me . . ."

Sin crept one eye open to find her in the throes of her own arousal, her head thrown back, her hardened peaks straining against the sheer fabric of her top.

"I know you're looking at me," she said over a moan. "Stop cheating. And close your eyes." Her lids fluttered open, and she shot him a hot glare.

Sin sucked his teeth. If she'd wanted to get off without him touching her, she could have simply teased him over the phone again.

"Now, Sin," she said forcefully.

"I want to fuck," he said, his voice hoarse with arousal.

"Patience."

"Fuck patience," Sin growled out.

"This pussy is for you, Sin," she murmured. "All night. After you follow my instructions."

Sin smirked. "All night?"

"Yes. Now eyes *shut.*"

"All right. Damn. And you better not run from this dick, either."

"I never run." It was more than a promise. So far, it had been truth. She took everything he gave, every thrust. She absorbed him, soaked him in.

Reluctantly, Sin gave in. Closed his eyes, and hoped her game ended soon.

"Now breathe in through your nose." Sin took a deep breath. "Can you smell it? My hungry need for you."

He grunted. Held in her scent, deep in his lungs, her intoxicating lust, until his own need for her burned. He was on the verge of erupting. Enough of this shit! He opened his eyes and leaned forward, prepared to—

"No," she quickly said, wagging a wet finger at him. "Don't move. Don't get up. Sit. Close your eyes. And enjoy."

"I need to *see* you."

"All you need is, to hear me, smell me . . . and allow your imagination to do the rest."

Sin nearly growled out his frustration. "You're fucking with me, baby." The sexual tension in the air was so thick. He inhaled the scent of her with every breath; every breath reminding him his dick was hard and throbbing, every breath filling his shaft with heat, demanding release.

Not from his hand, not from his imagination, but from the suck of her mouth, the clutch of her cunt, the feel of her soft body against the hardness of his flesh. That was what he needed.

Sin groaned again.

Patience. Let her have this moment, he kept telling himself. But—goddammit, fuck—the shit was killing him. He wanted to be inside of her body, pumping into her slick heat, melting deep inside of her, losing himself in her warmth. *Now.*

She made him wild with desire. Made him want to defy all logic, to do freaky things to her, with her. Seeing her—all alive and full of sensual feminine heat—made him want to fuck her raw, bust deep in her, and then lick her pussy until she came in his mouth. That's what this primal, sexual hunger between them did to him.

As if she could hear his thoughts, she called out to him.

"Sin . . ."

He opened his eyes, and took in the silhouette of her slick, swollen flesh, her glistening pussy lips splayed open, wet and ready, against the flickering candlelight.

"I'm coming . . . oh, oh, oh . . ." the first wave of heat gushed from her body, soaking her fingers, the counter, pooling around her ass. "Oh, oh, oh, oh . . ." she was on the precipice of another orgasm. "Come with me, Sin," she rasped.

"I'm with you, baby," he muttered. "Ah, goddamn, baby."

"Yes, yes . . . mmm . . . spill your sweet cum for me."

Sin groaned.

His strokes quickened, deeper, harder, faster. His fist tightened. "Aah, fuck. Goddamn, baby . . . ah, *shiiit . . .*"

His vision blurred.

His chest tightened.

The world evaporated.

And then he was growling, a sound so guttural that it echoed off the walls, and his milk—hot, thick, cream—was spurting out of his dick, like a firing cannon, aimlessly shooting up into the air, over his hand, landing on his chest, up over his head.

He stroked and stroked and stroked until he was spent.

When his eyes swam back into focus, they stared at one another for long, heavy, sensual minutes. He hadn't fucked her, and yet he felt sated. He felt filled by her heat. And he felt more drawn to her.

"Damn," he rasped, as he caught his breath. "That was . . . different. You're wicked, baby."

Dr. Dangerfield slid off the counter and stood on wobbly legs. "Oh, I'm just getting started." She went to him, no other words between them. He watched. Waited.

And then she knelt in front of him and licked over his hand, tongued around his balls, and then sucked his semi-erection into her mouth, coaxing out the remainder of his nut.

A hiss escaped Sin's lips, more pleasure searing through him. He gazed down at her, his toes curling as she looked up at him through a curtain of dark lashes.

She sucked him so passionately with a renewed purpose, sucking him until he came again, sucking, sucking, sucking, until she had emptied his sac, until his dick finally slipped from between her lips. Until all he could do was stare at her, his gaze drinking her in, his dick still throbbing for more of her.

TWENTY-EIGHT

FLAMES SHOT UP from the floor.

Red lights splashed over the crowd.

Colorful tribal-painted, loin-clothed bodies moved slow and nasty.

Club Passion's theme song, Byzantine Time Machine's "Adventure in Istanbul" greeted Sin as he made his way inside the island's extravagant club. Hips seductively swayed. Breasts swung. Pelvises thrust. Bellies rolled. Arms rhythmically moved up over dancers' heads.

Mesh mini-dresses clung to the hips of pelvis-thrusting women inside go-go cages situated atop massive alabaster pedestals.

Women wrapped in bright swathes of silk pressed their bodies into muscled, bare-chested hunks wearing leather briefs with zippers over thick bulges.

Sin couldn't deny the club's sensuality. Couldn't ignore its animalistic heat.

The club oozed of sex.

He couldn't deny the place was nothing short of carnal heaven, if such a place really existed. But if it didn't, Club Passion was the next best thing.

And, unlike the elegant masks worn by all members of The Pleasure Zone, most of the women at Club Passion wore beaded veils, while others wore Nairobia's signature jeweled-encrusted, custom-made face coverings, each mask alone worth thousands of dollars.

To the left of Sin, a bronzed, well-hung man threw his head back, the veins in his neck straining against his flesh, as he enjoyed the oral pleasure of three women squatting in their strappy heels. Two were on either side of him; their mouths and lips sliding rhythmically along the sides of his shaft, while a third squatted in front of him, suckling on his bulbous dickhead.

Sin swallowed back his own need for some good, sloppy head. He knew he couldn't get off here. If he were going to seriously take on the position of being the manager of Nairobia's Las Vegas club, fucking any of the patrons would be off limits to him, so he decided he'd might as well adopt that mindset now, in spite of his growing erection.

He grabbed a drink from a passing hostess wearing a glittered G-string and pasties. He glanced at her swaying ass as she balanced herself on seven-inch heels, snaking her way through the crowd.

How in the hell did she manage to find all these exotic-looking women, Sin wondered as he took a sip of his drink, *to work for her?*

It was the same question he'd asked himself when he was at the New York club. And he still had not come up with an answer, yet.

Sin scanned the club, taking in the nude sculptures of men and woman in various sexual positions strategically placed around the club.

Over in the far-right corner, he caught sight of a masked man on his knees, between the thighs of a buxom brunette, licking her pussy, while a statuesque blonde in a leather bustier and matching thong and a leather harness, slowly fucked him with a fluorescent dildo.

Sin cringed.

It never ceased to amaze, or shock, him what salacious vices the wealthy men and women who held the coveted gold-plated membership cards were willing to partake in.

He definitely made no judgment. It was simply another one of his observations.

A lopsided grin eased over Sin's lips as six candle tray dancers sauntered by, carrying burning wax candles on flat round trays on top of their heads, their flames dancing above their heads, as they swayed their hips. One in front of the other, their hips and arms moved in sync.

Sin moved further through the club, noting that its three-storied structure, although a very large space, was about ten thousand square feet smaller than the one in New York.

The sound of tambourines and mewling brought his attention back to the dance floor, where four dark chocolate beauties, their rich dark skin dusted in a metallic gold, danced to a tantric-induced beat. Gold leather straps wound seductively up over and around their calves, snaking their way up to toned thighs.

Their heads were shaven bald, their lips painted in gold. And in each hand, they worked a tambourine. Sin found himself transfixed to their movements. The way their bodies moved, almost possessed like, commanding the attention of everyone around them.

He stood there for a few moments, before he headed toward the winding glass staircase, where he made his way up to the second floor. He stood at the elaborate gold railing and looked down into the crowd.

A remix of "Wanderlust" played, and suddenly the club was drenched in ethnic sounds. Sin felt himself slowly becoming entranced by its beat, so much so that he felt an overwhelming urge to pull out his dick and swing it.

Had he'd come to the club to get nasty he might have done so. Instead, he suppressed his lustful feelings and stared at the larger-than-life penis situated in the center of the dance floor, adorned with two ginormous balls carved out of dark chocolate; its huge dickhead spilling out rivulets of white chocolate lava.

He pulled in his bottom lip, and bit down on it at the sight of beautiful naked women standing inside its enormous basin of melted white chocolate, covering their bodies with chocolate as they danced.

The sight made his dick swell.

The cleanup he imagined was a sweet sticky mess, but someone would happily lick over their breasts and along the seam of their candy-coated cunts.

When the sounds of cracking whips and sensual moans began seeping out from the hidden speakers, Sin knew it was only a matter of seconds before the long wall across the other side of the dance floor would slide open.

And when the wall finally did open, the dance floor would swell with naked bodies, brazenly fucking each other on the dance floor.

Sin leaned further over the railing, and waited.

TWENTY-NINE

"I KNEW I'D find you here," Sin said, leaning up against the doorframe, arms folded over a wall of muscle. He wore loose-fitting pants and a simple white T-shirt, and even dressed so causally he put the models on the cover of GQ to shame.

Dr. Dangerfield looked up from the folder on her desk.

"You know me so well," she said, closing the file. A small smile touched her lips as she looked at him, and then her eyes dipped down to his crotch—and the white linen pants that were doing very little to hide one of God's greatest blessings.

His bulge.

She cleared her throat. "Welcome to my world," she added.

Sin peered at her over the rim of his dark-rimmed shades, which somehow made him look sexier than he already was.

Lord, the man was the epitome of enticement and passion, everything dirty and dangerous. And Dr. Dangerfield felt the urge to slip a hand between her legs and stroke herself. But, instead, she drew in a breath, and hoped to hell she wouldn't soak her silky panties from the thought.

The man could rob a woman of thought, of reason.

"Nah, baby," he said, slicing into her musings. "This is only a small part of your world. There's so much more to you."

His eyes seemed to darken as he looked at her, and she suddenly felt heat washing over her. "And I'm here to uncover those other parts of you," he said before thinking better of it.

Dr. Dangerfield swallowed, and then stifled the smile that twitched at the corner of her mouth. She was glad he stopped by. He'd been on her mind all day, and—yes—she was happy to see him. She drank him in, soaking in every delectable detail of his sexy, masculine frame.

The fullness of his mouthwatering lips—God, yes. She licked over her mouth remembering in vivid detail how wicked his lips, his tongue, could be. Her gaze slinked over the coil of muscles that wrapped deliciously around his arms, and then her eyes journeyed down to his feet, his flip-flops, and those neatly trimmed toenails.

She pressed her thighs together, imagining Sin thumbing her clit before spreading her lips, stretching her. She bit back a moan. "I see why women can't get enough of you," she said over a smile. She stretched her arms out on her desk and clasped her hands in front of her. "You know all the right things to say."

Sin grinned. "Nah, sexy. It's not *me* women can't get enough of. It's the thrill of being brought to the edge, being pushed beyond their own limits that they desire most."

Dr. Dangerfield regarded him thoughtfully, and then she smiled. "And who pushes you beyond yours?"

His gaze latched onto her breasts, the hint of cleavage sexily peeking out from the opening in her ruffled sheer blouse, and then he lifted his eyes back to hers.

"No one," he said. He was still standing at the door as if he were trying to decide to enter, or leave, and Dr. Dangerfield hadn't invited him in. She didn't need to.

Sin needed no invitation. They both knew it.

"No? Shameful." She'd have to change that. "Everyone should experience the journey at least once," she said. He held her eyes, and in that moment, Dr. Dangerfield thought she saw something flickering in his eyes. Fresh heat. Lust.

Sin shrugged. "No one has been able to rise to the occasion."

"I imagine not, since that would require, however"—she lifted a brow— "giving up some control."

Sin frowned. And then he laughed. "Is that your way of calling me a control freak?"

"Aren't you? Has something changed that I'm not privy to?"

"There's nothing wrong with having self-control."

She cocked her head. "There's a fine line between having self-control and the need to *be* in control."

His grin revealed a dimple. "Well, maybe if you're nice to me, I'll let you show me the difference." His eye caught a marbled sculpture of a naked woman atop a pedestal on the other side of the room. The woman sat Indian-style, her back arched, head back, her arms spread open, as if she were offering herself to the world.

"New piece?" he said, jutting his chin toward the sculpture.

"A gift," she offered.

"Nice."

"Thank you. So, what brings you by?" Changing the subject was safer, for now—or she'd end up bent over her desk, her skirt hiked up over her hips. "Please don't tell me boredom." She raised a questioning brow. "I'll scream if you do."

Before showing up at her office, he'd started out walking along the beach to clear his head but, somehow, he managed to find himself here. As if he'd been pulled in this direction by some force greater than his own.

Sin smirked. "And what might you do if I told you I felt like being in the company of a beautiful woman?"

She scoffed. "I'll think you're so full of yourself."

Sin feigned insult, placing a hand to his heart. "I'm hurt."

Dr. Dangerfield rolled her eyes, and waved him on. "Oh, please. Just admit it. You're out prowling, and decided to stop by for a recess."

It was a statement that Sin answered in jest. "I'm always prowling, baby. Even when I'm asleep." He flashed her a grin. "My break begins when I'm six-feet under."

"Sounds like you've put a lot of thought into that," she said half-jokingly.

"It's a realistic plan. Don't you think?"

"I think it's nice to have a life plan. We all should have one."

She eyed him as he finally sauntered further into the room, oozing sex appeal, all self-assured and full of swag, and flopped into the chair across from her desk, his long legs sprawled out in front of him. She knew somewhere in the Bible he had to be listed as a cardinal sin.

She made a mental note to flip through the Scriptures for confirmation.

"Oh, yeah? And what's yours?" he asked, arching his hips up and pulling out from his front pocket his cell. Seconds later, he was turning it on SILENT.

She swallowed.

She'd never sucked on a man's toes before, but, goddamn him, she'd suck his—all ten of those beautiful masculine toes—deep into her wet mouth.

Sin's gaze caressed her face, his expression intense. "Well?"

Dr. Dangerfield shifted in her chair. Cleared her throat. "Well, what?"

"Don't do that."

She blinked and gazed at him coyly. "Don't do what?"

"I asked you what your life plan was?"

Oh, that.

To fuck you every chance I get.

The office door was still open. Someone could walk by at any moment, and the pulse at Dr. Dangerfield's neck beat quicker, the thrill of getting caught between his legs, his dick rammed in her mouth.

She shook the salacious image from her thoughts. "Well . . ."

she paused for a moment. She spent her entire career encouraging others to consider what their spiritual, physical, emotional, and even financial needs were; to consider their life plans; to consider their priorities; to determine their roles in the present and what they envisioned their roles to be in the future.

Life was constantly changing. People were always evolving—or at least they should be. And sometimes things didn't work out as planned. She believed that sometimes you had to change the life you planned in order to create, to find, the life you were destined to have.

Her life plan had been laid out for her long before she was born. From private schools to recitals; from cotillions to pageants; from Jack and Jill of America to all of the other trappings of America's black elite, right down to whom her first boyfriend would be—her parents had carved out her life in perfect fashion.

Her father, a summa cum laude Morehouse graduate, had graduated at the top of his class at Harvard Medical School, where her mother—a Spelman graduate, also attended two years later.

Spelman College was the only thing drilled into Dr. Dangerfield's brain early on. After all, it had been her grandmother's alma mater, and where all six of her own daughters had also graduated. So, it had been *the* only option. So was which sorority she would pledge. Again, it had been the *only* option. It had been ingrained in her long before she'd learned to take her first steps, or had spoken her first words.

Spelman. Her sorority.

It was her legacy. Her birthright.

Period.

And Dr. Dangerfield had pursued her doctorate because that, too, had been what was expected of her. Both of her parents, Drs. Charlton and Carlista Dangerfield, were renowned neurosurgeons in Los Angeles—no pressure there. Her father was the Chairman of surgery at UCLA Medical Center, and had been one of the first black men to own a seat on the NY Stock Exchange, where he'd amassed the majority of his fortune.

And her mother was Chairwoman of neurosurgery at Cedars-Sinai Medical Center, and had also been one of the past National presidents of Jack and Jill.

So, failure was never an option. Dr. Dangerfield had been surrounded by success all of her life. Medicine was in her blood. And although she too should have been holding a scalpel, she'd chosen the study of behavior and the human mind over becoming a surgeon instead. She'd become a psychologist, not because she wanted to, not because she had been fascinated by it, but because—if she wasn't going to medical school—then she had better be pursuing a career in the helping and healing of others.

It was what she had to do. It was what her parents had expected of her.

They'd rolled out the red carpet and made her future look easy. All she had to do was simply show up and walk the straight line, stay on script. So, she'd obtained her doctorate degree in clinical psychology, and then pursued a career in human sexuality, giving up on her dreams of ever becoming a professional ballet dancer, or a pianist.

Those were hobbies, not distinguished careers, so her mother had told her. And there had been no room for debate. Her life choices had been by design, not choice. And yet she was happy in her life. She had a thriving career she'd learned over time to not only enjoy, but to love as well.

And that she did. Loved every minute of her career, especially since she was afforded a front row view into the sexual lives of others. Yet, there was still that fleeting thought, that maybe she should have been more defiant (aside from having married two men who failed miserably at being proper husbands), been more of a risk-taker instead of doing what she knew was pleasing to her parents.

Maybe.

"Living my best life," she finally said. And that was true for the most part. "That's my life plan."

Sin nodded, and then scrubbed a hand down over his mouth. "And how's that working out for you?"

Dr. Dangerfield offered a smile. "I'm not complaining." She cocked her head to the side. "Do you have any regrets?" she asked quietly.

Regret?

Sin's eyebrow rose. It'd taken him years to learn how not to live his life in shame, to not blame himself for what others did to him, or didn't do for him.

Unease slinked its way over Sin's skin, and he dragged a frustrated hand through his locks. He didn't like that she tried to dissect him, tried to get beneath the layers of who he was. And, still, he enjoyed her company.

He was, his life was, one big contradiction.

Sin closed his eyes for a second and when he reopened them Dr. Dangerfield's gaze was piercing through him. She leaned forward; her arms planted on the desk.

Waiting.

He sighed, then said, "I regret nothing I've been through," he pushed out with more conviction than he felt. "What good would it do?"

Dr. Dangerfield shook her head. "Nothing. All it ever does is keep us stuck."

His swallow was audible. "You're right," he said. And then he went momentarily silent. He eased back in his chair and looked away; his gaze fixed on the erotic sculpture.

Dr. Dangerfield decided not to press the issue. She'd give him a moment to himself, in his thoughts. She'd simply sit. And wait.

The doctor had nothing but time on her hands. And she was more than willing to spend every ticking second with him.

Until he was ready . . .

THIRTY

"**TELL ME ABOUT** her," Dr. Dangerfield whispered, lifting her head from his chest. She'd been lying there like this, an Elhae mix CD playing low in the background, listening to the beat of his heart, syncing her breaths to his own; him stroking her shoulder, for what seemed like an eternity.

But it had been only for the last ten minutes.

She felt breathtakingly calm for someone who'd just been tossed around the room, fucked over every piece of furniture, up against the walls. Her slick pussy still throbbed; her breasts were still swollen, her nipples still aching, but she was glowing from the aftermath.

The room had been quiet save for the music and their breathing until she sliced into the silence, snatching Sin from the solace he'd surprisingly found in holding her in his arms. He'd wanted to hold her, and just lie still for a moment. But in true Dr. Dangerfield fashion, she wanted to *talk*, to probe.

He pulled in a breath, and then opened his eyes, catching her gaze. "Tell you about who?" He asked, already knowing *whom* she was referring to.

"Your mother," she answered. "What is she like?"

She felt him bristle at the question, and she took note in the way his body tensed. And now he was kicking himself for having ever mentioned her. He should have known she wasn't the type to let anything fly over her head without catching it.

For the most part, women never asked him about his past—that wasn't what they'd been interested in. And the few women who might have asked, more for having a reason to talk than being genuinely interested, he'd always been good at circumventing the questions about his mother or his life by encouraging them to talk about themselves instead. Or he'd simply tell them he didn't want to talk about it. What was really the point when they were only together to fuck, not get to know one another intimately.

Fact was, Sin hated talking about his *real* childhood—or even thinking about it.

Or his mother.

His recollections of her weren't good ones. They were dark and painful, and so he'd learned to block them from his memories. Though, every so often, traces of his tumultuous past had a way of clawing its way into his present. And he'd simply *fuck* it away. Pounding one wet hole after another, delivering mind-numbing orgasms with every deep stroke.

Sex in the beginning was more for survival than pleasure. It was an escape, a way to dissociate from his living hell. But then sex had become a sport that had eventually evolved into a passion. He'd become cunning in the art of seduction, skillful at pleasuring a woman in ways she could never imagine.

He'd had his mother to *blame* for his sexual prowess.

After all, he'd learned from the best.

She *was* . . .

Loose.

Mean-spirited.

Reckless.

Foul-mouthed.

And . . .

"*A temptress . . .*"

"*A man-stealing whore . . .*"

"*A sinful bitch . . .*"

He'd once overheard Pastor Meeken's wife hiss, *"Look at that street trash parading her bastard child in front of me—in the House of the Lord."*

She'd been sleeping with Pastor Meeken every Saturday night for nearly six years, and then sitting up in the pew directly in back of the First Lady every Sunday, brazenly hopping up throughout his sermons with her breasts spilling out of her short, sometimes too-tight, dresses, shouting, *"Preach, Pastor!"*

Sin was around four or so, when he'd clumsily walked in on her having sex with him, calling out his name. *"Ooh, yes, Pastor. God is so good. Bless me with your big, long dick . . .!"*

Two years later, Pastor Meeken was dead; his body naked in her full-sized bed, his semen still warm, seeping out from her well-fucked cunt.

He'd had a heart attack in the midst of his many orgasms.

Like wildfire, the scandal had hit the news headlines:

RENOWNED PASTOR OF LIVING IN GOD'S TRUTH FOUND DEAD . . . IN MISTRESS' BED!

PASTOR OF LIVING IN GOD'S TRUTH CAUGHT LIVING IN SIN . . .!

PROMINENT PASTOR SEDUCED BY CHURCH HEATHEN . . .!

Sin's mother's face had been plastered in every caption. She'd been marked by her transgressions. Shame and ridicule chased her out of the church, and right into the streets with a child she could no longer bear to look at, because he'd reminded her of everything she'd once had, and everything she'd lost.

Eventually twenty-eight-year-old Hope Saint-Michaels found comfort at the bottom of countless bottles of Johnny Walker.

Slowly she became bitter. Angry. Abusive.

And finally . . .

A drunk.

"She's dead," Sin finally said flatly, his expression emotionless.

"Ohmygod, Sin," Dr. Dangerfield said over a gasp, her heart suddenly aching for him. "How old were you when she died?"

He scrubbed a hand over his weary face. He felt a slight throbbing in his head, but he didn't have a headache. "Eleven."

Oh, God, he'd been only a baby. She couldn't begin to imagine what his life might have been like after losing his mother. She wanted to hold him tightly, rock him, and then smother him with kisses. "I'm so sorry to hear."

Sin shrugged. "Don't be." She'd done him a favor by dying. "It's inevitable. Death," he stated in a matter-of-fact tone, easing out from under her. She'd ruined his mood, fucking up a good thing.

Why couldn't she simply stay in the moment?

Goddamn. Why did her nosey-ass have to go asking about his mother?

Women.

He wanted to scream on her for not knowing when to mind her own fucking business, but the fear of saying something he'd regret kept him in check. Besides, he knew she'd meant no harm. Still, why hadn't he told her he didn't want to talk about her, as he'd done the last time she'd asked him about her?

Dr. Dangerfield peered up at him; saw an expression she'd never seen on his face.

Sadness.

Suddenly, there was an eerie draft in the room, chilling her to the bone. She sensed him slipping away from her. "Sin?" she said gently, unexpectedly feeling desperate to catch him before he pulled further away.

When he didn't respond, when he didn't look at her, she eased up on her forearm and lifted her hand to touch the side of his face, finally causing him to drag his eyes to meet hers.

His eyes darkened. "I don't wanna talk about it."

She nodded. Understood. "We don't have to, if you don't want to."

"I don't," he said harshly.

His brusqueness didn't sway her as she stroked his arm. "I'm here for you." And she meant it.

He didn't relax whatsoever, pain, conflict, clear in his expression. This was another side of him, the side he kept hidden so well. But something about her asking about his mother had unhinged his emotions.

She wanted to wrap her arms around him and press her lips to every part of his pain. Kiss him and kiss him and kiss him until it all disappeared.

His jaw tightened. And then between gritted teeth, he said, "I think you should leave."

Gaze fixed on him, she forced herself to not blink. Those words, unexpected, had stung her, but she managed to keep her voice steady, almost soothing. "I'm not leaving you; not like this." She felt a deep welling, an unexplainable sense, of . . . fear.

Maybe it was grief, for him, for his loss, for whatever else he might have gone through in his childhood. He needed space. She'd give it to him. But she wasn't going anywhere. Period.

He frowned. "I'm good." His voice was a rasp. "I just need to be alone."

He climbed out of bed and felt her eyes on his body as he stood to his feet. His dick hung, freely swinging as he walked toward the other side of the room.

She swallowed at the sight, the taste of him still lingering in the back of her mouth from earlier in the night. She swallowed again.

She eyed his chiseled ass, and then watched as he snatched open a drawer and pulled out a T-shirt. He hastily pulled it over his head, the muscles in his back flexing until it was finally down over his skin.

"Our past doesn't have to be who we are," she said. "We have no control over how someone else treats us." She assumed some form of abuse or neglect was at the root of his sudden turmoil. "Our future lies in how we deal with our past, in what we do with our lives in the present, in this very moment. *You*, Sin, are not your past. It does not define you."

He turned to face her. "It's who I am. So don't try to analyze me."

"It's not who you are, unless you want it to be." She swung her legs over the bed and then stalked toward him. "And I'm not analyzing you, or trying to."

Sin bit back a groan. Fought to keep his eyes from drowning in the sight of her breasts, her beaded nipples, the way the thin strip of red lace covered her sex.

She was suddenly crowding his space, clouding his senses, becoming a distraction. He couldn't think straight.

She stood in front of him, placing a hand on his chest, over his heart. Her touch warmed his skin. "No matter what happened in your past, you can get through it. You are a good man, Sin. And you have a good heart."

He scowled, grabbing her hand. "What don't you get, Doc? I *am* my past. And there's nothing good in it. There's no changing that—or me."

"Change is always possible," she said firmly, yet softly. She'd mastered keeping her voice steady and calm. "You just have to want it."

"Go home, Doc." He moved her hand from his chest. "I'm done talking." He was angry with her?

"I'm not leaving," Dr. Dangerfield repeated.

Defiant.

Stubborn.

The muscle in Sin's jaw twitched. His eyes narrowed. "It wasn't a question."

She raised a brow. "I didn't think it was. And like I said, I'm *not* leaving. You'll have to drag me out, if you want me gone."

Isn't this some shit? She knew damn well he wouldn't put his hands on her, wouldn't drag her out of his place, especially when he wasn't even sure he wanted her to leave.

He was frustrated. Turned on. Annoyed. Hungered.

He stared at her. He was seeing she was as insolent as she was sexy.

Never breaking his stare, she took his hand and squeezed it. "I want to help you." She eased up on the balls of her feet, and gently kissed him on the lips. He flinched, but didn't stop her. "Tell me how I can help you, Sin."

He stood in silence for several excruciating seconds, his stare unflinching. If he told her what he was thinking in that moment, she would think him maddened, crazed.

His mother had named him Sin, because his birth signified everything bad, everything dirty; everything wrong in *her* life. *He* was her devil child. Spawned from her sins. And in the end, she'd taken all of her hatred out on him. She'd done whatever she could to make him feel bad, dirty, nasty.

And still he'd wanted to love her. Had tried to love her. But all she did was hurt him, over and over until all he had left was his own hatred; until finally all he could do was wish her dead. To let death take her, and himself, out of *her* misery. Then maybe he'd be free.

Sin had reasoned in his young mind that whatever hell awaited him after she was gone couldn't be any worse than the one he'd already been living. She'd abandoned him long before she ever died. Her being alive had ruined him. Her death had been his salvation.

When he finally told Dr. Dangerfield, "You can't," and turned to leave the bedroom, she caught him by the wrist. She'd let the conversation rest for as long as he needed—but she'd be damned if she'd let him walk out on her, or give him the satisfaction of hurting alone.

"Then let me help you take your mind off of it," she said softly, dropping to her knees in front of him. She looked up at him, sexily, through her lashes, and Sin felt himself suddenly going weak with lust.

What the fuck?

The darkness in his eyes was now aglow with hunger.

"C'mon, Doc. Chill," he said, trying to ignore the heat rushing through his body at the sight of her on her knees. "Get up."

"No."

She licked his flaccid dick. Kissed its crown. Sucking his dick wasn't conducive to healing, but it was a sure way to ease away the tension that had quickly coiled its way around the room, nearly strangling out the air around them.

He hissed in a breath. "See what you do to me . . .?"

She moaned softly, and he envisioned himself spreading her legs, dipping his now growing erection back into her body, into her heat, where he'd kept it for most of the evening, instead of slipping it into her mouth.

"I'm going to make love to"—she tongued his slit— "this big"— she licked around the head—"beautiful"—her tongue flicked over his balls—"dick."

"Goddamn," he muttered.

She grabbed his ass, then slid her hands down the back of his thighs, caressing his hamstrings.

She caressed her face against it. Inhaled him. Smoothed kisses up and down the length of his shaft, sweeping her tongue wetly, lovingly, over the thick vein that pulsed over the top of his dick. His legs quivered.

His dick was so rigid, the head so broad. Arousal beaded the swollen slit as she whispered his name over and over. She flicked her tongue over it, causing Sin to hiss again.

"Shit." He gritted his teeth. That quickly, she was pulling him out of the shadows of his past, bringing him back to the present, flipping an on-switch in him.

Without thought, without hesitation, he slid his dick between her luscious lips. His breath hitched when he hit the back of her throat, and then she moaned over his shaft. Suckling him, taking every inch of him into her mouth in slow languorous sucks, deep sucks, her tongue working over every part of his dick as the fingers of her right hand fitted around him.

She stroked him. His stance widened. And then she sped up,

her mouth and fist working in time, meeting up at the crown, then back down to the base.

"*Fuck.* Ah, *shiiit . . .*"

With her free hand, she gently cupped his balls, heavy with cum and now aching for release. She touched him where he needed. Sucked him how he needed it. Licking him as she sucked him.

"Uhh, yes," he rasped. "Just like that. Don't stop sucking . . . oh, *fuuuck . . .*"

A low growl began to erupt from his chest. He grew incredibly harder in a rush, as she tasted more of his salted arousal.

She looked up at him, met his gaze. Hooded lids consumed her. Savoring the taste of him, she needed this, because it was what he needed. He needed calm. Soothing. Bliss. Special care.

And she was here to give it.

"Give me your pain," she murmured over his dick. "Let me suck it out of you."

He grunted, head falling back, tendons straining in his neck. She knew he was on the edge, she felt it at the crown, swelling against her tongue.

She sucked him harder, faster, siphoning out his anger, his need, the rush of swelling heat. With a ferocious growl, he climaxed, spurting hard jets of hot cum against the back of her mouth. She swallowed, gulped, sucked him harder again, until he cradled her face in his hands and rocked his hips, fucking her mouth.

She let him claim her mouth. She let him feed her, fill her, need her, want her. And the sharp rise of her own orgasm tightened in her belly.

She felt his body shudder. Felt him straining against the tide of another orgasm. He bellowed to the ceiling, his dick pumping frantically between her lips. More warmth—creamy and smooth, slid to the back of her throat. By the time she finished sucking him clean, Sin was breathless, in a haze of confusion and desire.

THIRTY-ONE

SHIT.

His dick was still hard.

It'd been hard all night, even after busting a nut in the shower, before climbing into bed last night. And so he'd reached into his nightstand and pulled out a bottle of Platinum wet he kept on hand for nights like that, for self-maintenance. He'd squirted a palm full of lube in his hand and then stroked out another nut—for relief; just so he could fall asleep; just to quickly empty out his balls so that his erection would go down.

But it hadn't. So he squeezed out more lube and took his dick in his fist again. That first stroke, his palm sliding up over his shaft then over and around the head of his dick always felt so good. All the way down, then all the way up, his fingers closed over the head. He'd spread his legs a little wider and had cupped his balls.

And came again. But even that hadn't helped with the erotic dreams that had followed.

All it'd done was ramp up his libido more.

Now, six hours later, and he was still hot, horny, and fucking frustrated.

With a grunt, he sat up and threw the sheet off his body and glanced down at his massive erection. What the fuck had she done to him?

More importantly than that, why the fuck had he let her get inside of his head?

He thrust his hand through his dreads, shoving the neatly woven locks from his face.

Dr. Dangerfield had sparked something inside of him, something deep and dark. Something he knew he needed to guard himself against.

He'd spent his whole life being detached, never getting too close to anyone, never allowing relationships with women to take root and bloom into anything of substance. Hell, he hadn't even entertained the notion of ever having a significant other. He didn't want one. Didn't believe there was a woman he could ever see himself wanting to build with, yet alone grow old with.

And now here he was second-guessing himself. Questioning his life. Flipping through his mental Rolodex, sifting through every fleeting memory of women whom he'd cut off, women who began to show signs of wanting more from him, women who might have shown any semblance of romantic feelings toward him.

They were a liability.

Emotional hazards.

And he had wanted no part of it.

So, he'd distance himself. Shut them out. Thanked them for a good time, then sent them on their weary way with a hug, perhaps one last kiss, and a "I wish you well, baby" spiel.

Truth was, he could fuck them. Make love to them. But he couldn't trust them to love him. And he damn sure couldn't trust himself to love them back. Many had proven themselves unworthy of his affection and attention outside of the bedroom. And so over the years, he'd made a concerted effort to never open himself up for any type of romantic involvement. He wasn't built for the potential headaches, the drama, or the crazy bullshit that went along with being in a relationship, or trusting someone to do the right thing in one.

Staying away from one—relationships, knowing when to cut ties, was the best thing for him, for anyone who tried to worm their way into his emotional space.

Sin knew he'd do well to remember that.

So then why the hell couldn't he get this woman out of his head?

It wasn't because she was beautiful. He'd had more beautiful women in his bed to last him a lifetime, hell two lifetimes. And it wasn't because she sucked dick and swallowed. He'd had hundreds of dick swallowers, and countless amounts of pussy, some better, wetter, than others.

He'd learned early on that no one did anything without wanting something in return; there was usually some underlying intent, and so he'd been suspicious most of his early life toward women, in particular. Which was ludicrous—almost laughable—because he loved every feminine part of who they were.

And still he did not trust them.

Yet, over the years, his suspiciousness managed to wane itself into cautiousness. Many were still suspect, still shady, and still . . .

He'd fuck them with abandon. Sometimes recklessly, other times not. But it was always purposeful. To give them something they'd never forget.

Him.

Sin shook his head. Tried to shake loose the dark thoughts, haunting memories.

He was fucked up. He knew it. He accepted it. He did whatever he could to protect himself from trusting someone, anyone, to share his deepest, darkest secrets with. And he had plenty.

He blamed his mother for that. For his dirty secrets, for his mistrust of women. He'd loved her, adored her, and even protected her. Even through her drunken tirades, he'd been loyal to her. Even when he'd find her lying in her own pool of vomit, when she'd shitted or pissed on herself because she'd been too damn inebriated to make it to the toilet, he'd cared for her unconditionally.

When she'd be passed out in the backseat of some car in some alleyway with her panties twisted around her ankles, he would rescue her.

But that hadn't amounted to nothing, but abuse—lots and lots of abuse.

Emotional.

Mental.

Sexual.

Incestuous.

"You black motherfucker! You ain't nothing but the devil's child. I shoulda aborted your ass, let them suck you right out of my pussy. Maybe then my life wouldn't be so goddamn fucked up . . ."

Whap!

"You make so fucking sick, boy! I can't stand your black ass."

And even when she'd climb into his bed in one of her drunken stupors, he'd made excuses for her. He'd close his eyes and pretend it wasn't her sliding her hand into his underwear. It wasn't her pulling out his dick and sucking it into her mouth until it hardened. He'd pretend he didn't like it, even when tears spilled from his eyes, his muddled mind racing with thoughts, with questions, searching for understanding. Why was she doing that to him? He'd known even at a very young age that it was wrong, that it wasn't right. And yet he'd become numb to the pleasure.

"Let Mommy make you feel good . . . C'mon, baby. Let mommy taste that sweet black dick . . . it's so big . . . mmm . . . just like Pastor's; so pretty, so good . . . "

Sin swallowed.

He'd forgiven her. Because that's what a child was supposed to do. Forgive. After all, he needed her, and she needed him. Right?

Shit.

He hadn't wanted to think about his childhood, to relive it. But all that clinical mumbo-jumbo bullshit Dr. Dangerfield spouted swirled around in his head.

"Our past doesn't have to be who we are. We have no control over

how someone else treats us. Our future lies in what we do with our lives in the present, in this very moment . . . we are not our past . . ."

But she was wrong.

Everything about who and what he was—his name, his conception, his life, his actions—was entrenched in sin.

Sin was his past. And his past was in every part of who he was. Although he fought to keep those parts of his past in check, it still had a way of creeping up on him when he least expected it to, like now.

"Mmm . . . c'mon, Sin, baby. Let Mommy show you how a woman should make love to you . . . let Mommy fuck you real good . . ."

Then she'd lift up her flimsy nightgown, reach between their bodies. Grasp his thick erection, and slide down on him. She'd ride him. And be wet, so, so wet, and Sin would feel like he was drowning in all of her wetness. He'd feel himself choking from guilt, choking from fear, choking from the strange sensations tingling over his nine-year old dick.

"Mmmm, yes, Sin . . . Mommy loves this big dick . . ."

Sin would always shut his eyes, squeeze out the imagery. Try to imagine it being one of the naked women he'd watch on some porn movie his mother kept playing on her VCR. Sometimes she'd make him watch them with her.

Slap!

Stars. Flashing white, bright and hot. Her hand would sting his face, even while she rocked her body down on his shaft, even as she swirled her hips, and soaked him.

"Open your eyes and look at me, you li'l dirty fucker . . . look at Momma . . ."

And Sin would open his eyes, wide with fear and anger and, and—God, help him—pleasure.

And then she'd cry out, pull out her breast and lower her nipple to his mouth. *"Suck my titty . . . Mommy has to teach you how to be a good lover . . . fuck a woman good, and you can fuck her whole life up . . ."* Then she'd whisper in his ear, *"Mommy's gonna come . . . this is our little secret, baby . . ."*

Sin would hold his breath. Struggling to block out the stench of Johnny Walker and weed and Benson Hedges cigarettes. Struggling to ignore the flood of sensations zapping though his body.

Struggling, struggling, struggling . . .

THIRTY-TWO

SIN STOOD IN the doorway and stared at her for several moments, admiring how sexy she looked in her plush, high-back leather chair, before she even realized he was standing there.

"Sin." He'd startled her, and yet she managed to not show it.

He smiled. "What's up, Doc? You busy?"

She closed her laptop, her gaze still on him, and said, "For you, no. How long have you been standing there, *stalking* me?"

He could definitely see how some men, and probably a few women too, with a few screws loose doing exactly that. Stalking her. He'd always found her too striking to be a psychologist, yet alone a sex therapist. At her height, she could have been on some fashion houses' runway, or on the cover of some Penthouse magazine.

He laughed off the thought. "It's called admiration. I was admiring you."

"Mm. Is that what they're calling it these days, *admiring?*" She watched him—his face, his movements—wanting to memorize him, to learn everything about him. He wore ripped jeans and a simple white fitted T-shirt that was strategically torn in all the right places to show the right amount of flesh. The sight of him alone fired her senses, and she felt the walls of her cunt slowly contract.

"Is everything okay?" she asked, pushing through her salacious thoughts, before she stood up and eased out of her panties. She removed her pink-rimmed glasses that complimented her face and somehow made her even sexier, and eyed him as he moved across the room. "Your energy feels heavy today."

He sat in one of the white leather chairs in front of her desk.

"Nah, I'm good." It was a lie, but he hadn't come here to dredge up any unwanted feelings. He hadn't come to talk. He'd come to get lost, to be distracted from his thoughts, from his past. Not rehash shit that he had no control over. And the truth was, Dr. Dangerfield was a beautiful distraction from the craziness inside his head.

She raised her brow, unconvinced. "Are you sure there isn't something on your mind? You do know I'm a pretty good listener."

He drew in a breath. "I appreciate it, Doc. But, I'm good." He ran his hands over his dreadlocks, and then clasped his fingers together. "No matter what, every day above ground is a blessing. So, what's there to complain about?"

She smiled. "Well, since you put it that way, nothing at all."

"Exactly. So I say let's seize the moment. Come play hooky with me," he said, standing to his feet, prowling the office suite from one wall to the other, taking in the wall of seductive artwork, colorful erotic oil paintings of half-naked couples in alluring poses.

The rain had stopped, and the sun had begun to peer through the enormous window that overlooked a lagoon and small waterfall.

The view was serene. And Sin wondered why he hadn't really noticed just how so before now. As much as he made it his business to stay *woke*, it was clear that there were definitely a few things he'd been sleeping on, like the picture-perfect sight in front of him.

"Hooky?"

"Yeah." He kept his eyes the view.

"And do what?"

He glanced over at her. "Be bad with me." He returned his stare out the window.

"Ooh, don't tempt me."

"Temptation is what I am," he said, dragging his gaze away from the window again to look over at her.

"Oh, really? And all this time I thought you were sin," she teased.

He grinned. "I'm both."

"Mm." The sound was sensual. "As tempting as you *and* your offer are, I—"

"Snatch the moment," he said, cutting her off and moving to stand behind her chair. He placed his hands on her shoulders, then slowly massaged them.

Dr. Dangerfield moaned as fresh desire coiled through her.

"There's someplace I want you to see," he said, bending down so that his mouth brushed against her ear.

Her breath hitching, she squeezed her legs together. "Where is it?"

He brushed a soft kiss against her cheek, then moved to sit on the edge of the desk, his scent warming her skin. "I'll have to show you." And then he slid off the desk, and she eyed him as his prowled back in front of her desk. Then took his seat again.

"Fortunately for me, I am not easily enticed." She leaned back against the chair, crossed a leg, and then swiped her bang from over her eye, and tucked it behind her ear.

"I'll tell you what." He stretched out his legs, and then dug in his front pocket and pulled out a quarter. "Heads, you get up and walk out to the car with me. Tails, I scoop you up in my arms and carry you out to my car." He flipped the coin high into the air and caught it in his left hand. Holding the quarter in his fist, he smiled. "You ready for your fate?"

Dr. Dangerfield narrowed her eyes at the challenge. "We create our own destinies, so do what you will." She said all this with a poker face.

"Oh, I plan to. Today, I'm orchestrating your journey." He slapped the coin on the back of his hand. "Well, well, beautiful lady. Looks like the gods have spoken." Grinning, he stood, stuffing the quarter back in his pocket.

She blinked. "Wait. Aren't you supposed to show me whether it was heads or tails?"

"Nah," his voice lowered to a mocking whisper, "it's whatever I say it is. Either way, you're with me for the rest of the day."

She rolled her eyes, and then laughed. "You do know that's called deceitfulness."

Placing his hands on her desk, he leaned in. "Nah, it's called doing whatever it takes to get you to spend the day with me." He glanced at his watch. "So, are you walking? Or will I have to carry you?"

"Sin," she said. "Thank you, but I can't."

The invitation was very unexpected. And, although she appreciated the gesture, it was not what she needed at the moment. She had treatment notes to finish. Had more files to close out. And then she wanted to get home to a glass of chardonnay and her hidden monitors. But, in all honesty, he'd piqued her curiosity.

Still—

She tried to think of all the reasons why she couldn't run off with him, but it was suddenly difficult to do with all the blood in her body rushing to places other than her brain.

Sensing her unwillingness to bend, to yield to his request, Sin stood again and then eased back around her desk. "You do know I am not above manhandling you to get what I want." He swiveled her chair slightly so he could stand directly in front of her.

Her pulse shot up in anticipation. "Oh?" He bent forward, putting his hands on the arms of her chair, caging her in. "Does that surprise you?" His lips were just a hairsbreadth away from hers, and their proximity to hers were beginning to make her wet.

The scent of him had ratcheted up her arousal exponentially. She now wanted some dick—*his* dick. Wanted to feel him inside of her. Hell. She was inclined to bend over her desk and tell him to pull her panties to side and just fuck her quickly, pound her pussy out real good, then leave her be.

She shook her head as her lips twitched as if fighting a smile. "Okay, you win. Now where are you taking me?" she asked in resignation.

"You'll see when we get there," he said smugly.

THIRTY-THREE

DR. DANGERFIELD LOOKED on in wide-eyed amazement, taking in the lush, green mountainside as she and Sin rode in a customized, safari-styled Range Rover. She was glad she'd acquiesced, and allowed Sin to have his way. She needed a change of scenery. Besides, she hadn't traveled to either ends of the island in months, so she welcomed the journey.

Admittedly, she was always in awe that the island was literally the shape of a heart. And for that, there was something magical about this place.

She loved it here, and she honestly couldn't imagine her life anywhere else.

"This island is truly beautiful," she said, more to herself than him.

On the left, was nothing but lush vegetation with pops of purple and pink flowers; while to the right of them was nothing but balmy beach.

Sin glanced over at her, and then reached for her hand. "Almost as beautiful as you." He brought her hand up to his lips and kissed it.

Dr. Dangerfield smiled. "I bet you say that to all your women."

Sin frowned. Yeah, he was guilty of telling women what they needed—even wanted—to hear to make them feel special, to make them feel desired. Feeling wanted was human nature, Sin knew. But most of those women he'd encountered who'd needed incessant assurance seemed to be fighting inner wars, psychologically and emotionally. They weren't comfortable in their skins, their sexualities. So they needed it. Reassurance. Constant stroking. But not Doc. She was different. He didn't feel the need to tell her anything she didn't already know. He didn't need to convince her of anything.

She already knew she was beautiful without flaunting it. She was already in touch with her femininity and her sexuality. She knew her wants, needs, and desires. Her confidence alone made her extremely desirable in his eyes. Sin was no fool. She was definitely in a category of her own. She wasn't afraid to dream. Wasn't afraid of living in the moment. She was unapologetic about her existence, for being a strong, beautiful woman.

Sin flashed her a smile, and then several more seconds ticked by before he finally answered, "I don't have *women* in my life. I have one-night stands."

Dr. Dangerfield laughed, letting her hand slip from his. "Oh, is that what we're calling it?"

"It is what it is. Nothing more."

"Do you ever think of love," she asked randomly. "You know, what life would look and feel like for you if you had someone to love in it?"

His brow rose. "Nah, I don't," he said as a matter of fact. "It's never crossed my mind." Truth was, love was for the weak. It made you vulnerable, left you exposed.

"Ever?" she asked, peering over the rim of her sunglasses at him.

"Nah." How could he when he'd never been exposed to it? He couldn't miss what he'd never had, let alone imagine it—even if he'd tried to. Daydreaming about intangible shit wasn't what he did. He saved that fairytale, fantasy shit for the helplessly romantic Harlequin types. Besides, the thought of even trying to imagine it felt exhausting.

Truth was, he believed you liked, you lusted, you even fantasized and, at times, obsessed. But loved? There'd been no moments in his life where love had touched his heart.

The concept was too foreign for him to conceptualize. Forcing anyone to believe in it was nothing more than a trap. And Sin refused to be caged to feelings he believed nonexistent.

During the years when he was growing up, he'd overheard random snatches of the word being tossed around by his mother whenever she screamed out in the throes of an orgasm, or lashed out in a fit of rage. Each event caused by the same man who'd filled her body with his seeds, planting the roots of their sin into her womb, then slid out of her body and bed, and snuck back to his life, back to his neatly constructed world. And Sin had become the end result, his birth the living proof of their sordid misdeeds.

But the word, *love*, itself had never been used toward him, that he could recall.

Not unless it referred to—

He shivered as memories sliced through him, razor sharp recollections so potent he could feel them nearly cutting him to pieces. Love was the definition of masochism. Driven by pain and humiliation.

If Dr. Dangerfield was put off by his assessment, she didn't let on. But something had tugged at her core that made her want to hold him in her arms. Strangely, her heart ached for him. Love, philosophical or not, was infinite. It was the key that unlocked hope, and bloomed endless opportunities. She believed in it, hoped for it, relished in the memory of it. Maybe he didn't believe in love. But she did. And she believed in its power to heal, and to turn a nonbeliever into a believer.

As if sensing her scrutiny of him, Sin glanced her way and she gifted him with a smile that momentarily robbed him of thought, of memory, pulling him—just like that—from the dark place he felt himself slipping to. Something tightened in his chest.

He'd have to end this thing between them soon, something

he should have already done. Before she became too attached. Before he hurt her. And yet he couldn't deny the physical attraction between them was stronger than he'd imagined it would ever be. Wherever they were, heat and passion followed them, flooding the space between them.

Eyes focused forward, his groin tightening uncomfortably. His dick needed attention. Unable to stop himself, he dragged his eyes from the road ahead of them, sliding his gaze over at her bare legs. Without words, she spread them for him, inviting him, daring him. He took the bait, his hand leaving the steering wheel and now on her knee, fingers slowly tracing the silky skin on the inside of Dr. Dangerfield's thigh.

"I believe in this," he finally said, his voice husky and thick, his eyes locking on hers as his fingers traveled higher, brushing the lace edge of her panties.

She was glad she'd worn the seductively short dress instead of her more conservative attire. But today when she'd awakened, she felt daringly sexy and had wanted to flaunt it. And now she sat in her seat, her skin slick with desire, her pussy wet and needy.

Sin's hand was close, so close to her throbbing clit. He could smell the spicy scent seeping from her sex, the wind stirring it around his senses.

"My dick is hard for you." He couldn't wait to part her slick petals and start tonguing her inner folds, savoring her rich, sweet taste.

She swallowed, embracing the swelling ache between her legs. Her lashes fluttered.

A hint of a smile played on his lips as they shared a seductive moment, before he wiggled his thumb past the lace and underneath her panties. Then he slid his middle finger against her slit. She was wet there. Oh yes. So wet and ready. She eased her body down in her seat a bit to give him more access. The excitement of being finger-fucked made her skin tingle and then her pussy grow wetter.

She could feel the wetness in her panties, her scent soaking into the lacy material.

Her cunt contracted in anticipation of his probing fingers.

She bit back a moan. She was glad he was behind the wheel instead of her because, if it were her, she'd have them veering off the cliff, plunging into that big beautiful ocean—roof first.

She drew gasping breaths. Her hips jutted upward. Heat flooded her. Her pussy was thick with lust, pulsating, begging for his fingers, his tongue, his dick.

The feel of her silken heat against his fingers elicited a groan from somewhere deep in his chest. "I want so badly to stop right here, and fuck you out in the open."

She swallowed, pressed her legs together, trapping his hand in heat and need.

"Who said I'd stop you?" she asked breathlessly. And then she giggled. "I know how nasty you like it." Her legs opened again.

"Oh, I'm tempted." His long fingers lightly brushed over her clit then, after several teasing strokes, disappeared. "All in due time." He pressed his fingertips to his nose and breathed her in.

"You smell sweet, saucy." His dick throbbed, hot and ready for release.

"I always am," she said, trying to tamp down the flames fanning out over her cunt. The sight of his tongue licking over his fingers nearly caused her to orgasm.

She smiled. He made her want to be nasty. She liked the way he made her hot, the way he made her pussy crave his touch. When she was with him, every nerve ending in her body came alive. And she couldn't wait to lay between his legs, her swooping bang brushing along his hip, her tongue licking over the crown of his thick, long dick, before sliding her mouth over him, taking the length of him deep in her throat.

"You're torturous," she teased, shifting her body in her seat, readjusting the hem of her dress. And he would soon be reminded of just how sweet and saucy she was.

"We're almost there," he said, as if reading her thoughts. His rich dark cocoa skin gleamed in the sunlight. "We have another ten minutes or so to go."

Dr. Dangerfield groaned inwardly. The wait would be hell, but she'd ride it out. She had no choice but to. She slid him a sideways glance. And then she reached over and grabbed at his crotch, sliding the heel of her hand over the lump in his shorts.

The SUV sped up. Satisfied, she sat back in her seat and took in the rest of the scenery. They traveled up a narrow road. A short distance later, the vehicle curved to the left, and on the south side of the island, the pink sand turned into a white sandy stretch of pristine beach with clear azure water, where coral reefs glowed in a kaleidoscope of vibrant colors. The array of coral served as home to sea horses, butterfly-and-parrot fish, and massive sea turtles.

Several moments later, the vehicle was coming to a complete stop. All that was around them was dense rainforest, grassy hills, and several trails leading to magnificent waterfalls.

After switching off the engine, Sin removed the key fob, then unhooked his seatbelt. "Come on," he said, looking over at Dr. Dangerfield as she unhooked her seatbelt as well. "Let me take you to my private paradise."

She smiled. "Mm. I can't wait." She opened the passenger door.

"Wait." He reached for her arm, feeling the need to clarify a few things before he took her to his private spot. "I dig you, Doc . . ."

She turned her head to him, and then swiped her bang from out of her eye. "I feel the same way." She smiled at him. "I—"

"All we're doing is having fun, right? We're keeping this thing we have going in perspective? I mean, no strings, no expectations, no feelings involved."

Dr. Dangerfield fought to keep from blinking at him. Why did he feel the need to ask her this, now? Had she said something in between him fingering her pussy and her promises of seduction once they reached their destination to ratchet up his morbid fear of commitment? Shouldn't he have asked her this *before* trekking her over a bunch of hills and mountains? Before inviting her to his secret hideaway?

Men.

She was quiet for moment. "Don't worry, Sin," she said calmly. "If I fall in love with you, I'll be certain to not ever mention it to you. In the meantime, I'll keep the switch to my heart turned off."

He narrowed his gaze, and she laughed at his expression. "Relax. I'm teasing. We're not only on the same page," she reassured, "we're reading the same paragraph. This thing we have going on isn't anything other than that—a *thing*. No commitments, no strings, no stress. Just lots of sexy fun."

"Good." He leaned over, closing the space between them, and when his lips touched hers, Sin couldn't help but wonder if all of his objections, all of his reasons to avoid getting too involved, would somehow come back to haunt him.

THIRTY-FOUR

SWEAT ROLLED DOWN his neck and soaked his muscle shirt that clung to him like a second skin. He'd gone running along the edge of the shore on the other side of the island early in the morning. And he'd run long and hard until his lungs burned and his muscles screamed. And yet he kept pushing himself until finally he had to force himself to slow his pace until he eventually came to a brisk walk.

Two hours later, he was sitting at one of the local restaurants waiting for Saint to join him. But of course, his brother was late—as usual.

He shook his head, glancing at the time on his Fitbit. 9:17 A.M. Saint was already seventeen minutes late. He'd left his cell—not that it mattered since service was usually shitty on the island—in his car. Still, he needed to call to see where the fuck he was.

He stretched his legs out, and then bent at the waist, touching his toes, stretching until the tension in his back uncoiled and loosened. He'd needed that run to clear his head. Thoughts of Dr. Dangerfield had been flooding his mind over the last several days, and it pissed him off.

He felt like one big walking contradiction. This *thing* between him and Dr. Dangerfield was starting to feel like more than just casual sex. And he knew the longer the two of them continued this dance, the more likely she was to end up catching feelings for him—if that hadn't already happened. And he'd somehow find himself sinking deeper and deeper into her seductive web.

Complications were the last thing he wanted in his life. He'd gone this long without any, and he wanted to keep it that way. Fact was, he didn't want to mislead her. And yet he wasn't ready to fall back from her either. Not yet.

But what was he waiting for?

Hell, it was only three days ago that he'd taken her to his sacred spot, where he'd then lost himself inside her sweet body. She'd so easily given herself to him—she always did, which for him wasn't anything short of what he was used to from every other woman he'd ever been with. But with her it was different. It *felt* different. Sure, lust arced between them. But there was something more that drew him to her. She was sexually aggressive, and yet submissive. And that turned him on. But, aside from being so sensual and extremely passionate there was something else about her that he couldn't quite put his finger on.

He didn't want to put too much energy into it. But all he knew was, every time he was around her, she made his dick hard. All she had to do was smile that sexy smile of hers, or look at him with those dreamy bedroom eyes. Eyes a man could drown in. And it was on.

Shit. That day in the rainforest, he'd wanted to feel himself raw inside her, to feel just how silky and wet her pussy really was. A thought he'd never entertained with any other woman. But there he'd been, overlooking a waterfall, wanting to claim her body in every way imaginable, marking her, staining every part of her core, with his seed.

That in itself was a very bad sign.

Sin inhaled.

A scented breeze drifted over him as he sipped his coconut water, trying to block out the sounds around him, trying not to think. He looked out over the beach. The sea lapped up on the sand several thousand feet or so away from where he sat out on the restaurant's patio.

With one of the ends of the towel draped around his neck, he wiped his face. The morning was an amalgamation of sounds, of clattering dishes, squalling birds, couples' chattering. A few lovers strolled along the beach, holding hands and laughing.

He took a deep breath. Clouds were swollen and suddenly growing dark. A storm was approaching. He closed his eyes and leaned back in his chair.

"Man, let me find out you out here sleeping," a deep voice drawled, pulling him from his thoughts. He looked up to see Saint staring down at him.

"It's about damn time," Sin snapped. "I was about to leave."

"Well if you'd had your phone on you, you'd have known I was running late."

Sin eyed him as he pulled out a chair and sat across from him. "My bad."

"So, what you out here brooding about?"

Sin forced a laugh. "Brooding? Man, that's bit of a reach. I was just tryna clear my head. You know, put some things in perspective."

Thunder rolled in the distance. The air carried the promise of a storm, and Sin wanted to be back on the other side before the sky opened up and dumped sheets of rain over the island.

Saint gave him a questioning look. "Oh? What's on your mind?"

"You know, I gotta make a decision about going back to the States. Nairobia's been hounding me real heavy. She wants an answer, like yesterday."

Saint nodded. "And?"

Sin shrugged. "No *and*. I'm still considering it."

He gave Sin a confused look. "Man, what's there to consider? Not to mention having Nairobia's sexy-ass close by."

He chuckled. "Yeah, I guess."

"Speaking of which, you ever wonder how she manages to keep that pussy so tight, after all the dicks she's had up in her?"

Sin shrugged. "Never really thought about it."

Saint *tsked*. "Well, I have. That bitch got a motor in that shit." He laughed. "Straight-out the box voodoo pussy. Have a nigga all fucked-up type pussy."

A tiny spark of irritation shot up Sin's spine. It wasn't the first time he'd heard Saint refer to a woman, as a bitch and he knew it wouldn't be his last, but it irked his soul every time he heard it, especially when it held such a derogatory connotation for him.

He glared his annoyance at Saint. "Yo, you need to chill with the *bitch*-calling. That shit's not cool, especially when referring to Nairobia—your employer, or any other woman."

Saint frowned. "You know what I mean. It's only a figure of speech."

"It's disrespectful."

"Says who? Women love it when a man calls her a *bitch*, especially when it's—"

Sin grunted. "That's some BS, man."

Saint's eyebrows lifted. "Okay, Mr. Sensitive. Right, right. I forgot you don't ever use the word."

"Unless it's requested, I try not to."

The waitress finally sauntered over to the table. She was a tall, ebony-skinned woman with a small waist, thick hips and a nice bubble ass. Sin didn't know her personally, but he'd seen her around the island a few times.

"Can I get you handsome gentlemen something to drink, before I take your orders?" Her golden eyes sparkled, as she looked them both over.

"You already know what I want," Saint said.

She smacked her lips. "Yeah, I do."

Saint winked and grasped her hand. "Cool. And I think I'll also have—"

She raised a brow, pulling her hand from his. "Um, no. Before you even say it—I'm *not* on the menu." Her island lilt was seductive, full of flirtatious connotation.

"Be nice to me," he teased, feigning insult. "I'm a good tipper."

She tilted her head and eyed him. "Oh really? I must have missed that part, because you definitely didn't leave me much of a *tip* the last time I saw you."

Sin glanced from the Saint to the waitress, curious to see how their little game was going to play out.

Saint laughed. "Don't front. You know I gave you a *lot* of tip and then some. You just didn't know what to do with it."

Sin shook his head in amusement at the sexual banter between them. It was obvious they were more acquainted than causally. And her teasing smile gave Sin a hint to what sort of relationship the two had.

"You know," she said, looking over at Sin, "you should really watch the company you keep."

Sin chuckled. "I wish I could. I'm kinda stuck with him."

She shook her head in mock sadness. "So sorry to hear that. My heart aches for you." And then she shot Saint a dirty look before she slipped back inside the restaurant after taking their drink orders.

"She wants me," Saint offered once she was out of earshot.

"Again?" Sin laughed. "It's obvious she's already had you."

"What can I say? I'm temptation in the flesh." He laughed. "I stole that line from you."

"Of course you did. But you might wanna come up with a more fitting line." He shook his head, "because from where I'm sitting, looked like baby girl is no longer *tempted* by the likes of you."

"Nah, she likes to role-play. You know, act like she's not interested. Give me lots of attitude so I can fuck the shit out of her later. She's in love with this dick."

Sin shook his head. "Whatever you say, man."

Saint leaned across the table and lowered his voice. "I'm telling you, bruh. She's a freak. You feel like getting in on some action?"

Sin's brow rose. "Action with who?"

"Me, you, and shorty. It's been a minute since we've tagged team some pussy."

Sin downed the rest of his water, and then set his empty bottle on the table. "Nah, I'm good."

Saint gave him a look. "Since when you start turning down an opportunity to get up in some freak's guts?"

Since—

Wait. When did it happen? Hell, he couldn't recall. He hadn't thought about it. It just happened. Somewhere over the last few weeks he'd somehow fallen back from threesomes. And most recently he hadn't been consistently living up to his role as a pleasure consultant.

Shit, he was slacking.

When the waitress reappeared Sin took her in again as she leaned over the table with their drinks, the generous cleavage nearly spilling from her blouse, and the stretch of black fabric over her curves.

She set a bottle in front of Sin. And a glass filled with ice in front of Saint. The ice crackled and popped, clinking against the glass as she poured the island's specialty tea. A passion fruit tea made with passionflowers and its small deep yellow fruit, along with rosehips, honey, and cinnamon, brewed out in the sun for hours.

Saint took a long sip, savoring the sweet flavor on his tongue. "Damn, that's good," he said, as his gaze trailed over her body. "I'm considering kidnapping you."

A hand on her hip, she rolled her eyes at him as he ran his tongue over his lips to collect the droplets. "And then do what?"

He gave her a predatory grin as his gaze traveled over her body again. "Well, baby, I was thinking of taking you on an erotic journey. Maybe invite my brother along for the ride."

Sin shook his head, opening the bottle of coconut water the waitress had set in front of him. And then he flashed her a smile. "No offense to you, beautiful. But I'ma need to pass on the ride."

She returned a smile of her own. "None taken," she said, before glaring at Saint. "But, you"—she shook her head— "are impetuous. And not even worth my time."

"I'm worth more than your time, baby." He licked his lips. "I'm worth your entire life."

She rolled her eyes again, and then quickly said, "I get off at three," before sauntering over to another table, leaving Saint's blood pounding hot in his veins as his gaze zeroed in on the extra shake she purposefully tossed in her walk.

Grinning, he said, "See. What I tell you?" He laughed. "Freak."

Sin gave him a look as he put the bottle to his lips. He took two long sips, and then swallowed. "Man, is sex *all* you think about?"

"Only when beautiful, freaky women are involved," he said as he savored another long swallow of his tea. "What more is there to think about?"

Sin snorted.

After draining his drink, Saint set his glass back down on the table and let his gaze wander over to waitress again. "I just wish she swallowed."

Sin frowned at the randomness of his remark. "You wish who swallowed?"

"Shorty," he said, thrusting his chin up in her direction. "She sucks dick like a porn star. Will let you bust all over her face. She'll even let you piss on her. But the freaky bitch won't swallow."

Sin shook his head.

"Speaking of freaks. What's up with you and sexy-ass Doc?"

Sin's water bottle stopped halfway to his mouth. "Nothing, man. We're chilling." For the most part, he'd managed to keep his *thing* with her under wraps. Quietly, discreetly, they'd managed to enjoy one another's company without it being public knowledge.

Saint laughed. "Oh, okay. That's code for *fucking*. I need to check her out."

Sin grimaced. "Check her out, for what?"

"For some more of that pussy, man. What else? That shit was good. I haven't had that since me, you, and Soul beat that shit down."

Sin tried to forget that night over a year ago. The sex had been bomb, no doubt. Seeing her handle three dicks with ease had been a major turn on in the moment. The way she'd surrendered her body to the fucking, the pleasure, had been enough to nearly send him spiraling. But now . . . the memory made his stomach knot.

"I tried to get up in them drawers a few weeks ago . . ."

What the . . .?

Thunder crashed, growing closer.

A tinge of jealousy singed hot in Sin's blood. He sucked in several breaths in an attempt to keep his composure. Damn, what was that about? That *thing* between them was nothing more than no-strings sex, after all. Hell, he'd been the one to set the ground rules. And she willingly obliged. So, fuck. She could give the pussy to whomever she wanted. It was her life, her body, and he knew that. And, yeah, his ego told him that whoever she fucked, they'd never fuck her as good as him.

Still, the very last thing he wanted to see flashing in his head was the visual of Saint's dick sliding in and out of her body. The idea of him touching her, of him being the one to dominate her . . . He cringed inwardly. What the fuck was he doing? She wasn't his to claim. And he didn't want her to be. Therefore, he knew he didn't have any right to feel any way about it. But—*goddamn it*—he did.

Sin dragged a hand through his locks and was tempted to pull them out in agitation, but he managed to scowl instead. "Oh word?" he said in a steely voice. "So y'all fucked?"

The word *fucked* came out thick, and burned the back of his throat as he said it.

"Nah, she said she wasn't interested in anymore random fucks." He scoffed. "Of course, she said it much nicely." He shook his head. "She was acting like I was some random-ass nigga."

Sin stifled a smile that twitched at the corner of his mouth. And he should have felt something other than annoyance from that knowing. But he didn't.

The sky opened up with a downpour.

And in that moment, he knew what he had to do. The realization was clear as day. He couldn't deny it, any longer. Yeah, he craved her. But he didn't trust himself not to hurt her. And what was worse than that—somehow, he didn't trust himself to stay away.

In the end, there was never any other choice save for the most obvious one. As the rain fell in torrents around him, all he could do was wonder.

Fuck, what had he gotten himself into?

Thirty-Five

"**Thanks for a** lovely meal," Dr. Dangerfield said, lifting her napkin and dabbing at the corners of her mouth. "Everything was delicious."

Not as delicious as you, he thought, feeling his dick slowly swelling. What was it about her that turned him on so deeply? The woman excited him and overwhelmed him beyond control, and those feelings made him feel vulnerable. They made him feel out of control.

He felt threatened by it. And he didn't like it one damn bit.

Still, he reached across the table and slid his hand over hers. "There's something I've been wanting to talk to you about."

She smiled at him. "I'm all ears; what's on your mind?" She swiped her bang over her forehead, and then tucked its curled ends behind her ear. Before flicking her tongue over her bottom lip.

He thought it so sexy that his thoughts blanked for a moment.

"Well, what is it you want to talk to me about?" she said, forcing his attention from her lips back up to her face.

"I want you to know how much I've enjoyed spending time with you," he started, before reaching for his drink, and then taking a long sip. And when he set his drink back on the table, his mouth still felt dry.

"Likewise," she said earnestly.

He reached for his drink again, and drained it. "You're an

incredible woman, Doc." Without thought, he began gently rubbing his thumb over the tops of her knuckles. "In more ways than I could have ever imagined, you have amazed me at every turn."

*Ohhh*kay. This was starting to feel awkward. She knew somewhere attached to his statement was a, *but* lingering. There always was.

She swallowed, and then gave him a slight smile that felt more forced than not. "So, what is it you want to tell me? The suspense is killing me."

"Well," he paused, as if trying to find the right words, or perhaps decide whether or not he was doing the right thing. And yet he knew in his heart it was for the best. "I'm leaving for New York."

Oh?

She blinked. "When?"

"In a few days."

"How long will you be gone?" she asked, shifting in her seat. She crossed her legs at the ankles.

"Well, if things go well . . . permanently."

Her lashes fluttered. "Excuse me?" She tilted her head, waited. Clearly, she'd misunderstood him. Had he said *permanently*, as in for good?

"I'm taking the job in New York until Nairobia's Vegas club opens," he firmly stated, clarifying any budding confusion.

She felt her stomach knot. "When did you decide this?" She pulled her hand away from his, dropping it into her lap. She kept her eyes on him, refusing to look away.

He shrugged. "About a week ago."

She pursed her lips. And the thoughtless motherfucker was just telling her, *now?*

"I didn't want to say anything until I knew for certain," he quickly stated, as if he'd read her thoughts.

She nodded, maintaining her poise and graceful decorum.

As calm as he was on the outside, he felt himself fighting emotions he hadn't expected. It was more than lust. Something much deeper was warring inside him. And he didn't know what to make of it.

"I know I should have probably said something sooner," he offered.

Oh, you think? She didn't say anything for a moment as she took a sip of her wine. When she tilted her head to the other side, staring at him, he figured her mind was at work, trying to analyze, ready to probe.

"I hope you aren't disappointed," he added, feeling his gut clench with want. He wanted to pull her into him, hold her in his arms.

She wanted to reach across the table and slap his face. He hadn't even left yet, and already she felt her pussy weeping at the thought of him taking that good dick along with him. Bastard!

"No, Sin," she finally said, staring at him, "I'm not disappointed. Why would I be?"

Control yourself. She inhaled deeply. *Remain calm.* She was too classy to lose control. But still—just *once*—she wanted to act a fool. Use a string of expletives, and then jump up from her seat and toss her drink in his face. Or maybe slap him, her nails dragging across his beautiful skin. Oh, if only she had a bit of ratchet surging through her blood, she could then tap into her inner ghetto child and turn this mother out.

"I completely understand. You're running."

Sin knew it wasn't a question. And yet he looked startled by the statement. "That's not what I'm doing."

She tilted her head. Gave him an "oh really" look. "Appears that way to me," she said calmly.

Sin swallowed, and then he shifted in his seat. "What exactly am I running from, Doc?"

Her gaze narrowed. And then she ran her tongue over the front of her teeth. She didn't want to have this conversation here, but since he'd opened the door by not having the decency to spring his sudden departure decision on her in private then oh-goddamn-well. He had to know things would have gotten heated, which is why he'd chosen to take her out for dinner, to be out in the open, as if she would dare stoop to making a spectacle of herself.

"Well for starters, from yourself. From something more than *this*," she said bluntly, lowering her voice. "You're running from the idea of ever getting close to a woman. Commitment scares you. The thought that you can feel something other than lust for a woman frightens you. It makes you feel out of control, doesn't it, Sin?"

Well, this was suddenly starting to become more uncomfortable by the second. Sin shifted in his seat again, leaning back in his chair. His gaze drifted beyond her for a moment before he allowed it to settle back on her face.

She leaned forward in her chair, head cocked to the side, scrutinizing him. It took every ounce of strength Sin had not to look away again. "You knew this was . . ." he paused, sighing. The night was quickly going to the left. Maybe he should have waited until after *dessert* to have this conversation with her. "Weren't you the one who said I should take the job?"

She blinked. Yeah, she had. Hadn't she? "Well, yes. And I meant it, as long as it is for the right reasons, Sin. Don't let your decision to leave be based on fear?"

He frowned. "Fear has nothing to do with this. I'm taking the position because I'm ready for change, because it's a good opportunity. And I thought you, of all people, would be supportive."

"I *am* supportive." She shook her head, and then swallowed. "I guess, I'm taken aback; that's all. I mean. I feel like it's all of a sudden."

Sin swallowed. "I told you about this months ago. You had to know it was bound to happen at some point. And you knew this thing we shared was temporary. Strictly physical," he said softly.

And yet his chest tightened. "No Strings-Attached. I thought we both understood the parameters of this. No feelings involved."

She blinked. Oh, so that was what this was all about. The fucker thought, *assumed*, she was somehow recklessly falling for his ass. She blinked again. And then she snorted. "Oh, how rich, Sin. In what world are you living in? Women catch feelings all the time. It's a natural process. And, yes, I care for you."

She placed her hands on the table and clasped them out in front of her. "But please do not think I was foolish enough to think anything more would come of *this*. I, unlike most women, understand the difference between good loving and *being* loved." Although her composure was calm and her voice low, her eyes flashed hotly over him. "Not once have I ever attempted to attach strings to my feelings, especially when we both know you aren't capable of loving *anyone* except yourself."

Ouch.

"I was never looking for love. Nor was I expecting it."

"That point," she said evenly, "was duly noted the moment I spread my legs open to you, Sin. Lucky for you, I had no intentions of ever loving you, not in *that* way. It seems obvious to me you have a problem with someone wanting to *love* you. And that's fine. But know this, Sin: wherever you go, wherever you end up, you're always taking *you* with you. And *that*, Mister Saint-Michaels, is something you will never be able to run from."

Sin glanced uncomfortably around the restaurant, then shifted in his seat. "Come on," he said, dragging his hand through his locs in frustration. "Let's not turn this into an argument."

Argument? Oh, he hadn't seen an argument. Hell, she hadn't had a good ole dirty verbal fight in years, not since her first husband, not since she'd forgotten all of her charm school upbringing and had gone upside his head with her twenty-thousand-dollar Hermès Birkin bag.

And it had felt damn good knocking him in his head. But this right here wasn't worthy of an argument. There was no need for turning this into one.

And yet she was *furious* . . . with herself.

She only had herself to blame. Inhale. Exhale. She knew things between her and Sin would have never worked out. And yet there had been a small part of her that had hoped, wanted, what they'd been sharing to somehow . . .

Fit.

To make perfect sense in spite of everything that was so imperfect.

He had been a challenge to her. One she had looked forward to conquering. That had been what had attracted her to him, to the idea of something special one day blooming between them. The beautiful flaws. She'd wanted the thorns *and* the roses. Not just parts of the bloom. But he continuously made it difficult for her to crack open his shell, to get to the core of the man beneath the surface.

So, if he wanted to go, then go—goddamn him!

"Sin, this isn't an argument. It's a conversation," she calmly said. She tilted her head. "It's what adults do when they are trying to communicate. But since you clearly aren't comfortable having *this* conversation, let me end it right here for you, and say congratulations to you." She lifted her half-empty glass in toast. "Much success, many blessings, Sin. And please know, I wish you nothing but the best." And then she reached inside her purse and tossed a hundred-dollar bill on the table. "This should cover my portion of the meal."

He gave her an incredulous look. "C'mon now. Don't do that. Take your money back." He was offended. "I got this." He picked up her money and tried to hand it back to her, but she shooed it away.

"I don't need it. Put it towards the tip." She eased out of her chair ever so gracefully, and then she went to his side of the table, leaned in, and kissed him lightly on the corner of his mouth. She straightened her back. "I hope New York *and* Vegas are everything you need it to be," she said, forcing a smile to her lips. And then she brushed fluttery fingertips along the side of his face, leaving her perfumed scent whirling around him.

Sin sat in his chair stunned, speechless, as he watched Dr. Dangerfield grab her clutch and then graciously saunter out of the restaurant, leaving him slack-jawed.

Head held high, Dr. Dangerfield waited until she was certain he wasn't coming after her, and then she sniffled. Her eyes glimmered with something, not quite tears, but there was a shimmer of emotion that made her vision a bit hazy. She blinked. And there it was. A lone tear slid down her cheek and then clung to the edge of her jaw. It wasn't a tear of sadness, more of a mixture of disappointment and happiness. She had to be honest with herself. In such a short time, Sin had reawakened her deepest desire—the need to love, and be loved.

She'd opened herself to the idea of love, allowed her heart to feel. And she'd proven to herself she *was* capable of still loving. And for that she was happy. She was happy that he was in search of ways to live his best life. Really, she was.

Still, she needed to rein in the left-side of her brain that controlled her logical thinking before she turned around and marched herself back inside the restaurant and cracked open the back of his skull with the heel of her coveted Louboutin shoe.

∽

Inside, Sin grabbed the nape of his neck in an attempt to squeeze out the tension that had suddenly coiled around his neckline. His jaw tightened. He felt like he'd just been bitch slapped. And he still felt the sting. What had she expected of him? She couldn't have thought what they shared would become something long-term.

Whatever they had was only meant to be temporary. He thought he had made himself very clear on that point.

She'd said she understood. *And yet she storms out, making a damn scene.*

Way to go, Doc!

He shook his head. Women. And that was exactly why he never kept any of them around long enough to become a headache. So why the hell was he sitting here feeling for her what he hadn't felt for another woman?

The shit unsettled him.

"Hi, sir," the waiter returned to the table pulling him from his thoughts. "Would you like anything else?" The lanky waiter glanced at the empty chair across from him, before his eyes landed back on Sin.

Sin shook his head. "No, thanks. I'm good."

The waiter nodded. "Very well. I'll bring you your check."

"Thanks." Sin glanced at his watch, and then around the restaurant to see who might have overheard the exchange between him and the Doc.

He dragged a hand over his face. No one seemed bothered by it, except for him. Guests were immersed in their own chatter to have even noticed Dr. Dangerfield had left him, abandoned him at the table.

For what? Because he'd decided to go to New York, and he'd hadn't thought to tell her right away?

He felt a tightening in his chest.

Nah, idiot! Your timing was way off, moron. Man, you really fucked this up. You really know how to be an asshole sometimes.

He sighed, waiting for the waiter to return with his check. And then he glanced over his shoulder, at the door, a part of him hoping she'd walk back in.

When he settled the bill, he stared at the empty seat across from him again, and then looked over toward the entrance behind him.

Several long seconds ticked by before Sin accepted that she wasn't coming back. And that was cool with him.

The time with her had been well spent, he admitted to himself. But it was finally time to move forward.

THIRTY-SIX

"**YEAH, BRUH, GET** that pussy," Saint grunted as he slipped the head of his dick between the lips of some random woman he and Sin had shared several rounds of drinks with. She was fairly attractive, with big breasts and a set of plump, juicy, dick-sucking lips. Sin couldn't remember the doe-eyed woman's name—it started with the letter *Q*—but he remembered her saying how she'd wanted two dicks, after sucking down her fourth drink. Said it had been one of her fantasies.

"To have two very handsome, very sexy men stuffing my mouth and pussy," she'd brazenly said. Tonight, she'd hoped her fantasy would come true. And, as always, Saint was eager to give her what she craved, promising her two big, long-winded dicks to stretch her out in any way she desired.

"It's what we do, baby," he'd added. "Give pleasure to the needy." And then he laughed. "Welcome to Passion Island, where all of your dirty fantasies come true. My brother and I will make your stay very memorable."

Although flattered, Sin hadn't been interested. They'd been at the bar having celebratory drinks. Jose Cuevo—shots, as a matter of fact. Sin's last hoorah before he headed back to the States to embark on his next adventure. He hadn't initially been in the mood when Saint suggested they hang out. "Man, let's get pissy drunk, and fuck the shit outta some horny bitch," he'd said.

Busting a nut had been the last thing on his mind. All he'd wanted to do was finish his packing and then chill at his crib, quietly, to clear his head. But Saint had other things in mind.

Pussy.

And so here Sin was. His dick sandwiched between her ass cheeks, spearing her cunt with deep, purposeful thrusts. It was a little after midnight. And the rain was pounding down outside. They were in her hotel room, all three, naked and reeking of alcohol and lust and steamy sex.

She was in the middle of the bed; on her knees, her back arched, her eyes shut, her asshole puckering, her mouth mere inches from Saint's long, thick erection, her nipples elongated from him sucking on them. They drew even tighter when he reached down and pinched them.

Her eyes bolted open as she hissed out her pleasure. "Yes, yes, yes," she murmured. And then she eyed Saint's dick. Looked at the swollen crown, and then licked the single drop of arousal that seeped from his slit. Saint groaned as her long tongue traced the crooked vein that ran down the side of his shaft.

Her body quivered with straining need. It pulsed through her. Although she'd hoped one, or both, of them would have blessed her pussy and clit with lush openmouthed kisses, they didn't disappoint in any other way, delivering dizzying, unbidden pleasure.

Both of their erections where rock-solid and powerful, Saint fucked her fast and hard, nearly ravenous and almost mercilessly, while Sin fucked her slower, more passionately. It was a delicious balance of naughty joy and delicious pain.

"*Unh*," she breathed as Sin's thumb slid over her asshole. And then he pressed it into her. "Mmm—*oh!*" she cried out.

A fresh burst of juices shot through her pussy as Saint reached between her legs and used his thumb and forefinger to pinch her clit, lightly twisting it.

"Oh God," she gasped as the pleasure swam through her, all the way to her toes. She heard herself panting, lost in the exquisiteness of two men, two sets of hands, two hard dicks—being at their mercy. Their dirty little plaything.

And then Sin slowed his thrusts, again, and found her sweet spot, his dick strokes brushing deliciously against the ridges. Sensations spiraled through her, the heat swelling sweeter than anything she'd ever imagined.

Tears sprung from her eyes, and she blinked through the haze. "Oh, God . . . this dick," she managed through clenched teeth. "Yes! Yes!"

Sin bit his bottom lip. Bit back a groan. This wasn't supposed to feel this good. "Aah, shit." He jerked his head back, flinging his locs from his face. And then the clothes strewn across the carpeted floor snagged his attention for a brief moment.

He spotted her lacy bra and black sequined thong

"This is what the fuck I'm talking about, bruh," Saint said over a grunt, pulling Sin back to the present. "Get up in them guts. Give this ho that dick-down, like old times."

"Yes, give it to . . . *me*. Oh, God! Fuck me . . . *deep*."

Sin pounded into her, the force of his thrusts causing her breasts to sway enticingly, her nipples so tight and beaded hurt her sweetly.

"Please, please, please. Oh, oh, oh . . ."

The needy sound of her moans echoing around the room turned Saint on more than it did Sin. His erection was in it, his dick sweeping over the walls of her pussy, his body giving her the performance of a lifetime, but his mind had been—and still was—somewhere else for most of the night.

And yet he continued his hungry thrusts followed by slow seductive hip rolls, giving her slow deep pleasure. His dick thickened inside her body, causing her to moan louder, as he watched her pleasure Saint with her drooling mouth. She sucked him with her eyes shut, one fist wrapped around the base of his dick, moving her plump lips vigorously up and down his veined shaft.

"Yeah, baby, suck that dick," Saint prodded, "while he's fucking you. You like the way he's making that pussy scream?"

She grunted. "God, yes," she said over the head of his dick as if speaking into a microphone. "Oh, yes." And then she lifted Saint's dick up and delivered a long, wet lick from his balls to the tip of his dick, causing the crown of his dick to grow wetter.

"Fuck," he whispered, the pleasure swelling in his balls. And then she did it again, pressing her tongue flat so that it covered more of his sac.

She moaned as Sin slipped deeper into her depths, his dick bumping the mouth of her cervix, his balls slapping up against the back of her pussy, with each deliberately hard stroke. Her body was aching, pulsing, and wet. Her hips moved frantically, desperate to meet his, her ass slapping against his pelvis.

"Damn, her pussy sound wet as fuck," Saint muttered. "Is that shit good?"

"Yeah," Sin said on a breath. "Nice and wet."

That part was true. But it—the pussy, *she*, wasn't—

He purposefully shoved away any thoughts of Dr. Dangerfield, not wanting to lose his erection. The pussy was starting to feel better than good, and he admittedly wanted to nut without thoughts of *her* fucking up his groove. And the day after tomorrow he'd be far enough away to not have to worry about being tempted to touch or taste or smell any parts of her.

"Fuck me," she cried out, interrupting his thoughts. Saint had already fucked her brains out, and now she wanted, begged for, his dick.

Sin pulled open her ass cheeks and withdrew until she could feel his dick barely touching her slit. He glanced down at his dick, his condom covered in creamy heat, and then he thrust back into her more powerfully than before, causing a gasp to escape from her as he dove into her deep and her pussy *queefed*.

And, then, immersed to the hilt in her wet heat, he went still for a moment, just letting his dick marinate in her juices, absorbing her heat, allowing her to savor the fullness.

Sin waited until she drew Saint's dick deep into her mouth and down her throat, and then—oh God, yes—he began thrusting. Hard, toe curling, mind-numbing plunges that made her body reverberate, and had her making high-pitched moans.

Saint groaned as she began to suck him hard, his hand clamped around the back of her head, his hips moving to the pulsing rhythm of her mouth. "Goddamn, baby. You sucking the shit outta this dick."

Sin slapped her ass, and then grabbed her by the hips, pounding her orgasm to the surface. He felt his own orgasm vibrating up his dick. He was close, so, so very close. He just wanted the night to be over. "Ah, fuck," he grunted.

Saint felt his own nut swelling, his midsection tightening. "You ready to bust, bruh? You ready to give this freaky bitch her late-night snack?"

Sin grunted his response, as Saint shot a big load of his cum into her wet, horny mouth. She sucked and groaned her delight, winding her hips into Sin's pelvis as she kept sucking Saint's still-hard dick.

"Yeah, greedy little cunt," Saint growled as she moved her pussy in rhythm with Sin's thrusts, giving as much as she was taking.

"God, oh, God, yes," she heard herself murmur.

Razor sharp, his orgasm splintered through him. Soon Sin fucked her harder in piston-like drives that—at times grazing deliciously over rigid, swollen flesh—made her crazed and made her cry out around Saint's dick, even as she vigorously sucked more of his nut out.

Sin was almost there, just a few more strokes. Harder, harder—
and then this shit would all be over.

Faster, faster . . .

Deeper, deeper—

"Aah, fuck," he growled, quickly pulling out and snatching the
condom off. His body jerked as he rapidly stroked his dick, his balls
swaying back and forth, his nut rushing out of his body in hot,
white ribbons, scorching the small of her back, and all over her ass.

THIRTY-SEVEN

"SIN?" DR. DANGERFIELD said, surprise registering over her face. She tightened the belt of her robe. "What are you doing here?"

"I needed to see you, before I—"

With raised brow, she tilted her head. "Why?" She hadn't seen or spoken to him since the night he'd told her he was leaving the island. And she'd purposefully been avoiding him. For no other reason than not wanting to be reminded of how foolish she'd been to fall for him.

"I was thinking about you. I wanted to see you before . . . are you okay?"

Of course, she was *okay.* Had he expected to find her slunk down in a tub with her wrists slit? *Arrogant fuck.* Still, she'd be better if she could reach up and slap his face one good time. She forced a smile instead. "I couldn't be better. Why wouldn't I be?"

He shrugged. "Just needed to be sure."

Fuck you, you sexy bastard! "I thought you'd be gone by now," she said calmly, nearly emotionless, changing the subject.

"My flight leaves early tomorrow morning. But I didn't want to leave without seeing you. I wanted to apologize."

"A phone call would have sufficed." Hell, even a damn note. She didn't need to see him. She didn't need to be reminded of how damn fine he was, and how much of a damn self-absorbed asshole he could be.

"You're worth more than a call, Doc."

She just stared up at him.

He swallowed in a breath. "I feel bad how things—"

"Don't," she said, cutting him off. He'd done nothing wrong. He hadn't hurt her. He hadn't misled her. He hadn't tried to string her along. On the contrary, he'd been honest, upfront—and very transparent—with her from the beginning. So whatever feelings might have come into play were of her doing, not his.

"There's nothing to feel bad about," she continued. "We were just fucking, that's all. No harm, no foul, right?"

Sin cringed. Damn, she made it sound harsh. *Fucking.* Like it had been dirty, vile, between them.

"Yes," he admitted softly. "At first that's all it was; that's all it was supposed to be. But somehow it became more than that. Everything we've shared over the last few months has been special to me. *You're* special to me, Doc."

She swallowed the knot forming at the back of her throat. "And you will always hold a special place in my heart as well, Sin. But I'm a big girl. I live with no regrets. I'm not shedding tears. I'm not on the verge of some psychotic meltdown. I went into this arrangement with both eyes wide open, without expectations, knowing what I was getting myself into."

Yeah, fucking a man who was afraid of giving up control, afraid of allowing someone inside the hollow spaces of his heart. She had no use for an emotionally bankrupt man, any-damn-way. She saw enough of them in her private-practice and in the island's couples' retreats to last her a lifetime, so she didn't want, or *need, that* in her personal life.

Sin stared at her, and she watched him uncomfortably as his gaze skated over her body. Aware of her arousal, she folded her arms over her breasts, over her erect nipples suddenly straining against her robe.

Damn those beautiful breasts. So pert, so perfectly shaped, her nipples deep brown, succulent, inviting . . .

The flicker in his eyes caught her breath.

Lust.

Her heart fluttered as he advanced toward her, his heat wrapping around her, brushing over her skin, thick and sweet, like warm honey.

She stepped back, but that only encouraged him to close in on her again, moving into her space until her back was up against the door. He pinned her there, with his eyes, with his body, with his overwhelming heat.

"You're an amazing woman," he whispered. And then he reached out and touched her cheek. "I can't lie, Doc. I'm going to miss you." His touch warmed her skin.

Dr. Dangerfield's pulse quickened, and yet she only offered a smile that hadn't quite reached her eyes. "I'll miss you, too," she admitted in spite of herself, in spite of the sadness swelling in her heart. Why had he come? Why didn't he board his flight without so much as a glance back?

Thoughtless bastard! Had he come here just to fuck with her? Hadn't he already done enough? He'd stamped his dick, his touch, all over her body. He'd be hard to forget, but she'd do it without a tear shed, without the blink of an eye.

"I want nothing but the best for you, Sin," she said in a low voice. And she meant it.

"As do I for you. You deserve everything your heart desires."

"So do you." She swallowed. Too bad it wouldn't be with her.

"If only . . ." his gaze never leaving hers, he shook his head, swallowing back a wave of remorse.

The heat of his stare unnerved her, but she stubbornly kept her eyes on him.

"I wish I could, wish I—" he continued, his words cut short by a finger to his lips.

"No need for any explanation. You are who you are."

He smiled, and then leaned in and kissed her softly on the lips.

For a long moment, Dr. Dangerfield closed her eyes, breathed in the kiss and imagined different circumstances—one in which he'd come to tell her he was staying here on the island. But that was pointless. His decision was made. His mind was set. There was no use exerting energy into wishing for things to be different.

And yet behind her lids pinwheels of desire spun in brilliant colors. She could feel every hard inch of Sin pressed into her belly. Her fingers curled into his locks as he suddenly pried open her mouth with his tongue and slid inside. It was only supposed to be a peck on the lips, a closed-mouth kiss, but Sin couldn't resist tasting her sweet lips one last time, he couldn't avoid the feel of her tongue against his one more time.

"Sin," she breathed out.

He licked her earlobe, then licked over her bottom lip, before capturing her mouth with his again. Why couldn't he resist her? Why couldn't she resist him?

"Oh, God," she moaned, her eyes fluttering open. She pulled away, breaking the kiss, panting, snatching back her control. "Don't."

"Don't, what?" Sin murmured against her ear, before brushing more kisses along her neck. Heat settled between her breasts. Her skin tingled, her nipples tightened, and she wanted to hang on to this feeling, freeze-frame it, stamp it to her memory, but the rational part of who she was wouldn't allow it.

"This. We—"

Her toes curled.

Her nipples pearled.

Her cunt ached for him one last time.

She hadn't given thought to fucking him, but the need was there, throbbing deep, ensconced in hunger and desire. The need for bliss; just one more passionate night with him—their goodbye-see-you-when-I-see-you fuck, that's what it'd be. And she could fuck him with everything that was in her, throw her wet pussy on him, give him a night he'd never forget, and make him regret the day he'd run from her.

Yes, she could fuck him with reckless abandon, fuck him with no cares, then see him to the door, slamming it shut behind him.

No. She'd given him enough of her, of her time, of her body. And she no longer wanted lust. She wanted love. She knew this now, more than ever, with all that she was. And if it weren't going to be from him, then she'd deny herself pleasure—with him, at least—until someone willing and able and ready found his way into her world.

Sin felt something tug on the inside of his chest, an ache he'd never experienced before, and it shocked and shook him. He inhaled, breathing her in. "I'm no good for you, Doc," he murmured, his gaze suddenly shifting from hers.

She hadn't asked for his confession. Didn't want it. Of course, he was no good, but she'd been willing to overlook that fact. She'd been willing to throw herself into the idea that he *could* be good for her, that *she* could be good for him—with work (lots of it!), with patience—lots of that, too. She'd been willing to surrender her body to him, completely, openly. But he'd closed himself off to her, shut out any chances of uncovering what they might have become.

"I know," she said softly.

"If you ever find your way to New York between now and the time I head out to Vegas, you know where to find me."

She slowly shook her head. She had no use in ever going to the city—or back to the States, if she could help it. And she wouldn't go looking for him. There wasn't anything there for her. She could get dick anywhere.

"My life is here," she said. "This thing we shared made me realize that what I want most is a forever. Not a fling, and definitely not some noncommittal sex. I've had enough of that." She eased up on her balls of her feet, and kissed him again.

The kiss started as a slow caress of her lips against his, then his tongue licked along the seam. She parted for him—one last time, and he tasted her, cinnamon, her breath so very sweet, that he pulled her harder against him, trying to swallow in her breaths. She took his kiss with a long, deep sweep of her tongue, and he felt her heart beat against him.

And then she backed away before she snatched her words back, before she opened her robe and slid her panties down over her hips. "You take care of yourself, Sin."

Sin nodded. Shoved a hand through his locks. Then stepped aside to let her by.

At the door, she gripped the handle and took several deep breaths before opening it. He watched her as she held open the door, wanting to memorize every curve, every dip, every stretch of skin—the very sweetest parts of her.

"Stay beautiful, Doc," he whispered, pressing his forehead to hers. He inhaled, held her in his lungs one last time, then swallowed in the memory, before walking out.

The door slammed.

The light went out.

And suddenly the world went black.

THIRTY-EIGHT

SIN STOOD ON her doorstep longer than he'd expected, his eyes closed, breathing, breathing, breathing. He thought seeing her would be of no consequence. And yet he felt fucked up. He'd felt as if he'd wronged her in some way, even though he knew he hadn't. Not that she'd said anything to make him feel that way because she hadn't.

No. It was what she hadn't said that was now fucking with him.

It was the silence of words he knew she wanted to say. Words he wanted to hear. Words he had no understanding as to why he needed to hear them.

But she'd held back. And it was probably for the best.

Some things were better left unsaid.

Wasn't that some wise man's motto?

Sin inhaled, then blew out a breath, before holding his head back and opening his eyes. Like brilliant diamonds, stars glistened back at him, but everything around him felt dark. This had turned out to be harder than he'd imagined.

She'd had him burning with desire. Had him wanting to lose control, wanting to beg her for the pussy. And Sin begged for nothing from a woman. It was either given to him or taken, freely. And she'd freely given of herself. Freely allowed him into every perfect space of her world.

So why hadn't that been enough?

He didn't want to ever be the man to ruin her, to break her. So, yes, this was for the best. He knew it. And yet he felt something welling up inside of him. A pang in the center of his chest, a tightening that nearly trapped the air in his lungs.

Admittedly, he'd wanted to taste her, one last time. The sweetness of her juice, the intoxicating scent of her cunt, fragranced by her own nasty need. God, he knew if he had tongued her, kissed her there— if she would have gushed into his mouth, he'd never be able to get enough of her. Her sweet pretty pussy all drenched in its flavored musk.

Her kiss, her taste, was still on his lips and her scent continued to cloud his mind with questions he had no real answers to.

But he knew he had to be honest with himself. What they shared was much deeper than anything he'd ever shared with any other woman. But it was only physical. A sexual attraction that was so primal, so intense, that the chemistry could be misinterpreted as something much more.

Something like love.

Sin snorted. *Not hardly.* Falling in love wasn't his thing.

He glanced back at her door. Then smiled, shaking his head. Dr. Dangerfield was one woman he'd never forget. A woman he'd never *want* to forget.

In another lifetime, she'd be everything he'd want in a woman, in a life partner.

She'd be all he'd ever need. Even he knew she was a woman most men would dream of having. But for now, what she deserved and what he was willing to give were completely two different things.

In the end, several thousand miles apart was best for the both of them, he mused as he glanced back at her shut door one last time, before finally walking off.

An hour later, Sin was back at his villa checking and rechecking his bags to make sure he'd packed everything. The walls were now bare of his artwork, and framed photos. His whole life was now packed away in boxes and suitcases.

Nairobia had told him he could hold onto the villa for as long as he wanted, in case he wanted, needed, to return. He'd told her that it wouldn't be necessary. He could always crash at Saint's or rent a suite if he needed to. And then Dr. Dangerfield's face had flashed in his head, which was what had really prompted him to go to her place in the first place.

She had a way of making him forget about everything, except the feel of her, the warmth of her. The lingering erection he'd gotten when the sight of her turgid nipples was showing through her robe was now beginning to throb all over again.

He knew he was bad for her.

His hunger for her was overwhelming, and he knew staying would be his undoing. Suddenly his pulse was racing, and his head began to pound with an ache behind his eyes. A headache. The last thing he needed. He had shit to do that didn't include succumbing to a fucking headache.

He closed his eyes, inhaling deep breaths, holding each pull of air deeply into his lungs before slowly exhaling. And when he finally opened his eyes again, he sighed and ran a hand through his locs.

Shit. What the fuck was wrong with him? Why was he feeling bad for doing what he felt was right? They'd fucked consistently nearly every day for *weeks*, true. And, yeah, he was feeling her. He'd already admitted that.

What did it matter, though?

He'd liked handfuls of women in the past and yet he'd severed ties without so much as a blink of an eye. And, yeah, a few had been hurt by the suddenness of it all when things ended—in spite of having been told that whatever they'd might have shared with him was only temporary.

It was always temporary. So, whatever hurt or disappointment or anger they'd might have felt at the time that, too, was only temporary. Then it was over.

Dr. Dangerfield was a resilient woman, Sin mused as he headed toward the bathroom, where he turned on the shower. *A man who is right for her will one day come into her life and be able to give her all that she deserves.*

He looked up at the ceiling in frustration. And then a tightness in his chest caught him by surprise. He clenched his fists at his side and then stretched his neck from one side to the other, his muscles bulging and flexing. It was all he could do to keep from punching a wall. He'd allowed her to get too close. Allowed her to seep too deeply in his thoughts. And that shit wasn't cool.

He muttered a curse under his breath, removing his clothes. He slid the shower door open, and then stepped inside.

～∽

Four hours later, Sin was up, staring up at his ceiling. He'd spent a restless night fighting with himself. Doubting himself, in some respects. Was he really ready to give up his life here in what many considered the world's greatest gem? Was leaving really about the need for change in his life, or the need to regain control of it?

"Who are you really running from, Sin—me, or is it from yourself?"

Dr. Dangerfield's words somehow managed to find their way into the forefront of his mind. And he'd spent the early hours of the morning walking along the beach, thinking. Trying to figure out what it was about her that kept him drawn to her, like a moth to a flame. He'd nearly laughed at the cliché.

And yet it held some truth.

He even, laughably, entertained the idea of staying on the island, just a few weeks longer to see if there was a remote possibility of having something more . . . a deeper connection with her.

He'd even wondered if he was even capable of that?

But then he felt himself choking on the thought, barely able to catch his breath. Not even the sounds of the waves rolling in helped him make sense of it all.

Then the answer became clearer along with the rising of the sun. It was, emphatically, no—hell no. He didn't want her. Couldn't want her in that way. So why the hell did the thought of *her* finding love with someone else bother him? Sin frowned. Love wasn't in his DNA. He hadn't known it. Not from a woman. Not from anyone. And, his own mother—*that sick, twisted bitch*—definitely hadn't shown him any.

Lust was all he knew. Sex was all he knew.

Fucking.

From his mother to every other woman he'd ever encountered in his life, he'd been the boy-toy, the fuck-buddy, the sex slave—for a lack of a better term. Until he'd finally been able to flip the bed sheets and take control of his sex life, his dick, and how he chose to give his good loving to.

Sighing, Sin shook his head. He couldn't believe he'd actually contemplated a relationship. The fact that he was trying to envision a life being committed to someone outside of more than a fuck or fling went against everything he believed in.

Hell, maybe he was losing his mind.

But the one thing he was most certain of, his time on Passion Island had come to an end.

THIRTY-NINE

NINETEEN HOURS LATER, Sin slid out of the backseat of a chauffeur-driven Bentley, and walked into the Ritz-Carlton, a large duffle bag hoisted up over his shoulder, and a carryon in his hand. He would have been satisfied with a simple hotel room at some other low-key location, but Nairobia had insisted on putting him up in the midtown hotel, which overlooked Central Park and was minutes away from Fifth and Madison Avenues, until he was able to secure a suitable place of his own.

He glanced around, taking in the sophisticated décor, as he walked over to the check-in desk, where a blue-eyed, thirty-something year old woman smiled at him. Her blonde hair was pulled back into a sleek ponytail. "Welcome to the Ritz-Carlton."

Sin flashed her a smile of his own. "Thanks."

Mm, he's a panty-wetter. "Will you be checking in?"

Sin glanced at the woman's gold-plated nametag. "Yes. I have a reservation. Sin Saint-Michaels." He watched as her manicured fingers quickly typed on the keyboard of her computer.

He handed her his ID.

"Oh, yes, Mr. Saint-Michaels. There you are," she said as she pulled up his reservation. She beamed at him. And then her eyes glossed with curiosity as to how he could afford the fifty-four hundred dollar a night rate. "Your reservation is for the Central

Park suite. Up on the twenty-second floor. You'll love the magnificent views of Central Park," she rattled on.

"Cool. I'm looking forward to it."

"How long will you be staying with us?"

He glanced at her nametag again, before looking back into her eyes. "I'm not sure. Might be indefinitely," he said. "All depends."

"Oh?" She swallowed. "So, are you here on business or pleasure?"

"Both. My business is my pleasure."

She caught the vein in the side of his muscular neck, and bit back the urge to lean over the counter to lick him there. She swallowed. "Sounds intriguing. Will you need one room key, or two?"

"One."

She cleared her throat. "Oh, okay. So, there won't be any other guests checking in with you?" Her subtle way of asking if he was traveling alone.

Sin smirked. "Not at the moment. But it's still early," he said, innuendo dripping in his tone. "Who knows what the day, or *night*, might bring." And then he winked at her.

Her cheeks flushed and heat suddenly pooled low in her belly as she handed him his keycard. And when his fingertips brushed over hers, she felt the walls of her cunt clench. "Enjoy your stay, Mr. Saint-Michaels. And if there is *any*thing you need, don't hesitate to call."

There went that panty-wetting smile again. "I will, Jennifer. Thanks."

When Sin finally reached his suite, he stood at the window and took in the spectacular view of Central Park.

This was it. The start of a new beginning, he thought to himself. And yet something still felt off. Something felt amiss.

Reaching into his front pocket he pulled out his cell, powering it back on. Taking a deep breath, he brought up Dr. Dangerfield's name and then hit connect. He knew it'd be late there, but—

She picked up on the third ring.

"Hello?"

And then he scolded himself for calling. Dr. Dangerfield sounded groggy. Oh, well. It was too late to end the call now.

"Hey, Doc. Just wanted you to know—"

"Who is this? Sin?"

"Yeah. I hope I didn't wake you."

There was a hesitation, and then what sounded like a sigh.

"Is there something I can do for you?" she said curtly.

His gut clenched. "Nah. My bad for calling you. Just wanted to let you know I . . . listen. I was thinking about how things ended, you know. I'm hoping we'd be able to work through this. Remain friends, you know."

He swallowed.

Dr. Dangerfield sighed again. "There's nothing to work through. All that needs to be said had been the night you left here, so there's nothing to work through. I'm glad you made it safely. But there's no need for any further calls. It's best I don't hear from you." She didn't sound bitter or angry when she spoke, just crystal clear—*stay the fuck out of my life!*

Sin scratched the back of his neck. "I hear you," he whispered. "I'll let you get back to sleep. Stay beautiful, Doc."

"You take special care of yourself, Sin."

And then it was over. Before he could respond, Dr. Dangerfield had already ended the call. Sin shook his head, unsure of how he felt about making that call. He simply knew it was out of character for him. However, he didn't regret making it.

Because, whether he wanted to admit it or not, Sin realized somewhere in the back of his mind, that Dr. Dangerfield had been good for him in a time he hadn't known he needed her to be. He'd never talked about his mother to anyone. Hell, he never really discussed in any full detail what living with her had been like for him with Saint. Yet for some reason, Dr. Dangerfield had managed to get him to open up to her.

Sin turned from the window and headed for the bedroom. If she didn't want to remain friends, then so be it. Wasn't shit he could do about it, except give her space and keep it moving. Because one thing he'd never done was throw himself at a woman. Point-blank. Period.

Sliding his phone back down into his pocket, he fell back on the plush bed and then stared up at the ceiling, understanding finally dawning on him. Over the years, he'd perfected an impenetrable persona that enabled him to compartmentalize his life. And in doing so, no one was able to pry into his past, or trespass on present. But he'd gotten too comfortable with Dr. Dangerfield. He'd lowered his guard. He'd revealed too much of his soul to her, and that shit was never good.

And yet he still wanted to be friends. Or if nothing else, be *cool* with her.

Yeah, give her space. She'll come around, he finally decided in his mind, before exhaustion claimed him and he closed his eyes, succumbing to sleep.

Three hours later, he was showered and had changed into a pair of faded Robins Jeans. He wore its matching denim jacket over a white Tee with a pair of white Buscemi sneakers.

Though being designer-cladded wasn't really his thing, especially since he'd spent the last several years of his life on an island mostly bare-chested, it felt good to throw it on from time to time. Besides, if he were going to be surrounded by jet setters and Manhattan's elite, then he might as well look the part.

Maybe, over time, it would become his new normal.

After all, he'd come to New York for change, hadn't he?

With a head turning swagger, Sin walked through the hotel's lobby like a man who had the world in the palm of his hand. The black-suited doormen held open the large glass doors, tipping their top hats to him as he stepped out into the city's light.

With no real destination in mind, Sin pulled his dark shades down over his eyes and strolled out the door, the scent of his Acqua di Parma trailing behind him as he hit the streets of the Big Apple.

FORTY

MATT BLACK'S "GOOSEBUMPS" poured out of the speaker of his Megablast.

And—*oh, yes, yes*—he was giving her goose bumps as his dick wetly slid in and out of her wet, tight, warm pussy.

"Is this what you came for?" Sin asked, husky-voiced.

"Oh, God, yes," she murmured, as she arched into his heat, welcoming his every thrust. This had been more than what she'd imagined it would be. Every touch, every exquisite thrust, was snatching her breath away.

He slapped her ass, *hard.* The loud popping sound echoed around the room, its after burn causing the walls of her pussy to tighten.

How many times have I wanted to do this?

Countless times. Creeping into the room of some tall, dark, and handsome stranger's room had been a longtime fantasy of hers. One she never expected to live out, let alone have the courage to follow through with.

Until him . . .

"Oh, God," she called out again, as his dick brushed over her G-spot.

She knew she was taking a risk being here, naked; her face pressed against the large wall of glass, the spectacular view of

Central Park stretched out before her blurring eyes, her pussy being speared from the back by a deliciously thick dick.

But, right now, she didn't give a damn. The way he was handling her body, her pussy, told her she'd done the right thing throwing caution to the wind.

The dick, the fucking, was worth whatever the consequence.

She knew better than anyone that fucking the guests was an absolute breach of contract. And yet the second his gaze had latched onto hers at the check-in desk she'd felt a jolt of sexual energy that had the muscles in her pussy rapidly clenching and her mind conjuring up all sorts of erotic images. Her cunt juices had already begun to seep into the crotch of her panties at the mere thought of him yanking her hair and pounding her from the back. Sucking her toes into his mouth while deep stroking her. Nothing like that had ever happened to her before. Not with that level of intensity.

And so she'd finished her shift a little after ten p.m., and then, instead of swiping out and catching the number two train to her modest, overly-priced Brooklyn apartment as she normally did, she talked herself into sneaking onto one of the service elevators, riding up to his suite, convincing herself that bringing him personalized room service was what he'd appreciate most.

So, when he'd opened the door and she'd walked in, no words were needed. She knew he knew what she'd come for. She'd boldly fumbled with his belt, and then attempted to unbutton his jeans. But Sin had pushed her hands aside and did it himself, lowering the zipper. Moments seemed to tick by before he'd finally yanked his jeans and boxer briefs down from his hips until his dick sprang free.

He hadn't kissed her, hadn't licked her pussy. And he didn't need to. She'd been already wet and ready long before she'd removed her clothes and sunk to her knees, sucking his sweet chocolate meat into her mouth.

And now he was wedged deep inside her aching cunt, absorbing every inch of him, melting over him. Loving the burning stretch of his dick as it stroked her walls.

She clawed at the fogged window, where her swollen red lips had been mere seconds ago, as he lowered his lips to her ear. "You've been thinking about me fucking you all day; you wanted this dick the moment you saw me."

It wasn't a question, but he pulled an answer out of her. "Yes. Oh, sweet God, yes." Shivers of ecstasy rippled through her as her dark pink pebbled-nipples brushed against the cool glass. "I fantasized about it all day."

"Well you have it now." He pushed in deeper, causing her to gasp. "All of it. So do what you do best, and fuck yourself on it."

He stared at her reflection in the glass. Her hair was messy, her lips puffy, her tanned skin flushed, her eyes practically rolling up in her head.

"Look at yourself," he bit out. "Watch me fuck you."

Her eyelids fluttered. Meeting his gaze through the window, she bit down on her lip at the sight of him. He looked like a chocolate god. A warrior, all chiseled, coated in primal heat.

A moan slipped from her lips. The pressure inside of her was building quickly as Sin's dick glided back and forth. And watching him watch her as he fucked her, purposefully, only pushed her closer to the brink.

Flattening both hands on either side of her head, he gave her free reins to ride his dick, to throw her ass up on him. She was tall, and her four-inch heels made her taller, giving her the perfect height to whine her pussy on his dick.

She moaned. More goose bumps covered her arms, her back. "Oh, fuck, yes. Mmm. Your big, black cock feels so good in my pussy."

Sin expelled a rush of air as she rapidly rolled her hips, her pussy throbbing around him, soaking him. "Yeah, that's right. Get nasty with it. Fuck the nut out of this fat dick." He inhaled. The living room of his suite smelled of feminine heat and wild sex.

Wet pussy clenching in time with her heartbeat, she continued bucking her hips, back and forth over his shaft, her heat warming the latex of his condom.

He slapped her ass, and then robbed her of her breath when he wrapped a hand into her hair and yanked her head back. "Fuck this dick." He slammed into her, biting down on the column of her neck.

She mewled, arching her back, wanting more, needing more.

"Get this nut." He tightened his grip on her hair, yanked her neck back harder, held onto her hair like a rein. And she grew wetter.

"Oh. Oh. *Yesssss* . . ." She closed her eyes as powerful sensations washed over her, curling up through her clit, causing every muscle in her body to clench.

By the time Elhae's "Love A Nigga" sliced into the air around them Sin had her screaming, her legs shaking, her slick pussy convulsing as her orgasm ripped through every part of her body.

Breathlessly, her body slid down the glass when Sin finally pulled out of her, making her dizzy as she fought to find her breath.

Her pussy pulsed. Her clit throbbed. She couldn't think. Couldn't see. Still couldn't breath as the air around her suddenly sizzled. She'd come for a taste of his heated sexuality, and he'd managed to wring her orgasm inside out and turn her into a ball of pulsing nerves, leaving her hungry for more.

FORTY-ONE

SIN WINDED DOWN into the Love Tomb, and suddenly the world changed color. Doja Cat's "Trauma" floated sensually out of from the lower speakers. Firelight flickered over and around the rounded walls.

The Pleasure Zone had taken the word *erotic* to another level. And he couldn't imagine what the club in Vegas would eventually be like once it opened. Because, if Nairobia's next venture was anything as erogenous as this club, he'd be literally *fucking* his life away.

There was a woman tied backwards over what appeared to be a huge black rubber ball. Several men were lined up stroking their dicks, waiting for their turn to use her mouth, while others took turns fucking her. Frolicking in the pool was a handful of naked couples. A few were kissing, their tongues sparring until they were nearly breathless. Others were in passionate embraces, hands descended to hips, bodies squeezing against the others. And stretched along a wall were polished wood benches, where a biracial couple was in the throes of oral sex. She on top, her pussy hovering over her Caucasian lover's face, her voluptuous ass spread open wide, his long tongue working in between her thick folds.

In nothing but black heels, a red garter, and fishnet thigh-highs, she rode his face, while she sucked him into her hungry, wet mouth, deeply, milking him, slurping and moaning over his dick.

Sin watched as he ate her, wetly, loudly, sucking and licking her with abandon until her legs trembled.

Grunts.

Groans.

Orgasms.

Sizzling bliss.

Bodies shuddering.

Dark chocolate melted over white chocolate.

Heat jetted to the back of her mouth, his mouth.

He drank.

She drank.

Until they were both empty, their bodies going slack from pleasure.

Sin regarded the lovers for several more seconds, before making his way down one of the many passageways, heading toward a cluster of chambers. Each chamber held an assortment of kink equipment—St. Andrews cross, a rack, bondage cuffs, An X-bar, pillories, stockade benches, spreader bars, spanking benches, and swings. Each chamber also held a table topped with an assortment of ropes, paddles, clamps, and various bondage gear.

This was his second week of training at The Pleasure Zone, and Sin was still amazed at the level of eroticism the club offered.

So sordid.

So kinky.

So feral.

So dark and mysterious.

Firelight captured his face, behind his mask, his eyes smoldering, and he looked deliciously wicked.

"Have you come to fuck?" asked a woman, sweeping in front of him. She wore an elaborate scarlet mask etched in rubies. At the sides, flowing swirls of gold formed around its edges. "Or are you looking to have your balls twisted and ass paddled?"

She ran a gloved hand through her hair, and eyed him

seductively. The sight of him made her breath hitch. His wide, chiseled-chest made her want to reach out and touch. Instead, she breathed deep and resisted the urge to tear open his shirt and pinch his nipples.

Sin's eyes gleamed as he stared back at her. In her right hand, she held a long black whip. Her breasts spilled out of a red leather bustier. A red spiked thong barely covered her crotch. Her long legs were stretched taller by seven-inch spiked heels. And around her neck she wore a spiked choker.

Sin appraised her lithe body, smiling appreciatively. She was beautiful, he admitted. But then he told her that she could save the ass paddling and balls twisting for someone more deserving of such torturous pleasure, that he'd only come down to browse—for now.

"Erotic pain is a turn on for most."

Sin raised his eyebrow at her. "I'm not most, baby."

"A shame," the woman said saucily; her big brown eyes flashing dark with desire. "I would love to paddle that sweet, muscular ass of yours until it welted, and then soothe it with my long tongue." She boldly flicked out her tongue for effect, extending it out until it touched the bottom of her chin and then the tip of her nose.

Sin cringed inwardly. It was no secret that submitting to a woman held no appeal to him. And there was definitely no way in holy hell he was ever letting a woman anywhere near his ass—with paddle, tongue, or anything else—except her hands to grab onto it while he was fucking her.

"Sorry, baby. That ain't my thing," he said evenly. "But I'll tell you what. If you wanna bend over and grab your ankles, I'll happily paddle yours." He flashed her a smile, and she felt her cunt clench.

Behind her mask, her dark eyes roamed over him as she moaned, and licked over her lips. "Mm. Only if you promise to fuck me in it afterwards."

Flashing her a smirk, he answered with, "If you're still here when I return, I'll do more than just fuck you in it."

Then, before she could speak, he backed her up against a wall under one of the torches, and slid a knee between her thighs, pushing her to a wider stance. Her mask glowed in the firelight. Her eyes flickered.

He cupped her spiked crotch, pressing his thumb over her clit. She grunted. "Ooh, you nasty fucker."

"Yeah, I'm nasty, baby," he said. And then he slipped his fingers in between her thong and inside her, stroking her there, making her hotter. Her pussy was trimmed. He fingered her until the musky scent of her arousal rose up to him, until she was on the verge of an orgasm.

One finger became two.

She lifted her hips to him, pumped her pelvis, taking his fingers deeper.

"Yes, motherfucker, yes."

Her clit throbbed. It burned for his touch, but he purposefully neglected it. She slipped her hand between them, to touch herself there.

"Move your fucking hand," he rasped, and her pussy fluttered at the harshness of his tone. "You don't get to touch yourself. You—"

A masked woman with spiked orange hair brushed past them, pulling her naked lover by a leash, his dick swinging as he trailed behind her, his eye locked on the sway of her ass. He was three-feet taller than her, and built like a linebacker.

You wanna nut on my hand?" Sin rasped, unbothered by the couple's presence.

"Yes," Spiked Panties croaked out over a moan.

Two fingers became three.

She cried out over the music, and soaked him with her desire. Sin glanced down at the rigid peaks of her chocolate nipples above the lines of her bustier. He bit back the urge to lean in and suck them into his mouth, bite them.

He hissed out a curse.

Fuck.

Now he wanted his own orgasm. But not with her. Moments later, he withdrew his hand from her wet pussy, raised his drenched fingers to her lips and slid them into her mouth. Breathing hard, she sucked them clean. Then she smiled.

"Imagine what I'd do to your dick."

Sin smirked. "Yeah, baby. Let's imagine." And then he walked off toward the cries of pain and pleasure emanating from various chambers. Some of the chambers looked like miniature dungeons where men and women were chained, naked, to the walls.

He'd even noticed a few of the chambers having medieval-style torture contraptions. *Goddamn, this is some real off the wall shit*, he thought as he continued his stroll. *All types of kinky shit.*

He stopped short at the eighth chamber. His eyes sparked in interest as he let his gaze drift over at a curvy-hipped, redhead lying on a bed, the red sheet beneath her was covered with rose thorns, hundreds and hundreds of them, sharp and piercing. Her hair, shiny red curls, flowed all around her, spilling out onto the bed like flames. Her milky skin glowed against the red sheets.

Covering her face, her mask was laced in gold and featured exotic peacock feathers.

Sin's dick pulsed against the front of his thigh.

As if she'd been waiting for him to appear, she raised her knees to her chest, and then slipped her thong—a string of black lace—to her calves. She smiled. And then boldly spread her bent knees, giving Sin a clear view of a patch of thick, reddish curls covering her pussy. He could barely see her tiny pink clitoris, but it was there, all swollen and glistening.

Sin inhaled, as if he could somehow smell her pungent scent through the glass, and then he swallowed. She stroked her labia, lightly caressing, teasing, herself. And then she took her thumb and index finger to pinch her pussy lips together. That fat, puffy pussy called to him. "Fuck me," she mouthed to him as she smacked her sex until her lips flared. "Fuck me," she mouthed again, running her hands up over her body.

She rolled her hips, and brushed her nipples over and over, then trailed her hand back to her pussy, fingers slowly fluttering to her clit. Sin licked his lips, and the woman moaned on the other side of the glass partition. She ground her hips down into the mattress and felt the bite of the thorns into her ass. Yet she didn't wince.

She groaned.

And in her smoldering eyes was her own wicked need. A deep yearning that called to him. She rocked her hips in time with Rihanna's "Skin".

"Come. Fuck. Me," she slowly mouthed again, dipping a finger into her slit and then winding her hips. Her sex growing wetter as the thorns pricked at her flesh. Sin took in every part of her pretty pink pussy. Another finger slipped inside. And then she was pulling those fingers out of her creamy heat, sliding them into her mouth. Her taste fueled her rampant need for pleasure.

And she cried out to him, her shouts blending in with the music.

Sin nearly groaned. Yet, a guttural moan from another chamber forced him to pry his gaze from the partition. He felt the head of his dick streaming pre-cum. And still he denied her, denied himself, fought back the temptation as Two Feet sang about twisted love, sinking love, about her being that type of girl.

Swoosh!

Swoosh!

The crack of a whip, and then came another piercing cry, and Sin finally walked off; the redhead, the thorns, and her pink creamy cunt quickly forgotten.

FORTY-TWO

"**GRETCHEN, DARLING . . . HOW** are things on the island?" Sin heard Nairobia say as the elevator doors opened and he stepped inside her penthouse.

She was standing in the foyer, again, under the chandelier, as she'd been the first time he'd come to see her here. Waiting to greet him. He'd been to her place several times since his first visit, strictly to discuss the construction of the new club, and what her expectations would be for him as its manager. And she was insistent on him being a part of every single phase of its development. He appreciated the gesture, but found no excitement in the whole process. Floor plans and contractors and meetings with architects held no real interest to him.

This was all her dream, not his.

"Mm, that is fabulous . . . Come, my darling," she said to Sin, motioning for him to come inside. "And the retreat, how are the couples doing . . .?"

Sin greeted her with a kiss to the cheek, and she breathed in his crisp, woody scent, a mixture of cedar and mandarin and leather.

"Darling, Sin just arrived. Shall I give him your regards . . .?"

Nairobia glanced at him. She found him irresistibly sexy in a pair of torn, faded jeans, white T-shirt and a thin leather biker jacket. He'd been in New York for a little over three weeks now, and he'd managed to not give much thought of her, or to reaching out to her. He'd decided it was for the best for the both of them.

To let space and time stay between them.

And, yet, hearing Nairobia say her name caused something in his chest to tighten.

Nairobia gestured for him to take a seat in the formal sitting area. He followed her as she led the way, keeping his eyes on the back of her head, instead of the curve of her hips or her swaying ass. All the while keeping his ear on her conversation with Dr. Dangerfield. He'd wished she'd had the phone call on speaker so that he could hear her on the other end of the line.

"Sounds like another successful journey. I love the work you do, darling. It is all because of you . . . *ja, ja* . . . the retreats have been a success because of your tireless dedication . . . nonsense, my darling. It was your vision, no . . .?"

Nairobia sat on the loveseat. Sin, instead, walked over toward the massive floor-to-ceiling window and looked out over the city.

"You are love, my darling . . . And you deserve good loving in the same fashion you give it, no . . .?"

Sin frowned. *Who was she talking about giving* her *loving to now, and so quickly?* And then he quickly shook the thought from his mind, scolding himself for even questioning it. Of course, she'd be *fucking*—someone else, already. She was an insatiable woman. A woman with wantonly needs, and sweltering desires.

Passionate and vibrant.

Was she fucking Saint now?

"Man, stop this shit. What the fuck is wrong with you?

"Bitches ain't shit, Sin. We are all whores . . ."

Sin swallowed. *Get the fuck out my head!* He thrust a hand through his locs, shaking the voice from his head. He was happy for her, finding someone she could share her life with, her pussy with, her good loving with—if that was in fact what she was doing. *The dick will never be as good as mine.*

It was his ego talking; the irrational, selfish part of his brain that wanted him to believe that he'd always be her greatest, the one lover in her past who'd never be forgotten.

Why the hell you care who fucks her?

Sin felt his chest tighten.

"Yes, my darling . . . you embody the essence of love. It will find its way to you. Trust me . . . And I will be there to greet it with you . . ." Sin swallowed. "Very well, my love. *Ciao.*"

Sin turned from the window as she set her phone on the sofa beside her.

"I am flying out to Vegas tomorrow," she said, rising to her feet, "to meet with the architects." She walked over to a long table and retrieved the most recent floor plans. "You will join me, no?"

Nah, I'm good. "I think I'll stay put, this time," he said coolly. "You know, keep my focus on learning the business."

She unrolled the plans and stared down at the drawings, without giving him a glance. "Very well then." She smiled at the layout. From its high ceilings, the cascading waterfalls to the huge gold chests that would be overflowing with gold-foiled condoms as if they were gold coins, The Pleasure Chest would be like no other club the world had ever seen.

Everything had to be perfect.

"What is on your mind, my darling?" She finally turned to face him, and started rerolling the drawings.

He gave her a confused look. "What makes you think something's wrong?"

"It is in your spirit, darling. You are restless, no?"

Aside from not sleeping through the night, Sin felt fine. He didn't feel any stress or pressure of sorts. "I haven't been sleeping much," he offered. "But other than that, I'm good."

Nairobia stared at him, her gray eyes burning over his skin. "Tell me what is missing?"

Sin frowned, finally taking a seat on the loveseat. *"Missing,* where?"

She shook her head and *tsked* him. "In your life, darling. Do not play coy with me."

He stretched his neck from one side to the other. "I'm being straight up," he said, keeping his tone even. "I'm not sure what it is you're asking." He stretched out his legs. "What is it you think is missing?"

"It is not for me to decide." She moved across the room to retrieve the tube the drawings had been sent in. She slid them down inside the cylinder, and then laid it on the antique table. "Are you not happy?"

What is that? Happiness didn't exist for a man like him. He was content. Sin shifted in his seat. "I'm good."

Nairobia flashed him a look, one that bordered more on sympathy than understanding. "Being good, my darling . . . is not being happy."

"Then what is?" he asked, leaning forward in his seat and resting his arms on his knees. He truly wanted to know.

Nairobia took the seat across from him. "Happiness is what you decide it to be."

"And what if you don't know what that is?"

"Then, my love," she said, crossing her legs so that the long slit of her dress opened, showcasing her thigh, "fate will decide for you."

Sin simply stared at her, wondering why the hell she hadn't mentioned anything about Dr. Dangerfield and whether or not she'd sent him her regards.

Obviously, he decided after several ticking seconds, because she hadn't.

FORTY-THREE

IT'D TAKEN HIM two months, but Sin had managed to quickly acquaint himself with most of New York's nightlife. And, tonight, he found himself sitting in Nightcaps—a trendy underground lounge in SoHo, a neighborhood in lower Manhattan, with all of its high-end boutique hotels, art galleries, luxury shopping, and fine dining.

He was seated on a barstool at the long bar that covered the entire length of the space, having shots of Jose. He was trying desperately to fit into this world, his new life, while trying to keep the purpose for being here, in New York, in perspective. But he felt nothing. No connection. No will to be here any longer than he had to be.

And he hoped Vegas would be different. Soon.

But, until then, he would do what he always did. Go through the motions. And perhaps have his wicked way with some unsuspecting, horny soul looking to unleash her dark hunger.

Nightcaps had a speakeasy vibe, hidden down in the basement level of a popular restaurant, with its dim lighting, flickering candles, and plush oversized couches and chairs.

The place was filled with beautiful women of varying shapes, sizes, and skin tones. And, along with the Wall Street and corporate lawyer types, most of the gym-bodied men looked like they were straight off the covers of *GQ* and *Playgirl*.

Tory Lanez's "Henny in Hand" poured out of the lounge's hidden speakers as Sin sipped on his drink. He glanced around the space and spotted a cocoa-brown woman sporting a short sassy pixie-style haircut at the other end of the bar. Sexy, he thought as the woman's eyes cut over in his direction, and for a moment their gazes locked. She was five feet, eight inches, but she stood taller in her four-inch heels. She wore a short skirt with a blouse that crisscrossed and tied in the back.

Her tongue traced over her cherry-red painted lips.

Damn.

And then she was weaving her way through the throng of men and women who were milling about, drinking very expensive drinks and socializing.

When she reached him, she sidled up on the barstool next to him. "I saw you staring at me," she said, staring directly into his eyes. "So, I figured I'd save you the trouble of stalking me from afar."

Sin laughed. "I don't stalk, baby. I admire."

She shrugged. "Same difference." She turned her attention to the bartender when he came to take her order. "I'll have what he's having."

Sin smirked. "You sure you can hang?"

She tilted her head and pursed her lips. "I'm a Scorpio, boo. I can *hang* with the best of 'em."

"And so am I," he said. "Now what?"

She pursed her lips. "Lucky you." When the bartender returned with her drink, she lifted it to her lips. "Take note," she said, tossing her head back and draining her glass.

"My kind of woman," Sin said over another smile as he eyed her as she motioned to the bartender with her finger to bring over another.

"Are you looking to get drunk?" he asked over the music.

She eyed him again. "I'm looking to get nice. And you?"

"I'm already nice." He glanced down into her cleavage. "I'd rather be nasty."

Now it was her turn to smile. "That's the only way to be. Isn't it?"

"Most definitely." And then he raised his glass. "To getting nasty." They both drained their drinks. Without prompting, the bartender knew to keep their glasses full as they got better acquainted.

"Is New York your home?"

"No. Jersey," she said.

"Oh, okay. So, what brings you out tonight? You looking for a man?"

"No. I already have one," she said. "I'm getting married in three weeks."

Sin gave her a solemn look as the bartender slid them another round. He lifted his glass to her. "Should I congratulate you, or give you my condolences?"

She flashed him a smile, and then clicked her glass to his. "He's a good man."

"And yet you're here—*alone.*"

"There's no crime in that," she said, eyeing him over the rim of her drink. She allowed her gaze to shamelessly wander up and down his body, before settling back on his face. "But you're sadly mistaken. I'm not alone, *now.* I'm here with you. Talking."

Sin grinned. "That you are, beautiful. You looking for some excitement?"

"I'm already excited. But I love exploring my dark, sultry side more. You love a tongue in your ass?" she boldly asked.

Sin laughed, nearly choking on his drink. He reached for a napkin from off the bar and wiped his mouth. "Nah, baby. Can't say that I do."

She raised an arched brow, and then tilted her head. "A shame."

He narrowed his eyes. "You're a li'l freak, huh?"

Her tongue flicked over her top lip. "I like pushing the envelope."

Sin liked her. "Is that so?"

"Yes."

He grinned. "You're on the prowl."

"Maybe," she said; her tongue flicked over the rim of her glass.

"It wasn't a question."

She batted her lashes. "I didn't think it was."

He put his empty glass on the bar. "And yet you're about to be married."

She took another sip from her drink. "He has my heart, but my body belongs to me. I do with it what I want, with whom I want."

"Ah, okay. Open relationship?"

She shook her head. "No. Opened legs when I want them to be, whenever the urges strike me."

Sin swiveled his stool in her direction, his legs spread open, giving her a full view of his crotch, an offering for the night, if she wanted. "And tonight, what urges are you experiencing?"

She glanced down in his lap, and then allowed her eyes to lift to his face. There, his dark, pensive eyes snared her, and Sin saw the lust in her eyes. She straightened her posture, her breasts springing forward in her form-fitting top. She felt the tequila sluicing through her veins, warming her, heating her low in her belly, straight down to her pussy.

"Depends."

Sin eyed her as she set her drink up on the bar, and then reached inside her purse, pulling out a tube of lip glass. She painted her full kissable lips with the shiny shellac, and then pressed them together.

Sin grinned. "What if I told you I wanted to finger you, right here? Would you let me?"

Her eyes lit with interest. "I dare you."

He kept grinning. "My name is Sin, baby."

"And I don't think you have it in you," she shot back.

"You don't know me, beautiful." His low voice sent a chill up her spine. "I dare do a lot of things, real *nasty* things." He ran his finger over her hip, boldly invading her space without care, without regard, for who might see.

Her eyes glittered, desire coiling around her body. She wanted to sling her drink into his handsome face, and then lick him clean. Everything about him was pushing her desire dangerously higher.

"So, can I finger you?" He stuck his middle finger, just the tip, into his mouth and then quickly pulled it out, suggestively waggling it as he swiveled his bar stool, causing his knee to lightly bump hers. A jolt of electricity surged its way up her leg, right to her center.

"You are so disrespectful."

"Not my intention. Tell me to stop. And I will." He swiveled back toward the bar.

"No," she said, placing a hand on his knee.

Sin smiled at her, his dreamy brown eyes becoming more intense as he stared at her. "Why not?"

She felt the warmth of arousal swelling inside her body. She swallowed. Then spoke as if she were a sinner at confessional, "Because I can tell you're a real nasty motherfucker. And my curiosity won't let me."

"I promise I won't kill the cat"—he glanced pointedly at her crotch— "I'll just stroke and pet it."

My God. But with the booze sloshing through her body, the devil propped up on her shoulder, and her panties now wet, she was too disoriented by desire, by fascination, by the slow sweet throb in the pit of her pussy, to resist him. And yet she had promised herself she'd only come out to have a few cocktails, maybe flirt a bit, and then head home to her man, where she planned to fuck him and his long West Indian dick all night.

She was trying to be good. Trying to be faithful. Trying to keep her legs shut, and her tongue out of another man's mouth. But her dark urges made it difficult.

And this man—

"Turn back toward the bar," Sin said, twisting his stool so that he was facing her as they spoke. Her heart beating in her ears, she did as instructed. "I want you to look at me."

He reached over and ran a hand up the inside of her skirt, stared deep in her eyes and smiled. "I bet you taste sweet," he murmured. His lower lip was wet. He licked it. And now she wanted to lean in and lick over it too.

"Are your panties wet?"

"Find out for yourself," she murmured, brazenly. And then he boldly caressed the inner part of her thigh, his eyes flickering heat. Her skin was warm. Her breath puffed as he held her gaze, his hand creeping up to the top of her thigh. He smiled when he reached her thong and found it drenched.

He stroked her there, and she nearly toppled off her barstool.

She knew she was a slutty bitch, who loved doing freaky shit, especially with a sexy chocolate motherfucker who could match her nasty. She felt her skin overheating the closer his hand climbed up her thigh.

She opened her mouth. He lifted a finger. "Don't say a word. Just nod. Okay?" He petted her wet panties, leisurely, skillfully. "It's just you and me. Ignore everyone else around you."

She swallowed, closed her eyes and nodded.

"Spread your legs for me," he said, lowering his voice so it could only be heard over the din of conversation and music.

"Don't start what you—"

He stopped her with his finger slipping in between the leg of her panties, his probing finger brushing over her clit, and suddenly she was gasping for air.

Leaning in, he whispered, "See I knew you were naughty. See how wet you are."

She nodded.

"It wasn't a question." His thick finger slipped inside her pussy, and she nearly spilled over her drink. An open hand on the bar, her nails curled into the granite slab. She threw her head back and clawed at the bar, squirmed in her seat and moved against his hand.

"Yeah, that's it. Fuck yourself on my hand. Give into it. Soak my fingers with this warm, juicy pussy."

"*Aah*—"

"Careful, nasty girl. They'll hear you." He pulled his finger out and pinched her clit, and she gasped. Then panted, hovering over the edge when he said, "Let me fuck you deep, beautiful. Let me give you a night you'll never forget, before you run off and get married. Would you like that? Me, you, and this big hard dick?"

She nodded, and groaned.

Satisfied, he freed his hand from her wet clutch, and turned a crooked smile to her. "Let's ditch this place."

"Let's," she said saucily. She took his hand, and then boldly sucked his fingers into her mouth. When she was done, she licked her lips.

"I didn't get your name," he finally said as he helped her off her barstool.

"I didn't give it. But you can call me Pain," she said, huskily. And then she was leading him toward the exit. And, in less than ten minutes, they were in the garage's parking lot. Naked. In the backseat of her tinted Range Rover, going at it like two horny teenagers. Hot and hard, Sin rode her G-spot, angling her hips so that his dick stroked over every part of her inner flesh. Her sheath clutched him, wetly, greedily as he bucked and thrust into her.

She gasped and welcomed him, absorbing every part of him, throwing her head from side to side, mewling, screaming, crying out, begging for him, for it—harder, faster, deeper. And he delivered, each thrust more powerful than the last. He was much more long-winded than she had imagined, delivering toe-curling stroke after another, causing her to shudder in delight. Ooh, the dick was good. Random dick always did it for her. It fed the slutty part of her soul.

She wrapped her legs tightly around his waist and sunk her nails into his flexing ass muscles. "Gut my pussy, you nasty fucker," she hissed, and then she rocked her hips in time with his strokes.

All thoughts escaped her, a heartbeat away from another orgasm. She saw stars.

Orgasm swept her up in another breathless frenzy.

Sin grunted, then quickly pulled out and snatched off his condom and tossed it to the floorboard of her SUV as he rapidly stroked his dick multiple times and exploded, his orgasm gushing out in thick streams of heat that jetted out over the woman's head, then onto her face, her neck, her breasts. His seeds scorching her flesh and the leather seat beneath her as she moaned and writhed.

FORTY-FOUR

A SENSUAL TUNE melted over the dance floor as bodies bumped and grinded erotically to its beat. Overactive libidos were in overdrive.

Temptation swirled all around Sin.

All this sucking and fucking, all this pussy and ass and beautiful breasts on display, made it difficult to *not* have an erection. But Sin managed to keep his hard dick in check in spite of the eroticism around him. Still, the temptation was real and never-ending.

The Pleasure Zone was a freak's never-ending sexual playground, and as badly as he wanted to throw some sexy-ass, masked woman over one of the leather sofas and give her a hard, balls-deep pounding, he had to keep reminding himself of why he was here.

Work.

He'd been shadowing the club's manager over the last several months and, quite frankly, it was turning out to be more work than he had expected. The hardest part being unable to revel in the debauchery around him.

The sights, the sounds, the smells . . . it all licked at his libido. And, as much as he enjoyed watching all the beautifully exotic-looking women unleashing their hidden, freaky desires, all of the erotic visions and sexual energy floating around him was slowly driving him nuts.

He wanted to *fuck*.

He wanted to *forget*.

Forget about his throbbing dick, forget about his need for pussy, forget about his need to nut, forget about his need for some sense of calm; forget about what he'd had back on Passion Island.

Peace of mind.

Truth was, a big part of him missed the warmth of the sun, and the smell of fresh coconuts and hibiscus. He missed his runs along the pristine beach's shoreline, the peace and quiet he found being on the island.

New York was too loud. This club was even louder.

And now a part of him was beginning to second-guess his decision to come here. But he wasn't planning on reneging on his agreement with Nairobia, especially not after she'd sweetened the deal by offering him an additional hundred-grand a year on top of what they'd already agreed on once the club in Vegas opened.

The money alone was too good to pass up. And the opportunities were endless. And the decision to move forward in his life had been made.

Bottom line, there was no turning back. And there was no sense in dwelling on what had been. What counted was what he chose to do in this moment. And he decided to enjoy the ride for as long as it lasted, and then move onto whatever other adventure life presented him.

Wearing a pair of black jeans and the club's signature black V-neck T-shirt, with the words THE PLEASURE ZONE scrawled across his chest, Sin sauntered through the club, the muscles in his chest flexing as he weaved in and out of the crowd toward the glass-encased elevators.

When the doors opened, he stepped in. Seconds later, the elevator stopped, and then quietly slid open on the fourth floor, where Sin stepped out, making his way down the carpeted corridor, passing several *play*rooms. He found himself wanting to find a way to become immune to the incessant moaning and groaning and animalistic mewling.

All around him were men and women fucking—lots and lots of fucking. All he saw whenever he walked through the club at any given time were tongues—licking over pussies, over clits, over puckering assholes, tongues swirling around nipples and hard dicks.

Instead of stopping to take in the salacious action, he kept his eyes forward, walking past a condom and lube station on the right of him, followed by the Cognac lounge, where whirls of cigar smoke floated around the space. To the right of him, a trap soul song—some pussy-popping anthem—seeped out from the beneath the closed door of what had been coined as the Stripper Room, where horny men and women embraced their wannabe-stripper alter egos.

Sin glanced at the time on his watch. It was almost three in the morning and, with only three hours left before the doors closed, and yet the club showed no signs of slowing down, or thinning out, any time soon. The later it got, the thicker the sexual energy became, the hungrier the club-goers became for more untamed pleasures.

This shit is crazy. He made a quick left down another hall, then stood in front of thick sliding glass doors. *Don't these freaky muhfuckas ever sleep?*

He shook his head.

To the right of the door was a keypad. He punched in his four-digit passcode.

Seconds later, the doors slid open and he stepped through, the doors swooshing shut behind him. The red painted walls and red lights shining overhead were dramatic, yet sensual.

The area was soundproofed and the only area where he could hear himself think. He hadn't had a moment of down time from the moment he walked through the club's doors, nearly five hours ago.

He breathed in the quietness momentarily. And then he sighed, finally removing his silk mask as he made his way toward a set of offices.

He walked into the largest of the three. The door had been open, which meant it was cool to walk in.

Behind a large sleek, glass and chrome desk, Sin found Josiah shuffling through a pile of invoices and membership applications. Despite the club's expensive price tag, its membership continued to soar exponentially. From high-profiled politicians and television personalities to professional athletes and Academy-award winning actors, the club's membership roster was filled with a long, illustrious list of freaks.

"Man, with all that ass out there. How do you do it?" Sin asked as he walked further into the office.

Josiah looked up from the keys of his MacBook, rubbing his eyes. "How do I do what?" He eyed Sin as he plunked down on the red leather sofa.

"Stay holed up in here, instead of"—he gestured with his head toward the door, stretching his long legs out— "being out there getting in on the action?"

He shrugged. "Self-control, basically. I've been around it for so long that I'm mostly immune to it." He glanced in the direction of several surveillance monitors strategically placed in his office for viewing every inch of the club, so that nothing went unnoticed. "I care a lot more about building my reputation, than busting a nut in one of the members."

Sin shook his head, scrubbing a hand over his face. "Yeah, I hear you. But"—he whistled— "damn. Night after night—this shit is torturous."

Sin let out his breath in a long exhale, running his hands over his locs, pulling them to the nape of his neck. He tightened his grip.

"Should I remind you of house rule *numero uno*?"

"Nah, I got it," he muttered. "Never engage in sexual acts with any of the members."

"Exactly." Josiah narrowed his gaze. "And, bro, I'm telling

you—you'd be wise to adhere to it. The last thing you want is to get caught up in some workplace drama."

Sin unfolded his body from the plush leather, rising to his feet. "Yeah, I hear you."

He eyed Josiah as he pressed a button on a remote, zooming in on a curvy brunette, wearing a black mask with multifaceted colored stones. She was on the third floor, bent over an oversized burnt-orange sofa, a dick in her mouth, a dick slicing into the back of her pussy.

"Trust me, man," Josiah said. "You wanna get a nut, look into one of these monitors, and rub one out in one of the spare offices." He opened a bottom drawer in his desk and pulled out a pink box. "And when you do, use this." He tossed the box to Sin.

Sin frowned, catching it in midair. He stared at the image of Nairobia's half-naked body wrapped around the box like wrapping paper.

"What's this?"

"Nairobia's portable Chocolate Pussy. It has a rechargeable battery, and a four-speed setting."

Sin laughed. "Man, you're crazy."

"Laugh if you want. I'm telling you, man. Warm the removable sleeve up, add some of that Pleasure gel, and"—he shook his head, then shuddered— "I promise you, that right there is the truth."

Sin continued laughing. "Whatever you say, man. I'm out." And with that, Sin headed for the door with his new Chocolate Pussy tucked under his arm.

Just in case he was ever in need of an emergency release.

FORTY-FIVE

With shopping bags in hand, Sin slid his keycard into the door, and stepped inside his suite once he heard the lock click open. He tossed the key card on the credenza and then headed into the living room. He'd been out for hours in and out of Flagship stores on Fifth Avenue in search of something to wear to a formal affair Nairobia had invited—on second thought, summoned—him to.

He disliked suits and ties, so being stuffed in some penguin suit wasn't going to happen. But he eventually settled on Versace—all black, from his jacket, shirt, and pants right down to his underwear and socks. The black patent leather Ferragamo slip-ons would set the ensemble off. He'd spent a small fortune on the ensemble, but he'd step up in that piece *GQ* down.

Dropping his bags on the sofa, he divested himself of his leather jacket, tossing it over the back of the suite's loveseat, and then he kicked off his boots and stripped down into his boxers, before walking over to the window and staring outside. He hadn't been to The Pleasure Zone in over a week, for no other reason than just not feeling it. He was getting restless. And feeling trapped. Something he'd feared would happen.

The days and weeks were haphazardly colliding into one another, and now it was the first week of November. As a result, Daylight Saving Time had ended, and the skies darkened early. And with that came chilly weather, something he wasn't looking forward to. All he knew was, the weather in New York could be brutal and unforgiving.

Sin sighed. It'd been a long-ass day, and now all he wanted to do was take a long, hot shower, and chill before he had to be ready. The party started at ten, but he'd opted to be fashionably late and had asked Nairobia to have her driver pick him up at eleven.

He muttered a curse as he stared out of the suite's living room window because he hadn't given complete thought as to how he'd manage the City's approaching winter months. Fighting through its biting cold, and sloshing through slush and snow wasn't exactly what he'd had in mind when he'd agreed to come here. Truth was, he'd hoped to be in Vegas by now. And yet Nairobia's new sex club was *still* nowhere near completion. Something about codes and politics, shit he had no concerns with.

Pensively, Sin stared out at nothing in particular, and emitted a weary sigh. The moon shone bright, casting a glow over Central Park, and yet all he saw was darkness.

He shoved a hand through his locs, then finally stepped away from the window and headed toward the bedroom. The hairs on the back of his neck stood on end. He put his hand at his nape and rubbed as he entered the bedroom.

He flipped on the light and was startled by what he saw.

Jennifer—naked, her back up against the headboard, her hips moving against the bed as she stared over at him through half-lidded eyes. She greeted him with her musky scent and a smile.

He blinked.

What the fuck?

She wet her lips. "Hey, Big Daddy," she murmured, her hand slinking between her spread legs. "I've brought you room service." And then she spread her legs wider. Her clit poked out from its hood, firm and hard, like a thrusting pistil among wet, thickened petals. "I've been thinking about you making love to me all day. I think I'm becoming addicted to you. All I want to do is be fucked by you."

Sin frowned. He wasn't impressed by her attempt of seducing him. He wasn't the least bit turned on by the sight of her. He had no desire to touch her, taste her, or fuck her.

Truth was, he'd already fucked her twice. Big mistake.

Still, had he'd been in the mood, had this been someone else, perhaps under different circumstances his dick might have swelled against his thigh. But this shit right here was an unwelcomed invasion of his space. And his dick was as limp as a wet noodle.

And yet for a long moment he simply stood there staring at the deep pink peaks of her breasts, before he finally spoke. "Yo, what the fuck are you doing?" Then he shook his head for asking the obvious.

Her face went slack, the blood in her cheeks draining, and then her lips quivered as she threw her arms up over her breasts. "I-I thought you'd be happy to . . . you know, be surprised to find me here." Her breath came in shallow gasps as she looked at him.

Sin fought to not breathe in her scent, but there it was. Clinging thickly in the air. He swore under his breath, flexing his fingers back and forth. He wanted to snatch her by her shoulders and shake the living shit out of her. Instead, he curled his fingers into his palms to keep from choking her.

He scrubbed a hand over his head and breathed in a steadying breath, he caught himself before he slipped and called her the B-word. "I am surprised. But I'm not happy," he said, fighting to rein in the bite in his tone. He walked over to the chair in the corner of the room and grabbed her uniform and her silky undergarments and tossed them over at her, her panties floating like pink wings as they fluttered to the bed. "You need to put your clothes on, and leave."

She blinked in shock, and directly on its heels came embarrassment and regret. He didn't want to fuck her. How could she have been so damn stupid sneaking up here? She'd been certain they'd had a connection.

She closed her eyes, tears stinging her lids.

"I-I'm sorry," she stammered, finally opening her eyes and then scrambling to her feet. "I'm such an idiot." She fastened her bra in front of her then twisted it around her body until its clasp was at her back. She waited a beat. "I thought we had lots of sexual chemistry. Was I misreading the connection?"

Sin watched as she packed her breasts inside each C-cup, almost feeling sorry for her. Maybe he'd come off a bit harsh, he thought. But then he thought better of it. Fuck no. She was moving like he was her man. Getting the dick twice didn't give her carte blanche to creep into his suite whenever her pussy tingled.

Sin kept staring at her, his jaw set. "Whatever connection you feel, it isn't reciprocated," he said honestly. "And it damn sure isn't real. If I mislead you in anyway, I'm sorry. But I'm not here to get tangled up in an affair. And I'm not looking for drama."

"Are you going to report me?" She swallowed. "I won't blame you if you did?"

"Look," he said softly. "Let's forget this ever happened. Just get the fuck out, okay? I'll wait for you to finish dressing in the other room."

She nodded as she slipped into her blouse and then haphazardly slid her pants over her hips, mindlessly leaving her panties behind.

Sin walked over toward the window and stared out at Central Park again, and then he paced the floor, wondering what the fuck was wrong with him. There'd been a beautiful, buck-ass naked woman in his bed, offering up the pussy and he'd turned it down—wet, tight pussy at that.

Maybe I should let her suck this dick one last time for the road. Yeah, let her take it to the back of her throat and suck out this nut.

He could let her caress his dick with her tongue.

Nah, fuck that. That broad is obviously nutty enough.

Sin glanced over and eyed her as she finally came out of the bedroom. She dropped her heels to the carpeted floor and then shoved her feet into them, shame painted all over her face. *Good.* She should feel fucked up, he thought as he walked her to the door, and then held it open. *Crazy-ass.*

"It'll never happen again," she whispered, sheepishly.

"Cool," was all he said as he watched her tromp down the hall, before slamming the door shut. He should have been relieved she was gone, but the empty suite and the growing ache in his balls suddenly made him angry.

He wanted to fuck. Hard. Bust his dick inside something warm, tight, and extremely wet. But what he wanted, what he craved, wasn't anywhere near.

That, alone, pissed him off.

And he had no one else to blame but himself.

FORTY-SIX

AT EXACTLY TEN p.m., a black Rolls Royce pulled up to the curb of Sin's hotel. The driver stepped out and then briskly walked around the vehicle to open the rear passenger side door.

The driver, who identified himself as Samson, tipped his hat. "Mr. Saint-Michaels?" he greeted.

"The one and only," Sin said light-heartedly. He was in a shitty mood and didn't feel up to being out, but he'd convinced himself a night out mingling around the rich and freaky was what he needed to shake himself out of this sudden funk.

The driver gave a slight nod of his head. "Ms. Jansen has sent me to drive you to your destination." He held open the door.

"Appreciate that," Sin said as he slid into the backseat." He sank into the butter-soft leather and inhaled the cabin's smell in appreciation as the driver closed the door.

As they pulled off from the curb, Sin gazed out the tinted windows. He sighed inwardly. He was thankful for breathing, for being on earth to live his life. But he was beginning to feel like he wasn't *alive*.

This wasn't his world. He didn't fit. And he knew he was fooling himself into thinking that he could, happily, become a part of it.

He was a misfit.

Being here, driven in this chauffeured car, in these expensive-ass clothes, his feet stuffed in a pair of overrated loafers that were already hurting the top of his feet, all felt fake to him, and he didn't want any part of it.

The shit was becoming exhausting, and downright sad. And the painful truth of the matter was, it took this very moment, peering out of the window, watching the streets whir by for him to realize that he had no real purpose in his life. And he wanted it. He wanted a reason to stay put somewhere. Someplace where he could finally feel at home.

But he couldn't think about it right now though. He had to shake off this foul mood and get his mind in party mode.

He rubbed his forehead, feeling a slow throb beginning to bloom into a full headache. It was the last thing he needed. All he wanted to do was lose himself inside some pussy. He didn't want to have to think. Just fuck. Fucking didn't require thought. All it required was his hard dick and lots of hip thrusts.

Maybe tonight he'd get lucky. Connect with one of Nairobia's freaky guests—preferably from out of town, someone he wouldn't have to run into again—and then give her nine thick reasons to give herself to him—all night.

Yeah, that's what he needed. Or did he? There was a time when sex was all he needed, all he ever thought about. But now it didn't consume him the way it used to.

If he were being perfectly honest with himself, meaningless sex was starting to feel overrated. Shit. Who was he kidding?

It *was* overrated.

But so were relationships.

Weren't they?

"Have you ever wondered what it would feel like to be in love?"

He frowned.

Love wasn't in his DNA.

Lust was all he knew.

Sex was all he knew.

Fucking was all he knew.

Sin couldn't believe he was actually sitting here thinking about all this. The fact that he was trying to envision a life being committed to someone outside of more than a fuck or fling went against everything he believed in.

Yeah, he was definitely losing his mind.

Opening yourself to someone, allowing oneself to be vulnerable, came with choices. Consequences. Sometimes disappointment crept in, not always flowing or ebbing. There were risks. And rewards. Sometimes it all swirled together, drifting dangerously into a burst of vividly painful colors. But it took courage, unwavering determination, to embrace the challenge, both feet firmly planted. Loving someone was a choice, not always conscious, not always easy.

He'd never shared that sentiment. The idea of coming home to the same woman, the same pussy, day in and day out seemed monotonous, tiresome, and . . . *boring.*

He hadn't been interested. He preferred a revolving door of women—preferably ones who were nameless and easily forgotten—rather than having one woman trying to smother and trap him.

But now, it sounded rather pathetic.

As the car moved through Manhattan, Dr. Dangerfield's words about running from himself kept coming back to him. Maybe running was all he'd been doing. Maybe running was what had saved him from himself. Or maybe it simply kept him sane.

"You're running from the idea of ever getting close to a woman. Commitment scares you. The thought that you can feel something other than lust for a woman frightens you. It makes you feel out of control, doesn't it, Sin?"

Spine stiffening, Sin winced at her words. What she'd said that night in the restaurant held truth. But, either way, he was now starting to feel tired from running. He was getting old—*er.* That glaring reminder had come to him while he was standing in the mirror staring at his reflection in the mirror while he brushed his teeth this evening. And all he saw staring back at him was another version of himself: an old, lonely man. Sad.

He shook the image from his head, and tried to focus his attention out the window. But his mind kept wandering back to Dr. Dangerfield. The way she laughed. The way she smiled. The way she tilted her head in question. And—God help him, the way she tasted. Why had he let her into his space?

Because—

The sound of Darion Ja'Von's voice poured out through the speakers. "Too Late" began playing and Sin suddenly found his thoughts replaced by the lyrics of the song.

"I cannot replace your lips and the way that they taste . . ."

Sin closed his lids, and pinched the insides of his eyes together.

"Is it too late . . .?"

He felt his stomach knotting. He'd never lived with regret. No woman controlled him, his mind, his dick. And yet Dr. Dangerfield had somehow been able to make him want to give up control.

All this time, he thought he wanted more, but all along he'd already had all he needed. His life had been complete, or so he thought until this very second.

Sin hated to admit it, but what he needed, what he wanted, what he craved, wasn't in New York City. It wasn't in Vegas. It wasn't running some sex club. It wasn't in the company of Nairobia or any of her freaky, exotic friends.

It was—

"Yo, what's good, my beauties, cuties, hookers, hoes, pimps, and playboys, it's ya boy, Mar*Sell*, coming at you live 'n' direct with another steamy night of *Creepin' 'n' Freakin' After Dark* . . ."

Sin shifted in his seat.

"If you're just tuning in, Wel*Cum*. You already know how it goes down here at 93.3 The heat: hot, raw 'n' ohhhhh so nassssy . . . So, drop them drawz, sit back . . . relax . . . light a candle . . . pour yourself a glass of your favorite bubbly 'n' prepare to be stimulated beyond your own imagination as we get into tonight's segment: Good lovin'.

"That's right my, freaky peeps. You heard it right. Good lovin'. And, tonight, we're gonna delve into what good lovin' is, what it feels like. So, holla at ya boy 1-212-FreakMe . . ." A few seconds later a female caller was on the line. "Yo, what's good, beauty . . . you're on the air with ya boy, Mar*Sell*. Whom am I speaking to 'n' where you calling from?"

"Oooh, *yassss*, godda—*bleep*—it. It's Cassandra, from Brick City, sugah-boo. It's about time you picked up for me with ya fine, big di—*bleep*—ck self. You coons stay doin' me. I've been tryin' to get me some airtime wit' you for weeks."

The radio personality laughed. "Well, you got me now, baby. So, tell us. What's your definition of good lovin'?"

"*Mmph,*" the caller grunted. "Good lovin' is when the dingaling makes the cootie-coo whistle 'n' you start skeetin' 'n' pootin' at the same damn time. And then he lays them good coins in ya purse, happy you spread it wide 'n' low for him."

What the fuck?

Sin frowned.

"Sounds like gold-diggin' to me, baby." The radio personality sighed audibly over the airwaves, ending the call. "Next caller, you're on the air."

"Yo, what's good, my nigg—*bleep*—a? It's ya boy, Supreme, from Long Island. Yo, that broad you just had on was wildin' son. Nutting 'n' farting, word? Yo, where they doin' that at? Nasty ass. She sounded ratchet as hell."

"Man, what can I say? She's livin' in her truth, playboy. Now tell us yours."

"Man, good lovin' is when a b—*bleep*—itch got you wantin' to climb up in that sh—*bleep*—it 'n' lay up in it all night. It got ya heart beatin' hard 'n' you seein' stars 'n' shit 'n' thinkin' about killin' a muhfuc—*beep*—kah for even tryna think he can get what's yours. That good lovin' make a muhfu—*bleep*—kah wanna set her wig on fire if she even try'n leave. It'll make you wanna cut out the cookie 'n' carry it in ya pocket so no one else can't get it. Ya heard?"

Sin cringed inwardly, shaking his head. He didn't need to listen to this dumb shit. He knew without question what good loving was. He'd had lots of good pussy in his life, but good loving went much deeper that what was between a woman's legs. It was in the chemistry, in the connection, in the touch. It was selfless. It was loaded in the way a woman looked at you; in the way she gave herself to you.

Sin swallowed. And then he felt his chest tighten.

What the fuck was I thinking?

He didn't know what was happening, but he finally had clarity as to what he needed, what he desired, what he longed for, what he'd been denying himself. What he'd been too afraid of allowing in his life.

Sin groaned as he tapped on the glass partition of the privacy window, and waited for it to slide down. "Yo, my man," he prompted, his chest burning. "Turn around. Take me back to the hotel."

"Sir?" the driver said, adjusting his rearview mirror and meeting Sin's eyes.

"Take me back to the hotel," he repeated. "And hurry. It's an emergency."

"Very well, Sir." And then he floored it, weaving in and out of traffic and through intersections. And as the car made a left turn, then a right, before racing through a yellow light, heading back in the direction it'd come, Sin held his hands in tight fists, certain he was going completely out of his mind.

When the driver finally arrived at the hotel, Sin was already hopping out before the car had a chance to pull to a complete stop, hoping like hell he wasn't too late.

FORTY-SEVEN

"SIN," DR. DANGERFIELD said, startled by the sight of him. In haste, he'd come back. Not wanting to travel on Nairobia's dime, he'd booked a last-minute flight to Fiji, and then caught the ferry to the island. It'd been an expensive and very long journey, but well worth every dollar spent. But none of that had mattered. He would have gladly blown his whole life savings if he'd had to.

Dr. Dangerfield blinked, taking him in. And then she shook herself free of any thoughts of how damn fine he was. She wasn't about to let this sexy *fucker* blur her focus. She'd almost allowed that to happen, once before. And look where that'd almost gotten her—all up in her feelings. But she'd had herself to blame for that. However, she'd forgiven herself for that mishap. And she promised herself that she wouldn't let it happen again.

Yet she felt heat washing over her as her gaze soaked him in. But she shook it off, and something clicked in her mind, flicking on her other switch. The therapist. The clinician. Not the woman whose loins ached for the loving caress of a man. *This* man. No, she would not allow herself to be *that* type of woman.

She shut her file cabinet. "What are you doing here?"

Damn, she's still pissed. "Hey," he said, sheepishly. He'd grovel if he had to, he decided. And then he grinned. "You busy?"

She tilted her head. "Maybe," she said, the word sounding garbled in the back of her throat.

"Can I come in?" he asked, ignoring the statement.

"Make an appointment," she said, only half joking.

His smile widened and for a moment she forgot to breathe. Damn him.

"Yeah, okay. I'm still coming in." He stepped further into her office, gently shutting the door behind him. "With*out* an appointment."

She shrugged. "Suit yourself."

He stopped several feet away from her, and then spread out his long arms. "Can I get a hug?"

"Not without an appointment," she said plainly. And then she rolled her eyes at him. How dare he show his face after being gone for nearly four months without a single word? No phone call; no telegram, nothing. And then he showed up in all of his fineness empty-goddamn-handed. And, yeah, she could have reached out to him, could have called or texted him. But that was beside the point. Where were her roses, or her beautifully wrapped box of "I'm-sorry"?

She had the mind to question him about it, but then thought better of it. It was better to feign indifference when it came to men like him.

He stalked closer. "You've missed me. I can see it all in your face."

Her eyebrow went up and then she stared him down. Cocky bastard. "No. What you see is a woman busy. Now if you'll excuse yourself. I have things to do."

He smirked. "Not until I get my hug." And then he was wrapping those thick arms of his around her, pressing her warm, soft body into the wall of his chest.

It was then she let out the breath she didn't realize she'd been holding in her lungs. She breathed him in, deeply. Not seeing him for all those months had done nothing to fan out the torch she still held for him.

And, for Sin, having her in his arms only solidified what he'd been trying to ignore, what he'd been trying to avoid.

He missed her. More than he'd wanted to admit.

He inhaled, then groaned inwardly. Damn she smelled good. Felt good, too.

Dr. Dangerfield pushed back from him, prying herself from his embrace. She moved to the other side of the room, to put space between them. She needed space, needed more air to breathe. His presence, his overpowering masculinity and sensuality, was suddenly suffocating her, making her feel claustrophobic.

She stared at him with questioning eyes.

"What are you doing here?" she asked. "Don't you have a *club* to manage?"

Sin shoved his hands down into his front pockets. No woman had this kind of effect on him the way she did. And he had his growing arousal to prove it.

"Nah," he said. "Construction won't be completed for another six months."

She tilted her head. "Okay. So why are you *here?*" She sat on the edge of her desk, crossing her legs at the ankles. Sin's gaze dropped to the red-lacquered soles of her four-inch white booties—the word LOVE printed on the side in multi-colored letters, the irony not lost on him. It was a word he'd never used, a word he'd struggled to recall hearing as a child, a word he'd always felt disconnected from, and yet the word now had meaning to him.

Damn, she looks hella good, he thought as his eyes took in her white jumper, the way the expensive material molded over her hips, without clinging too tightly.

It was a perfectly sexy fit. Like she was.

"Well," she said, bringing him back to her question. And then she folded her arms over her breasts, in an attempt to hide her protruding nipples. They suddenly ached.

His gaze met her questioning one. "I left something behind," he said coolly. "Had to come back to claim it, before someone else got their hands on it."

Her brow rose. "So, *you* flew thousands of miles just to come back for this *thing?*"

"Yeah."

Her head tilted again, in disbelief. "And you mean to tell me you couldn't find *any*one to ship it to you?"

"Nah." He stalked closer, pinned her with his stare. The intensity in his eyes made her shiver. "What I came for is too precious, too valuable, to trust anyone else with."

His fingertips touched her temple as he brushed her bang off her forehead.

"Aren't you gonna ask me what this thing is?"

She shook her head. "No. It's none of my business. And quite frankly I don't care to know."

He smirked. "That's too bad." He brushed her cheek with the back of his finger, and she swallowed. "But I'm gonna tell you anyway," he murmured, his gaze was heavy, thick-lashed. "I came back for your heart."

"Well isn't that—"

Wait. She blinked in surprise. Had she heard him correct?

She swallowed. And then she steadied her breathing. "My heart? And what exactly do you want with it?"

"I wanna spend my life listening to its beat."

She swallowed hard. "I don't have time for this, Sin. My heart isn't available," she said, hoping her voice hadn't cracked when she said it. "And it isn't on the market. Nor are my emotions to be toyed with."

"I'm not looking to play with your emotions, or toy with your heart. I'm looking to get inside of it, to be a part of every single heartbeat."

She gripped the edge of the desk to keep from swooning. It all sounded good, too good. But she wasn't about to get sucked into false hopes that would later turn into broken promises, leaving her brokenhearted and potentially homicidal. She'd have to kill him, or damn near make him wish he were dead, if he were to ever play her.

"Sorry, but I'm not interested in a man who isn't capable of giving anything other than his dick to a woman."

Sin's mouth went dry, and yet he managed to swallow the lump in his throat.

"Teach me how to love you then. Show me." He suddenly felt a desperate, urgent, need to make her see him in his most vulnerable state. "I never had that—love—in my life, never felt it. But being in New York—and away from you, made me realize what it is I've been missing, what I've been needing, my entire life."

"You can't love me, Sin." Her head had told her early on, long before she'd ever slept with him, that he wasn't the type of man a woman should ever get attached to. And yet, in the end, her heart had somehow wanted . . . *him*. In her bed, her body, her life. In any way he was willing to give of himself.

He was everything sinful and yet she'd been willing to open herself to him. But he was too broken. Too damaged. Too guarded.

"And if I'm really honest with myself," she continued, "I can't love you, either."

He swallowed. "You don't mean that."

Didn't she?

He felt an ache in his chest that had him struggling to breathe. Waiting. And when she didn't respond, he felt himself fumbling for the right words. Shit. He should have written everything out. He stifled another curse.

"I don't have enough energy for you, Sin," she finally said, shaking her head. "You require too much. And I simply don't have it in me."

Her words cut him to the quick. It physically pained him that she'd already given up on him. "Don't say that," he said. And then he sighed. "Look, I'm flawed. I'm scarred. And—shit—I'm scared as fuck of putting myself out here like this. I'm not perfect. And I'm not sure if I'm even perfect enough for you. I have secrets. I have nightmares—at times. But if you're willing to be patient with me, I know I can get this shit right. All I'm asking from you is a chance . . ."

She closed her eyes for the briefest of moments, her attempt at not letting the switch in her mind click to that woman aching for a love of her own; her attempt at willing him away, making him invisible. And yet when her lids opened, again, he was still standing there.

Her voice trembled as she said, "I'm not looking for a project, Sin. Nor am I looking to be your experiment, to see if you have the ability to attach, to connect, to another human being. I want more than great sex, Sin. I want more than good dick. I want a man who wants to love and be loved back. I want a man who can commit to me, surrender to his feelings for me. I want a man who isn't going to hide his fears, his emotions, his thoughts, or his sorrows from me. So, again, what exactly brought you back here?"

Sin swallowed. His lip twitched. He felt himself becoming lightheaded. It was either now or never.

"My heart," he whispered. "My heart brought me back." He paused, trying to steady his racing heart. Damn, this bearing his soul shit was a lot of work. "It hasn't beat right since I left. No games, no BS . . . I'm here for *you*. Only you."

His words touched her, deeply. She closed her eyes and willed the tears not to come. But one slipped down her cheek. And her knees would have buckled had she not been sitting on the edge of her desk when he leaned in and kissed away that lone teardrop.

"Look at me," he said tenderly.

She blinked, and then looked up at him, refusing to shed another tear, refusing to allow him to see her becoming emotional. She was always strong, always well put together, always calm and collected, always the voice of reason. Just once, she wanted to fall apart, to not give a fuck, to be an emotional fucking mess. But pride wouldn't let her. Ego wouldn't allow it.

Maybe she'd rejoice in her tears later. But for right now—

"I fucked up," he said softly, disrupting her thoughts. "I should have never left."

"No, Sin. You didn't leave. You ran off."

"Yeah, that part." She narrowed her gaze at him. And he put his hands up in mock surrender. "Okay. I ran. I was a scared fool. But I'm back to get it right. I'm not looking to experiment with you. I'm looking to grow with you. To build with *you*. All of you." He ducked his head and kissed her, warm and breathless. When he pulled his head back, Dr. Dangerfield's eyes were shimmering, but she hadn't kissed him back. "Tell me you don't want this too."

She'd wanted to hear this from him months ago, but he'd been too closed off, too unbothered by the possibility. And now he was here professing things she wasn't so sure he was prepared for. She needed to know what had changed, what had him wanting all of *this* now?

She swallowed, her chest tightening as she drank in his words.

"I don't know." She shook her head. "I can't trust—"

He cut her off, feeling his gut clench. "I can be the man you need—I know I can, if you'd let me," he said as he pulled away. He wasn't a man who begged for anything, but he'd get down on his knees and beg her for a chance to get it right if he had to. All he needed was one shot. He smiled down at her and then pressed his forehead against hers.

"I've missed you."

"And what about your new life, back in Vegas, or New York . . . or wherever the freakfests lead you?"

He gathered her hands in his and lifted them both to his mouth. He kissed her right hand and then the left. "The only freakfest I'm interested in is right here with you. I'm not going back, unless you tell me you don't want me here."

Her expression was disbelieving.

"I'm an idiot, even an asshole sometimes," he admitted. "And, yes, I'm difficult and distant. But the fact is, you are everything I've always needed. You bring me calm and peace."

She shook her head. She wanted to believe him, wanted to trust his words. "This is a lot to take in all at once. I need some time to process." She swallowed. "Alone."

"Cool." He sighed, feeling relieved that she hadn't flat out told him to kiss her ass, or to fuck off. That was definitely a good sign. "Take all the time you need." He touched her face with his fingers, and then tipped her chin. "You're so beautiful." He pressed his lips to hers, again. And she felt her toes curling, felt her heart beating in her ears. And when he pulled away, her cunt was suddenly moist and they were both breathing heavily. "Talk later?"

Still dazed from the kiss, she simply nodded.

"I'll let you get back to your work then." He started for the door but when he got there he paused and turned to face her. "You once asked me what made me smile. I told you then, half-joking, good pussy. But the answer is, *you*. You make me smile."

Dr. Dangerfield felt her skin heat, her cheeks now flushed. He caught her totally off guard by his admission.

"I—"

"I don't want you to say anything. Not now. Just don't count me out, Doc. That's all I ask."

She swallowed as she watched him reach for the doorknob. But then her voice halted him before he opened it and stepped out into the hallway.

"Sin?" she asked in a low, shaky voice.

"Yeah?"

"Can I ask you something?"

He gripped the doorknob and breathed deeply. "Of course. Anything."

Dr. Dangerfield hesitated, not sure if she should voice what she wanted to ask.

"I want something real, something meaningful," she said, piercing into every part of him with her gaze. "I want a man willing to be vulnerable, willing to allow me into the deepest parts of who he is, because I won't ever deny him those parts of myself."

"I can—"

She shook her head. "No, let me finish. I want a lover and a partner. And, ultimately, I want a husband, someone I can build a life with. And, eventually, I want to be pumped up with babies—three, to be exact, by *one* man. I want forever, Sin. So, tell me. If I give myself to you, this time, will we just be . . . *fucking?*"

He shook his head. "Don't you get it, Doc. You've always been more than sex. I just didn't know it until we started spending more time together. Honestly, that scared me. And I wasn't ready to deal with that, let alone accept it."

There, he'd said it. The idea of falling for her had frightened the shit out of him. The fear of hurting her, unintentionally, had been even more frightening, to him. And he didn't want to ever be the cause of her hurt or pain. So, leaving—okay, *running*—had been, what he'd thought to be, the best thing, for the both of them.

"But I didn't know not having you around, not being near you for these last few months, not feeling your skin against mine, or the feel of your lips against mine, would have me feeling so empty. So, to answer your question, baby. You are more than fucking. *You* are the pieces of what's been missing in my life."

He paused to let his words sink in. "I'm making an appointment for Sunday. One p.m. That gives you two days to work out your schedule," he said. "And, Doc, the whole day is mine."

She swallowed in his words, whole, digesting every single syllable. She was too full to speak, so she simply nodded her head, and then eyed him as he finally opened the door to her office and walked out, leaving her swimming in his every word.

FORTY-EIGHT

SUNDAY AFTERNOON, THEY'D walked thirty minutes through a lush garden of mosses and ferns and colorful flowers, with Sin carrying her in his arms—because of the heels she'd refused to part with—until they'd reached their destination.

Surrounded by coconut and palm trees, sugar cane and natural springs and rivers, they stood in the middle of a rainforest, watching the most stunning view of a series of lakes falling into one another, creating a variation of waterfalls and cascades tumbling down into a breathtaking basin.

She drank in nature's beauty, soaked in the splendor of this magical place; Sin's secret hideaway. He wrapped his arms around her waist and pulled her back hard against him. He leaned in, nuzzling her ear. "The first time I brought you here, I was sharing a very small part of me with you."

She swallowed. "And now?"

"And now I've brought you here to share every part of me."

Dr. Dangerfield kept her gaze trained on the view, but her lips and her heart trembled. She craned her head and looked up at him. "But why now?"

"Because there's no other woman on this earth more deserving than you." He pulled her in tighter. She tried to turn to face him, but he held her in place, holding her tighter around the waist. His lips flush to her ear, he whispered, "I don't know what it is about you, Doc, but you make it easy for me to forget."

She craned her neck again. "Forget what?"

"No questions," he murmured. "Not today. All I want you to do is listen and feel. Feel the energy around us. Listen to the melody around you. Can you do that?"

She nodded. "But why am I here now? What has changed from the first time you brought me here?"

He sighed. Always the inquisitive one, he thought. "Everything," he said softly. "I'm changed. Being with you changed me. Being away from you changed me. Everything that I am has changed because of you." He slowly turned her to face him, and Dr. Dangerfield felt her heart stutter.

He saw the skepticism burning in her eyes, and he felt the need to extinguish any doubts blazing in her mind. He reached for her and pulled her to him. Then he took her with his mouth, gently sucking on her bottom lip, before his tongue was greedily prying, probing, around in her mouth, his tongue dancing with hers.

The melding of mouths, the touching of lips, the dancing of tongues, he kissed her until she couldn't breathe, until she felt *his* heartbeat thumping between her legs, until she heard *his* groans and thought they were coming from her own chest, until her kiss was melting his soul.

Sin's hands roamed over her body, grabbing her ass, holding onto it, squeezing.

With a groan, her body writhed against his until his dick throbbed with the threat of exploding just from her rubbing against him. His whole world narrowed so that he could see only her, breathing her in, savoring the sweetness of her kiss, feeling her quivering flesh against his.

God, he wanted her. Not just sexually. He wanted her in every way possible. He wanted her heart, her mind, her body, and every part of her beautiful soul.

He knew Dr. Dangerfield wanted more than mere human touch.

She wanted more than unforgettable fucking.

She wanted intimacy in its purest, simplest form.

She wanted love.

And he wanted to be the only man to give it to her.

Dr. Dangerfield had pulled that out of him. She'd managed to stretch out his needs, to untangle his wants, to twist loose his desires for so much more than he'd allowed himself to imagine. And he was ready to spend his entire life making sure she knew that being right here, with her—his heart beating wildly in his chest, was where he wanted to be.

Reluctantly, he eased his lips from hers, gazing down at her. "I've never met a woman like you. Someone who I feel connected to," he said in a shaky voice. "You make shit feel easy, uncomplicated. I'm not gonna front, this is all new to me. It's overwhelming. And I'm gonna fuck up, sometimes. And I might even try to push you away. It'll never be personal though, not with you. But I'll work through it if you'll work through it with me. Everything about you makes me want to be a better man, a greater lover, and . . ."

She looked up at him directly in the eyes, and then started to speak, but he laid a finger over her mouth. "Let me finish," he said softly, letting his finger fall away.

She nodded.

"I can't imagine life without you in it," he said, his voice catching with emotion. "Everything I've ever needed is right here, with you. The last four months away from you were the loneliest I've ever been. I don't ever wanna feel that type of emptiness again."

"Sin—"

He shook his head. "No, let me finish. I crave you, ache for you. I want it all with you. I'm ready, baby. To be vulnerable—with you. To be in love with you. I'll never leave you, or run off on you, again. Ever. You have my word." He took a deep, shuddering breath. "I want you." He sighed, shaking his head. "There's no other woman who will ever compare to you. You are the other half of me. The puzzle pieces that I've been missing."

He framed her face in both hands, his need to let her see him, through him, every part of him. "You fill my soul with things I never knew possible—hope, joy, and promise. I'm not gonna front. My feelings for you scare the shit out of me. But I'm not running from them. I'm not running from you—or us. Trust has never come easy for me. But I trust you, Doc. I trust you with my darkest secrets, and with my heart. I'm ready to give you everything that I am . . ."

Dr. Dangerfield swallowed back her emotions as Sin took her hands in his and lifted them both to his mouth, kissing the first one and then the other. "I never knew love. I never thought I could, or would, ever feel love, until you, baby. No matter where I've gone, I've never felt like I belonged. It never felt right. Until you—you changed that, Doc. When I'm with you, holding you in my arms, it feels like home. It feels safe. And I can't imagine being any other place in this world, except right here with you."

The tears came. And then she blinked, his face becoming a shimmery glare as she stared at him, her mouth now open, her whole-body trembling as Sin reached into his back pocket and pulled out a tiny box.

Dr. Dangerfield's melting heart nearly stopped as he opened the box. She felt the earth shift beneath her feet, her breath catching as she stared down at the exquisite diamond ring. It sparkled and caught the sunlight streaming through the trees, blinding her with its brilliance. "Ohmygod, Sin . . ." And then a shaky hand flew up to her mouth.

Sin took her left hand and lowered himself to one knee. "Will you marry me, Gretchen Dangerfield? Have my babies and give me forever?"

Nothing ever felt more right than this very moment. His hand shook as he slid the large rock onto her finger, but as she stared down at him with a tender smile, she lost herself in his gaze, his dark brown eyes pooling with something much deeper than lust. So deep that she nearly drowned in them.

He found himself holding his breath as he waited, his heart beating wildly, as he waited for her response.

Tears fell from her cheeks as she finally nodded her answer. "Yes, Sin. Yes."

He smiled and pushed himself back up, and then leaned in and swiped his tongue over her cheek, catching her tears and then kissing her tenderly on the lips, before gathering her in his embrace. He buried his face in her hair, breathing her in.

Moments ticked by before he gently pulled away, and then he turned her back around to face the waterfalls.

"Close your eyes, baby."

"Sin—"

"No buts, no questions. Agreed?"

She murmured her assent, rubbing her ass against him. Sin waited for her to close her eyes, and then he slipped his hand beneath the front of her dress. Her pulse quickened. Her pretty silk panties were now damp from his proposal, from the four carats on her hand, and from his confession of love. She writhed in anticipation. She was here for it, for whatever sensual play he wanted to share.

There was magic in receiving pleasure as well as giving it, and she welcomed his probing fingers as he worked over her clit in slow, circular motion.

"You're mine now, baby," he murmured, leaning in so that his mouth brushed against her ear. "This fat pussy is so good, I want to lose myself in all this wet heat, bury this hard dick deep inside you," he said, with a bolus of heat peppering his voice. And his erotic words sent a flutter of butterflies twirling in her stomach.

Her breath hitched, the sound of his voice, the stroke of his fingers on her swelling clit, sending fresh desire spiraling through her.

She bit into her bottom lip.

Slowly—so very slowly—he slid his middle finger against her slit, and she bit back a moan. "Right now, this is all about you, Doc. You like that?"

Oh God—

Her knees trembled. "Yes. I like—*mmm . . .* love—*uh . . .* it."

"Good," he murmured. The warmth of his breath spread over her cheek, causing her face to flush. "I like knowing you love me touching you, stroking you."

His finger slid inside her, and her lids shot open. Her head fell back, the tendons in her delicate neck straining, her eyes rolling up in her head.

"Unh-uh," he warned. "Close your eyes."

"I need—*mmm . . .* want—*oh . . .* to see."

"Use your other senses," he said, thrusting his fingers deeper inside her. "Concentrate on the sounds around you. And focus"— he slipped another finger inside her—"on this." Her pussy clenched in response. And then she moaned low in her throat, her body humming as he used his talented fingers to do sinful things to her.

Sin nuzzled her neck, her ear. "Your pussy's so wet." His balls tight, aching, he pressed his dick into her back again, and murmured, "You feel how hard you got this dick?"

"Yes," she said, breathlessly.

"I could nut right now, just by the feel of your sweet pussy milking my fingers."

His words alone turned her molten, liquid heat sluicing over his fingers. She wanted release, needed it. And so did he.

"Don't stop," she murmured. "Please." But he did, withdrawing his hand from her wet pussy, and she groaned in protest at the sudden loss. He raised his fingers to her lips and instinctively she flicked her tongue over his fingers.

He smiled.

And then she felt him reach for her zipper. Felt his dick grow harder against her body as he tugged it down to the center of her back.

"I can't wait to see this beautiful body naked," he said, his voice a mixture of lust and adoration. "I'm gonna kiss over every delicious inch of your skin. I've missed fucking you, baby. I've missed being inside you."

Her mouth opened, but no words came for she could barely breathe from his seductive promises. Sin gently brushed his hands over her skin, easing the material down over her shoulders, slowly revealing the swell of her breasts, the tight brown of her areolae, the delicious peaks of her nipples. The air felt cool against her heated skin.

She tried to turn to face him, but he stopped her. "Stay still. Close your eyes back."

Reluctantly, she acquiesced. Surrendered to his will, his want, as he tugged her dress down, and then watched it spill off her, pooling around her feet, leaving her clad only in red panties and a pair of red bottom heels.

He heard the sharp intake of her breath, felt her shiver. Nearly naked, she felt feminine, and so powerful.

"This dick is all yours," he promised. His dick ached, and he couldn't wait to unload. He pulled her back into him, reaching around her body, between her legs. "What do you smell?" His fingers moved over her clit again.

The air seemed thicker, full of seductive power. Dr. Dangerfield drew in a breath and she caught the scent of him. The fading woody amber of his cologne was overpowered now by a sensual musk that made her nipples tighten, and made her want to turn around and taste him.

She felt a fresh tingling in her cunt that had nothing to do with his fingers dancing circles over her clitoris, but everything to do with him; his masculine ruggedness and the lusty thoughts of feeling the bulbous head of his dick brushing against the walls of her cunt swirling around in her head.

"I smell you," she murmured, suddenly feeling lightheaded.

Sin pressed his himself into the small of her back again. "That's not the answer I was going for, Doc. Try again."

She squeezed her legs around his hand, her body clenching, drawing him in deeper, her greedy cunt wetly swallowing in his fingers. She moaned, feeling her orgasm building, getting stronger by the second. Over her beating heart in her ears, she heard screeches and squawks and the ritual calling of tropical birds echoing around them. Her eyes opened again, and through a lusty haze, she spotted a pink and green dove, watching, waiting—two lovebirds sitting in a tree.

The sun was beginning to set, the world giving way to a golden glow.

Again, he told her to close her eyes as he cupped her breast with his free hand. Her skin felt hot to his touch. "Now tell me, again"—she gasped as his thumb flicked over her nipple— "what do you smell?"

Fingers stretching her, she cried out. Her orgasm crashing against her pelvis, then tumbling out of her body. She waited for her body to stop trembling, and then she inhaled. Breathed in the freshness of the air, richly scented by gardenia, frangipani, and hibiscus.

"Desire," she finally murmured, her body riding wave after wave of another orgasm. "I smell heat and longing," she said, breathlessly.

"Bend over," he told her. And she did. Eagerly. Excitedly.

She heard him unzipping himself. Heard the tear of a condom. In her mind's eye she saw his dick spilling out of his underwear, saw him rolling on the condom.

"Spread open your ass so I can get up in that pretty pussy," he said hoarsely, smearing the lone drop of precum beading at the slit of his crown, before rolling the condom down over his shaft.

With her feet at a wide stance, Dr. Dangerfield reached behind her and pulled open her cheeks, her ring sparkling on her finger, exposing her glistening lips, all slick and sticky.

Sin groaned at the beautiful sight, bending at the knees. She heard him moan, and she gasped as he put the crown of his dick to her and rubbed her pussy. Purposefully, he slid in. And she came again as he slid inch by inch into her body, slowly, deeply, pulling out and then plowing back in, stealing her breath with each thrust.

"Fuck," he hissed, grasping her hips. "So fucking tight." He pulled out again, just to the head, and then drove back in, his shaft powering through, stretching her heated sheath. "Goddamn, you feel so good."

Good pussy always does, she thought, a smile curving her lips, but it was quickly replaced with an opened mouth when he stroked over her sweet spot. Again, and again, he brushed over her inner flesh, causing heat to rise. She gasped. Then her breath caught in the back of throat as her orgasm rolled out of her body in waves of wet flames, curling up through her clit.

"That's right, baby," he said, his voice raw with desire, "come on *your* dick. It's all yours. *I'm* all yours . . . if you want me."

If?

There were no ifs. There were no maybes. She was surer than she'd ever been about anything in her life. Yes, she wanted it—*all* of it. Every damn beautifully flawed inch of it. She wanted it unsheathed and needy and, so, so thick.

She wanted *him*.

"Give me all of you, Sin," she murmured over her shoulder. And then her breath caught. "Take off . . . *uhh* . . . the condom . . . *oooh* . . . and fuck . . . *aah* . . . me. With all . . . *mmm* . . . of you."

His heart beat rapidly in his chest. "You sure, baby?"

"Yes," she said breathlessly. "Take me raw."

And he did, gladly, proudly. Pulling out, removing his condom, and quickly slipping back in; hissing at the feel of her wet, silky walls; the warm, velvety grip, the slippery slide, more delicious than he ever hoped for.

Flesh to flesh, everything inside of Dr. Dangerfield spun tighter as she moved her hands to her breasts, pinching her own nipples, and feeling herself grow wetter with every stroke, every pound, every inch of Sin's dick. The exhilarating rush of sensations rose higher and higher like waves crashing against a jetty. She was sure she'd be tossed over the cliff had it not been for the possessively tight grip Sin kept around her waist, drawing her in with each thrust.

She was right there with him, wanting to feel the essence of him flooding deep inside her, coating her walls with his seed, and his very own desire for her.

She clenched him as his body twitched and convulsed. His toes curled.

Sin's head dropped back. He looked up through the foliage and spotted a flaming orange dove. And overhead, flying over the treetops were huge golden hornbills.

His growl echoed skyward, the pressure building inside him. "So fucking wet." And then he began to thrust long, hard and as deeply as he could. "I'm *cum*ming. This nut is for you, baby. *Uhh . . . shiiiit . . .*"

And then he moaned deep in his throat, his orgasm ripping through his body. Body trembling, knees going weak, Dr. Dangerfield's eyelashes fluttered upward as another orgasm rolled around inside of her.

Sin's eyes opened.

And there it was, slicing through the mist, a magnificent rainbow. And in that very moment, Sin Saint-Michael and Gretchen Dangerfield both felt it.

Love.

And forever . . .

Made in United States
Orlando, FL
13 April 2024

45775843R00203